MALLORY

BILLIONAIRE ROMANCE SERIES

MICHELLE LOVE

HOT AND STEAMY ROMANCE

CONTENTS

Made in "The United States" by:

Michelle Love

© Copyright 2020 – Michelle Love

ISBN 978-1-64808-802-5

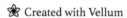 Created with Vellum

BLURB

When art student Quilla Chen bravely dives into a Venetian canal to rescue a suicidal man, she has no way of knowing the man she has saved is the eldest son of one of America's wealthiest families. But Jakob Mallory has his own dark secrets—an addiction to cocaine which has fueled his epic rise to the top, but now threatens everything as his addiction grows stronger. Their attraction to each other is palpable, and soon, they become lovers.

PART ONE: TORMENT ME

"**B**ella, bella, bella!"
Quilla ignored the calls of the gondoliers as she walked quickly over the bridge. It was dusk, and Venice was readying itself for the nightlife, but at this moment, on this particular bridge, it was quiet. Quilla kept her focus on her destination; she'd had good practice at tuning out the incessant catcalls and whistles that followed her. Even dressed as she was, simple white shirt and cargo pants, the Italian boys would make their appreciation known. It had annoyed her at first—her American sensibilities offended by their objectification—but now she just ignored it.

Every morning she woke up in this glorious city, Quilla Chen would spend a few seconds in wonderment. Italy ... she never thought a working-class girl like her would get here. Oh, she'd worked eighteen hours days to fit in both work and college, ending up with a Fine Arts degree, but when her professor at her alma mater had called and told her she'd won the scholarship to go spend the summer painting in Venice, she could hardly believe it.

"And when you get back," he'd said kindly, "we'll discuss your Ph.D. thesis."

Her. Quilla Chen, soon to be Doctor Quilla Chen. "I'll make you proud, Mom," she'd said the day she'd found out. The photograph of her mother, five years dead, didn't make up for the loss, but Quilla had felt happier than in a long time. 'Do something' were her mother's last words to her, and she had. She had done something. At twenty-four, Quilla was looking at a future which had some value, some meaning.

Now, as she walked towards the north of the city, towards Cannaregio, away from the tourist track, she wondered idly if she could make a life here, in this glorious city. There seemed too much to discover for one summer; she wanted to immerse herself in the culture, the language, the beauty. Since arriving a week ago, she had already sketched and painted a number of pieces, so inspired had she been. Tonight, her mission was to sketch and photograph dusk falling over St. Dell'isole Michele and Murano from the Ponte de la Sacca de la Misericordia.

The bridge was quiet when she got there. She settled down on a small stone walkway at the side of the bridge and looked out over the Venetian Lagoon. It had been a typical sweltering day but as the sun began to set, the colors that spread across the sky were heaven. Soon Quilla was so lost in her work that she didn't even notice the last of the boats coming out from under the bridge and that the streetlamps were turning on.

It was only when she heard the scrape of shoes that she looked up. A man, tall, wearing a suit, stood at the pinnacle of the bridge, staring down into the water. He was handsome—if a little red-eyed and unshaven—Quilla judged him to be in his early to mid-forties. It was the expression on his face that made her heart twist with sadness. Hopelessness, utter, complete hopelessness ... she drew herself back into the shadow of the bridge, not wanting to intrude on the man's privacy, but she couldn't tear her eyes away from him. As she watched, he slowly, carefully, took his jacket off and laid it carefully on the bridge. With mounting horror, she saw him lay his wallet and phone on top and then his shoes. Oh, God no ... before she could scream out, he leapt in one movement, plunging into the murky depths of the water.

Quilla reacted in a flash. Wrenching off her sneakers and shirt, she dived into the water. Opening her eyes, she could see nothing in the dark waters of the lagoon; instead, she stretched out her arms, searching. She knew it was probably hopeless, but something in the man's face made her want to find him, want to save him. She broke the surface to suck in some air, then, out of the corner of her eye, she saw something. Without thinking, she made a grab at it and felt an arm. She pulled on it and the man broke the surface, too, spluttering, cursing—in English. An American.

"No, you freaking don't," Quilla gasped, as he struggled to free himself, and using all of her strength, she hauled him to the side of the canal. He was a big man, so all she could do was pin him to the side of the canal and hope someone would come help them both out.

"Let me go," he murmured, his voice breaking and cracking.

"No, never ..." Quilla had no idea why she said that with so much feeling, but her whole world was now about saving this man. She yelled out, hoping one of the people in the houses at the edges of the canal would hear her. A minute or two passed and then there were two young men scrambling to help. "Get him out first," she ordered them, and though they looked unhappy, they did as she said, dumping the crumpled American to the stone walkway and lifting her out.

"Thank you," she gasped, "Thank you."

They asked her, in broken English, if she was okay—did she want them to call for an ambulance? Quilla, panting hard, looked down questioningly at the American, who shook his head.

"No, please, no ambulance, no police, no press."

No ... press? Who was this guy? Quilla put her shirt back on her damp body—clearly to the disappointment of the two boys. She shook her head, laughing. "Look, can you watch him for a sec while I grab his stuff from up there? Might tell me who he is and where we can take him."

She climbed up onto the bridge and grabbed his jacket and personal items. She bent down to wrap his jacket around him and for the first time, he looked at her properly. Their eyes locked and Quilla felt something shift in her soul. He slowly lifted his hand and cupped her cheek, stroking the soft apple of it so tenderly, she thought she might cry, looking at her as if he couldn't believe she was there.

"Okay," she said, embarrassment making her cheeks flame. "Let's see who you are ... Jakob? Jakob Mallory?"

"Yes, I ..." He gave a big sigh and she was struck again about how hopeless he looked. "For what it's worth, I'm Jakob Mallory."

"Jakob, do you have somewhere you're staying?"

He shook his head. "I flew in this afternoon. I wasn't planning on a vacation." He gave her a wry smile then, the first sign of his personality, and she found herself smiling back.

"Well, then ... can you walk? You can stay on my couch tonight, and then we'll get you a room tomorrow."

He was still staring at her and for a moment she wasn't sure he had heard what she said.

"Okay."

It wasn't until they were walking back into the city that she realized what she was doing. She'd just saved this dude's life ...and what, now she was taking him back to her apartment? You are insane. But her gut told her that he was no danger, and jeez, she felt a responsibility for him. Besides, she was pretty damn good at martial arts and if he tried anything ...

"What's your name?"

She smiled. "Quilla. Quilla Chen."

"Quilla. Unusual."

She said nothing, used to the reaction. They walked a little in silence for a little way, then he put a hand on her arm and stopped her.

"I can find a hotel ... it's okay."

She looked up at him. His eyes were the same deep hazel as her own, his close-cropped hair a few shades lighter. He towered over her and was a pretty impressive physical specimen, she had to admit, but it was the look in his eyes that still spoke to her. Loneliness. Despair.

"I don't think you should be alone, tonight," she said simply, and Jakob smiled softly.

"You might be right."

Quilla drew in a deep breath. "Look, come back to my apartment, take a hot bath. On the way back, there'll be some tourist shops. We can skip in, get you some clean clothes. You need food, warmth, and someone to talk to. You're not a homicidal maniac, are you?"

She asked the question with a grin on her face but there was still a little bit of her that was wary—he was a stranger, after all.

"Not lately," he said, "Although there was that time I got stuck in an elevator listening to Justin Bieber."

Quilla laughed, relaxing. "Completely understandable. Come on, then."

SHE CRUSHED the garlic cloves and added them to the pan. If there was one thing she loved in this world as much as art and books, it was cooking. And here, in this city, she had access to the farmer's markets selling ripe and luscious fruit and vegetables and endless little delicatessens where they sold every kind of meat and cheese. It was nice, she reflected now, to have someone to cook for. A simple tomato and basil pasta dish it might be, but with crusty bread and a good red wine, and the sounds of the Venetian nightlife drifting up through the large open windows, it was a perfect evening. As the sauce bubbled away on the stove, Quilla leaned out of the window to see the lights of the city.

"Beautiful."

She started. She hadn't heard the tub drain or the bathroom door open. Jakob Mallory was grinning at her from the doorway, dressed in the light cotton T-shirt and shorts they'd managed to get from a tourist shop. They showed off his long, long legs and well-muscled calves. The T-shirt fit loosely on his big frame and the khaki reflected his eye color. Those eyes, still troubled, still so sad, met hers, and crinkled wonderfully at the edges as he smiled. "The food, it smells beautiful."

Quilla rolled her eyes, blushing. "It's just pasta." But she was absurdly pleased. "Please, sit, it's almost ready."

She loaded his plate as he poured the wine, looking around her apartment. It was shabby, rustic, and she loved every inch of it. All spare surfaces were laden with her books, her paints, papers and pencils. At the end of the long kitchen table, there was a pile of books and he picked up the top one.

"The Story of Art. Huh, Gombrich. You'd get along with my pa."

Quilla, balancing two plates laden with food, tottered to the table. She placed one in front of Jakob with a shy smile.

"Enjoy. Simple, but I think it'll do you good. If nothing else, the garlic will be enough to kill any bacteria we might have picked up in the Lagoon." She grimaced and he grinned.

"Sorry about that and ... thanks. For the food, for saving my life, for your kindness."

Quilla, flushing again, shoved a forkful of pasta into her mouth. "So..."

"Why did I try and kill myself?"

Quilla swallowed her food. "Not that it's any of my business. You don't have to talk to me about that ... we can talk about something else."

Jakob nodded, appearing to consider her words. After a pause, he attacked his food again. "This is damn good, Quilla. So tell me—do you live here?"

Quilla told him about the scholarship. "I never, in a million years, thought I'd ever come here. It's like a dream."

"Where are you from?"

"Seattle."

Jakob put his fork down. "You have to be kidding."

Quilla frowned. "No ... why?"

Jakob grinned. "My family, all of them, live and works in Seattle. Born and bred."

Something was ticking over in her brain but she couldn't quite get there. "Your family?"

Mallory. Mallory. Something in that name ...

Jakob looked vaguely uneasy. "My dad is Randall Mallory."

Holy. Fuck. Balls. Quilla gaped at him. "There's no way—you're making this up."

Jakob, still smiling, got up and went to grab her iPad, handing it to her. "The name of your scholarship award is..."

"... The Ran Mallory Award for Excellence in Art." Quilla typed Jakob's name into the search engine and a second later, her screen filled with images of the man sitting across from her. "This is too much ... your dad is a legend. He came to talk at my graduation ... damn, Jakob ... this is too weird." She shoved the iPad onto the table like it burned her to touch it. She narrowed her eyes at a laughing Jakob. "Was this a test? I get the grant, so ..." She immediately regretted her words as a shadow passed over his face. "God, I'm sorry, that was an idiotic thing to say."

Jakob put a hand on hers. "Don't worry. So, we're both Washington natives then?"

Quilla smiled at him, grateful. "Looks like. Well, now I know you're a Mallory, which kind of negates any questions about what you do ... although I suppose I could ask which branch of the billion-dollar conglomerate you run."

He grinned at the dubious amazement in her voice. "Sadly, not art. That's my dad and my youngest brother Grady's domain."

"You have another brother, right?"

"Two. Kit's the one you're thinking of, actor, model, and major pain in the ass. His twin brother Joel coaches tennis, mostly his kid ..."

"Skandar Mallory!" she said, suddenly making the connection. "Wow. My best friend and I always go see him play when he's playing in Washington."

He raised an eyebrow at her. "Schoolgirl crush?"

"No," she said, but she grinned, "So he's your nephew, huh?"

Jakob laughed. "I feel so old right now."

Quilla started to apologize but he held his hand up. "Please, I was kidding ... though, do you mind if I ask?"

"Twenty-four."

He looked her up and down. "Twenty-four, maybe five-five in

your bare feet, and yet you dragged a two hundred pound, six-foot-five man out of a canal."

"Adrenaline," she said quickly. "Plus, you know, mad skills."

He laughed. "You know, Quilla Chen, I'm not sure I've met anyone quite like you."

"Good job. You'd need therapy." There I go again, Miss Foot-in-Mouth. "Sorry, I have very little filter and clearly no tact."

"I was lost," he said suddenly. "I forgot what it was to have fun, to laugh, to enjoy anything. For months now. At that moment, I just thought ... so quick, so easy."

Quilla leaned on her elbows and studied him. "But you flew here with no luggage, on a whim?"

"Not exactly ... I had a layover to Paris. My luggage is probably enjoying a trip to the Eiffel Tower right now. I thought I'd come into the city and waste a few hours, then ..." He trailed off. Quilla was sure he was keeping something back but she bit her tongue. He drew in a deep breath. "What about you? Family? Husband?"

"Neither. Just me."

"I'm sorry."

"Don't be. I have friends, good friends, amazing friends. And I'm good at being alone."

He smiled at that but didn't say anything. Quilla toyed with the stem of her wine glass.

"Jakob?"

"Yes?"

"Would you like some more food? More wine?"

"No, thank you. It was beyond delicious, but I couldn't eat anything else. If it's not too much to ask, I just want your company for the evening."

"Of course. Let's go sit on the balcony—and I'm bringing the wine, no matter what you say."

"Alcoholic."

"Shut up."

She was amazed how easily they could talk—he must be a good ten, fifteen years older than her, maybe more, but she didn't feel the age gap at all. They seemed kindred spirits, talking about music, Italy, books, food. It was nearly midnight before Quilla suddenly yawned.

"Sorry."

Jakob looked amused. "It's late."

"It is." Suddenly there was a little tension in the air. "Look," she said eventually, "you're a big guy and my couch is tiny. I'll sleep on that; you take my bed." She was blushing furiously but she didn't know why. Bullshit, she said to herself, you're attracted to him, is all.

Jakob shook his head. "No way. You've done far too much for me already. Do you have a sheet I could borrow?"

She pulled some sheets and a pillow from her cupboard and gestured towards the kitchen, suddenly so bashful she couldn't meet his eye. "Help yourself to anything you want. Oh ..." She disappeared into the bathroom, then came out waving a toothbrush still in its packaging. "Lucky I just picked this up."

Jakob took it from her. "I really can't thank you enough, Quilla, I mean it."

"It's really okay. It's been an unexpectedly lovely evening."

JAKOB LAY ON HIS BACK, staring at the ceiling, wondering how he got here. He hadn't planned on seeing this night or any other. But that tiny girl in the next room ... damn, when he'd felt her small hand pulling at his arm, her body pressing him up against the side of the canal, yelling with all her might for someone to help save him, he'd almost wanted to push her away and tell her he wasn't worth it. Then he'd seen her face. Her ethereal beauty had sent a jolt through his soul, her soft smile, the dark hair hanging in bedraggled strands around the most exquisite face, the flush in her cheeks from the exertion—from saving his life. Jesus ... his frazzled, delirious mind hadn't known anything but that he would do whatever she asked.

And when he'd calmed himself, talked himself out of the hole, he'd found something new—a new friend, a chance at a new life.

... If it wasn't for the millions of bugs crawling under his skin right now, scratching and clawing at his nerves, screaming for their medicine. Cocaine was an evil, insidious mistress and over the last year, he'd succumbed. Slowly it became a necessity, rather than a pleasure; something he thought that he could control. When it became clear it couldn't ...

He'd walked out of the lounge at Venice Airport, leaving his luggage and his flight to Paris, where his brother Grady was waiting for him. He should call him; let him know he was staying here for a few ...

Wait, what? He pushed aside the sheet that covered him and sat up. Green eyes, pink lips, that smile ... He didn't even know the woman who had saved him, not longer than one day, and now he was what, planning on staying and dragging her into his fucked-up life? Shit, no ...

He got up and went to check on his clothes, clean and drying on the balcony. Dry. He took them inside and dressed, shaking his head. The hell was he thinking? He glanced around for paper, a pen.

Sweet Quilla, there are no words to tell you how thankful I am to have met you tonight, for you being so brave and selfless. Allow me to be the same by not dragging you into my mess, but know I will never, ever forget you. Jakob.

He ignored the sadness pounding at his heart and left the note on the kitchen table. Unable to resist, he pushed her bedroom door open a crack and looked in. She lay on her stomach, her dark hair clouded around her on the pillow, her dark lashes resting on her cheek.

Brave, smart, funny, and beautiful, Jakob thought as he closed her door, feeling bad for intruding. He slowly padded to the door and stopped. No key. The door was old, no deadbolts, just a good old-fashioned lock and key. He glanced around for the missing key, felt above the lintel, moved some papers around on the cabinet by the side of the door. Nothing.

He checked the kitchen and now his pulse quickened. Quilla's apartment was on the third floor, so he couldn't get out via the balcony. Suddenly all the adrenaline came flooding back into his body, and he was desperate, needing to go find a fix from somewhere.

He had people he could call who would know where to go here in Venice, but it was useless if he couldn't even get out of ...

"Looking for this?"

He spun around to find Quilla standing at her bedroom door. In her hand, the key. Jakob met her gaze, all ready to make up a story, but then she smiled sadly.

"What is it? Vicodin? Coke? I know it's not heroin. You don't have any track marks, at least from what I could see."

She walked towards him, slightly unsteady from sleep, and handed him the key. "You can have this; you can go, get high, get depressed, and jump in the canal. If that's what you want. Or you can stay here with me for a few days, get straight, and get some space, just chill out. I'll help you through withdrawal; I've done it before for someone. It would be easy for us to just say goodbye now—we don't know each other. So, I'll leave it up to you. I'm going back to bed. If you're here in the morning, I'll be delighted. If not, well, you made your bed. Goodnight, Jakob."

She turned and walked back into her bedroom and closed the door. Jakob, the key cold in his hand, stared after her with only one thought on his mind.

I'm going to marry that girl.

"Come on, faster."

"God, I hate you ..."

Jakob grinned at her as she panted for air. "This was your idea, remember."

Quilla squinted up at him.

"I said "let's go for a stroll in the cool Venice evening, not, hey, let's race across the city in hundred-degree heat'."

Jakob laughed, handing her a bottle of water from his backpack. "Hush your grumbling." Quilla stuck her tongue out at him, tilting her head back to drain the bottle in one go.

It had been a week since she'd pulled him out of the lagoon and Jakob could hardly believe the change that had come over him. In that week, Quilla had become his friend, his confidant, his challenger, his rock. Jakob Mallory had reached the age of forty-seven without forming any serious attachments beyond his brothers and a few friends. Probably why his closest relationship up to now had been his business partner Gregor, an ambitious Harvard grad. Gregor had been the one who shared his 'secret' with Jakob, the way he found the energy to work eighty-hour work weeks and still screw his way through the A-list of Seattle's elite.

Still, Jakob thought now, all that was going to change. This tiny Asian American woman in front of him had changed all of that. When she'd come back into the living room the morning after they'd met and seen him still there, his long body cramped up on her couch, the smile on her lovely face had been all he had needed to know his decision to stay was the right one. That day, he'd called the airport to find out his luggage had been taken off the plane when he hadn't checked in. Then, on the way to get it, he'd called Grady in Paris and said three words. "Met a girl." Grady had laughed in his gruff way. "Hey, man, go for it. About damn time."

Quilla blew out her cheeks. "God ... I need a shower."

Jakob shook his head. "Not yet, wise one. I've just seen a gelato cart over there." He smiled as she looked excited. Food had been one of the highlights of this past week—she had taught him to cook with fresh ingredients and he had taken her out to some of Venice's most high-end restaurants. They would sit at the outdoor tables long into the evening, talking about their lives. On the days he hadn't been able to leave the apartment, the comedown from the coke fever too much, she had kept him cool, distracted him, and at one point, as his body became wracked with shivers, wrapped her arms around him to keep him from thrashing about.

That had been a bad night, with the delirium that came with withdrawal agony. He'd sweated and spasmed until finally falling asleep on the floor, in Quilla's arms. When he had awoken, the fever had passed, and they were entangled on the floor, Quilla still asleep. Gently, he had laid back down next to her and studied her face, so peaceful when she was asleep. God, he had wanted to kiss her, that gorgeous, blush-pink mouth.

Jakob Mallory had never been in love—and he didn't even know if this was love—but damn it, it felt good. Despite the difference in their ages, they connected on so many levels. This was all going through his head when Quilla had awoken herself with a gigantic sneeze, taken one look at him and dissolved into such infectious giggles that he could not help but laugh. It broke the tension. She had pulled him to his feet and sent him to shower while she made coffee.

The gelato guy grinned at him approvingly as Quilla debated over which flavor to have. "Pistachio," she finally decided and Jakob nodded.

Carrying the over-filled cones away, they started to stroll back toward Quilla's apartment. Casually, Jakob let his hand brush hers, then he took it, not glancing down at her to see her reaction. She didn't pull her hand away. He risked a sideways look and saw a flush on her cheeks—which could be from running, he told himself—but she seemed very concentrated on the ice cream, all of a sudden. They walked slowly back through the tiny streets, over the bridges, stopping to watch the tiny boats and gondolas that traversed the canal system.

Jakob brushed his thumb over the back of her hand as he held it and he felt her squeeze his fingers just briefly. He looked down at her and she smiled at him, their eyes locking, a moment of understanding passing between them. As the streets grew quieter and night fell, Jakob saw a dimly lit street to the side of them. He glanced at Quilla.

"Adventure?" he said, his voice low, seductive. He saw her breathing quicken, the blush deepen, and she nodded once. He led her down the street, silent, with the noises of the city far away. A light breeze blew along the narrow street, washing over their hot bodies, giving some relief to the sultry evening. They walked slowly, taking their time before Jakob could bear it no longer and stopped, slipping his hands onto her waist.

Quilla looked up at him, her eyes almost shy, but as he bent his head to kiss her, he felt her relax into the embrace. Her lips moved against his, slowly at first, then as his big hand fisted her hair into a knot at the nape of her neck, he heard her give a soft moan of desire. His cock was hard against the fabric of his shorts and as Quilla pressed her body against his, he could feel her trembling. As they broke away from the kiss, breathless, he stroked her face.

"Quilla ... are you sure you want this?"

She leaned into his touch, nodding. "I'm sure I want you..."

He grabbed her hand and they were running then, back to her apartment. Tumbling in the door, they were kissing and tearing their clothes off.

"Wait, wait, wait," Quilla said, putting her hands against his chest, "I seriously need a shower first or ..."

As Jakob swept her up into his arms, she shrieked with laughter as he carried her into the bathroom.

Under the cool spray of the shower, they explored each other's bodies, kissing, stroking, caressing. Quilla moved her hand down to cup his cock, stroking the hot length of it along her belly as Jakob, trailing his lips along her shoulder, slipped his fingers along the slick crevice of her sex. As he massaged her clit, she ground against his hand and with a growl, he tumbled her out of the shower onto the floor.

"I have to be inside you, beautiful ..." and he hitched her legs around his hips. She helped guide him to the entrance of her cunt and as he thrust into her, she gasped at the quick pain of his rigid, huge cock slamming into the core of her. They fucked hard, furiously, as if they had no time and were so desperate to be joined that all their feral animal needs came flooding out of them.

Quilla gripped his buttocks, moving her own hips to meet him, angling them up so he could drive himself into her. Jakob, his gaze focused totally on her, marveled at the way her breasts, so full and ripe, and her softly curved belly, undulated under their movements as he fucked her.

"Jakob, Jakob ..." Her urgent whisper made his body react, his thrusts becoming fiercer, deeper. Inexorably he drove her towards a shattering climax and when it came, he marveled at the way her lips parted, her eyes closed, and her head rolled back. He kissed her throat, feeling the vibration of her cry of pleasure shimmer through the delicate skin.

"Quilla ... my God, Quilla ..." His body was no longer his; it belonged to her and he came, shooting hot semen deep into her core. She tightened her thighs around his hips, running the tips of her fingers up and down his back, the delicious sensations prolonging his orgasm.

As they caught their breath, Jakob gathered her to him. "God, Quilla, I've been wanting to do that since we met."

She chuckled shyly, laying her cheek against his hard chest. "Me too ... but that's not why I ..."

"I know that. Look at me."

She looked up and he smiled down at her. "You are the best person I've ever known, Quilla Chen. You saved me—not just that evening at the canal, but in so many ways over the last few days."

Her eyes filled with tears. "That's such a lovely..." she got choked up then and he kissed from her forehead down, trailing his lips across her soft cheek until his mouth covered hers.

"Jakob?"

"What is it, baby?"

She gave a little chuckle. "This bathroom tile is really hard."

He laughed and got up, pulling her to her feet. He ran a leisurely hand down her side, admiring the way her full breasts fell, the soft belly, almost but not quite flat, the curve of her hips. "You really are just beautiful," he said idly, and she kissed him again.

"Come with me." She took his hand and led him to her bedroom. "Our playground," she said with a grin. "Bet you're glad you're off the couch from now on."

Jakob grinned back and swept her legs from under her, laying her back on the soft bed. "Hey, I like that couch. I fully intend to fuck you on that couch."

"Oh, you do, do you?"

"Hell, yes. Then I'm going to fuck you on the kitchen table and on the living room floor ..." He was lifting her legs over his shoulders, trailing his lips down the valley between her breasts down to the soft rise of flesh around her navel. His tongue circled and dipped into her bellybutton and he heard her drawing in a very shaky, excited breath. "Oh, you like that, huh?"

"Where else are you going to fuck me, Jakob Mallory? Jesus ..."

His mouth was on her sex then, tongue sweeping along the soft folds of labia, lashing around her clitoris. He paused for a beat to answer her and she moaned.

"Impatient girl ... well, Miss Chen, you have that wonderful balcony. I'll wait until the early hours of the morning, when the city is quiet ..." He bent his head to taste her again and felt her fingers knot in his short hair, "then I'll taste every part of you, kiss very inch of your skin until you beg me to fuck you so hard, I'll have to muffle your screams with my hand in case we wake the neighbors ... but ..." He was moving up her body again so he could kiss her mouth, "we'll wake the neighbors anyway and silently, they'll watch us, marveling over your beauty, the way you blush and moan as my cock slams into you again and again and again ..."

He plunged into her swollen and ready sex, his cock straining to find the center of her. Jakob put all his weight of his hands, on either side of her head, and locked his gaze on her face as he thrust into her. Quilla, her limbs liquid under him, gazed back at him as if drinking him in, wanting to memorize his face. She clung to him, her legs moving with him, her breasts pressing up into his chest. He smiled down at her as their bodies became damp with sweat from the exertion, from the hot Venetian night. Jakob glanced over to the large, dusty freestanding mirror and smiled.

"Look how beautiful you are," he said, and lifted her leg so she could see his thick, long cock sliding in and out of her swollen cunt. It was a mesmerizing sight and soon they were clawing and tearing at each other as they came, pausing only to catch their breath, before beginning again, long into the night until the dawn began to break over the city.

. . .

QUILLA OPENED ONE EYE. She lay on her stomach in her bed, her limbs pleasantly sore. Her thighs were aching in a way that made her smile. Jakob wasn't beside her in bed but she could hear him whistling in the kitchen. Quilla glanced over the clock. It was afternoon, but she didn't care. Last night—and this morning—had been the most erotic, most exhilarating night of her life. Only exhaustion had stopped them eventually and she had fallen asleep, wrapped in his thickly muscled arms. She closed her eyes, recalling every part of the night, the way he'd kissed her in the darkened alleyway—she knew without doubt that if he had taken her right then, she would not have turned him down. The idea they might be caught was thrilling to her.

She felt cool lips against the small of her back then, and smiled as they trailed up her spine. The bed dipped as Jakob lay down with her and she turned over. He smiled appreciatively as he ran a hand over her belly and dipped his head to kiss both breasts, teasing her nipples with his tongue.

"Good morning," she said lazily and felt his laugh rumbled through his big chest.

"Good afternoon, gorgeous. Damn, look at you ... even super-models don't look like this when they get up ..."

Quilla rolled her eyes. "Sweet talker. Perhaps you like the way the pillow seems to have made my face into this abstract artwork." She turned her far cheek to him and he grinned when he saw the soft skin rumpled from the pillow's creases.

"I love every line," he said, kissing her. "I bought you brunch."

She heaved herself into a sitting position and looked over to the nightstand. Two long glasses of orange juice stood on a tray with croissants and fresh fruit. "Oh, yum, I am parched."

He handed her a glass and she drank half of the cold juice in one go. "So hot."

"Yep." He wiggled his eyebrows and she laughed.

"I mean the weather. Thank you for this; I needed this." She drained her glass and smacked her lips together, smirking at him. He was looking at her with a strange expression.

"'Sup?"

He didn't answer, but instead grabbed her ankles and pulled her flat on the bed again. She giggled as he pushed the sheet away from her. "What are you doing?"

Playfully, he put a finger to her lips, silencing her. She took her cue, watching him lazily as he fished an ice cube from his untouched glass and placed it on her throat. With his thumb and forefinger, he gently traced a pattern with the cube around her breasts, taking his time with each, finishing by holding the cube on her nipple until it became painful, then taking each nipple into his mouth to warm it. Then, he drew it down the center line of her stomach, circling around her navel again and again, dipping into it, letting the icy water run into it, and then dipping his head to drink it from her.

The ice cube, melting against her hot skin, was trailed lower until it was on her clit, Quilla's legs parting gently as his hand slipped between them. All this time, Jakob never broke eye contact with her and Quilla, being silent, held in her moans of pleasure. She felt the ice against her now as he brushed it up and down her sex until it finally melted away. Then, so gently, his long finger slipped inside of her while his thumb brushed a steady rhythm on her clit. Quilla felt her vagina clench and tighten around his finger, responding to him, and a small moan escaped. Jakob gently placed his free hand over her mouth, smiling, a question in his eyes. She knew without doubt that if she said "Stop", he would do so immediately. She at once felt so vulnerable and yet safe under his caress.

Jakob increased the pressure on her clit and slipped another finger, then another, inside her, pressing upwards against her g-spot until she tensed and shuddered, the mellowest yet most all-consuming orgasm of her life rippling through her body. It seemed to go on and on. From somewhere, Quilla remembered the French saying La petite mort—the little death—and that's what that felt like, a scintilla, a moment where she didn't care if she lived or she died.

As her breathing returned to normal, she smiled up at him. "You have mad skills."

He touched her cheek with the back of his hand. "I love watching you come," he said simply, "it's the most exhilarating thing in the world to me."

Quilla shook her head. "Jakob Mallory ... I'm going to wake up in a minute and discover I'm in a fever dream." But she loved the way he looked at her, loved being naked and totally vulnerable with this man.

"Quilla?"

She locked her fingers with his. "Yes, lovely man?"

"Will you come back to Seattle with me? I mean, when your scholarship is done. Will you come back and live with me?"

Her eyebrows shot up. "Live?" She was silent for a moment and Jakob, his eyes wary, tried to smile.

"I'm not trying to freak you out. And if you say no, if you think it's too soon, that's okay."

Quilla sat up again, studied his face. "Jakob ... I really, really,' she exaggerated the word and he smiled, "want this to work. I do. It is a little fast to live together ... and we come from such hugely different worlds— seriously, look at this place, it's luxurious compared to my actual one bed in St Anne's. I'm a grad student; I work in the art department of the university and just about make rent and food. I'm crazy about you, but I think we should date a bit first."

Jakob nodded, only wincing slightly. "I always go all in—it's a character flaw – "

"No," she interrupted, "It isn't at all. Better to do that than always hold back. I've done that in the past, with ..." She sighed, hugging her legs to her chest. "My mom was a heroin addict. I helped get her clean, the last time and stupidly, I thought we'd actually made it. I didn't get her the follow- up care she needed. And she started using again, but she hid it. I found her dead, overdosed. So, no, don't hold back, please. It's just I'm not ready quite yet."

Jakob pressed his lips to hers. "Quilla Chen, you are wiser than your years."

"Grandpa."

"Ouch." But he laughed. "So, you'll think about it?"

Quilla grinned and slid her hand around to the back of his neck, leaning her forehead against his. "Yup. And what's more, I'll think about it while sucking your big, delicious cock ..."

"You are a filthy, filthy girl ..."

"Oh, I know ... I know ..."

IF I HADN'T MET Jakob, Quilla thought as she stared wide-eyed out of the window at a rain-drenched Seattle, I'd be sitting on a steaming, stinky bus instead of this air-conditioned behemoth of a town car. Next to her, Jakob was clearly enjoying introducing her to the luxuries in his life. He'd insisted on changing her plane ticket to a business class one—next to him, of course—and they'd arrived back in Washington rested and without a hint of the jetlag she'd expected. And of course, being with him had made leaving Venice easier—although she still felt a pang. She'd spent the last three months there, met Jakob there, and fell in love with ... everything. Oh, to hell with it, she smiled to herself, I fell in love with him. She didn't mind admitting that to herself, even if she was holding back from saying it to him ... yet.

Jakob reached for her hand. "So, you want to go home, get changed? Get some rest?"

She nodded. "I think I need to. Do some laundry, call my friends. Just for today," she said hurriedly, not wanting him to think she didn't want to be with him.

He nodded. "Of course. Look, take as long as you need—but I would like to take you to dinner, meet my family. Separately, if you like. Then it's not too scary."

"That sounds perfect ... I'd like to meet your dad at dinner, it seems respectful and appropriate. Then maybe we could do something more relaxed with your brothers, your friends."

"Good call. Kit and Grady are still abroad, anyway, but Joel is around. Skandar, too," he added with a grin, and she shrugged good-naturedly.

"I've moved on from my crush. I prefer his uncle now."

"Damn straight."

Later, at home, she suddenly missed his company—after all, they'd been together day and night for nearly three months—and after loading her washer with her clothes, she snagged her phone from her purse and dialed her best friend.

Marley Griffin yelled a hello down the phone that made Quilla laugh. Marley, a science nerd who was currently wowing the science world with her research, was a Canadian émigré who Quilla had bonded with at college over their loathing of the cafeteria's food. The dark-haired, pale-skinned, hard-bodied Canook had been Quilla's confident ever since, but when she was in Venice, calling each other had been a case of when they had the money to call Emails just weren't the same, Quilla realized now, as she listened to her friend's happiness at hearing from her.

"I've been saving up," Marley told her now, "So that the day you came back, we could go out and blow it all on drink and loose men. Or was it loose drink and men? Either."

Quilla giggled. "God, I have missed you. When can we start drinking?"

JAKOB STOPPED by the office before heading to his father's house. His assistant Miles was there and the two chatted.

"You back to work?"

"Not for a couple of days, Miles, as long as there's nothing too urgent."

"Nothing that can't wait." Miles was a slight man of Iranian and Irish heritage, with effortless poise and grace and a razor-sharp intellect. Jakob thought again that he was wasted as his assistant and had offered to fund further education for him, but Miles insisted he was happy where he was—for now.

"I might change my mind on it, so keep that offer open," he'd said with a grin and Jakob had reassured him that it would always be open to him. He liked that Miles didn't defer to him or kiss his ass if he disagreed with him. Gregor, Jakob's business partner, loathed Miles—which was always a reason to keep someone around. Miles had no time for Gregor either.

"How is Gregor?"

Miles sniffed. "Busy spreading STDs as usual."

Jakob snorted with laughter. "No change there."

Miles made a face. "Ugh, can you imagine?"

Jakob grinned. "I hear women find him attractive."

Miles mumbled something and Jakob was pretty sure he heard the words 'Helen Keller'. He tried to look disapproving but failed.

"For someone as misogynistic as Gregor, he sure does enjoy having a lot of bad sex with as many women as he can. Oh, I'm assuming it's bad," Miles waved a hand dismissively, "because it's him."

Jakob laughed and right on cue, Gregor himself came through the door.

"Miles, can you send these by courier?" He threw an envelope down on the desk.

No please, no thank you. Jakob's eyes narrowed, but Miles, as unflappable as ever, merely ignored the envelope. "I'm sure Mandy will send it for you in the morning."

"I'm asking you."

"Hello, Gregor."

Gregor turned and blinked, obviously amazed at seeing him. "Hey, I didn't know you were back. To be honest, I didn't expect you back ... your dad said something about Venice and a girl?"

Miles' eyebrow shot up and he suddenly seemed very interested in their conversation. Jakob tried not to grin.

"Something like that. Anyway, I'm back."

Gregor chewed his lips, then tapped the envelope. "Send that out. Tonight, Miles. Jakob, a word in private?"

Jakob winked at Miles, who made an obscene gesture behind

Gregor's back but did it with such a cheesy grin on his face, Jakob had to smother a laugh.

Jakob followed Gregor back to his office and sat down. He already knew what was coming.

"So ... Venice. For nearly three months? Could have given me some notice, Jake."

Gregor knew Jakob hated his name shortened. He looked over at him now, obviously trying to figure out where this new relaxed Jakob had come from.

"So, who is she?"

"My girlfriend."

Gregor shook his head. "Man, I thought we had a silent agreement—no long-term things, no commitments to interfere with the business."

Jakob gave a hollow laugh. "I seem to remember us saying that once, in college, stoned out of our minds. Didn't think it was binding."

"How do you think we built this business, Jake? Work. Eighteen-hour days."

"Which we had the energy for twenty-five years ago. Jesus, Gregor, how much more money do you need? This place and the people we invested in are the top picks from every grad scheme in the country; hell, the world. You and me, we don't even need to show up for work anymore."

"So that's it? That's why you dropped everything for some Italian pussy?"

Jakob's dark green eyes took on a dangerous gleam. "Watch yourself, Greg. And she's American, actually, from here, too."

"How'd you meet her?"

Jakob hesitated, then decided the truth was the best way to go. "She dragged me out of the Venetian Lagoon after I jumped in. I was coming down, Greg, hard. She nursed me back to health."

Greg sneered. "So, she saves you from the drink, recognizes you, and thinks 'hey, meal ticket'."

Jakob moved suddenly then, diving across the desk and grabbing

Gregor by the throat. "Gregor, you don't ever talk like that about her again, okay? Or we are done." He studied the other man's eyes then released him in disgust. "You're high at work?"

Gregor gave a laugh. "Seriously? You're judging me? Did you think no one noticed at that benefit in January how wasted you were? Don't be a hypocrite, Jake. You know how much we built because we could use it to fuel our energy."

"Yeah," Jakob said, bleakly. "I remember, and I can tell you now ... it's over. You need to get clean or I'm walking away with my share and you can do whatever the hell you want."

He got up and walked to the door. "And I mean it, Gregor, you will speak about and to Quilla with respect, or not at all."

He slammed the door behind him, stalked down to the car, and drove out to his dad's place feeling irked and tired and ... pissed. Why was he still in business with that clown? It wasn't as if he even liked Gregor—the dude was snaky as all hell. Fuck it. He'd talk to his dad —who had warned him about Gregor from the beginning—and work out a way to separate from him without risking the jobs of the people who worked there. Buy Gregor out, maybe. Mallory Fisk didn't need him anymore and Jakob didn't need someone like that—such a malevolent presence—in his life.

As he drove out to the big house, he pushed Gregor to the back of his mind and focused instead on Quilla. He already missed her. Tomorrow he would go over early and see her before work. He still couldn't quite believe she was his ... or that he had fallen quite so hard. He'd always been such a workaholic, but the last three months he realized how much of life he had been missing.

He steered the car up the long driveway of his father's home. Despite his billions, Randall Mallory's home wasn't a tacky monolith to bad taste. Instead, it was a two-story ranch-style home—large, yes —but not over the top.

Jakob didn't bother to knock—it drove him mad that Ran never locked the door, but today he didn't care. He found his father reading in his library, his beloved dogs asleep at his feet.

"Hey, Dad."

Randall Mallory looked up and smiled, putting his book down. "Well about time, Jakob, come on in. I'll call for some coffee."

The dogs, two loopy Labrador retrievers, jumped up to greet Jakob and he wrestled with them while his dad ordered their drinks. Ran batted the dogs away affectionately and gave his son an awkward hug. He stood back and studied him. "Well now, you look good, Jakob. Healthy. Rested."

They sat, Jakob relieved to see his father looking so relaxed himself. Since their mom had died, Ran had gone through life with his usual stoicism but with a stoop to his tall frame, a sadness, an almost palpable sense of bewilderment. Francis Mallory had been the love of his life and without her, Ran wasn't sure how to exist. His father had never been the archetypal patriarch; he was kind, considerate, brilliant—and lonely and Jakob hated to see him so depressed.

Now, he smiled at his eldest son.

"You really do look good, Jakob. Now, tell me about this remarkable young lady."

BACK IN HIS OFFICE, Gregor Fisk had done little work since Jakob had left. He knew his time at the company was at risk and that Jakob held all the cards because at the beginning, it had been the Mallory family who had bankrolled Gregor.

He hated it. He hated being in debt to a family who, for the most part, hated him. He'd had a plan to change that. Had a plan. And mostly that plan had had to do with Jakob being deemed unfit for service by the Board. Gregor had invested time and had risked everything to procure the highest quality coke. When he'd persuaded Jakob to use a little pick-me-up—the night his mom was buried—he'd had no idea how quickly Jakob would become addicted. He had been using the drug to fend off the pain of losing his mom, of working to prove to his dad that he could take care of the business. Gregor had been waiting ever since to see Jakob fall.

And now, damn it, he was clean. Gregor had seen it in the healthy pallor of his skin, the clear sclera in his green eyes. All that work wasted. His interest had been piqued when Jakob had admitted the suicide attempt. That would have been … helpful. None of Jakob's brothers were interested in property—or were qualified to fill his position. It would have been Gregor's 'honor' to take the reins.

Now this girl had screwed up his plans … twice. Quilla. Gregor smirked. It shouldn't be too hard to find out who she was, with a name like that. He picked up the phone to call the person he knew could find her, wherever she was in the city.

QUILLA FLOPPED BACK on her bed, Marley beside her. "God, that was fun." They had been out at a local bar, a band playing in the background, and Quilla had told Marley everything. Almost. She'd edited the way she had met Jakob—she just said he fell in the water by accident. Normally she would have told Marley everything, but she felt disloyal about discussing Jakob's pain when they had never met.

"I still can't believe it … Jakob Mallory. Damn, girl," Marley propped herself up on her elbow and looked down at her friend. Quilla looked … amazing. That was the only word for it. Her eyes sparkled, her skin glowed … "Ugh, you are a living loved-up cliché," Marley grumbled and Quilla laughed.

"Yes, I am." She gave Marley a very cheesy, smug grin. "I got mine."

Marley snorted. "And then some, by the sounds of it. So, what now? I mean, you lived together for three months so …?"

"He asked me to move in with him—I said I needed time. That was then, though," she admitted, "and I thought I was being mature and sensible. But fuck it, if we can go through all of that and be …" She trailed off when she saw Markley's doubtful expression and sighed. "Yeah, I know. I just …"

"If you say 'miss him already', I will vomit on you." Marley growled, and pretended to throttle her friend. Quilla giggled and Marley relented.

"Well," she sat up, adjusting her T-shirt. "I'm going to get a cab. I need to meet this man of yours before you decide to move in with him and be all like 'Oh we must register for dishware, darling."

Quilla pushed her off the bed with a foot. "Yeah, that'll never happen."

"You don't know. When you're all Mrs. Billionaire, you can spend your days buffing your nails and giving him blow jobs that you've learned from his personal sex sensei."

Quilla was crying with laughter. "Yes, because that's what they do. God, you are a lunatic; my ribs hurt."

Marley leaned over and hugged her friend. "I am happy for you and not at all jealous. Nope, not one bit." She grinned wickedly at her friend, before waving. "I'm outty."

"Later, dude."

QUILLA HEARD her friend close her front door but lay on her bed still, catching her breath and thinking of the evening and her friend and Jakob—of course, Jakob. She rolled over onto her back, kicking her shoes off and easing out of her jeans. She grabbed her phone. Eleven p.m. There was a message she'd missed.

Thinking about your lips right now ... thinking about what I'm going to do to you tomorrow ... J xx

Quilla grinned. God, why had she said she wanted today to take a breather? She wanted him here, now ...

She shook her head and went to run a bath in her tiny tub. If nothing else, she needed to shave her legs and primp herself for tomorrow. She took her phone in with her—just in case—setting her iPad on the sink to play soft music. She had nearly drifted off to sleep when her phone buzzed.

She smiled when she saw the caller ID. "Hey, I was dreaming about you ..."

Jakob gave a throaty chuckle. "Must be catching. How was your evening?"

"Fun, but it was missing something." There was a chuckle in her voice.

"And what would that be?"

They both laughed. "I hear splashing. You in the tub ... naked?"

"Nope, fully clothed."

"Funny girl."

Quilla grinned. "You still at your dad's?"

"No, on my way back into the city. He wants to meet you."

Quilla felt a shiver of nervousness and when she didn't reply, Jakob reassured her. "You'll be fine; he's a kitten, really."

"I'll take your word for it."

"Anyway, this tub ..."

She laughed. "You know, it's small, but it could fit two people if they were very, very close ..."

Jakob growled. "Woman, I'm already on my way."

"I'll leave the door open for you."

JAKOB PUSHED OPEN the door to the apartment building and quickly ascended the two flights of stairs to Quilla's apartment. 3E. He pushed on her door and let himself in. Down the hallway, then he was into the living room. There were dimmed lamps on and Quilla, naked and wet from the bathtub, sat on a chair, waiting for him, her posture upright, and a small smile playing around her lips.

"Hello, baby," she said softly and slowly, and deliberately spread her legs so he could see her wet, slippery cunt, swollen and ready for him. Jakob let out a long sigh of longing and moved toward her. When he reached her, he bent his head to kiss her and felt her hands at his crotch, unzipping him. She smiled up at him. "Stay still, handsome."

She took his already stiffening cock from his pants and glided her lips over the wide crest of it, teasing the ultra-sensitive tip with her tongue. Her hand stroked up and down the length of his shaft while the other cupped his balls and massaged them gently.

"Jesus ... Quilla ..." Jakob closed his eyes and let the sensation of her mouth and hands take over his body. God, this woman ...

In moments, he was on the edge and made to move to pull away, but her hands clamped onto his buttocks, keeping him rooted there until, with a moan, he came, shooting into her warm, wet mouth.

As soon as he could gather himself, he reached down and took her in his arms. "Now that is a wonderful, wonderful way to be greeted."

He pressed his lips to hers and wrapped his arms around her small body. "God, I missed you today, Quilla Chen ..."

"Me too, baby," she whispered. "Come, let's get reacquainted ..."

Gregor walked out into reception the following Monday, on his way to a meeting. He was already annoyed; now that Jakob was back, it was seriously curtailing his usual method of business. Plus, all his private detective had been able to find out was that his girl-friend was a grad student. Gregor had been obsessing over the woman all weekend, sure she was the reason that everything was changing.

Now, on his way to a meeting, he glanced over to the couches in reception – and stopped. A gorgeous girl was sitting there, waiting, her long dark hair pulled up into a messy bun at the nape of her neck, her slim legs in flared jeans and sneakers. Gregor felt his groin tighten. Glancing over at Maxine, the receptionist, who ignored him, he strolled over to the young woman.

"Hi."

She looked up and smiled. God, beautiful. "Hi."

"Can I help you with something?"

She shook her head. He guessed she must be part Asian; her eyes were a beautiful shape, her features delicate. "It's okay. I'm just waiting for Jakob."

Gregor rocked back. "Jakob ... Mallory?"

She grinned. "Is there another?"

This couldn't be her, she was way too young for Jakob ... wasn't she? Gregor stuck his hand out. "Gregor Fisk, Jakob's business partner."

The young woman, who had been sketching, shoved her pad to one side and stood up, taking his hand. "Quilla Chen, Jakob's ... friend."

Gregor had to smile at that. "Jake and I have no secrets, Quilla. I know you're fucking him."

Quilla rocked back a little and her smile faded. "It's Jakob," she said finally, "and that is none of your business." She dropped her hand.

"Everything okay here?"

Gregor looked around to see Jakob descending on them. "All good. Delighted to meet your beautiful friend."

He noticed Jacob move to Quilla's side and put a protective arm around her. "Hey, baby."

"Hey," Quilla said, her narrowed eyes fixed on Gregor's. "Let's go, shall we?"

Gregor watched them walk away, amused. Quilla Chen wasn't going to be a problem, he decided. Her clothes, though she wore them well, were cheap—when you put that together with the studentship, the artist ... hell, this was going to be easy. He'd pay her to disappear; he knew her type. Always using that off-the-charts beauty to snag themselves a rich one. And by the look of it, Jakob was in deep. Deep, deep. Her leaving would be a body blow. And if she wouldn't?

Gregor watched as the couple got into Jakob's car. Quilla Chen was slightly built. If she wouldn't go voluntarily ... there were other ways.

Ways that would break your little heart, Jakey boy. Gregor smirked to himself and went to his meeting.

QUILLA DREW IN A BIG, shaky breath. Any minute now they would meet with Jakob's father, and she could feel her palms sweating. She rubbed them on her jeans. Jeans? What had she been thinking? Jakob had said the dinner would be casual, but maybe she had taken him too literally.

"Stop panicking." Jakob was watching her, his grin wide. He was enjoying this.

"Jerk." She stuck her lower lip out.

Jakob laughed. "You can punish me later, woman. We're here."

Randall Mallory was waiting as they got out of the car and he walked down, smiling to meet Quilla. "Quilla, I've heard so much about you." He stood only an inch or two smaller than his son, his dark blond hair worn in a flowing, pushed-back way. Elegance screamed from every pore. His handsome face showed little of his age —late sixties—and his smile was genuine and welcoming. His voice was warm and deep and he shook her hand before clapping his son on the back. "We're barbecuing. Come around back."

We're? Quilla shot a panicked look at Jakob—who seemed to be looking everywhere except at her. Sneaky son-of-a ... half grinning to herself, she managed to kick the back of his calf and heard his low chuckle. Ran led them around the house into the huge and beautiful garden. There, she saw a group of people sitting, laughing with each other. A very familiar blond young man was teasing the dogs. Skandar Mallory. Quilla's nerves came racing back, but she wondered if she could surreptitiously call Marley—she would die of envy. The thought made her grin and she was still smiling when they reached the group. Jakob's brother Joel, a tall, rangy man, his long blond hair tied back, shook her hand—she was surprised that he appeared shy. Completely unlike his son: Skandar Mallory was everything she expected, confident, arrogant, and a whole lot of fun. Ran introduced her to a gorgeous woman with caramel-colored hair and dark brown eyes. She shook Quilla's hand. "Asia Flynn. Technically not a Mallory anymore, but they have trouble letting go," she stage-whispered, winking at Ran, who rolled his eyes. Quilla laughed; she liked the woman immediately.

In fact, as she met other members of the family, cousins, friends, she wondered at how unlike the stereotype of a rich family they were. If it was possible to be so alike in their temperament and yet so different at the same time, the Mallorys had it down.

Joel, she discovered, was looking for a new career. "I've gone as far as I can, coaching him," he told Quilla, gesturing at his son, who was now wrestling both the dogs and his uncle. Quilla saw Jakob was losing and grinned at him. Help me, he mouthed to her, and she shook her head, smiling triumphantly. Ha, ha, payback. Skandar raised his arms in victory as Jakob gave up.

"Isn't he number one in the world?" Quilla asked Joel, who shrugged and smiled shyly.

"Yep, but I don't have the experience he needs now to help him stay there. He's enjoying it at the moment but it's only going to get harder. Tennis players have a short shelf life past twenty-five."

Quilla groaned. "Too depressing." Joel grinned and tapped her beer bottle with his. "Preach it, sister."

Asia, she learned, was Kit's ex-wife. Very recent ex-wife. An entertainment lawyer, she'd married Kit Mallory in Monte Carlo on a whim, five years previously.

"It was good for four and a half of those years," Asia told her with a wry grin as evening drew in. "Just didn't go the distance. I might have left Kit, but I couldn't bear to leave the family." She patted Quilla's hand. "I'm glad Jakob has you. We were worried."

RANDALL MALLORY ECHOED that sentiment an hour later. Feeling brave, Quilla had gone to seek him out and found him in his library. He stood up when he saw her and invited her to sit. He poured some wine for her.

"Whatever you did for my son, I want to thank you."

Quilla flushed. "I didn't do anything, really."

"You are too modest." Ran's voice was so soothing, so mellifluous, that it was impossible to feel tense in his presence. "I know my son. Before he met you, before he went to Italy ... he was breaking. He was breaking, and I didn't know what to do. What happened in Venice, Quilla?"

Quilla shifted in her seat, uncomfortable. "Mr. Mallory—"

"Ran."

"Ran ... I respect you very much, but it's not my place to tell you that. Please, I don't want to offend you."

"Quilla, my dear, if anything, you have proved his faith in you. I'm sorry, but in my position—in his position—I had to be absolutely sure. Jakob told me what happened."

Quilla didn't know how to respond to his testing of her. She chewed her lip. "Ran, I want you to know, I never did anything for any ... gain of my own. It was all for him."

Ran smiled. "Quilla, believe me when I tell you, I never thought any different. One only has to be in your presence to know your genuine empathy. Your love."

He got up, and nervously, she followed suit. He placed his hands on her shoulders and she was surprised to see tears in his eyes.

"You saved my son," he said, his voice breaking. "Thank you."

Quilla wanted to cry at the emotion in his voice. "I guess I did gain after all, because I couldn't imagine a world without him."

Ran hugged her tightly. "From now on, Quilla Chen, whatever happens, you are a part of this family. I will never forget what you've done for my boy."

SHE WAS STILL FEELING the warmth from that hug when Jakob took her back to his apartment. She walked into what could only be described as a page out of a catalogue. Muted colors, black, white, gray blended perfectly. She nodded approvingly at the stuffed bookshelves and of course, his art. She looked at one piece, then turned to gape at him. "That's a Hopper. A. Hopper. Please tell me it's a print ... no, don't, I don't want to know."

Jakob grinned. "Come here, wench." He opened his arms and she went into them, tilting her head up for a kiss.

"My family is crazy about you," he murmured, trailing his lips down her neck.

"It's mutual." She wound her arms around his neck and pressed her body against his. "I adored them. Asia is great, too; Kit must be a fool."

Jakob laughed softly. "Don't be too hard on him; the divorce is hitting him hard. Yep, he's an idiot, but he still loves her."

He took her hand and led her into his bedroom, Quilla nodding approvingly at the massive bed. "Well, lookit, our playground."

Jakob laughed as he slid his hands under the straps of her top and pulled them down her shoulders, stopping to kiss each one. "Quilla?"

She moaned as he freed her breast from her bra and took the nipple into his mouth, sucking and teasing it until it became so sensitized she could barely stand it. "Yes, babe?"

"I'm in love with you."

A delighted smile spread across her face. "And I am in love with you, Jakob Mallory."

Jakob chuckled. "Thank God."

Quilla shrieked with laughter as he pushed her back onto the bed and started to tug her jeans and underwear from her, burying his face in her sex for a second before covering her body with his. She freed his quivering, rigid cock from his pants and stroked it while he kissed her.

"I'm going to fuck you all night long, Quilla Chen ..." And as he thrust into her, Quilla sighed happily, knowing that there would be endless nights like this, with this wonderful, sexy man.

She didn't know just how soon the fairytale would end ...

Jakob dropped her off at home before going into work. "Shall I pick you up from college later?"

"I'd love it, thank you." She kissed him before regretfully breaking away and opening the passenger side door.

"Hey," he said as she got out, "Call the movers." He grinned, and she laughed.

"Don't worry, I will."

She went back up to her apartment, still smiling. Yesterday had been a momentous day—meeting his family, finally declaring their love, and then, later, after marathon sex, Jakob had asked her to move in with him. This time, she hadn't hesitated.

Back in her apartment, she dropped her purse and looked around. They'd joked about movers, but really, they wouldn't have that much to move. Books, records, art supplies, her clothes. All the furniture had come with the apartment. Quilla realized how compact her life had been before. What would it be like now? She still felt that vague uneasiness over the chasm between their lives, but she loved him. She didn't want his money, she wanted him. Screw what anybody else thought.

A knock at the door. She grinned—Jakob, back for another kiss? She was still smiling as she yanked the door open, but it faded swiftly.

Gregor Fisk stood in her doorway, his face hard. "Hi, Quilla. I think we need to talk." And before she could react, he pushed his way inside.

JAKOB GOT to the office and greeted Miles with a beaming smile. His assistant looked amused. "I take it the family meeting went well?"

"Very well ... plus, she's agreed to move in with me."

Miles, never one to avoid a spotlight, stood and did a celebratory dance. Jakob shook his head, laughing.

"Miles, never change."

In his office, he sat and reflected. His life was so totally different from six months ago. And he hadn't finished yet. When Quilla had agreed to move in with him, he'd lain awake, with her sleeping in his arms, and thought about the one thing he still had to change—his work. He was so tired of property. Even though it had made him billions, it no longer satisfied his soul. And then there was Gregor. Jakob shook his head. The best thing he could do was cut him loose; buy him out or vice versa. He didn't need Greg's sneakiness, his duplicity, in his life. Quilla clearly hadn't liked him from the start, even though she refused to tell him what Greg had said to upset her. She was protecting him, Jakob, he knew that, but still. Gregor had to go.

Jakob picked up the phone and asked the company's head of HR to meet him as soon as he could.

GREGOR SAT WITHOUT BEING ASKED, looking around her apartment with a sneer on his face. Quilla felt her face flush with anger.

"What do you want?"

Gregor smiled. "I'll make this simple. I will give you a quarter of a billion dollars to leave this city and never come back."

Quilla gaped at him. "What the fuck?"

"Come on. Don't act innocent, Quilla; I really don't have time. You've played the game perfectly. Jakob is crazy about you. But I need his head in the game, so to speak, and that means you," he pointed at her as if she didn't know whom he meant, "have to go. So ..."

Quilla stood and up and went to open her front door. "Get out. Now."

He didn't move. "Come on, now. Two-hundred and fifty million dollars. Just looking around here, I can see that kind of money would be life changing."

"That kind of money would be life-changing for anyone," she retorted. "Get out."

Gregor stood, shaking his head, smiling. "Don't be naïve, Quilla. This was your one chance for this not to turn nasty. Last chance. Take the money. It'll be quite the step up for the daughter of a heroin addict and deadbeat dad."

Quilla's eyes filled with tears of anger, disgust, and humiliation. "Go fuck yourself, Gregor. You don't know me or anything about me, and anyway, coming from a coke junkie, you have no room to talk. I don't give a fuck about money; I just care about Jakob. And I would appreciate it if you didn't have me followed or whatever it is you're doing. Leave."

Gregor stood up as if to leave. Then, in a flash, he was pressing her body up against the wall, his hand slipping between her legs. "And yet you spread your legs for the nearest billionaire."

Pushing his hand away from her, she slapped him across the face, hard, and with a roar of rage, he grabbed her and threw her to the floor. "Fucking bitch!"

He kicked her, hard, in the stomach and she curled up into a ball. Gregor stood back, trying to calm himself. "Take the deal, Quilla. And I wouldn't bother to tell Jakob about this—or it's going to get a lot worse than that, little girl."

He left her still curled up and not believing what had just happened. She eventually staggered over to her door and slammed it, shooting the deadbolt across before sinking to the floor. She had never been more terrified in her life—terror mixed with anger and disbelief. *Fuck you, Gregor, I won't be threatened.* She got unsteadily to her feet and stumbled over to grab her phone.

When she heard Jakob's voice, she couldn't hold back the tears.

GREGOR DROVE BACK to the office. *Damn it, that shouldn't have gone that far ... not yet.* He sighed. *Maybe he'd scared her enough that she'd leave anyway, now.* He had to admit—Jakob knew how to pick them—Quilla Chen was beautiful, but he knew a gold digger when he saw one.

Lost in his thoughts, he didn't notice everyone staring at him as he made his way back to his office. When he got there, he stopped. Jakob, Randall, and the Head of H.R., Paul, were waiting.

"What's going on?"

Ran put a hand on Jakob's arm as Jakob, his face full of rage, stepped forward. Ran spoke, his eyes hard, and he held out a sheet of paper. "Gregor, this is a notice of your termination. You will leave here, after we have spoken, and you will not return. Your name will be removed from the company, and you will receive no financial reparation. In return, we will not contact the police and report your assault and attempted blackmail of Quilla Chen. Do I make myself clear?"

Gregor smirked. "You cannot do that. I have a contract—and half this company is mine."

Ran's smile was icy. "Actually, we can." He looked over to Paul, who nodded.

"Because you were loaned the money to pay for your side of the business—and you have yet to fully repay the Mallorys for that loan, we can default you. Also—there's an 'appropriate behavior' clause in your contract. We have deemed you in breach of that."

"Put simply, leave now or we will ruin you." Jakob's voice was scratchy with rage and Gregor looked at his partner.

"Over some Asian pussy?"

It took both Ran and Paul to hold Jakob back. Ran narrowed his eyes at Gregor. "Get out and don't ever come back."

Gregor, realizing they meant what they said, shook his head. "This isn't over."

Randall Mallory let go of his son's arm. "Oh, it is, Gregor. It is."

"So you fired him? Just like that?"

They were sitting in a crowded bar in the city, at a booth with a table full of empty bottles. Joel and Marley, their drinking companions for the evening, were at the bar, getting along famously. Quilla was tucked into the crook of Jakob's arm, his lips against her forehead.

"Yup," he said, drawing away and looking down at her. "Good riddance. I should have done this years ago."

"What will he do now?"

"I really don't give a fuck. Besides, Gregor's got enough money that he'll never have to work again."

Quilla shook her head. "I still don't get why he wanted me out of the way so badly."

"Christ, who knows what's going on in that junky head? Drugs have fucked him up. He was always a tool, but never like this. And I might have turned out like that if it wasn't for you, beautiful, so thank you again."

She kissed him back, her mouth curving up in a smile. "You could never be like that."

Jakob looked her over appreciatively. She had a white, floating dress on which made her look ethereal, her hair bunched up in a messy bun. The dress fell to her mid-thigh, her golden-skinned legs so tempting to him. He ran a leisurely hand up her inner thigh and she wriggled with pleasure.

"That dress is driving me crazy," he murmured in her ear and she chuckled, sighing with pleasure as his fingers made contact with her panties. "I want to fuck you so bad," he said, nipping her earlobe with his teeth. She grinned.

"Later, gator ... our friends are coming back."

THE BAR WAS STILL PACKED at nearly midnight. Quilla excused herself to go to the ladies' room, and Jakob was being grilled by Marley. They were all a little tipsy and Jakob, Marley, and Joel grinned as Quilla made her unsteady way to the bathrooms. Jakob listened to Joel and Marley argue with each other. He liked Quilla's friend very much—so did his brother, by the looks of it, but Jakob couldn't tell if it was the teasing between soon-to-be lovers, or two future best friends the first time they met. He'd had way too much champagne, he decided. As his vision blurred, he looked out over the crowded bar, waiting for Quilla to return.

Then his heart began to beat faster and he sat up. Gregor. Gregor was in the bar. The other man saw him and saluted sarcastically. Shit. As Jakob looked on, he suddenly saw Gregor turn and he followed his gaze ... Quilla.

God ... Jakob stood suddenly, startling the other two who followed his gaze. Joel, knowing Gregor's face, jumped up too, and all three of them dived into the crowd. With a wrench of pure terror, he saw Gregor get to Quilla first. He saw her turn and register Gregor's presence with a look of alarm. Then Jakob lost sight of them in the crowed.

Someone screamed. "He's got a knife!"

No, no, oh God, no ...

"Out of my way," Jacob shouted in desperation and a path started to clear. He got to Quilla just as Gregor disappeared. For a second, Jakob felt relief, but then, as Quilla turned to him, her lovely face pale, her eyes confused, he saw the blood. Her hands clutched to her belly, her white dress turning red.

Blood. Her blood ...

As Quilla began to collapse, he raced forward to catch her ...

2

PART TWO: TOUCH ME

Joel Mallory leaned his head against the cool wall of the hospital waiting room. Next to him, Marley Griffin was sitting hunched over, jiggling her legs up and down. It was three a.m., and they'd been waiting for a couple of hours while the doctors assessed their friend, Quilla Chen.

Joel thought back over the last few hours. The laughter, the fun of hanging with his brother and Quilla and her friend in their favorite bar, then the utter horror when in an instant, the world had changed and his eldest brother, Jakob's, girlfriend was stabbed by a vengeful ex-partner of Jakob's.

The mad, panicked dash to get help, the flashing lights, Quilla passed out and bleeding in a terrified Jakob's arms—God. Joel felt sick.

He looked over at Marley. They'd only met that night, but already they'd become good friends, but now the young woman looked hollow and scared. He took her hand and she half smiled at him. "Don't worry, sweetheart. She'll get the best care, I promise."

Marley smiled gratefully. "I'm going crazy waiting. I'm going to find some coffee."

Alone, Joel sighed. He'd called his dad, who was on his way.

Skandar had wanted to come, too, but Joel, mindful of the constant press that followed his son everywhere, told him not to. "Last thing we need, pal, is a media circus," he told him. "Quilla knows you care."

The door to the waiting room opened, and a young woman with messy blonde hair to her shoulders came in. She nodded at Joel, then took a seat on the far side. She looked exhausted. In her hands there was no purse, just a set of car keys. Joel realized that she was wearing a nightshirt over her jeans, obviously having had to come out in a hurry.

"Hey," he said, "you okay?"

The woman looked up, her eyes red from crying, and tried to smile. "Yeah, thanks." She hesitated. "Teenage sister thought it was a good idea to go out, drink, then got in a car with a guy who was also drunk."

"Damn ... she okay?"

The woman sighed. "Yeah, she's just getting stitched up now. Scared the shit out of me." She studied him. "How about you?"

Joel shifted in his seat. "Friend got stabbed. We don't know how she is yet."

"God, I'm sorry."

Joel nodded, then got up and held his hand out to the woman. "Joel Mallory."

She smiled. "Nan Applebee. That's awful about your friend ... what happened?"

Joel sat down next to her, shaking his head. "Hell, if I know ... she's my brother's girlfriend and the dude that stabbed her was trying to get back at my brother for firing him. Damn coward. She's tiny, too; you should see her."

The enormity of what had happened seemed to be hitting him now, after hours of disbelief. He clenched his fists tightly to stop his hands trembling. "Sorry," he said when he noticed her watching him. "It's the cruelty of it, you know? Never seen anything like that before."

Tentatively, Nan put his hand on his back and rubbed it to comfort him. Joel blew out his cheeks, then looked up as first Marley, and then Jakob, came back to the room. Joel stood and hugged his brother, introducing the others to Nan Applebee.

"Quilla's going to be fine," Jakob said, his voice scratchy from stress. "One stab wound, clean, not too deep, but nasty enough. Painful. It didn't hit any of her major organs. She'll be here for a couple of days, then they'll let her out to recover at home."

Marley stood at his side, dark purple shadows under eyes. Jakob looked down at her and put his arm around her shoulders. "Hey, kiddo, do you want to stay at mine for a couple of days?"

Marley, pale and drained, move away from him, her entire body rigid with tension. "No, thanks. I'd rather be at home."

Joel nodded. "I'll take you." But Marley shook her head.

"No ... I'll get a cab, thanks. I just ... never mind." She turned to go, then stopped and looked back at Jakob. "I don't want to be the person who assigns blame ... but make this right, Jakob."

Joel stared after her. "Man, she's angry."

"She has every right. Look, they say I can stay with Quilla but ..."

Joel nodded. "I get it. Look, I'll update Dad and the others. What are we going to do about the press?"

Jakob rubbed his face. "God, I hadn't even thought ... look, we say exactly what happened. We fired Gregor Fisk because of gross incompetence and his behavior. He got angry and tried to get revenge."

"They'll dig up everything on Quilla they can find—it might get rough."

Jakob smiled humorlessly. "Not as rough as being stabbed. She's a fighter; a little press intrusion is something we can protect her from. Can Skandar run some interference?"

Joel nodded. "I'll talk to him. He'll get questions, no doubt, and someone from here's bound to leak it."

"Maybe we can ask them to sign some NDAs?"

"No." Ran Mallory walked through the door at that moment and heard them. "We've never been the sort of family who runs and hides. We ride ..."

"... out the storm," said his sons in unison and Ran smiled.

"That's right. How's Quilla?"

Jakob told him the news and Ran nodded. "Good. That's good to hear. Damn that Fisk ... I have everyone out looking for him. Hello ..."

He suddenly noticed Nan sitting behind Joel, trying to make herself invisible. Ran smiled and shook her hand. "I'm sorry; we seem to have taken over the waiting room."

"It's no problem ... oh, hey." Nan looked over at the door, where a young blonde teenager hovered, her face crisscrossed with butterfly stitches. She glanced shyly at the three men, then at her sister.

"Doctor says I'm good to go."

Nan got up and smiled at Joel. "It was nice to talk to you."

Joel nodded. "You, too. Glad the kid's okay."

"You wait till I get her home," Nan muttered with a wry grin. Joel laughed, but didn't envy the younger woman.

"Look, can you get home okay?"

Nan, at the doorway with her sister now, turned. "Yeah, I have my car, but thanks. I hope your friend is okay."

HAYLEY APPLEBEE GLANCED over at her elder sister as they drove home. So far, Nan had said precisely nothing, but Hayley knew that just meant the build-up of magma under the volcano was just getting bigger and soon Vesuvius would explode.

To head at least some of the eruption off, she sighed. "Look, Nan, I'm sorry. It was a dumb thing to do."

"So dumb."

"I know." Hayley waited. Nothing.

"Aren't you going to yell at me?" She frowned at her sister, weirdly disappointed. Nan, who looked drawn and tired out, shook her head.

"Hays ... I was all ready to rip you a new one, but then ... that dude I was talking to, his friend got stabbed by a guy because her boyfriend fired him. He stabbed her. Not the boyfriend. When we live in a world like that, you doing something most teenagers have done at one point or another and getting off relatively unscathed—well, now, I can live with that."

She shot a side look at her sister. "Doesn't mean you're off the hook entirely, though."

Hayley smiled. "Didn't think so. Nan, you know who those people were, don't you?"

Nan looked blank. "I know the first guy's name was Joel but ..."

Hayley sighed. "Nan, please, occasionally read a gossip site, okay? The Mallorys? The richest family on the west coast? Kit Mallory, the actor? Skandar Mallory, the tennis player?"

Nan looked confused. "He wasn't there."

Hayley muttered something under her breath, then said, "I know. The dude with the long blond hair? That's Skandar's dad."

Nan shook her head. "No way. That guy is way too young."

After trying to explain who the Mallorys were, to no avail, Hayley gave up. At home, she apologized to her sister again, hugged her, and went to bed.

NAN FLOPPED down on her bed and checked the time. Just after five a.m. She groaned. In a couple of hours, she'd have to be up and ready to teach a class full of eighth graders about Hemingway. Why couldn't Hayley have decided to do this on a weekend? Nan realized the absurdity of what she was thinking and sent an apology into the cosmos.

She plumped up her pillow and closed her eyes, but sleep would not come. For some reason, she was thinking about the tall, blond, impossibly handsome Joel Mallory. And you've just answered your own question, she grinned to herself. She couldn't believe he was the son of a billionaire, the father of another. He had such a plaid-wearing homeliness about him. She could imagine him chopping down trees or bringing in the cattle, but not coaching a world-class tennis player. She wondered if the dark-haired girl with him was his girlfriend—she hadn't seemed like it, but who knew?

She fell asleep eventually and was only ten minutes late to her first class. She called that a good day.

．　．　．

TWO WEEKS LATER, Joel sat, watching Skandar's practice session with his hitting partner, barely registering the skillful shots his son was hammering down the other end of the court. Soon, he wouldn't need to do this, get up early to fly off all over the world. It had been his decision to bow out of Skandar's training at the end of this season, but as his responsibilities had lessened and his time freed up, he'd been flailing around for things to do.

Before Skandar had been born, he'd started at college, intending to get an architectural degree, to go into business with Jakob, building and designing exquisite homes at affordable prices. But when a one-night hook-up with a girl called Felicity had resulted in a pregnancy and subsequent maternal abandonment, all that changed. He'd given his son both his own grandfather's and his son's grandfathers' names, and Skandar Randall Mallory was born. And he had honestly loved every moment. His bond with his son had been one of trust and love and laughter. Skandar, as soon as he could run, was a bundle of energy, and when Ran had bought him a tennis racket for his sixth birthday, it was obvious to everyone that Skandar's future career path was pretty much set.

Now, Skandar was twenty-five and the number one tennis player in the world. His matinee idol looks meant he was never off the front page of the tabloids and his dad, not a slouch in the looks department either, garnered almost as much attention. Joel, unlike Skandar, didn't relish the attention, and he was looking to go back to relative anonymity when he left the coaching team.

"Yo." Skandar nudged him out of his reverie, holding out a cold bottle of water to him, then cracking one open for himself and draining it. The morning was warm for a Seattle fall day, and Skandar's shirt was drenched with sweat. Peeling it off and dumping it on the ground, he yanked another from his bag.

"You okay, Pa? You've been quiet all morning. I hit a pristine backhand down the line earlier, see it?"

"Good job," Joel said automatically, then blinked, coming back to the present. "Sorry, my head's not in the game today."

Skandar sat down next to him. "Pa, I've meant to ask ... what are you going to do now? It's been a couple of months since you said you were going to hand over to Carlos."

Joe shrugged. "Honestly, I'm not sure. I was talking to Jakob about it ... I thought maybe I could go back to college, finish my degree, partner with him on some project."

Skandar tipped half a bottle of ice water over his head. "Sounds good. What's stopping you?"

Joel smiled, sheepish. "This sounds crazy, but my confidence in my ability to do that, now that I'm older, has taken a knock."

Skandar studied his father. "What about taking a couple of adult courses at night school? See if you like that, before you commit to college."

Joel squinted at his son. "When did you get so smart?"

Skandar grinned. "Just occasionally, I can bring my A game. Although, really, I'm thinking, you're a freaking billionaire, just enjoy life. You did all the heavy lifting bringing me up on your own."

"Never felt like heavy lifting, and it's Dad who's a billionaire; it's you, not me. I need to make my own way," Joel said, and Skandar clapped him on the shoulder.

"Dad, I know. Regardless, it's not easy ... I'm not sure I could have done it. Anyway, I'd better get back to it. Think about the night classes, yeah?"

The kid was right, Joel thought. A tester class might be the way to go. He grabbed his iPad and started to research as Skandar destroyed his hitting partner with a vicious serve.

JAKOB STARTED to laugh as soon as he got home. Quilla, obviously bored after being house-bound while she recovered, had built a fort out of the boxes of her stuff he'd arranged to have picked up. She lay in the middle of it, propped up on pillows, reading, and a half-drunk cup of tea beside her. He peered over the ramparts of the fort and grinned at her.

"Didn't the doctor tell you not to lift anything heavy?" he said in mock-disapproval.

Quilla stuck her tongue out at him. After the horrific night, the terror of not knowing if she was going to be okay, Jakob had been afraid her natural merriment would be subdued, but no, she was astonishingly resilient.

Quilla had talked about the attack—she'd had to go over and over it a hundred times with the police, after all—and she seemed remarkably practical about it. "Weirdly, I didn't even realize he'd stabbed me until I saw your face, and the blood," she told Jakob. "I thought he'd just punched me. My body knew something was very wrong before my brain did ... then, that's when the pain hit. I don't remember anything after that, until I woke up in the hospital. Did the police find Gregor?"

Jakob had shaken his head, his face grim. "No. He's still out there, somewhere. But I promise you, Quilla, he won't hurt you again."

She smiled, touched his face. "I know that."

She'd been released from the hospital a couple of days after the stabbing, but on the understanding that she was to take it easy. 'Taking it easy' had meant being spoiled by Jakob, he'd told her, and he had. He'd arranged for all of her possessions to be moved to his penthouse, had made sure his home was turned into their home now, making room in his closet for her clothes, room on his bookshelves for her beloved books. He'd even cleared out a guest room and made it into an artist's studio for her. There were tears of gratitude and love when she saw it.

Now, though, restricted by her injury to sitting for most of the day until it healed properly, Quilla was being to get stir crazy.

Jakob helped her to her feet and led to the couch, pulling her onto his lap and kissing her. "How was work?" Quilla asked between kisses.

"Same old, same old."

"So you're not extra-busy because Stabby McDouchebag isn't there?"

Jakob winced and laughed at the same time. Only Quilla could make light of something so serious. His arms tightened around her, but he kept his tone light. "Nope. To be honest, the place runs itself now. If I'm honest ... you're not the only one who is bored. I'm thinking about stepping back, letting the executives run it, and concentrating on smaller projects ... affordable housing, places for the homeless. Stuff I—and Dad—always wanted to do."

Quilla stroked the hair back behind his ears. "If I didn't already love you more than it was possible to love someone, Jakob Mallory ... "

She kissed him, her lips moving firmly against his, her fingers knotting in his hair. Jakob closed his eyes, enjoying the feel of her skin against his, tasting her, his tongue moving against hers gently. Then, as the heat began to build, he pushed her away, gently. "Quilla ... you have to take it easy. Seriously, we have to wait at least six weeks, the doctor said."

"God." She was annoyed now. "I feel fine. It doesn't even hurt anymore; my stitches are coming out in a few days."

Jakob is grinning at her sulky face. "Nympho. I'd rather wait a few weeks, then have you healthy for the rest of your life, rather than risk anything ... tearing."

They both winced and Quilla shrugged. "Fine ... but after six weeks, you'd better be ready for some seriously dirty sex."

He grinned, leaning over to kiss her. "Damn right, I will be.

JOEL PUSHED his way into the community center slowly. The place was quiet this afternoon—there was a school across the street, and he could hear the kids playing in the sun. Joel went to the reception and pressed the bell. A kind-faced woman in her sixties smiled at him as she came around the corner.

"Hi there ... you need something?"

Joel half-smiled, cleared his throat, nervous. "Yeah, um, I was wondering if you had any fall evening classes with any places left?"

"Okeydokey." She sat down at her desk and wiggled the mouse to wake the computer screen. "Well, let's see ... what kind of thing were you looking for?" At Joel's blank face, she smiled. "Okay, let's just see what we've got available first, then go from there. Just a minute, dear."

The phone rang on her desk and she picked it up, balancing it on her shoulder and chin. She spoke quietly into it at first, then glanced up at Joel. "Actually," she said to the other person on the phone, "I could use some help. I have a very pleasant young man at reception who wants to know if we have any places left in the evening classes. No, that's just it, I don't think he knows, so maybe you could talk ... that's wonderful, see you in a minute."

She put the phone down and smiled. "We have our career advisor coming to see you; she may be able to help you chose the right course for you. Take a seat, hon."

Joel thanked her and went to sit down. He grabbed a magazine from the pile on the table and saw Skandar's face on the cover. He never stopped feeling proud of what his son had achieved. Ever.

"Joel?" He looked up to see a very attractive, very familiar blonde woman grinning at him.

"Nan?" His voice broke in amazement. Dude, you sound like Scooby Doo.

Nan obviously had a similar thought and smothered a grin. "Come with me." She nodded towards the inner sanctum. "I have an office with air-con we can talk in."

He hadn't noticed the reception was stifling until she said it. He followed her down a long hallway and into a small office at the far corner. As they sat, he smiled at her.

"It's good to see you again ... how's your sister?"

Nan rolled her eyes. "All teenager. Shouldn't say that. Apart from the odd aberration like that night, she's a good kid. Cares about people, about the world. How about your friend?"

Joel smiled. "Well on the way to recovery. My brother tells me she's bored out of her mind on bedrest."

Nan laughed. "Maybe you should have brought her, too. Which brings me to my next question—Joel, Hayley told me who your family is, what they've done, so I guess my question is: What the hell is a billionaire doing asking after night classes?" She had such a sweet grin that Joel couldn't help but join in with her laughter.

"My son needs more intensive coaching than I can give him and, to be honest, I'm sick of traveling around the world."

She looked at him askance, and he held his hands up. "Sorry, that didn't come out right. What I mean is ... I need to do something for myself now, and I'd like to be closer to my family."

"And you didn't want to go into the family business?"

"That's just it—the family business isn't just one thing—it's art, it's property, it's acting, it's sport. I'm trying to find where I fit in."

Nan nodded. "I understand ... well, what is it you're passionate about?"

Joel was silent for a moment. "I can't remember anything past caring for my son. Is that sad?"

"Definitely not," Nan said with feeling, her cheeks reddening. "That's wonderful. I kind of get where you're coming from—Hayley and I are a self-contained unit. Of course, that doesn't help you now," she admitted with a grin.

Joel smiled. He liked this woman very much, her humor, her intellect, her easy smile, her caramel-blonde hair falling onto her shoulders ... concentrate, Mallory.

"Is this what you do then, give career advice?" He looked around the room at the information posters; the books stacked high, battered old file cabinets with drawers that didn't quite close. There was something comforting about the room—about Nan too, he realized.

"No," she said. "I just do this once a week when I have free time. I teach eighth grade at the school across the street."

He blinked. "And on your free period, you volunteer here? Wow."

Nan smiled shyly. "I like to give back. Hey, look, why don't we start by talking about what qualifications you do have and see what comes up in the mix?"

Joel smiled gratefully. "Thank you. I really appreciate it and ..." he hesitated, not used to this anymore, "if it's not wildly inappropriate, can I take you out for a drink to say thanks? You can say no, if ..."

"Yes, I'd like that," she said, blushing furiously, and Joel grinned. "Good. Now ... my qualifications."

. . .

HE HAD no idea what prompted him to ask Nan Applebee out; it was just that second, a lock of hair had fallen over her face, the ends brushing her rosy cheeks, and she had looked so entirely adorable that he couldn't help himself.

They'd arranged to go out the following Friday. She refused his offer to pick her up—sensible girl—and arranged to meet at one of her favorite bars in the city.

Joel smiled to himself now as he dressed to meet her. Of all his family, he had always been the one to enjoy simple things—not simple; he amended, just more natural—plain, hardy clothes rather than tailored and expensive suits, a good burger, beer straight from the fridge. He'd always felt the disenfranchised brother, the one who didn't bring home the supermodels—he immediately felt bad at that thought. He loved Asia and Quilla, and neither of them behaved like some of the women his twin brother Kit dated. He still thought Kit was a fool for letting Asia go.

Nan Applebee was just the kind of woman he liked; smart, funny, kind. The fact was that he couldn't stop thinking about her soft skin or the clean, fresh laundry scent of her.

Ease on down, tiger; you don't want to scare her. But Joel grinned to himself. He was looking forward to tonight.

"ONCE AGAIN, YOUR DRIVER IS WAITING." Hayley Applebee flopped down into the chair in her sister's bedroom, watching her dress.

Nan flashed a panicked look at her as she stood in her underwear, chewing her lips. Hayley was wearing skinny jeans, a T-shirt, and a wooly hat pulled over her long blonde hair and looked like a page straight out of an Abercrombie and Fitch catalog. She grimaced at her.

"Which one?"

Hayley glanced over with a bored look. "The lilac one."

Nan picked up the dress and slid it over her head. It was a casual summer dress, spaghetti straps, and loose fitting. The color suited her skin tone, but Nan still wasn't convinced. "It's awfully short," she muttered, turning to look in the mirror and catching Hayley rolling her eyes.

"As long it covers your biscuits, who cares? You're twenty-nine, for the love of God; I swear, sometimes you act like you're fifty-nine." Hayley stifled a yawn and went back to texting on her phone for a second. "I've just put it on Facebook that you're going out with Skandar Mallory's dad."

Nan whirled around. "No, God, Hayley, delete it. I don't want him to think ... Jesus, is it gone?" She looked so wild-eyed that Hayley looked at her in alarm.

"I was joking ... jeez." She let out a long breath. "Do you honestly think I don't know the way the world works?"

Nan sucked in a breath. "Tell me, oh wise one, how does it work? Little jerk."

Hayley grinned. "If you don't hurry up, he'll be long gone anyway. You look great. Can we go?"

In the car, Nan tried to stop her palms from sweating. Hayley glanced over at her.

"Stop panicking. Have you got everything you need? Money, phone ... condoms?"

"Hayley, stop." Nan felt embarrassment spread through her.

Hayley shook her head. "I'm serious. A girl's gotta look after herself, and you never know." She glanced at Nan's dress and hid a smile. "After all, if things get too hot, that dress at least gives him easy access."

"Turn the car around," Nan ordered, and Hayley laughed out loud.

"Chill, sis. Enjoy the moment. Go with the flooowwwww ..." She elongated the word and made it sound much filthier than it needed to. She really wasn't helping Nan's nerves. As Hayley pulled the car up to the sidewalk outside the bar, Nan got out and then stuck her head back to glare at her still-grinning sister.

"By the way ... you were adopted—they found you under a bridge. Wearing Crocs," she added, and Hayley laughed again.

"Go meet the hottie," she ordered, and as Nan shut the door, she wound down the window and called out. "Remember, a girl's got every right to get hers."

Nan scowled after the car as Hayley drove off. Her emotions in a whirl, her stomach roiling with nerves, she took a deep breath and pushed open the door of the bar.

JOEL STOOD as he saw Nan walk into the bar, her long legs trembling like a newborn foal, her lovely face nervous. He pushed away his nerves and crossed the room to greet her. When she saw him, she grinned with relief and something shifted inside him. Desire.

"Hey," he said, smiling down at her, admiring the curve of her shoulder, the hollow of her throat, the way the lilac dress warmed her pale skin. Her warm dark eyes shone as she looked up at him.

"Hey, yourself. You look great. I love The Grateful Dead," she said, nodding at his classic T-shirt. Joel put his head on one side, amused.

"Really?"

She giggled. "Nope. Couldn't pick 'em out of a line-up, but you do look good."

He laughed and held out his hand, and she took it. "Come," he said, "I've snagged us a table ... what's your poison?"

He ordered their drinks and sat down next to her. "Well ... hello."

She laughed, relaxing. "How's the soul searching going? Any progress?"

Joel grinned. "Well thanks to my awesome career advisor, I'm knocking a few ideas around."

"Like what?"

Joel leaned forward. "Well, I've been coaching Skandar for going on seventeen years, so I thought, maybe teaching Phys. Ed.?" He looked at her as if to gauge her reaction. Nan, her expression smooth, nodded, but he could tell she had reservations. "Just say whatever you're thinking, Nan, I want your advice."

She half-smiled. "I think if you want to teach Phys. Ed., that's great —that's wonderful, especially if you can commit to the four-year degree course, then to continuing your studies of the subject as you teach. You're in an ideal situation—with those credits from college you already have, they'll help—and it's not as if you can't afford it."

Joel nodded. "But ...?"

Nan took a deep breath in. "I just think ... it's not big enough for you. I think you need to build on what you've already done, not start over, albeit in the same field."

Joel nodded, but then admitted "I'm not really following you."

Nan smiled. "Not really sure what I mean, either. Just that, I think you're meant for bigger things."

Joel sat back and smiled. "You think?"

The waitress brought over their drinks then—two cold beers—and a cocktail. Nan looked bemused as Joel handed it to her. "Sip."

She did as he said. "Man, that's good ... what is it?"

"Appletini," Joel said, grinning. "I thought I'd get extra points by getting an apple for the teacher."

Nan laughed. "That, Joel Mallory, is adorable. Or cheesy. I can't tell."

"Funnily enough, I was going for cheesily adorable, so ..." He put his hand up for a high-five, and she returned it, giggling.

"Anyhoo," Nan said, relaxing back into her seat, all trace of nerves gone, "tell me about you and your family ..."

SKANDAR MALLORY GRINNED TO HIMSELF. He was flying across the Atlantic and had just logged onto his iPad to check his emails. He saw one from his dad and opened it.

Have a date. With a girl. Feel free to mock.

Skandar choked out a laugh. Thank God, he wrote. I was beginning to wonder whether it had fallen off.

He couldn't actually remember the last time his dad had dated—or even who he had dated. He just hadn't seemed bothered about it, but now that he was free of coaching duties. Skandar had tormented himself over his dad's decision, wondering if he had somehow caused the sudden outcome. They both knew Joel had taken him as far as he could, but it was a big change for both of them.

He was on the way now to play in a David Cup match in Paris, the first big match since his dad left him. His new coach, the mercurial Carlos Sosa, the Argentinian legend, was sitting across from him, texting furiously, his permanent glower having etched deep lines on his handsome face. Skandar, while delighted that he'd managed to snag the un-gettable Sosa, hadn't quite gotten the measure of the man yet. He had a feeling that his more social activities and his fun-loving approach to the game might come into conflict with the older man's low tolerance approach.

Yup, he was definitely moving into new territory here. Skandar Mallory, at twenty-five, was the wealthiest sportsman in the world—it didn't hurt that he'd inherited his father's movie star looks. Sponsorship deals abounded. Cologne, watches, sports cars—they all wanted him. For the last two years, he'd ridden the wave of being completely untouchable at the top of the rankings, but now there were one or two newcomers—men in their late teens, who were coming from behind him. Fast. Skandar wasn't naïve; he knew in a couple of years they'd leave him behind, but he was damned if he'd lie down and take it. He glanced back at Carlos. His first words to Skandar had been "I don't give a fuck who you are; you will listen to me." Yeah, scary as hell but exciting, too. He hoped his dad would be okay and wondered how his date was going. His own love life was a riot of ... well, basically, whoever he wanted, but it was a lonely existence. Always being out on the road. Still, there was enough time for love.

Right now, all he wanted to do was win.

ALL RIGHT, so Joel Mallory was ... delicious, Nan, four Appletinis on an empty stomach, decided. True, her head was a little woozy, but God, the man could bring the funny, the handsome, and the drop-dead sexy.

"How come you're not married?" Oh, hell. Blabbermouth.

Joel didn't seem to mind. "Just didn't happen. Skandar's mom skedaddled pretty soon after he was born, more fool her. Then I just got busy. Now and again, I would go on dates, but not for a while. But then, I was never interested in anybody until now."

Nan flushed pink and couldn't hide her smile. "Okay." Deep breaths, deep, deep.

"Nan?" Joel's mouth curved up in the sexiest smile she'd ever seen. "Are you free tomorrow?"

Saturday. Nan ran through her day in her head.

"I think so ... why?"

Joel took a sip of his soda—he'd had one beer, she noticed, and stopped. "Oh, just to go through some college applications."

Her face fell, and he laughed. "I'm kidding. I'd like to ... oh, er, I hadn't thought what, but I'd like to take you out again."

"Love to." She braved a grin. "How about you give me a tennis lesson?"

Joel looked relieved. "Good thinking. Note to self, always plan what you're going to ask a woman to do."

Nan grinned wickedly. "Sometimes ... other times, you can wait until the moment is right, like ..."

She was hushed by his lips on hers, tender, hesitant, and then, when she responded, his hands slid around her waist. When they broke apart, she laughed.

"Just like that. Yes, very well done, illustrating my point."

Joel grinned. "Glad you think so." He drew a fingertip down her cheek. "Nan ... .is it short for Nancy?"

She shook her head. "No, just Nan."

"Nan ... this is going to sound like such a line, but would you like to come back to my place?"

Yes, hell, yes. But Nan wasn't drunk enough to be reckless. She hesitated, and he saw the doubt on her face.

"Hey, look, I'm not expecting anything. Just drink and talk, is all, I swear." He gave a rueful grin. "Seriously, I have no game. I think Kit stole of all mine when we were in the womb."

Nan laughed. "That scoundrel."

"He is a cad and a bounder."

Nan chuckled then sighed. "Look, I'll be honest ... I want to. I want to like you wouldn't believe. But the Mary Sue in me is going 'on the first date, you harlot?" Even if it is just drinks and talk."

Joel nodded. "Understood. Can I at least give you a ride home?"

"That, you can do."

She smiled as they walked, hand in hand, to his truck. "1963 Chevy C-10 pickup," she said, running her hand over the hood. "Gorgeous. You refurb this?"

Joel smiled. "I wish. I'm afraid this is one of the perks of being a Mallory. I couldn't resist."

Nan hugged the hood. "It's not a luxury, but a very expensive necessity." She sighed and stood, getting into the passenger seat. Joel was laughing at her appreciation of the vehicle.

"I never took you for a gear head," he said, getting into the driver's seat and re-fastening her seat belt for her.

"My dad loved cars," she said. "Hayley and I used to help him ... well, I did, Hayley was too young."

"Your parents still with you?"

Her face clouded a little. "Mom is. Or rather, she's remarried and has a new family now. She lives in Florida.

Joel nodded, understanding, and changed the subject. "Now, at the risk of ending up in Tijuana, I'm putting navigation in your hands. Point the way."

HAYLEY HAD LEFT her bedroom door open a crack before she went to bed and was even now watching videos on her iPad as Nan opened the door. Hayley slid out of bed and over to the door, but she couldn't hear anything. She opened the door wide, flooding the hallway with light —to see her sister, sitting on the floor, a huge, stupid smile on her face.

"Hi," was all she managed before dissolving into giggles.

Hayley crossed her arms. "And yet they put the children of our future in your hands."

Nan put her hand up for silence and Hayley tried not to laugh. "I might be drunk."

"Disgraceful."

"I know."

"I'm judging you."

"Julie no-shed."

"Is that your new name?" Confused, Hayley eventually figured out she meant 'duly noted'."

Nan tried to focus on her sister. "Can you lift me up?"

Somehow, Hayley managed to wrangle her sister into bed. "I'll put a bowl next to your bed, for if you need to hurl."

Nan grunted and let out such a long moan that Hayley was alarmed, shooting up from the bed to avoid anything projectile coming her way. "What? What is it? Don't you dare hurl until I get a bowl ..."

"No." Nan rolled onto her back and opened her eyes. "It's not that ... oh, God, this is why I shouldn't drink."

Hayley's interest was piqued now, and she sat back down on the edge of the bed—out of the splash zone, of course. "What? Did you screw him in the bathroom of the club?"

"Eww, no ..." Nan did look like she was going to hurl then. She struggled into a sitting position. "I hugged his truck."

Hayley looked blank. "Is that some weird Kama Su ...?"

"We didn't have sex!" Nan yelled, then winced. "I mean, he had a great '63 Chevy truck and I hugged it. Like a lunatic."

Hayley's interest faded. "Seriously, that's it? You got the most action from a truck?"

Nan shook her head. "We're supposed to be going out tomorrow ... what's the betting he gets home tonight and thinks 'Jeez, she's kinda weird, maybe this isn't the best idea'?"

Hayley sighed. "Well, if he does, then he's not worthy of you."

"And if he doesn't?" Nan asked in a small but hopeful voice. Hayley smiled.

"Then next time," she got up and pulled Nan's shoes off and tucked her into bed, "fuck him, instead of molesting his motor vehicle."

Nan was already asleep by the time Hayley closed her bedroom door.

QUILLA CRAWLED across the gigantic bed to where Jakob was typing on his laptop. He looked up ... and saw she was completely naked. Damn. His cock responded immediately but he still shook his head at her, with a smile.

She sighed. "Two days," she grumbled, "two freaking days before our six weeks is up and still you make like a Maryknoll nun."

Jakob laughed and then relented. "Come here." He pushed the laptop aside and drew her to him, stroking her body. The scar on her belly was healing; the stitches had come out weeks before. He stroked the soft skin. "Tell me honestly. Does it hurt at all, ever? Even a twinge?"

She took his face in her hands. "Not at all, I promise."

He searched her eyes for a long moment, then with a swift move, laid her back on the bed, covering her body with his. "Even a twinge and you tell me, swear?"

"I swear."

Jakob kissed her mouth, then moved down to her throat and took her nipple into his mouth. God. He had missed this. Quilla hooked a leg over his back and tilted her hips to grind against his thigh. He could feel how warm her sex was and his cock thickened and lengthened, desperate to be inside her. He kissed her stomach, her belly, circling her navel with his tongue, running the tip against her scar, then down to the mound above her sex, shaved and smooth.

He grinned up at her as he moved still lower and caught the sensitive clit between his teeth, biting down gently, feeling it twitch and swell at his touch. His tongue lashed around it, probing and teasing, and he felt her become wet and swollen. He brought her to orgasm with his tongue and then moved up to kiss her.

"No pain?"

Her skin was damp, her hair sticking to her face as she panted, but her eyes shone. "No pain."

He nuzzled her nose with his, fixing his eyes on her. "Spread your legs for me, my beautiful Quilla ... wider ... as wide as they will go ... that's it ..."

Her breathing quickened under his will. Jakob sat up and peeled his T-shirt from his chest, all the time gazing down at her. He pulled his belt from his pants and bent down, twisting the leather around her small wrists and lashing her to the bedframe.

"Are you mine, Quilla?"

Breathless, she nodded, and he smiled, his eyes sleepy with desire. "Are you hot, my love?"

Another nod. He picked up the glass of champagne he had on the nightstand, fisting the root of his cock as he did, and poured some wine into the hollow of her belly, catching the liquid with his tongue as it dripped down her side. Quilla wriggled with pleasure then moaned, as, taking a mouthful of champagne, Jakob went down on her again, letting the bubbles fizz against her clit as he slid a long finger into her cunt, and pressed upwards to massage her G-spot.

Quilla bucked, her body taking over as Jakob unrelentingly took her with his hands and mouth. He spread the swollen lips of her sex and slid his tongue up and down the slick cleft, moving between her clit and her cunt. He felt her body tense, nearly at orgasm, and with lightning speed he drew himself up and entered her, his cock almost desperate to be inside her. He gazed down at her, her arms on either side of her head, her hands gripping the bedframe they were lashed to, her eyes shining up at him.

"Remember when we were in Venice, my love? That night we fucked so hard, we thought we'd wake the neighbors?"

Quilla smiled, laughed a little. "How could I forget?"

"Remember we watched ourselves in the mirror, my cock sliding in ..." he thrust hard, and she moaned, "and out of your perfect cunt?"

"I do ... God ..."

Jakob smiled, quickening his rhythm. "Remember that night we talked about fucking on the balcony, about how I wanted everyone to see how beautiful you when you come?"

"God, yes, yes ..." Quilla arched her back, pressing her sex onto him as he thrust harder and harder and deeper and deeper ...

"And we did that, didn't we, Quilla?"

She nodded her head, now panting so hard she was unable to speak. Jakob drove her on and on until she moaned and came, her body vibrating as Jakob grinned in satisfaction. He pulled out just as he reached his own climax and came on her belly, shooting milky white fluid onto her skin. She smiled up at him as he massaged it into her skin.

"I love you so much, Jakob Mallory ..."

"As I love you, my darling, darling Quilla ..."

He released her hands, and she wound her arms around his neck and kissed him tenderly. "I have missed that so much ... that was incredible."

Jakob gathered her to him. "Quilla ... would you like to go back to Venice, to our little apartment, for a time?"

She looked surprised. "I'd love to, but ..."

"You have work."

"I do, and I love you for asking, but I can't let them down, especially now that I've been ... sick."

Jakob nodded and then gave her a guilty smile. "Sweetheart, the thing is, I kind of talked to them already."

Quilla drew back and looked at him. "What?"

Jakob nodded. "I'm sorry ... it happened when you were still in the hospital. I was crazy scared and angry ... I went to your boss and told him that ..."

"What?" Quilla sat up in bed. "You told him that I couldn't make my own decisions anymore?"

Jakob rocked back from the anger in her voice. "Honey, I was acting crazy, I know, and I overstepped the mark. But the only thing I care about is you and trying to make up for what Gregor did to you because of me."

Quilla contemplated for a moment then sighed. "Jakob, what Gregor did ... it wasn't your fault. He's a psychopath; I knew it the first day I met him. A sociopath. Do you know one of the first things he said to me? He said 'I know you're fucking Jakob." This is a man who'd known me all of five seconds."

Jakob watched her in silence. She pulled her knees up to her chest unconsciously. "But that doesn't mean you get to organize my life for me. And why the hell didn't my boss—or you—mention this before? God ... look, I'll let this one go because of the circumstances, and I love you for wanting to make me happy, but please ..."

"I understand, and I'm sorry." Jakob sighed. "Look, I've been messing up my whole life with the drugs. And I haven't had a real relationship in a long time, so I'm relearning some of this stuff. Forgive me?"

Quilla smiled. "This time, Mallory. Now, show me again how much you love me

"Seriously, dude, give it up. We've been doing this for a month, and I haven't gotten any better." Nan twirled her tennis racket at Joel, who grinned back. He held his hands up.

"You're right. Man, you suck at this."

She hit a tennis ball at him which he dodged, laughing. "Come on, Martina, let's get some lunch."

At the little lunch place he took her to (which, she noticed, had no prices on the menu), they ordered. Then, as they waited for their drinks, Joel laced his fingers in hers. The last month had been blissful, fun, exhilarating—and chaste. What she'd found in Joel Mallory was a best friend, a confidant, a soulmate. He got along with Hayley, he talked to Nan about her work—he had fit so easily into their lives, and she couldn't remember a time when he wasn't around.

Now, as they ate their crab salads, she was nervous. Because today, she was going to his place for the first time ... overnight. And God, she desperately wanted to sleep with him, but the whole idea of being naked with this man was terrifying her and she didn't know why.

She told him that, and he frowned. "Why?"

Because look at us, look where we're both from. Different worlds.

I'm a schoolteacher; I live in a two-bedroom chalet. But she didn't say any of that to him. "Maybe it's just first-night nerves," she joked awkwardly. He squeezed her fingers.

"You're thinking about it too much." He moved his chair so he was next to hers, looping his arm along the back of her chair. His fingers slid along the exposed skin under her arm, drifted up and down slowly. Nan shivered; the feeling was blissful. Joel calmly continued to fork his food into his mouth with his free hand, but now the other hand had moved down to cup her buttock, his large thumb stroking the curve of it. Nan smiled at him. His hand moved to hold her thigh, and his fingertips traced a pattern, sending her blood racing, her breath quickening.

Joel put his fork down and nuzzled her ear. "Nan? Would you like something more to eat?"

She shook her head, concentrating on the furious pulse beating between her legs, his fingers so tantalizingly close to her sex, she wanted to scream.

"Nan ..." God, his voice, so low, so melodic. "Shall we go back to my place?"

She turned her head then and pressed her lips to his. "Yes. Yes."

THE NEXT TWENTY minutes were a blur of cabs and streets and elevators and now, in his bedroom—his surprisingly modest bedroom—Joel slid his hands to the nape of her neck and untied her halter, letting her dress slither to the floor. With her small, perky breasts, she hadn't bothered to wear a bra, and he cupped them in his big hands, kissing them as if he were worshipping them. Nan ran her hand through his hair and pulled out the band holding it back. It was silky, and she let the blonde strands fall through her fingers as Joel took her nipple into his mouth. She wavered slightly, and he gathered her into his arms. "Lay back on the bed for me, sweetheart."

She did so and watched him as he stripped off his T-shirt and jeans. Undressed, he was even more unbelievable, taut chest, broad shoulders, thickly muscled arms. She could see his cock outlined in his underwear, already hard and long. She sat up as he moved to strip his underwear off.

"Wait ..." she said, her nerves gone. "I want to do it."

Joel let go of the waistband with a smile and she slid her fingers over the top of them and slowly peeled them from him. She gave a sigh as his cock, ramrod hard and erect against his belly, swelled and quivered. She stroked her fingers up and down it, feeling the silky-smooth skin move under her touch. She smiled up at him, then took the sensitive tip into her mouth. She could already taste the pre-cum, salty and rich, and as her tongue flicked around it, she heard Joel suck in a deep breath.

After a few moments, he moved her head away and laid her back on the bed, hitching his fingers around her panties and freeing her from them. He pushed her legs up to her chest and buried his face in her sex, teasing and tasting until her labia swelled and pulsed with desire. Then he took her, sliding in so gently, so slowly, she cried out as he filled her and began to move.

"Joel ... oh God, Joel ..."

They moved together, skin on skin, finding their rhythm easily and rocking their hips in unison. Joel kissed her, his tongue massaging hers, exploring her mouth. Nan clung to him, her legs wrapped around his hips, moving up to his waist as she tilted her sex to meet him, allowing him to drive himself deeper into her. God, yes, this was what she had been missing, the connection, the human touch, and the passion. Joel looked at her as if she was the most beautiful creature ever to walk the Earth and at this moment, this wonderful, sensual moment, she believed she was.

Her climax, building, building, building, slammed through her, and she let out a cry of "Oh!" and felt as if she were flying as Joel came, his groan like music to her.

Afterward, they lay side by side, facing each other and talking. She grinned at him.

"Why was I so nervous?"

Joel laughed. "Can I tell you a secret? I was scared to death."

"No way."

"Way."

Nan sighed. "My whole body feels like it's been rehabilitated. I wasn't even aware of some of the sensations you brought out in me."

"Right back at ya," he said, and kissed her. "Hey, I do have something to talk to you about. An idea I've been kicking around for a couple of weeks."

"Tell me."

"Remember we had that conversation where you told me teaching Phys. Ed. was a bad fit?"

"Kind of."

"Well, while I've been trying—and failing—to teach you how to, you know, hit a tennis ball." He laughed and ducked away as she swiped at him. "I got to thinking ... you're right. That was thinking too small. I was thinking— what if we built community sports centers— somewhere where anyone can come and fulfill their curiosity or gain access to the equipment they need? What do you think?"

Nan nodded, her eyes excited. "That's more like it. I think that's great—have you talked about it with your family?"

"Not yet, but I'm going to. It really is a basic idea at the moment, and I wanted to run it by you first."

She smiled. "Really?"

"Really. You, Nan Applebee, in less than a month, became my person. You kind of became my person when you hugged my truck on our first date."

Nan groaned and covered her face. "God, don't remind me."

Joel laughed, then gathered her to him. "Wouldn't change a thing. Will you help me with this?"

She nodded. "Of course." She laughed, then rained kisses down on him, making him chuckle. "Of course, I will," she said, calming down. "I'm your person."

Joel rolled on top of her. "Well, then, my person, let's see how else we can celebrate this new partnership ..."

.   .   .

IT WAS the phone call in the middle of the night that woke them both. The landline in Joel's apartment. For a second, blinking sleep from their eyes, they looked at each other. Then Joel scooted out of the bed and went to answer it. After a few moments, Nan got up too and went into the living room. Joel was sitting, his head in his free hand, talking in a low tone into the phone.

His whole body seemed to have slumped, his demeanor one of defeat. Nan sat next to him and put her arm around him. God ... she knew all about the midnight phone call—it was never good news. She remembered the night the police had come and told her and Hayley that their dad had died suddenly. No accident, no suspicious circumstances, he had just ... stopped. The grief was still raw five years on.

Joel locked his fingers between hers. "Okay ... right. Thanks. Call me as soon as you know anything more." He put the phone down and groaned. Nan, her heart pounding.

"What? What is it? Is it that psycho who stabbed Quilla? What?"

Joel shook his head. "No ... no, it's not. A girl's been murdered, a German tennis player, at the match in Rome. God...Nan ..."

Nan saw the fear in his eyes. "What, baby? What is it?"

Joel closed his eyes. "It's Skandar. He's been arrested ..."

3

PART THREE: TRUST ME

I t seemed to Skandar that even through the walls of the jail cell, he could still hear all the reporters that were outside the Rome police station, clamoring for news on the biggest story of the year. Annika Hahn, dead, murdered, and Skandar Mallory arrested. He kept repeating it to himself, because he couldn't believe what had happened. Annika was dead. The German tennis ace had only been nineteen. Dead. It didn't seem possible.

But then, neither did Skandar being awakened early that morning by the door of his hotel room being kicked in and guns aimed at him, cops yelling at him in Italian.

The door outside the cell opened, and his father came in, looking harassed, angry, scared—everything Skandar was feeling. The police officer with Joel opened the cell and nodded for Skandar to step out. Bail was set and paid.

He fell into his dad's arms, and Joel hugged his son. "Are you okay?"

Skandar shook his head. "I don't know what the fuck is going on, Dad. Annika's dead."

Joel silenced him with a look. "Later." He didn't want Skandar to say anything in front of the Italian police.

Skandar noticed a young blonde woman hovering awkwardly behind his father. Joel introduced her. "Skandar, my girlfriend, Nan."

The woman had a kind face, and she put a hand on Skandar's arm. "I'm so pleased to meet you, if not under the greatest circumstances."

Joel was antsy. "Come on, let's get out of here. We have a suite at the Hassler."

In the cab to the hotel, Skandar stared out of the window, hollow-eyed. He felt like someone had taken a baseball bat to his head. Joel, not the most effusive father, nevertheless had his arm casually draped over the top of the seat, his fingertips resting lightly on his son's shoulder. It was a tiny gesture that meant everything to his son. At the hotel, they gave the few paparazzi who were stationed outside the building the slip by sneaking in through the kitchens.

Skandar raised his eyebrows at the opulence of the suite Joel had procured for them. Very unlike Joel Mallory—the most down to earth one of them all—and seeing his reaction, Joel grinned. "Jakob's idea. Give the impression of huge influence and possible backhanders without ever saying a word."

Skandar snorted. "Jakob's a genius." He grinned a little at his dad. "I thought this was a bit too over the top for you." He glanced at Nan. "He's probably showing off for you."

"Okay, that's enough." Joel rolled his eyes as Nan giggled, but then his smile faltered. "Skandar, sit. I'll order some food, then we're going to talk."

"HAHN, nineteen, was found strangled to death in a hotel populated by her peers. More than one witness has come forward to say they saw Hahn enter the hotel room of American tennis superstar, Skandar Mallory, hours before her body was found. Mallory, who is the nephew of actor Kit Mallory, was arrested and bailed. He has not yet been charged but has been asked to stay in Rome until the investigations have concluded. Harry Aries is our reporter in Rome. Harry?"

Nan flicked the television off and grabbed her cell. Dialing, she tapped her fingers on her leg, agitated. So much stress—so much had changed in a flash. Still reeling from their first incredible night together, she'd immediately offered to come with Joel, seeing how devastated he had been by the news, although not realizing, she knew now, how much of a big deal this would be. Skandar was in trouble, serious trouble.

"Yo." Her sister sounded sleepy, and Nan felt guilty about calling her, but Joel and Skandar were with the police, and she was antsy.

"Hey, you. I'm sorry, did I wake you?"

"It's okay, hang on ..." Nan heard Hayley cough and then the rustle of blankets as she sat. "How's things? Did you break Skandar out of the clink? Are you on the lam?"

Nan suppressed a smile. Even thousands of miles away, Hayley could cheer her up. "Yeah, he got bail—I didn't ask much. Joel had to lay down for that. Not my business. Skandar is shell-shocked ... well, it's hard to say, since I've never met him before, but he's definitely subdued."

"He didn't do it, though, did he?"

"Of course not. Skandar's admitting to sleeping with Annika, but says she left after a couple of hours."

"Is Joel doing okay?"

Nan sighed. "I don't know. Listen, this has all happened so fast ... are you sure you're all right there?"

"Hell, yeah. I have pizza on speed dial and Netflix. I'm good. Just ..."

"What?"

"Are you sure you want to get so involved with that family? I know Joel's great, but from what you've said, he's the exception."

Nan frowned. "I didn't mean to infer the others are shady ... just that they're more focused on what they do. Joel's more relaxed about things—apart from this, obviously. Skandar's a good kid, a bit arrogant and careless, but ..."

"I'll say," Hayley muttered. "Even if he didn't do it, he has a reputation for screwing around, doesn't he?"

Nan couldn't argue with that. After she had said goodbye, she wandered around the suite, feeling out of place. Maybe she should fly home and leave Joel to deal with his son's predicament.

The door opened, and Joel smiled at her, his face tired. "Hey, gorgeous."

"How did it go?"

"Well," he dropped onto the couch, and Nan sat beside him, linking her fingers with his. "They have no physical evidence to prove Skandar had anything to do with the girl's death. The trouble is, they have no physical evidence of who did kill her either, nor a motive for the murder. So far, it all comes down to the word of a couple of witnesses; who, by the way, have gone to ground. They're not part of the tournament and no one seems to know who they could be, not the hotel, no one. So, at the moment, Skandar remains the sole suspect based on the fact he was the last person to see her alive."

"Apart from her killer," Nan added gently, and he smiled.

"Apart from the killer." Joel sighed and leaned his head back on the couch. "What's more of a problem is the press. They're working up to trying Skandar themselves; he'll be crucified, no matter the outcome of the investigation."

"Where is he now?"

"The pool, doing laps. Carlos—who is as terrifying as he looks— bawled him out after the police interviews. They're replacing him in the team for the tournament."

"Temporarily?" But she knew the answer already. Joel leaned over to kiss her.

"Thank you for coming with me, Nan; it's made all the difference."

She gave him a shy smile. "I haven't done anything; I wish I could make you feel better."

Joel gave a small chuckle. "Well ... I know a way we could relax for a few hours."

Nan grinned. "Hours? That's ambitious."

He laughed. "Give an old guy a break. It would be a shame to waste that enormous bed, wouldn't it?"

Nan pressed her lips to his. "Why, yes, it would. It would indeed ..."

SKANDAR PUSHED himself harder and harder into the swim until, at last, exhausted, he hauled himself out. At least the pool was off limits to the press. His publicist, Zoe, a bulldog business person with the face of an angel, was scheduled to fly in tomorrow morning to start on a strategy. Jesus, a strategy. Annika was dead, and he was thinking about a PR strategy. Is this what he'd become?

He could still remember Annika's smile. She was so much fun, so full of life. God. He refocused, remembering how her athletic body had curved against his, the way her skin felt on his, the way she moaned when she came ... he'd had a crush on her since she'd exploded onto the tennis scene two years previously. But, of course, he had to play the cool dude. He unashamedly slept around—the same as any young guy would, and certainly, his cohorts were no angels. But he was Skandar Mallory—Superstar, Billionaire, The World's Hottest Bachelor, and People Magazine's Sexiest Man of the Year (beating his uncle Kit into second place—that was satisfying, he grinned to himself). His smile faded. Shit, he thought now, how did I ever think any of that mattered? Annika's dead. He squeezed his eyes shut, trying not to let the grief overwhelm him. What he wanted, more than anything was to go home and wall himself up in his large condo. With a pang, he realized, even if all the charges were to be dropped and he could go back to the US, that the press would not let him alone.

Skandar went back up to his room and shut the door. He lay on his bed and took stock. Carlos was this close to quitting; although the Argentinian had committed to at least six months with Skandar, he had a feeling the man would drop him like a stone if he thought his own legacy might be tainted. Fuck him, Skandar thought, if he's that flighty, good riddance.

He needed a distraction. He grabbed his iPad, then logged onto the sci-fi forum of which he was a secret member. His nom-de-plume was goofy, chosen when he was a fifteen-year-old—SkunkMalady-Bibble. It had always made him smirk. He logged in now and checked who was online. He dismissed a couple of the ubergeeks—the ones who corrected anyone and everyone who got any sci-fi fact even slightly wrong—those people were nuts. Skandar smiled suddenly.

This was more like it—Samadamadingdong was online. "Yes," Skandar hissed in delight, and started typing.

SkunkMaladyBibble: Yo, Dingdong, how's it hanging?

Samadamadingdong: Hey, Bibs, slightly to the left. Good, thanks, just trying—and failing, obviously—to focus on a paper. Where are you at this time? Mars? Jupiter? Atlantic City?

SkunkMaladyBibble: Would you believe, I'm on Uranus?

Samadamadingdong: Why, why would you go there? I'm disgusted at your obvious joke.

SkunkMaladyBibble: But you're snickering, aren't you?

Samadamadingdong: Yes, I am. And I'm judging myself.

Skandar grinned to himself. Yes, this was what he needed, unadulterated silliness and mockery with his favorite online pal. They had agreed at the start, no real names or details, no flirting, no flaming. It had been a couple of years now since they started chatting—and whoever she was, she had been a constant source of escape. Strangers into friends, he thought, now, the power of the Internet, and he settled back to chat with her some more.

Nan laid her head on Joel's stomach, feeling the rise and fall as he breathed. She adored these moments after they had made love, calm, peaceful, together. He held her hand—which always made her tear up a little. This man, she thought, this man feels like home.

"Hopefully, in a couple of days, the police will be able to let us take Skandar home," Joel said now, apparently deep in thought.

"Then maybe you should both stay with me for a while—he obviously can't go home."

Nan turned her head to look up at him. "Maybe it's not such a great idea for me to stay with you. I have Hayley to consider—if the press starts digging into my background as your girlfriend, then I don't want her in the firing line. Does that make sense?"

Joel considered. "I never thought of that ... huh."

She rested her chin on the hand splayed on his stomach. "I know you've probably got all the security covered and if it were just me, then I'd—what was it your Dad said—ride out the storm with you." She grinned as he stroked her cheek. "But Hayley never asked for this, so ... '

"I get it. Man." He shoved himself into a sitting position and pulled her to him. "This got more complicated than we expected. Thank God for you, though." He kissed her forehead. "I'm serious, Nan. I could not have coped these last few days without you."

Nan reddened to the roots of her hair and smiled. "No problem ... it's ..." She hesitated, dropping her eyes to her hands, "it's what I would do for anyone I loved." Her heart was thumping ferociously against her ribs, and when he didn't immediately react, she risked a glance at him. His eyes were soft.

"Right back at ya, kiddo," he murmured, and Nana felt the relief flood through her. He loved her. Good, she thought, thank God.

Because I am in way too deep ...

IN BREAKING NEWS, tennis ace Skandar Mallory has been given leave to return to the United States by the Italian police investigating the murder of nineteen-year-old Annika Hahn, the young WTA player ranked fifteenth in the world, who was brutally murdered at her hotel last week. Mallory, the grandson of wealthy Seattle business and philanthropist, Randall Mallory, was arrested, but has not been charged with any crime. The twenty-five-year-old is known to have been with Miss Hahn on the night of her death, but so far, no evidence has been found to link him to her murder. The Italian police say Mr. Mallory understands that he may be extradited back to Rome, should formal charges be made in the future.

SKANDAR FELT like kissing the Washington ground as he landed back in Seattle. The flight from Italy had been one of dodging the press—which meant change after change in remote parts of the world to get back home. Instead of the usual transatlantic route, he and Joel had taken the longer route—across Europe and Asia and finally down through Anchorage to Seattle. They'd sent Nan back a day before they themselves had left Rome, so the press wouldn't get used to her being with them and follow her home. He had to admit; he'd seen parts of the world even he had never visited, but it had taken four days, and he and his dad were exhausted and sick of fast food, grabbed at weird times of the night.

His grandfather, Ran, had arranged for a town car to pick them up and they flopped into the air-conditioned car, and both of them fell asleep immediately.

SOMEHOW, they'd gotten back to his grandfather's house, because the next reasonable cognitive thought he had was that he was in a soft bed, and it was evening again. He got up and stood under a refreshing shower, sighing with relief at feeling vaguely normal again.

Downstairs, he heard voices from the dining room and followed the sound. He found Ran, Joel, Nan, and Quilla sitting eating pizza straight from the boxes—he loved that his billionaire family didn't have graces—and a young girl he didn't know with long straight blonde hair, almond eyes a dark brown, and long, long legs. Jakob was on his cellphone on the other side of the room.

Quilla got up to hug Skandar. "You okay, bug?" She wrapped her arms around him—quite a feat when he stood over a foot taller than her. He lifted her off her feet and swung her. She giggled as he set her down.

"Well, that's more like it. Come sit."

Nan leaned over to kiss his cheek. "Skandar, this is my sister, Hayley—she doesn't need me to tell her who you are."

"Quite. Hi, Skandar."

He liked that she didn't look star struck the reaction he was used to getting—and it was a relief. If she was nice as Nan, then ... he sat down next to her.

As if reading his mind, she grinned. "If you're wondering if I'll be as sweet and comforting as my sister, you're wrong. I will shamelessly mock you like we've known each other forever."

Skandar burst out laughing. Ran, at the other end of the table, grinned. "You tell him, Hayley."

Jakob finished his call and came back to the table. "Hey, Skan, happy to see you, buddy."

"Hey, Jakob ... how's everything?"

Jakob exchanged a glance with Quilla, who smiled. "Actually, we might have some news."

"Oh, my, you're ..." Nan started, but Quilla quickly waved her hand.

"No, God, no, nothing like that. Joel ... remember that you talked to Jakob about building sports centers for the communities in Seattle without access? We might have found your first site."

Jakob smiled at his lover. "Quilla's been scouting for places in her lunchbreaks—never let it be said this girl doesn't commit."

"That's great ... wow, I hadn't even thought past the initial idea, but damn, Quilla, Jakob, that's amazing."

Skandar looked at his father, bemused. "What's this?"

"Your dad's going to build community sports centers," Nan said proudly. Skandar smiled.

"You gonna find the new ... um ... me?"

Hayley snorted, and Nan scowled at her. Skandar raised an eyebrow and Hayley shrugged.

"Sorry, just warming up to that mockery I was talking about."

"Hayley," her sister's voice carried a warning, but Skandar grinned.

"You are one weird girl," he said to Hayley, who smiled with her mouth full of pizza.

Soon they had broken up into groups and Skandar and Hayley went outside to play with the dogs. He sized her up as they ran around. She was tall, almost six-foot, he guessed, slender but not skinny. Her long blonde hair hung in a straight curtain around her, topped with a wool hat. Her willowy body was clad in skinny jeans and a loose-fitting tee. Skandar realized he was staring—and that she'd noticed. He grinned guiltily as she stuck her hand on her hip and struck a pose.

"I know, it's impossible for you not to look, what with all this going on," she waved her hand up and down her body, then laughed. "Dude, we're practically brother and sister."

He followed her over to the swing set which had been there since his dad was a toddler. "How'd you figure that one?"

"Well, if my sister and your dad are dating ... I'm wrong; I'm your aunt. So behave." She pulled a serious face, which turned quickly into duck face. Skandar grinned.

"Dude,"—she looked like she didn't mind being called dude, so he risked it—"You are so nutso. So come on, get serious, tell me about you."

Hayley swung gently back and forth on the swing. "What do you want to know?"

"You work?"

She nodded. "Part time at a comic store downtown. I'm at college most of the time."

"Studying."

"Sports psychology."

"Seriously?"

"No."

"Jerk. So come on, what?"

"Architecture."

"Jakob's field. He could help you out."

"I intend on picking his brains. His girlfriend is cute."

"Quilla's a peach, yeah. Still can't believe what happened to her."

"That's the night my sister met your dad. At the hospital."

Skandar raised his eyebrows at her. "Really? Smooth moves, Pa, macking on the patients while your brother's girl is bleeding to death."

Hayley winced then rolled her eyes. "Nan wasn't the patient, I was, and he wasn't macking on anybody."

"Chill, I was kidding. Why were you there?"

Hayley didn't answer for a second, and a myriad of crazy reasons ran through his mind. Then she shrugged. "Potted version, got drunk, got in the car with drunk, drunk rolled car. Got lucky, minor cuts and bruises and no charges." She looked at him and for the first time, she saw a vulnerable side to her.

"Hey," he said gently, "no judgment here. We've all done dumb stuff ..."

They were quiet for a moment. The evening was mild, and a fresh breeze blew in from the lake on the property.

"So," Hayley's voice was hesitant. "Do you want to talk about it? I just thought someone around your age, not family, maybe ..."

Skandar grinned sideways at her. "Didn't you just tell me you're my aunt?"

She didn't smile. "Skandar."

He looked away. "I ... jeez, I don't even know what to tell you. Annika and I had been flirting a while, you know. She never knew this, but I had the biggest crush on her for years. Of course, being a douchebag, I never let her know, played the field, tried to make her jealous. It worked. Now ..." He shook his head. "Wish I hadn't waited. I thought we had forever."

"I'm sorry."

Skandar squinted across to where the dogs were busy digging up his grandfather's prized rose bed.

"She was a sweet kid, you know? Why anyone would want to do that to her ..." He trailed off, looking inside at his family, talking and laughing. "They think it's all going to be okay, I can tell."

"That should give you some comfort."

"I honestly don't know. A part of me feels I should be punished for not protecting her."

Hayley was silent. "Were you together long?"

Skandar shook his head. "Just that night. We'd been flirting and building up to it through the whole meet, then that evening, she came to my room. Said she was tired of waiting."

"Why'd she leave, then?"

Skandar looked desolate. "Carlos Sosa. He has me on a strict no-carbs, no- sex, no-fun regime. He called me that night, said he was coming up to see me, so I had to send her away. If I hadn't, she'd be alive now. God."

He put his face in his hands, trying not to scream. Hayley was quiet, leaving him to get hold of himself. He looked up eventually with red eyes.

"Thanks for listening. We don't even know each other, but it's been good."

Hayley, never shy, grabbed his phone from his back pocket and programmed her number into it. "Call whenever. If you just need to shout and curse, call me. We'll drive up into the mountains and find a quiet spot and howl and curse to our hearts' content."

She held her hand up for a high-five, which he returned, and handed his phone back. "I'm getting cold, so I'm going to head in. Coming?"

"In a sec." He watched her lope back to the house. Good kid, he thought. Real good kid.

He looked forward to having her as a friend.

Quilla Chen rested her hand on Jakob's thigh as he drove them back to their apartment, gazing out at the lights of the city. She heard him sigh and turned to him. His brow was furrowed, his eyes uneasy.

"What are you thinking about?" She stroked his hair back over his ear. Jakob flashed a smile at her but it faded, and he shook his head. "Skandar. Damn kid would get himself into trouble."

"To be fair," Quilla said gently, "he didn't do anything wrong. In fact, listening to Joel and Nan tell it, it just seems weird all around.

Have you considered that someone might be out to frame him? A rival?"

He gave her a sharp look then, and she realized he hadn't considered it. "I'm just giving you a for instance." She tried to get him to smile, but his eyes were hard. "What? I didn't mean to upset you."

His face softened. "You could never upset me, beautiful. I just had never thought ... we'll talk about this at home, just give me five minutes. I don't want to be driving when we talk about it."

Confused, Quilla nodded, but twenty minutes later she understood. They were sitting in their living room, lights dimmed, and as Quilla kicked off her shoes and curled her legs underneath her, Jakob said the one word that made her skin crawl and her stomach drop. "Gregor."

Quilla felt the blood drain out of her face. "What?"

Jakob, seeing her distress, sat down next to her and pulled her into the crook of his arm. "It's just a theory," he said, kissing her temple. "But we can't find him; the police can't find him. If he thinks —and God, I hate even saying this out loud—if he thinks he hasn't got 'enough' revenge on me, he could be going after the rest of the family. He knows he won't get near you again."

Quilla didn't say anything, and he tightened his arm around her. "Sorry, baby. I might be totally paranoid, but it's worth looking into, right?"

She nodded. "God, yes, anything to help Skandar. I'm a year younger than him, but I feel like a momma bear when he's around."

"You're an old soul, Quilla Chen. Something else made me think tonight."

"What's that?"

"When Nan thought you were pregnant."

Quilla laughed. "Why is it that whenever a woman says she has news, it's always presumed she's either pregnant or engaged? I might be climbing Everest or ... ' she cast around, "giving an enema to a Blue Whale."

Jakob shook his head, still chuckling. "Only you could think up something like that. No, what I mean is ... for just the briefest second when Nan thought you were pregnant, a part of me wanted you to say 'Actually yes.' Then, of course, I got it together and told myself ... we haven't even had that conversation."

Quilla chewed her lip. "We've been together for what now? Six months? Do you think it's too soon? I mean to discuss in the abstract, yes, but I'm not ready to have kids yet."

Jakob nodded. "Which was my first thought, and there's something else we've ignored up until now. There're twenty-three years between us, Quilla. We've glossed over that fact so far, but it is a consideration we have to deal with."

Quilla suddenly felt tears threatening. "I love you; I don't want to be with anyone else."

He kissed her. "Me neither. This is it for me. But ... I have, to be honest. Children have never been high on my list. So if we reach a point where it becomes an issue, we need to face it. Although for a second, I was swayed by the idea of you being pregnant. In all honesty, I can't see it happening."

Quilla nodded, her throat thick. She snuggled into his chest so he couldn't see the sadness in her eyes.

Because she had thought about children—way off in the future, yes, but his children, green-eyed and beautiful. His revelation struck deep inside her. No kids? She heard him sigh, felt his chest rise and fall against her cheek.

"Anyway, my beauty, I've got an early meeting so ..."

IN BED, they made love slowly, and later, when Quilla had fallen asleep, Jakob slid out from the covers and went into the living room. Sleep had been avoiding him lately, and he felt the build-up of those sleepless nights now. The reason was simple—and one he kept to himself—he was pretty sure Gregor was waging a campaign against his family. After Quilla had been stabilized, her surgeon had spoken to Jakob privately.

"The stab wound isn't deep, nor was it violent enough to cause extensive bleeding. From the circumstances you've described ... it sounds like the attacker meant to wound and not kill. If he was standing next to her, he could have easily stabbed her multiple times in a few seconds and deeply, too. He could have easily murdered her, but he didn't. I don't get what his motive was."

For a time, neither did Jakob. It wasn't until he got the first email —sent through an anonymous IP address—that he knew.

Next time, she dies.

It has been a warning, the stabbing. A vicious, nasty, painful warning but just that. Gregor would never stop until he brought Jakob and his family low. Which was why, tonight, when Quilla theorized that someone was framing Skandar, the pieces had fallen into place.

Jakob looked at the clock. A little after midnight. He knew his dad would still be up reading. He grabbed his cell—then, hesitating, crossed the room and looked in to see if Quilla was still asleep. Her face rested on the pillow, her eyes closed, her hair tangled around her. So beautiful. Jakob leaned against the doorframe and watched her breathing for a few moments. I love you, Quilla Chen, so, so much.

NEXT TIME, she dies.

JAKOB SWALLOWED the knot of fear in his throat and went to call his dad.

SKUNKMALADYBIBBLE: Hey, Boo.
    Samadamadingdong: 'Sup? You're online late tonight.
    SkunkMaladyBibble: Had a strange day. Met someone.
    Samadamadingdong: Whoa. Do tell!
    SkunkMaladyBibble: Not like that. She's just the coolest person—
apart from you, of course.

Samadamadingdong: I'm only your imaginary friend, though. What's she like?

SkunkMaladyBibble: Funny, smart, gorgeous. And someone I think could be a true friend one day. I wish I were able to say more.

Samadamadingdong: You know the rules. But I'm glad you have someone like that, dude. I think I may have met that person as well.

SkunkMaladyBibble: Spill it.

Samadamadingdong: Nah, too early to say for sure. When and if things progress, etc. He's kinda messed up at the moment.

SkunkMaladyBibble: Bad news. But I know how he feels, so don't be too judgy.

Samadamadingdong: Judgy's my middle name.

SkunkMaladyBibble: Some days I wish you were here, so we could really talk.

Samadamadingdong: I know. Me, too, but then we wouldn't have the luxury of spilling our darkest moments to each other without fear of recrimination or exposure. God, that's deep for this time of night. Willies, bum, pee pee.

SkunkMaladyBibble: Lunatic.

Samadamadingdong: Ya, bruh.

SkunkMaladyBibble: The fuck? Is that some young person's talk I don't know?

Samadamadingdong: Ya, bruh.

SkunkMaladyBibble: Anyway, should probably get some sleep. Just wanted to check in.

Samadamadingdong: Ya, bruh.

SkunkMaladyBibble: Stop that. Sweet dreams.

Samadamadingdong: Right back at cha. Night, dude.

SKANDAR WAITED as his car was brought around to the back of the house. His grandfather, tense and antsy, shook his head at him. "This really isn't a good idea."

"I'm going stir-crazy, Pops. Just sitting here listening to Zoe plot out pre-canned sound bites and statements, waiting for the Italians to drop the bomb on me. The press is already eviscerating me. I need to get out, even for just a few hours."

Ran sighed. "Just don't bring Hayley into it. I don't want those girls harassed. And if Jakob is right, if this is all Gregor Fisk's doing, I don't want him targeting Hayley or Nan."

Skandar put his hands up. "That's why we've planned this down to the last detail. Hayley will meet me there."

"Halfway up a volcano, in a visitor's center."

"Exactly. No one will think to look for us there. And they have a great little café." Skandar, rich beyond his wildest dreams, still had enough of his father in him that he enjoyed a homemade bowl of soup in a family-run café.

Ran nodded. His grandson was willful, had always been so, and besides; he was an adult.

"Okay, but, and I mean this, any hint of paparazzi, you hightail it out of there."

"Like Road Runner, Pops, I promise."

THINKING about what his grandfather said, Skandar got an unexpected jolt of pleasure when he saw Hayley waiting for him. His pulse raced, his stomach warmed when he saw her, regulation wooly hat pulled down over her hair, bundled up in a parka, skinny legs in her usual jeans and boots. Up this high on Mt. Rainier, even in the summer, the snow fell relentlessly, densely packed and towering above the few people that were milling around.

Hayley waved at him as he parked the car and got out. Already, they felt like real friends—since the first night, they had talked on the phone a few times, late into the evening.

She hugged him now, and Skandar relaxed into her embrace, breathing in her clean scent of her hair. "That's a good, strong hug you have there, Miss Applebee."

"Oh, shut up," she said good-naturedly. "Can we get inside? It's freezing."

They lined up with the other visitors, Hayley opting for the tomato soup and hot chocolate, Skandar grabbing a salad to go with his soup, and a bottle of OJ.

They secreted themselves away in a far corner of the restaurant, away from the other patrons.

"So, got tired of holing up in the castle?"

Skandar nodded, swallowing a mouthful of soup. "I'm sorry for complaining about being captive in a luxury mansion, but yeah. And I wanted to see you."

Hayley grinned, completely guileless. "Of course. Why wouldn't you?"

"How's your sister?"

"Desperately in love with your dad. It's quite revolting, really."

Skandar laughed. "Nauseating stuff. How about you? Seeing anyone?"

"Oooh, details. Okay, well, yes and no. Yes, I'm seeing someone. No, I'm not seeing anyone."

Skandar, ignoring the sting that passed through him, shook his head. "That makes no sense."

Hayley rolled her eyes. "It's complicated ... his name is Tim; we dated a while back, last year of high school. He turned up at my college this year, and we reconnected. Now it's getting where we have to decide whether we're a couple or just friends."

Skandar speared a tomato with a little too much force, and it burst, spattering him with juice. "Shoot. Well, how do you feel?"

"Weirdly obligated." Hayley admitted, handing him a napkin. "I think it's a case of..."

"He's more into you than you are him."

"Yep. And he's the nicest guy, too, so ..."

Skandar pushed his plate away. "Want my advice?"

Hayley grinned, and Skandar knew she was about to mock him. "I'm just saying, as a friend, you deserve better."

Hayley shrugged. "Truth is ... unless I feel a real connection, a meeting of minds, I can't be bothered. Do you know what I mean? In that case, sex is just sex, not anything of worth."

Skandar was surprised. "You believe it should be?"

"Well, yeah. Look, I'm all for 'in the moment' stuff, don't get me wrong, but there comes a time when a girl needs to connect with the mind as well as the body."

Skandar shook his head, grinning. "How'd you get so wise at nineteen?"

Hayley smiled. "You sound like an old man."

"I feel it, at the moment."

Hayley reached over took his hand. "Skan, this will pass—you did nothing wrong, and they've already admitted that they have no evidence. As for your grief, ride it out. I'll be here for you, and your family, too, but it's not something we can make go away."

He twisted his fingers between hers. "I'm damn glad my dad met your sister, Hays."

She smiled, but after a beat gently withdrew her hand. Skandar felt bereft, but hid it with a smile. "So, tell me more about this mind/body thing you have going on."

Hayley grinned wickedly. "I could show you a thing or two, Mallory. Um, I mean ... God ... deploy filter," she muttered to herself, tapping her temple, as Skandar laughed out loud. Hayley's face was red. "You know what I mean." She waited until he'd stopped laughing and her face had returned to its usual color and heat. "What's your kink rating, Skandar Mallory?"

Skandar, his mouth full of orange juice, had to swallow before answering. "We're really talking about this, huh?"

Hayley shrugged. "Hey, look, I was brought up in a very sex-negative environment. It wasn't until I got to college and read The Story of O and Anais Nin that I realized what a beautiful thing sex could be, almost like an art form."

Skandar shifted uncomfortably, starting to get turned on. "Dude ... you really into being pierced and led around by a chain in your hoo-ha?"

Hayley grinned. "Firstly, I'm impressed you've read O, and secondly, nope. But they did set something free in me."

"So, that being said, have you 'connected' with anyone who satisfied you like that?"

"Oh, I haven't slept with anybody yet; this is all just a theory." She said it so nonchalantly that it took a moment for him to process what she'd just said.

"Wait, what? You're ..."

"A virgin? Yep."

"Wow."

"Why 'wow'?"

Skandar blinked at her. "Have you seen you?"

"What do my looks, good or bad, have to do with it?"

Skandar didn't answer her for a moment. "Nothing, I'm just ... you talk about sex as if you've really thought about it ... so, why?"

"I told you. I'm waiting to have that connection. And I have thought about it."

Skandar smiled at her. "You are something special; you know that?"

Hayley's eyes narrowed. "Mocking me?"

"I swear, not at all. Impressed. Really impressed. I hope whoever you do decide to sleep with first, deserves you."

"Thank you. You didn't answer my question."

"My kink?" He smiled at her. The restaurant had emptied out now, so he felt more relaxed. "Well, okay. Let's start with my history. Cashed in my v-card at sixteen. Haven't formed any lasting attachment—until Annika. That night was the best one of my life—my sex life. And, of course, the worst." He felt hollow again. Hayley pushed the rest of her hot chocolate over to him.

"It's only lukewarm now, but it helps, the sugar helps."

He smiled at her gratefully. "Can we do this again?"

"Of course. Anytime. Next time, how about we meet in a mall, get some pretzels, and hang out like teenagers?"

"You are a teenager."

"Only my body is. I'm actually forty-nine in maturity."

He laughed. "I can believe that. And pretzels sound good."

. . .

SKANDAR DROVE BACK into the city, feeling more relaxed than he had in weeks. Hayley Applebee was enchanting. That was the only word he could up with. And, damn, if she hadn't turned him on with her brutal honesty about sex. A virgin at nineteen, these days? Alone now, he allowed himself a little fantasy about kissing that rose-bud mouth of hers, twisting his hands in her long hair, letting the fine blonde strands running through his fingers. He thought about the weight of her slender body on top of his, straddling him, her full pert breasts bouncing as she rode him ...

Jesus, man, pull yourself together. You cannot fall for your dad's girlfriend's sister. God, that was way too complicated. Still, he felt lighter, almost high, a smile plastered on his face. At the turning for his grandfather's place, he let the car drive past the entrance to the property, knowing where he really wanted to be. Home. His condo, where all his stuff was. Yeah, there might be paparazzi, but it had been weeks—maybe they had better things to do now. If nothing else, he needed to grab some more clothes. With that in mind, he turned the car and drove into the city.

HAYLEY GOT HOME, and distracted, walked into Nan's bedroom without knocking. "Hey, I ... oh God ..."

She turned around quickly at the sight of Joel Mallory orally pleasuring her gasping and moaning sister. Seeing her, Joel leaped up, off the bed, and Nan shrieked in shock.

"I'm sorry, I'm sorry!" Hayley made a dash for her bedroom and shut the door behind her. God, to unsee that. Luckily Joel had yet to remove his pants, so she was spared the sight of ... Little Joel. Despite herself, she giggled but straightened her face when her sister knocked on the door.

"Come in."

Nan, scarlet, wrapped in her robe came to sit down on the bed.

Hayley waited a moment then asked 'Where's Joel?"

"Um, he left."

"Okay."

For a moment, they avoided looking at each other, then Hayley could stand it no longer, and a laugh escaped. Nan stared at her in horror for a beat, then her own face crumpled and soon they were both laughing hysterically.

"Stop, stop, my insides hurt," Nan pleaded after a while, and Hayley dragged some air into her lungs.

"I'm really sorry, Nanny," Hayley said, using her childhood nickname for her sister. "I didn't think." She smothered a grin and started to sing, "Skyrockets in flight, afternoon delight ..."

Nan swiped playfully at her. "We thought you were out with Skandar all afternoon."

Hayley looked at her watch. "It's seven p.m."

"We may have gotten distracted. How was your date?"

Hayley got up to find some food. Nan followed her into the kitchen as Hayley grabbed a box of pop tarts. "Want one?" Nan nodded. "It wasn't a date; we're friends. It turns out I think we'll be good friends. So, Mommy, you don't have to worry."

"Not your mommy," muttered Nan, but she smiled.

"No, you're not," Hayley suddenly grabbed her sister and hugged her. "You're better than she ever was. Ever."

Nan hugged her back. "You too, weird butt."

"Have not got a weird butt."

"Have too."

Hayley gave up, laughing. She grabbed the pop tarts from the toaster, cursing as the hot sugar burned her fingers. She dropped one onto a plate and handed it to her sister.

"How was Skandar?"

"Fun," Hayley said, gingerly biting into her pastry. "I think he's coming out of the slump. I wish they would hurry up and let him know where he stands. He needs to grieve that poor girl and get on with his life."

Nan waved her into the living room. "Sit. I need to tell you what Joel said to me."

Hayley grinned wickedly. "How could you hear? Wasn't his voice muffled?"

"Oh, ha ha. Annoying brat. Anyway, here's the thing ... they think it might be tied to the ex-partner of Jakob's, the one who attacked Quilla. They seem to think he might be targeting all of the family as revenge."

Hayley put her pop tart down. "Asshole. And they still don't know where he might be?"

Nan shook her head. "He has unlimited funds to hide himself away with, plus, Jakob thinks he was planning to usurp Jakob or the Mallorys for years. Getting Jakob hooked on drugs, weaseling his way to the Board, positioning himself for a takeover. When Jakob fired him, he went insane—or was already halfway there. Gregor Fisk is a billionaire—and a corrupt one, at that; he could literally pay anyone to do anything. Which is why the Mallorys' homes are like Fort Knox now."

Hayley frowned. "Has he told Skandar any of this? Because him tripping up alone to meet me today probably wasn't the wisest thing."

"Probably not, but hey, the guy has to live."

LATER, when Hayley crawled into bed and switched on her iPad, there was an email from Skandar.

Had a blast today, thank you. Let's do it again very soon, deal? S.

She grinned and typed back. Deal, I had a great time, too. Here for you whenever. H.

She sat back and thought about him. There was no doubting Skandar Mallory was drop-dead gorgeous; his dark blond hair cut short was never tidy, and she loved the undone-ness of it—nothing less sexy than a young man who spends more time doing his hair than his girlfriend—his crooked grin, his little-boy swagger. She loved that when he smiled, his eyes would crease so much they would almost close. God. A small heat shot through her groin. Yeah, that smile could ruin a woman, and he damn well knows it too, she thought to herself. Do not fall for him.

Do not fall for Skandar Mallory ...

·   ·   ·

HE'D GOTTEN AWAY with it by the skin of his teeth, had to lose a couple of paps, but Skandar was home. Before he switched any lights on, he regretfully closed the drapes—with drones nowadays, even a condo as high up as this one could be spied on—but it shut out the view of the city that he loved so much. The place smelled dank and unlived in. He was used to leaving it for extended periods of time when he was on tour, but this seemed different. He walked around the place, trying to get the feel for it again. This had been his solace, his cave, but now ...

It's not the place that's changed; it's you, he thought to himself. The condo seemed empty; hell, his day seemed empty—without Hayley in it. Shit. He didn't want to complicate their friendship by having feelings for her; he really didn't. And after what had happened to Annika—he was gun shy and a little paranoid.

He took a shower and went to bed, logging on to see if Samadamadingdong was online. No dice. Damn. He could do with someone to talk about Hayley with. Hayley Applebee.

"Virgin," he said out loud, shaking his head. He still couldn't believe it—but he did think she was telling the truth. He thought back to what she'd said and on a whim, downloaded Delta of Venus by Anais Nin to read in bed.

And when he went to sleep that night, he dreamed about Hayley Applebee in his arms, sweating, panting, crying out his name, and definitely no longer a virgin ...

Quilla looked up from her paperwork as her boss turned off the lights in his office. Gerry smiled at her. "It's after seven, Quilla, go home."

She smiled, waved a wad of paper. "I will. Just want to finish this before the weekend. Jakob's coming for me in twenty minutes, anyhow."

"Well, goodnight."

The art department at the college was quiet in the evenings. Occasionally a student would pop by for supplies or to borrow some equipment and they would always stop and have a chat with Quilla. She was one of the most popular grad students to go to for advice.

Tonight, though, all was quiet. Good, I can concentrate, and then she groaned as her phone rang. I jinxed that. She shook her head ruefully and picked up the phone.

"Hello?"

Nothing. She heard the line crackle.

"Hey, I can't hear you, so ..."

"Quilla."

Her palms started to sweat. Gregor. "What the hell do you want?"

He laughed. "I'll tell you that in a while. For now, I wanted to apologize for ... hurting you."

"Hurt me? You stabbed me, you son of a bitch." She was mad now, and her voice rose. "And you killed that tennis player, that poor girl. Why?"

His chuckle made her want to scream. "No, why would I want to do that?" So fake—he wasn't even trying to convince her. Bastard.

"To set Skandar up, to punish the family, because of the pathetic psycho you are."

"You listen to me, you little whore," he spat out suddenly, and Quilla's body started to tremble at the hatred in his voice. "You tell that boyfriend of yours that I will never stop until I've destroyed everything he loves. Everything and everyone. And Quilla?"

She didn't answer him, her throat closed. She heard his breathing, hard and enraged.

"Tell him soon, very soon. Because when I come for you next time, Quilla, I'll make damn sure that you don't survive my knife again."

The line went dead. Quilla froze and dropped the receiver onto the desk, hearing the dial tone. She wasn't sure how long she stayed frozen like that, but it wasn't until Jakob came to get her that she moved. He took one look at her terrified, stricken face and dashed to her side, locking her into his arms.

"What is it, darling? What is it?"

She mumbled something, and he smoothed the hair away from her face. "I'm sorry, sweetheart, I didn't catch that."

She stared up at him. "I said, he's going to kill me ..."

. . .

THE POLICE WERE KIND, but Jakob could see their hopelessness. Gregor was in the wind. Quilla told them about her accusation that Gregor had killed Annika and was setting Skandar up. She saw them exchanging glances and desperately blurted out everything she could think of to help, but eventually one of them calmed her down.

"Miss Chen ... it's okay. Mr. Mallory came to us a few days ago with his theory, and in concert with the Italian police ... well, we think it has some credence. Skandar Mallory should hear something in the next few days, but we can't, for legal reasons, confirm that yet. It's entirely up to you whether you pass that information on to him."

LATER, Jakob and Quilla were in the bathtub, Quilla's head resting back against his shoulder. The fear that had been roiling in Jakob's gut since the phone call hadn't abated and now, stroking his long fingers down her belly, he couldn't help but picture her dead, stabbed not once but a hundred times, bled out in his arms, her lovely eyes staring and sightless for evermore.

Fuck. He squeezed his eyes shut. He should have told her about the messages earlier. He'd had to admit to receiving them when they were interviewed and the look of surprise, of betrayal on her face, he would never forget. She hadn't said anything to him about it afterward.

Now, they bathed in silence; he heard her sigh. Pressing his lips to her temple, he asked her if she was okay.

"I'm mad."

"I'm sorry."

"Not at you, baby. At that asshole. For making me afraid again. Fuck, I'm so mad." She sat up and turned around to face him, straddling him. Not for the first time, he was struck by the beauty of her, her face, her breasts, and the way her belly curved out slightly as she sat on top of him. There was fury in her eyes. "Jakob, will you do something for me?"

He slid his hands onto her face. "Anything, anything."

"I need angry sex," she said. "I need to fuck and be fucked, hard. All night. In this tub, on the floor, against the wall. Fucking do what you want to me, just nail me right."

At her words, he felt his cock respond, and she slipped her hands between his legs. "You're so fucking beautiful," he growled and pulled her to him, kissing her until they both tasted blood.

She pulled and massaged his cock until it was pulsing with the desire to be inside her. Jakob lifted her so she could guide him in. Then, with one furious thrust, she impaled herself on him, taking the long, thick length deep inside her, grabbing the back of his head with her hands to kiss him as they fucked. His cock drilled into her as she moved and he could feel the muscles in her cunt constrict and pull at him, sending glorious sensations through his body. He clamped his hands around her waist, his fingers biting into the soft flesh there.

"When we get out of this tub," he growled as his lips found her throat, "I'm going to lick your pussy until you cannot stand it any longer. Then my fingers are going to go deep inside you as I fuck you in your perfect ass."

Quilla moaned. "More." She slammed her hips onto him and threw her head back. Jacob molded her breasts in his hands, feeling the weight of them, stroking his thumbs over her nipples. He smiled at her. "You want more?"

He tumbled them out of the tub onto the floor and pressed her down on her stomach. Grabbing the belt from his robe, which hung on the door, he bound her hands behind her. "You like this, Quilla?"

She nodded, her breath quickening as he pushed her legs apart and eased into her ass. Bracing his hands on either side of her head, he began to thrust slowly, listening to her moan and say his name over and over.

"You're mine to do with what I like tonight, Quilla Chen."

"Always yours, always..."

They fucked until the sun came up, the rays of light streaming across their aching bodies as Jakob took her against the bedroom wall, holding her small frame easily as he slammed into her. His eyes were full of her; he could not get enough of this goddess in his arms. Finally, exhausted, they fell into bed, wrapped their arms around the other and slept. Neither of them noticed—again—the tiny camera that been planted in their bedroom for months now, watching them fuck and kiss and sleep.

THE MAN WATCHING the feed smiled as he watched them, marveling over the body of the woman, so curvy and ripe. He stared at the man, his old friend, his former partner, and wondered to himself how he would feel when she was dead. He would soon find out ...

This just in ... all charges against Skandar Mallory have been dropped after the murder of Mallory's girlfriend, Annika Hahn last month in Rome. Police are now satisfied that Miss Hahn, a former Wimbledon Juniors champion, was killed in a random act of violence by an unknown assailant sometime after leaving Mr. Mallory's room on the seventeenth of the month. The Italian Police Association has offered an unequivocal apology to Mr. Mallory for the inconvenience caused and asked for anyone with any information to come forward ...

"HOLY SHIT," Hayley said, shooting upright in her bed, and grabbing the remote. "Holy shit, holy shit." She turned the volume up and listened for a few seconds more before raising her arms above her head and whooping loudly. She muted the TV. and grabbed her cell. Skandar's line was busy. It clicked onto voicemail.

"Yo, dude, I just heard. God, I'm so happy for you, Skan, so, so happy ... ' She found herself choking up as the house phone started to ring. "I'll try and call you back in a few but ... baby, you made it. You made it!'

Still half crying, half laughing, she grabbed the house phone. "Hello?"

"Get off your phone, I'm trying to call you," yelled an obviously deliriously happy Skandar, and she laughed through her tears.

"I was trying to call you! It was just on TV. God, Skan ..." She did cry then, and he laughed.

"I know, I know, that's how I feel ... look, there's only one person I want to celebrate this with, but my family is making me have a celebration dinner with them. Say you'll come and we can make our escape later."

"Of course, of course. God, I can't believe it. When did they tell you?"

"They called about five minutes ago. My dad and my grandfather are dancing. It's quite a sight to see."

She laughed. This family, with her sister dating Joel, had felt more like a family than she'd ever experienced and now that she and Skandar were best friends—they spent nearly all of her free time together now—it just made this all the sweeter.

"Skan, I want to do something special then, something mad, just the two of us."

"Hmm, mad—for us that's not a stretch. Come over soon and we'll discuss it."

As soon as the cab pulled up to the Mallory homestead, she raced up the driveway. Skandar must have been watching from inside because as she reached the huge wooden front door, it was flung open, and Skandar scooped her into his arms and spun her around so fast she started to laugh. Finally, he relented and put her down, and she staggered, still laughing. He locked his arms around her to steady her, and she caught her breath.

"It's over," she said, grinning, touching his face. He grinned that crinkled smile of his and nodded.

"It's over, boo." They both laughed breathless, then, as if it were the most natural thing in the world, his lips found hers and they were kissing. Hayley closed her eyes and sank into it, his mouth as sweet as she had always thought it would be. His fingers slipped into her hair, gentle, the pads of his fingers stroking delicious patterns on her scalp.

She slid her arms around his waist, fingers running over the taut, hard muscular body.

They broke apart just as she was about to pass out from oxygen deprivation, but his hands stayed on her face, his thumbs gliding over the apples of her cheeks. His eyes, that warm brown color, those long, long dark blond lashes, gazed down at her, his smile, his beautiful smile, breaking across his face.

"They're waiting for us inside," he said softly, with regret. She nodded, unable to tear her eyes away from his. He took her hand, and they walked inside slowly.

Their family greeted them, and Hayley could see Nan trying not to grin at their clasped hands. She was grateful her sister didn't say anything about them to her; this was brand new, and she didn't want to share it with anyone else, yet. Skandar stayed at her side for the whole evening as they toasted with champagne, his hand resting lightly on the small of her back.

Hayley knew that in a few short hours, her life had changed forever and when, finally, Skandar drove them back to his condo in the city, top down in his Mercedes, she felt something shift in her soul.

IN HIS HOME, she walked around the vast living space, looking around. It was surprisingly chic, and of course, she nodded approvingly at the game consoles. Skandar handed her a cold soda and grinned as she pored over his games collection. "Wanna play?"

She grinned at him, relieved that he was so relaxed about the change in the status of their relationship. Reading her mind, Skandar put his soda down, then took hers and put it next to his. He took her hands. "Hayley, nothing needs to happen here until you're ready. We can just hang out and have fun and talk. I wouldn't mind another one of those sweet kisses of yours, but if you're not ready, that's okay."

Hayley's eye filled with tears, and he stepped towards her, but she smiled, waved him away. "I'm fine. These are happy tears, I promise. I have a confession. I Googled you after we first met and all I read were these articles on how much you were a player and this and that. When we became friends, I thought 'Give him a chance' instead of judging you. The man those articles described—I've never met him. All I know is you, Skandar Mallory. The funny, sweet guy who became as important to me as my own family."

Skandar simply held out his arms, and she went into them. He buried his face in her neck his lips against her throat.

"You changed me," he said, his voice cracking with emotion. "You gave me back hope. You made me believe in goodness again."

Both of their faces were wet with tears when they kissed again. "But I meant what I said," he said finally, "nothing needs to happen unless you want it to."

"Is it okay that I'm scared?"

Skandar grinned. "Hell, yes. I'm terrified. I don't want to screw this up."

Hayley laughed. "In that case, how about we game for a bit, relax us both?"

"You got it. Choose your poison."

She settled on Red Dead Redemption. "Nice," he approved, and they scooched down on the couch to play.

By the time they finished, she was barely able to keep her eyes open. He smoothed her hair back from her face. "You can have my bed; I'll sleep in the guest room."

She rested her head on his shoulder. "No," she said sleepily. "I don't want to be alone."

She couldn't bear to think of him not being next to her. He didn't reply, but got up and hoisted her into his arms.

In his bedroom, he removed her sneakers and jeans and tucked her into bed; she turned over to watch him undress. He stripped down to his boxers. God, he's magnificent, she thought, his athlete's body honed and cut, the broad shoulders leading down to the deep vee of his hips. He was watching her watching him, a strange smile on his face. She took her time drinking him in, every curve of muscle, every soft silky inch of his skin. He made to move to get in bed, but she sat up.

"No."

His eyes were sad, disappointed, but he nodded. "It's okay, I'll ..."

"No, that's not what I meant. I meant ... don't stop ... there." She blushed, but suddenly it was imperative she see him ... all of him.

He got it. "Off?" He gestured to his boxers, and she nodded. "Okay."

Slowly, he peeled his boxers down his legs, stepped out of them, and stood. Warmth flooded through her as he stood there and let her study him. His cock, beginning to stiffen, was thick and long, beautifully shaped. Slowly she crawled to the edge of the bed and he moved so she could touch him. She ran her fingers lightly down the shaft, marveling at how silky it felt and how it quivered and grew under her touch. She heard him pull in a ragged breath and looked up at him.

Their gazes locked and at that moment, a silent agreement was made. Hayley peeled off her T-shirt, then unhooked her bra. She was astonished that she didn't feel self-conscious or embarrassed—she wanted him to look at her, to touch her. Skandar gently cupped each breast in his hand, and then bent his head to plant a kiss on each one. Hayley felt herself get wet as he slowly climbed onto the bed and pushed her back onto the pillows. She reached down to stroke his cock again, feeling the heft of it in her hand.

Skandar kissed her mouth. "You want to stop, you just say stop, and I'll stop, okay? No matter when, baby ..."

Hayley pulled his head down so she could taste his lips again. "I don't want to stop; I want you so much ... '

Skandar smiled and Hayley gasped as he slipped his hand into her panties and began to stroke her. "Is this okay?"

She nodded, feeling her clit harden under his touch, and when he bent his head and took her nipple into his mouth, she gasped, the rush of arousal, the depth of her feeling scaring her and thrilling her at the same time. Her hands, still stroking his cock, brushed over the sensitive crest of it and he shuddered. "God, Hayley ... that feels so good..."

He moved down her body, trailing his lips down her belly, his fingers hitching under her panties and pulling them down. He parted her legs gently, then looked up at her. "You're beautiful ... don't be scared." She nodded and he bent his head and took her clit into his mouth.

Hayley let out a cry that turned into a giggle of pleasure. Skandar laughed and she felt the sensation rumble through her sex. His tongue teased and lashed around her clit and she felt her sex flood with desire. She closed her eyes and gave herself up to the pleasure. Skandar brought her to near orgasm, leaving her panting and needing more as he leaned over to the nightstand and retrieved a condom from the drawer. He sat back on his haunches to slip it on— he even made that look sexy—and smiled at her.

"Remember, you say stop, we stop."

She nodded, panting, wanting to feel him inside her. Skandar gently moved the tip of his penis up and down her slit before nudging at the entrance of her vagina. "Okay?"

She nodded, and he pushed inside her. Her eyes widened at the quick sharp pain but as it faded and Skandar began to move, finding his rhythm, her legs wrapped around him and she began to move her hips along with him. Skandar locked his gaze on hers, and they rocked gently, the pace quickening as they both drew near climax. Hayley's vision exploded in bright sparks, and she thought she would pass out as her orgasm ripped through her and she clung to Skandar as he thrust harder once more and came, shuddering and groaning her name over and over. Her body, still vibrating with pleasure, felt different, as if finally, she fit her own skin.

Skandar excused himself to use the bathroom but was back in a flash, climbing into the bed with her and gathering her to him. "Hey, beautiful."

He kissed her. "You okay?"

She nodded, her eyes shining. "More than okay, Skandar Mallory." She ran her finger down his cheek. Skandar nuzzled his nose against hers and smiled.

"Tired?" She nodded, and he pulled her to him. "Sleep now, baby. I'm not going anywhere."

She thought she might not be able to, given the delicious tempta-

tion of his skin next to hers, but soon found herself drifting off, knowing, without any hesitation that she was in love with him.

NAN ROLLED over in the bed to find Joel away and furiously texting.
"Morning, baby."

He turned and smiled, but she could see the worry in his eyes.
"What is it?"

Joel shook his head. "Fucking Kit. Now that Skandar's in the clear;
he wants to do a joint interview with him. Diane Sawyer, for
chrissakes."

Nan frowned. "Why?"

"Because," Joel pushed the sheet back and got up. "Kit is a narcissistic asshole who will exploit his own nephew to get publicity."

Nan slid out from the bed and went to him. "I'm so sorry, Joel." He
gathered himself.

"I better call Skan."

She gave him some privacy, wondering what would happen. She
had never met Kit Mallory, box office superstar actor—or Joel's
youngest brother Grady, for that matter—but Joel and Kit were
fraternal twins and to hear Joel tell it, polar opposites. She had met
Asia, Kit's gorgeous ex-wife, and found her to be down to earth and
professional, as well as warm and generous, and could not reconcile
the two personalities.

"I fell in love with him,' Asia had told her quietly. "But sometimes,
love isn't enough. Not with Kit."

She had piqued Nan's interest, but she hadn't felt she could ask
Joel more— there was obvious some sibling tension there.

Which reminded her ... last night Hayley and Skandar had not
taken their eyes off each other. Admittedly, it was a bit weird seeing
her boyfriend's son so obviously smitten with her sister, but they'd
looked so happy. She retrieved her cellphone and called her sister.

"Hey, bug," she said when Hayley answered. She could hear the
TV. in the background.

"Hey, you okay?"

"Sure, just calling to see if you got home okay."

"Um," Hayley hesitated and in that second, Nan knew.

"Hays ... are you at Skandar's place?"

"Yeah, we came home to play PlayStation, and you know, it got late, so I crashed here."

Nan smothered a smile. "Well, that's cool. Look, I don't want to disturb, just to say I have that parent/teacher thing tonight so I'll be late home. Call if you'll be out, okay?"

See, she could do 'cool older sister' in her sleep. To be honest, she was relieved that Hayley was with Skandar—he could keep her safe, at least.

"Sure thing," Hayley said, catching onto her tone. She lowered her voice. "Thanks, sis, love you."

"Love you, too," Nan replied and saying bye, she put down her phone just as Joel reappeared, his face grim.

"Kit's flying in to try and persuade Skandar to do the interview."

Nan nodded. "Will he do it?"

Joel sighed. "I honestly don't know."

"Sure, let's do it," Skandar shrugged nonchalantly later that day. Kit Mallory grinned at his family.

"See? The kid's up for it, so what's the problem?"

Hayley glared at the man. She didn't care if he was the most famous actor in the world; he was a giant douchebag. That was her first impression, and she wasn't changing it in a hurry. Yes, he was staggeringly good-looking (although nothing on Skandar, she decided somewhat smugly), his long blond hair coiffed perfectly into perfect surfer style, his blue eyes enhanced with contacts. Skandar, his usual easygoing self, who was still living on the high from the charges being dropped, and from their lovemaking, didn't see the harm but Joel, Randall, and Jakob were dead set against it.

"It opens you up to any questions they want to ask about your relationship with Annika," Joel told his son, but Skandar grinned good-naturedly.

"It'll be fine, Pa. I haven't got anything to hide."

Kit grinned his thousand-watt smile and clapped his hands together. "Good, that's settled. Cherry," he barked at the poor PA, who looked exhausted and hungry. "Get that confirmed."

"Maybe Cherry would like something to eat and some rest first." Randall Mallory was usually a calm, warm center but his voice, this time, took on an edge. Hayley watched as Kit graciously inclined his head in agreement. Ran Mallory's words apparently carried some weight with his famous son, if no one else's did.

Nan stood and held her hand out to Cherry. "Come, let's grab some food and I'll take you up to your room."

Cherry followed her out, as did Hayley. Nan nudged her sister. "I got the good twin," she muttered, and Hayley snorted.

"Word," she shot back, and she saw Cherry nod, her tired eyes amused.

"You're not wrong," she blurted out, then looked alarmed, as if she'd said too much. Hayley tucked her arm under hers.

"What's said here stays here. How the hell do you not beat his ass with a baseball bat?"

They were in the kitchen then, and Nan made a sandwich and heated some soup. Cherry smiled at them gratefully. "He pays very well," Cherry admitted, "and he's not always like that. Sometimes I get to see the real Kit—he's not so bad."

Nana and Hayley exchanged a look, and Cherry chuckled. "No, it's not like that, I don't have a crush. I have a very patient, very understanding wife at home."

Hayley grinned. "Then pretend you're having a crush on Asia—that'll get to him."

"Hayley," Nan warned, and Cherry shook her head, smiling.

"I'd never do that. That was one time Kit genuinely was crushed. He still loves Asia."

SKANDAR AND HAYLEY drove out to Discovery Park then hiked the mile and a half to the West Point Lighthouse. The weather had turned cooler, and the fall leaves were flaming red and gold. They found some driftwood to sit on, Skandar with his arm around her, looking out to the lighthouse and the water. Hayley leaned her head on his shoulder and Skandar pressed his lips to her forehead.

"You okay, Hays? After last night, I mean."

She looked up and smiled. "More than, Skandar Mallory. You made everything so ... natural, and easy and exhilarating. You made it perfect."

Skandar nodded. "You're the perfect one," he said, his voice thick. He cleared his throat, then grinned his wicked smile. "Although you are making me all mushy, which is not acceptable at all."

"It's revolting, isn't it?"

"Totally." He laughed along with her. "Actually, I do have an admission ... there's someone else."

Because he was grinning, she knew not to be shocked or scared, but still, it stung a little. "The floozy."

"Want the story?"

"Well, I'm going to need to know whose ass to kick, so yeah," she pretended to be angry. He grinned.

"Jealous. You don't need to be; I've never met her. I'm even presuming she's a 'she', although I'm pretty sure. Promise you won't think I'm the biggest geek?"

"Too late."

"Ha ha, funny girl. Well, it gets lonely on tour, especially when Carlos has the key to my chastity belt."

She stuck her tongue at him.

"So, I found this forum, this sci-fi nerd heaven and starting lurking on it. After a while, I found this thread where this person was posting, and we got to talking on the forum, then later, private messaging."

Hayley was staring at him in shock. "Skan ... which forum is this?"

Skandar looked sheepish. "Battlestar Galactica and Cap ..."

"Caprica," she finished for him.

He looked amazed. "Yeah, you know it?"

She nodded, trying not to grin. "Yeah, I love it. Ask me who my favorite character is, Skandar."

Something was tugging at his brain. "Who?"

"Sam Adama."

It hit him then. "You're Samadamadingdong?"

"You're SkunkMaladyBibble."

"Holy shivering fuck," he said and started to laugh. "Of all the ... wow. We were really meant to be, huh?"

She flushed with pleasure at his words. "I think so."

Skandar kissed her, tilting her chin with a gentle hand. "Hayley Applebee, you are my world now. I am away a lot—do you think you could live with that? You're always welcome to come with me, of course, but I know you have college. I want to make us work. Can you trust me?"

She nodded. "With my life," she said and wrapped her arms around his neck, kissing him fiercely. "Hey, ... so ... it's getting cold and um, well, I need ... practice so ..."

Skandar grinned. "You got it, beautiful ... let's go back to my place."

HAYLEY LAY BACK in Skandar's arms, sweat-drenched, her body reeling from making love. God, if this was what it was like ... she grinned at him. "You may have turned me into a nympho."

He laughed. "That's just because you have no one to compare me to." His stomach growled, and she giggled. "Well, thanks, belly, that's ruined the moment. God, I'm starving. Pizza?"

"Hell, yes."

Skandar scooted out of bed and threw on his jeans. "I'll order some." He went out to grab his phone and Hayley got up and reached for her clothes. Then something caught her eye, and she stopped and smiled. When she walked out to join Skandar, she was wearing a white shirt of his, halfway buttoned up, the length of it falling to just above her knee. Skandar was just finishing up ordering and grinned.

"Wow."

Hayley posed for him. "I just always wanted to wear a guy's shirt and look sexy for him. Like in the movies."

"It worked ... come here."

TWENTY MINUTES LATER, when the pizza arrived, they fell on it like savages. Skandar picked up the remote. "Wanna watch some TV while we eat?"

Hayley nodded, her mouth full of food. Skandar flicked it on and scanned through the channels, settling on the news. They watched as the anchorwoman talked, not really taking anything in. It was only when they heard his name that they looked up.

"Skandar Mallory, recently exonerated in the murder of German tennis star Annika Hahn, now faces a new crisis as gossip sites have published photographs of the twenty-five-year-old superstar in bed with another woman. The woman, seen here, is believed to be nineteen-year-old UW sophomore, Hayley Applebee. Karl Harlow reports, with images that some viewers may find offensive."

Hayley dropped her slice of pizza, nearly choking on the mouthful she was eating.

"What the actual fuck?" Skandar growled. He turned the TV up. A reporter, standing outside the very home they were in, was talking to the camera.

"The photographs, which are explicit, show Mallory with a young woman. Both are naked, and as the sequence continues, it is clear they are having sexual relations. This comes just a day after Mallory was cleared of suspicion in the murder of Annika Hahn, his then-girlfriend. Some say the timing is suspicious ..."

But Hayley stopped listening. The photos—thankfully, her breasts and genitals were blanked out—were obviously taken last night—the most wonderful, erotic, private night of her life. She felt violated, exposed. Shamed.

Skandar looked horrified. "God, Hayley, I'm so sorry ... what the fuck?"

"How the hell did they get pictures, Skandar? Did you tape us?"

She stood and fled to the bedroom, yanking off his shirt, not caring if she ripped it. She tugged her clothes on as he followed her. "Is that what happened? You taped us, and they hacked your hard drive?" She was pulling on her sneakers now as Skandar held out his hands.

"Sweetheart, no, I would never ..."

"Then how did they get the fucking pictures?" she screamed, then burst into tears, sobbing, humiliated. "God, what am I going to say to Nan? To my friends? My God, I'm going to have to drop out of college —if they don't throw me out first."

"Hayley, calm down. We'll get to the bottom of this ... you haven't done anything wrong. I have no idea ..." He looked around the room then started to open closets, drawers. She knew what he was looking for. Cameras. She searched, too, then, desperate for proof that he didn't know they were being watched. God, she wanted to throw up.

"Here," Skandar said in a dead voice. He stood back from the closet and let her see. A tiny recording device with a feed lodged in the door, directly facing the bed. She stared at it.

"And it's not part of your security system?"

"No."

"God." She watched as Skandar ripped it from the wall and stamped on it. "You shouldn't have done that. There might have been fingerprints, evidence the police could use."

She went to sit on the bed and after a second, Skandar came to her. "I swear, I didn't know. I would never do anything to hurt you like this."

She couldn't speak, couldn't reassure him. She wanted to believe him but he had been so reckless in the past. She looked at him, studied his face, his dark, hurt eyes and knew that even though she loved him, she didn't quite trust him.

"I have to go."

Skandar put his arms around her. "No, please, stay and let's figure this out. I'll get Zoe to come over and—"

"This isn't about public relations, Skandar. It's about whether I can trust you with my heart."

He followed her out to the doorway. "You can ... you can trust me."

She couldn't look at him. "We'll see. I need some time."

Skandar nodded. "Okay ... okay..." He opened the door for her but then shut it again, his face creasing with emotion.

"Just, please remember this ... I love you."

Tears were dropping down Hayley's face. "I love you, too ... but I need some time. I'm not saying forever, but ..."

Skandar took her face in his hands. "Kiss me before you go..."

She pressed her lips to his, her resolve nearly faltering but then she pushed him away and fled, banging down the stairs and out onto the street. The paparazzi assailed her immediately, and she kicked and fought her way through them, cursing them out, not caring that it was all being captured on film.

She ran three blocks before stopping, bending double to sob her anger, her hurt out. She managed to hail a cab and almost fell into it.

"Where to, Miss?" The cab driver had a kindly face—which made her sob even harder. As he waited, she managed to choke out. "I don't know ... I don't know ..."

4

PART FOUR: TAME ME

I t wasn't the first time Joel Mallory had punched his twin brother across a room, but it was certainly the hardest.

To be fair, Kit Mallory deserved it, stalking into his father's house with an entourage the size of a small army and yelling at his nephew in front of everyone. "What the fuck are you doing with this tramp, Skandar? Are you trying to ruin the whole family? What next?"

It had been a race to see who could punch Kit first, but Joel beat his son out by a hair. Randall grabbed hold of Skandar while Jakob hauled Joel off his brother. Ran nodded at Kit's entourage. "Please wait in the library, folks; we'll get you some refreshments. Thank you."

As Jakob hauled Kit to his feet and blocked him from going at Joel, Ran released his grandson, giving him a meaningful look. "The rest of you, sit down."

Skandar, struggling to simmer down after hearing Kit insult Hayley, slumped back in a chair. "Don't you ever call her a tramp again, you fucker," he hissed as Ran put a cautioning hand on his shoulder.

Kit was unrepentant. "You can forget about Diane Sawyer now; I can't have you crapping all over my career as well as your own."

"Kit, shut the fuck up," Jakob had heard enough. "Skan's done nothing wrong—we have to figure out who put the cameras in his condo, and why."

Kit rocked back a little. "Wait ... I thought this was a sex tape you released."

"No," Skandar's voice was like ice, "unlike you, I actually have respect for the women in my life."

Kit gave a hollow laugh. "I'm sure Annika ..."

"Do not finish that sentence; do not finish that sentence, cocksucker," Skandar was up again. This time, it was Jakob who body-blocked him.

"Enough!' Randall Mallory roared, and his three sons and one grandson looked at him in amazement. Jakob tried to remember when his father had raised his voice in his lifetime. He couldn't remember such an occasion. His father, looking drawn and exhausted, sat down and motioned for his family to follow suit.

"I am tired,' he said, "The last few months have been difficult enough without us imploding, too. Kit, you will never again refer to Hayley with anything but respect, do you understand?"

Kit rubbed his face. "Of course, ... look. Skandar, I'm sorry, I didn't mean that. It was wrong of me." His swagger had disappeared now and he was genuinely contrite.

Skandar nodded stiffly.

"Good, now, let's see if we can't come up with something to control this idiocy, this disgusting violation. First, we need to make sure that Hayley is protected ... Skandar?" Ran looked at his grandson and noticed a shadow pass over his face. "Where is Hayley now?"

Skandar sighed. "At home, holed up, I think. I've tried to call her a couple of times but ... she's distraught, Pops. What we did ... it wasn't a one- night stand, or anything tawdry. I love her. I hope to God she still loves me."

Joel looked at his son and gave him a proud nod, a half smile.

"Nan told me this morning that Hayley's regrouping. I'm going over there later; I'll see if she wants to talk."

Skandar dropped his head into his hands, and Joel put his arm around him. Kit sat forward.

"So, what can we do? What with this, the murder, Quilla's stabbing, this family has been through the mill. It's already impacted on my work—not that I don't realize how much worse it's been for you all," he added, hurriedly.

"Look ... we call it what it was—a disgusting invasion of two people's privacy, call the person who did it scum, say we'll spend every penny, do everything to bring that person to justice." Ran let out a tense sigh. "I could do with a drink."

"Good thing I brought you some single malt back from Scotland then," said a familiar voice.

They all turned around in surprise. Grady Mallory, his grin wide, raised his hand. "Hey, folks. What did I miss?"

KIT MALLORY WENT BACK to his hotel. Unlike his brothers, he didn't own a home in Seattle, preferring to be in L.A. It was more convenient for parties and attending red carpet events, he told them, but over the years he'd begun to feel the disconnect, and it had made him resentful, even if it was his own doing.

He gave Cherry, his PA, the night off and ordered room service. He sat down and flicked on the TV, not really watching it.

He shouldn't have insulted Skandar's girl—that was wrong. He'd just come from a meeting with his people and found out he was being dropped from the Oscar presenting roster—humiliating when he'd already announced it. To do damage control, he had to agree to appear in a British singer's music video—filming at the same time as the Oscars. It gave him a good reason to miss the Oscars without losing face.

Trouble was the singer herself. Bo Kennedy. They'd clashed once before over Twitter over a throwaway remark he'd made about ... God, he couldn't even remember now. Bo, a no-nonsense Londoner with strong feminist credentials, had ripped into him ... eviscerated him, and done it with a great deal of humor. He had a grudging respect for her. She wasn't like all the cookie cutter Barbie dolls clogging up the music; Bo Kennedy had the soul of Billie Holiday inside her and the voice to match. Everyone loved Bo. She'd bucked the trend of stick-thin singers by remaining curvy—by Hollywood's standards she was on her way to being obese, but in real world terms, her curves were the stuff of Marilyn Monroe and Jayne Mansfield and many a man's fantasies.

Her people had reached out to him to be in her video ... the pitch being he would play the handsome rogue boyfriend she was about to leave in a very public, very embarrassing fashion. He'd said no, at first —actually; it was more like "Fuck, no, with that ballbreaker?" - But when he thought about it, there was something that made him laugh about the offer. It was as if she was challenging him to prove he was the douchebag she thought he was. So when the whole Skandar/Murder Suspect/Sex Tape debacle had forced his hand ...

Shit. His guilt over abandoning his family had only gotten worse when Grady had shown up. Of all his brothers, Grady was the one who never put a foot wrong in his father's eyes. Mostly, that was because ... Grady never put a foot wrong. He was solid, dependable. Kit had always resented him because Grady had been in love with Kit's wife, Asia. To be fair to Grady—he had met Asia first and when he had brought her— just as a friend—to a family barbecue, Kit had taken one look at the gorgeous young woman and made his move. Grady had forgiven him, but it didn't stop Kit from being paranoid every time the golden boy was around Asia.

Stop going over the same crap, he told himself. He was rethinking the interview with Skandar and Diane Sawyer—maybe it would be good to do and act righteously indignant—especially when it came to the filming of a vulnerable young woman. Yeah, perhaps.

His food arrived, and he ate quickly, showered, and went to bed. In the morning, he would get Cherry to confirm the interview with Sawyer. Then, after that, he would fly to England and see about Bo Kennedy. He had to admit; he was rather looking forward to it.

· · ·

SKANDAR LEFT his grandfather's house just past midnight. Grady's arrival had been a relief to them all; he had idolized him when he was young, and because they were closer in age than his father and his brothers, Grady had always filled the big brother role for Skandar.

He'd asked his advice about Hayley. His uncle, who'd married his childhood sweetheart, Molly, only to find after the honeymoon she had Stage IV cancer—talked to him and told him to give Hayley her space. "But not too much space, kid," Grady had smiled. "You don't want to pressure her; just let her know you'll wait."

Skandar opened the windows of his car and let the night air flood over him. He couldn't stop thinking about Hayley, her hurt, and humiliation. Damn the fucker who did to this her, to them. But it wasn't just them. The police had gone to his house, scoured it, and found hidden cameras everywhere. On their advice, the rest of his family had their homes checked. Jakob and Quilla were horrified when the police found cameras in their home, too. Quilla had sobbed, and Skandar's heart broke for her—they all knew what it meant.

Gregor. That son-of-a-bitch. If Skandar could get his hands on him, he'd ripped him apart with his bare hands for what he had done to Hayley, to Quilla, to them all. He had no idea why Gregor would go after him, though. The answer came back to him: he was an easy target. Skandar shook his head in desolation. *Am I truly the weakest link in our family?*

His cellphone rang, and he pulled over to the side of the road to answer it. His heart leaped when he saw the call ID.

"Hey, sweetheart, it's so good to hear from you."

He waited, but Hayley didn't reply. Instead, he heard her sob. It made his chest hurt. "Oh, baby ... '

"I'm sorry," she said through her tears, "I promised myself I wouldn't do this, but I miss you, I just miss you."

"I love you. I miss you every minute," he said, his own voice cracking. He hesitated then, "Samadamadingdong, can I come see you?"

He heard her laugh softly through her tears. "Yes, please, SkunkMalady."

"Don't forget the Bibble."

"SkunkMaladyBibble. Nan is at Joel's."

His chest tightened. "You're on your own? She left you alone?"

"I'm a big girl, Skan. Nan offered to take me with her, but I wanted to be on my own ... except I don't want to be on my own. I want to be with you." She sighed.

"Darling, I'm coming over now. Lock the doors, the windows. I'll call you when I'm outside." His heart was thumping unpleasantly, his adrenaline flooding his veins. He kept picturing Gregor hunting Hayley down, stabbing her like he had done to Quilla, but then was aware he might be scaring Hayley. "Just to keep the paps out, you understand."

"'K. Hurry."

"I will, baby, I promise."

HE WAS at her door within a half hour. As soon as she opened the door and saw him, she burst into tears. Skandar pulled her into his arms and closed the door behind himself.

"It's okay, baby, I'm here now ..."

She nodded as he smiled down at her, brushing away her tears with his thumbs. "God, you look beautiful."

She laughed through her tears then. "You never told me you had a kink for snot. I need a tissue."

He followed her into her bedroom, looking around approvingly. Every surface was stuffed with books and records; her laptop opened on her desk. Her closet door was open, and it looked like she'd taken everything out—searching for more hidden cameras. She followed his gaze.

"All clear," she sniffed, rubbing at her eyes. He sat down next to her.

"Hayley ... I cannot begin to ..."

"Ssh, don't say sorry again. I'm sorry for even accusing you of..."

He caught her mouth with his, and she responded, her lips hungry against his. "I love you so much, Skandar," she said when they broke for air. She stood and lowered the blind on her window, then stripped her T-shirt off in one fluid movement. Skandar's breath faltered. God, just to see her ... so lovely, such a turn on.

"Sweetheart, are you sure?"

She bent down and kissed him again, then pulled him to his feet and slid her hands under his T-shirt. As she pulled it over his head, she smiled up at him. "No more talking."

He grinned. "Yes, ma'am."

She took his nipple into her mouth and teased the small nub as he unzipped her jeans and slid his hands into the back of her jeans, his fingers sweeping down to cup her perfectly rounded buttocks.

"I want to be on top," she murmured against his lips.

"I have no problem with that," he chuckled, then grinned as she pushed him back onto the bed. She pulled her jeans and panties off, unhooked her bra and straddled him, gloriously naked, her pale skin almost luminous in the dull light of the room.

"In an act of supreme defiance," she said, "and after torturing myself by checking every gossip site, I decided my time was better used researching technique. If the world's going to label me a whore, then I'm damn well going to live up to that label."

Skandar caught her wrists and made her look at him. "You are not a whore. I will kill anyone who calls you that." His voice was rough, cracked, and she smiled down at him, her eyes soft.

"I'm reclaiming the word," she said confidently, her hands at his fly. "Whore being your lover, whore being the girl who thinks about you all day, every day ... "

He nodded and as she reached in free his cock, already pulsating and thickening, he stroked his thumbs over her nipples, let his fingers drift down her belly. "I love you, Hayley Applebee."

"I love you too, Bibble," she grinned, and then her mouth was on him. As her tongue, hesitant at first, swept over the head of his cock, he shivered with pleasure, his hands in her hair, letting the soft strands fall through his fingers. He drew in a deep breath, his head falling back as she sucked gently at him, his cock, his entire body at her mercy.

After a few moments, he lifted her up so he could kiss her mouth, his hand drifting between her legs to feel her already wet for him. Hayley leaned over and grabbed a condom from her drawer, and helped roll it onto him before she straddled him again and guided him inside.

God, it felt like coming home, making love to this gorgeous girl, his best friend, his compadre. Skandar felt like all his limbs were being made numb with pleasure, all his blood rushing to his cock as she moved on top of him, her slick sex enveloping his size. He stroked her body as she began to breathe hard, his fingers sliding into her bush and feeling the engorged clit swell and pulse under his touch.

He came, his body arching up, slamming his hips against hers as she cried out and he felt the hot rush of her orgasm. As she wilted, panting, he sat up and rolled her onto her back, hitching her legs over his shoulder and burying his face in her sex. For a moment, she moaned—"God, Skandar, I don't know if I can"—but he was unrelenting, sweeping his tongue the length of her slit until it lashed mercilessly around her clit again and again until she nearly screamed as she came for the second time.

This time, she did beg him to stop and he grinned and complied, taking her into his arms. He smoothed the damp hair from her forehead, and they gazed at each other.

"This is all that matters,' he murmured. "You and me. Forever."

KIT SHIFTED UNCOMFORTABLY under the studio lights. He never gotten used to that heat, even as experienced as he was. Skandar was sitting next to him, texting, a sleepy grin on his face. He didn't even look nervous.

"Five minutes," the floor manager called, and Skandar looked up, finally putting his phone away.

"Stay on script," Kit muttered as Diane Sawyer came towards them. He didn't miss Skandar rolling his eyes.

The interview itself began well, comfortable, discussing Kit's latest film and the fact he was about to work with Bo Kennedy. Diane brought up the Twitter spat and Kit, ever magnanimous, laughed it off as a way to meet new people. He felt Skandar snort under his breath and surreptitiously kicked him.

Diane turned to Skandar, and as they discussed Annika Hahn, Skandar told her how he had felt about the dead girl, that he missed her, that he wished her family didn't have to go through the pain of her sudden and violent loss. Diane was gentle but thorough, and Skandar was honest and touching. Kit was impressed. It had been a good idea not to cancel the interview.

"Now, Skandar, in light of what you've just said ... we can't not talk about the photographs seen on the more salacious gossip sites."

Skandar drew in a deep breath. "No, I don't suppose we can gloss over it," he said with a rueful smile. "Diane, I'm used to the public eye, the intrusion, the loss of privacy. It comes with the territory. This, however, was such an intrusive, despicable, heartless invasion of privacy that I don't even have the words for how angry I am. It is inexplicable to me why this happened—what has anyone gained from it? The woman in those photos, Hayley Applebee, the girl I love, deserves to be treated with respect and love. She is a brilliant, smart, funny, beautiful student who is worth ten billion of any of the scum looking at, commentating on or publishing these photos. We were engaged in a private act of love. If the person who broke into my home—and, I have to add," – and he looked straight into the camera, "the home of my brother, and installed these cameras is watching, just know this. We will stop at nothing to find you, and you will be brought to justice."

His whole body was trembling. Diane looked at him with renewed respect. Kit, sensing a moment, threw his arm around his nephew. "And as his uncle, I have to speak up and say here that privacy is the watchword of our family, and we will vigorously defend it."

Diane blinked, then her professional smile returned. "Quite. That was an impassioned speech, Skandar; you must be serious about your lovely new girlfriend."

"I am. Very serious. This is it for me."

Even Diane was taken aback by his words for a second. "You do seem very happy."

"It would be impossible not to be with Hayley."

Kit could swear that Diane almost swooned at that. Jesus, kid, laying on much?

FINALLY, to Skandar's relief, Diane turned to Kit. "And how about you, Kit? I know you're still reeling from your divorce from the gorgeous Asia Flynn, you saw the photos of her at the Met Gala with Sebastian Winter, I presume?"

Kit's face went red, but he gave her a strained smile. "We remain on good terms. I'm glad she's finally moving on."

Skandar shot his uncle a hard look. Low blow, Unc, he thought, feeling sorry for Asia. Diane looked equally unimpressed by the childish slight.

"And what about you, Kit? Have you moved on? Apart from the dalliance we all know about, of course, with Lulu Florentine? Have you and she reconnected since your divorce?"

Ouch. Kit, his eyes wary, shook his head. "No, we're still friends, but no, we're not together. To be honest, Diane, I'm at a time in my life where I just want to be alone, really work on myself, find out who I am when I'm not 'Kit Mallory, superstar'"

Skandar gazed in horrified wonder as his uncle made air quotes around his name. Skandar met Diane's eyes and the corner of her mouth hitched up. Skandar thought he might lose it.

"Well, that's all the time we have." Diane was clearly dying to get away from Kit and howl with laughter. "Thanks so much for talking to me; it's been fascinating."

"Thank you, Diane."

"We're out." The floor manager called, and Diane shook their hands--giving a wink to Skandar and a slight nod to Kit. Good luck with that. Skandar decided he liked Diane very much indeed.

"TALK ABOUT HOGGING THE LIMELIGHT, jeez, Skan, let a guy get a word in." Driving them away from the studio and to the airport for Skandar to get a flight back to Seattle, Kit's perfectly-styled hair whipped around him as they sped along the freeway in his convertible.

Skandar grinned to himself. "This was your idea, Kit. I was answering the lady's questions."

"And declaring endless love. I'm surprised she didn't throw her panties at you, like every other woman in America will want to now."

Skandar shrugged. "I thought it went well. Asia will probably want a word, though."

Kit didn't reply. Skandar studied his uncle's profile. How was it that he was so entirely different from Skandar's dad, his twin brother? Where Joel was humble and low-key, Kit was vain and extroverted. He wondered if he had always been like that or whether his chosen career had made him like that.

Skandar thought back to some of the times he himself had been arrogant or careless with others. He knew one thing: Kit had loved Asia, really loved her, but he couldn't control his baser instincts or eschew the stereotypical life of a global film star. Lulu Florentine (seriously, that was her real name?) wasn't the first.

When they got to the airport, Kit surprised him. "You know, you should marry that girl. Don't let her go, if she means that much to you."

Skandar smiled. "I won't. Thanks."

Kit nodded once, then turned to leave him. He stopped. "Skan ... if you see Asia, tell her ... tell her hi from me. Hope she's good. Sorry about the ... you know."

Skandar could see the sadness in his eyes. "You could call her yourself, you know."

Kit laughed softly. "If I were her, I wouldn't take my call. See you when I get back from London."

· · ·

TWO DAYS LATER, after a long transatlantic flight, he was finally being driven to the video set. Kit stared out of the window at the sunny streets of London, packed with workers, tourists and shoppers. Living in L.A., he wasn't used to seeing people walking around the streets, and he found it fascinating to watch the interactions of different people—the exasperated stressed faces of the city workers, pushing through slow crowds of tourists, the determination of the shoppers.

At the studio, he was greeted with brisk efficiency by a P.A., Sindy, who had long legs and a great rack. He smirked to himself—shouldn't be too hard to find some after-hours company. Sindy led him into makeup and introduced him a huge man, who waved his makeup brushes at Kit.

"Wotcha," he said in a broad London accent, straight out of a Guy Ritchie movie, and steered Kit into a chair. "Nice to meet ya. Right, what are we doing? Full glamor puss?" His dark black eyes twinkled and his smile beamed through the thickest beard Kit had ever seen.

Kit blinked. "Um ..."

Sindy punched the giant playfully. "Terry, don't tease. Mr. Mallory, we'll call when Bo is ready, okay? Can I get you anything?" She pronounced it 'anyfink'."

Kit cleared his throat. "Tea, perhaps?" He was suddenly aware he was speaking very, very correctly—in a faux English accent. Damn it. "Tea would be great, thanks," he said, relaxing and speaking in his regular American accent. "What time do we start?"

Sindy beamed. "When Bo arrives. I'll be back with your tea."

Kit had to admit twenty minutes later that Terry, while he looked like a Sasquatch, had a supremely light touch with makeup. Kit now looked awake and fresh-faced without looking at all ... cakey. Dewy fresh, even. He nodded at Terry in the mirror.

"Dude, if Hollywood isn't already banging the door down, they should be."

"Cheers, mate." Terry gave him a thumbs up.

"Seriously, it takes a lot of skill to make me look good." Kit could afford to be generous in this mood.

"Cool. Look, I have to get ready for Bo so ... '

"She's not here yet?"

"Dunno, mate. Bo is Bo. Wardrobe should be coming for you soon. See ya."

Kit waited for anyone else to come and see him but after ten minutes, he decided to go out and see the set-up of the shoot. To him, there were a lot of people hanging around, talking, and not much work being done. Well, maybe things worked differently here in the UK. Wardrobe came to find him and after that, he grabbed his iPad and answered some emails. He checked the gossip sites to see the reaction to his and Skandar's interview, which had aired in the US the previous evening—and wished he hadn't.

They loved Skandar and his emotional declaration of love for his girlfriend. There were pictures of Skandar and Hayley walking in the park, gazing at each other—obviously, pre-set up by his publicist Zoe —who Kit immediately considered poaching. She was clearly a genius.

Kit, however, did not come over well. Passive-aggressive much, Kit? Star disses ex-wife in a tell-all interview. Sour Grapes of Wrath! Mallory seethes as Winter sets his sights on the beautiful ex-wife. Pictures of Sebastian Winter kissing Asia. Fucker. His mood plummeted as he looked at Asia, so gorgeous, her warm, easy smile lighting up the red carpet. There was a time when she lit up his red carpet.

He switched off his iPad and went to find Sindy. She was chatting to the lighting guys. Kit drew her aside. "Look, anyone have any idea when Bo will be here?"

She looked blank. "Dunno. She doesn't have a manager, so she sets her own times. She'll 'ere, don't worry."

"I'm not worried," he hissed and turned away from her. Fuck, why did I agree to this? He stalked off and sat in the chair with Bo's name on it. A minion approached him but he scared him off with a stare. How long was he supposed to wait for this woman?

An hour and a half later, just when he was seriously considering ditching the whole thing, there was a commotion. Laughter, raucous cackling and cursing, and there she was. For a second, all Kit could see was fake fur coats and fingernails, then finally, she reached him. He stood up, fury racing through his veins.

"Where the fuck have you been?"

Everything went silent. Bo looked at him, expression blank, but with her eyes challenging him to shout at her again and see where it got him. She was gorgeous, Kit reluctantly admitted. All breakneck curves, soft pillowy breasts with a cleavage you could lose yourself in, and the face of an angel.

"'xcuse me?"

"You were supposed to be here two hours ago! Do you think I have the fucking time to waste waiting around for some torch singer?"

Silence again. He seethed, refusing to back down. Not looking away from him, Bo called to the rest of the room. "Who got the time?"

"One minute twenty," said a voice from somewhere in the back. Bo smiled.

"Fucking brilliant. I win!" She turned and raised her arms to the room, and they all cheered. Kit had no idea what was going on and it showed in his face. Bo turned back to him smiling. "I bet these fuckers that I could get you to lose it in less than two minutes. You've just won me a hundred bloody quid!"

Again with the cheering. Kit drew in a breath, trying to calm himself. Losing it now—again—would not help anything.

"Look, can we just start?"

Bo waved him away nonchalantly. "You take your shirt off and look pretty; I'll just be a minute in makeup, then we can get down to it."

Hell, why, why, why did his cock just jump to attention when she said that? This bitch was insane, a pain in the ass, slovenly, over-the-top, spoke like Dick Van Dyke in Mary Poppins ... Fuck. He gave a stiff nod. "Fine."

She was true to her word this time and when she emerged, in a stunning red dress which clung to every curve and lit up her face, her honey-blonde hair falling in soft waves to her shoulders, it didn't do his erection any good. And of course, as soon as they got into their first clinch as the music played back, she would sing along with the backing track and her voice was so smoky, so divine, that, despite himself, he lost himself in the role. Bo was utterly professional—and a great actress, he was surprised to find—and their chemistry was undeniable.

At the end of filming, there was a scene where his character, dejected and abandoned by his love, sits alone in their bedroom (all artfully shabby chic, of course) only to look up and find her waiting in the doorway for him. Kit played the part perfectly, glancing up as Bo waited. He stood and walked to her and took her in his arms.

The moment their lips met, it was as if lava covered their bodies and they kissed passionately, for real. She tasted so good, so sweet, and God, the scent of her skin was driving him mad. He pulled her closer, not hearing the director shouting cut. Bo, her lips curving up in a smile, made no effort to pull away. Unseen by anyone else, she slipped her hand down to his pants and cupped his cock, squeezing the hot length of it through the fabric. A small growl escaped Kit and he fisted her hair in his hand and ground his mouth down on hers.

"Guys ... guys? Yeah, that's a wrap." The director coughed awkwardly.

Kit released her and Bo stepped back, grinning. "Get what you needed?" she said calmly to the red-faced director, who nodded. "Good." She looked back at Kit then very deliberately looked down to his groin and smiled. "Thanks for coming. You were great ... impressive."

She turned and walked off the set, shouting her thanks to everyone, who applauded her as she left.

Holy fucking shit. Kit couldn't believe what had just happened—and now she was just leaving? The hell? He obviously couldn't go after her—what, was he supposed to chase her? Him, Kit freaking Mallory? Hell, no.

Instead, he plastered on his best smile and thanked each and every member of the crew before leaving. He toyed with the idea of taking the PA back to his hotel-- she'd looked at him eagerly when he'd shaken her hand, but he found he didn't want to—despite the necessity of getting rid of the worst aching boner he'd ever had. Damn you, Bo Kennedy, ballbreaker and prick tease.

It was only back at his hotel that he felt bad. Why are you such a douchebag all the time? he said to himself as he looked into the bathroom mirror. You never used to be like this. The truth was, ever since he lost Asia, he'd been lost. He'd covered up his devastation and guilt by becoming this unbearable untouchable pig. Bo Kennedy was neither a ballbreaker or a tease. She was a goddess who had now bested him three times.

And, God, he'd absolutely love it if she did it again ...

Bo Kennedy was, at that moment, back in her massive home in the north of the city. Face and body scrubbed clean in the shower, she went back downstairs and grinned at the woman sitting on the floor with an angelic blond-haired toddler playing with some trains. Bo sat down with them.

"Thanks, mum." Bo kissed her mother's cheek and then tickled the little boy's feet. 'Ello, you. Got a kiss for Mummy?"

The boy, Tiger, threw himself into her arms, and she rolled back, cuddling him and blowing raspberries on his cheek until he screamed with laughter.

"He did drawing at school today," her mum, Daphne, said proudly, "and he won a prize. Show Mummy what you won."

Boo made an excited face. "Oo, what did you win? Show Mummy, go on."

Tiger skipped merrily up to his room to find his prize. Bo sat back against the couch and sighed. "He's been okay, Mum? Have you?"

"We've been just fine, darlin'. You look exhausted. How was the movie star?"

Bo grinned. "Movie starry. Big-headed, bit of a wanker, but very, very shaggable."

Daphne went red but giggled. "Bo, you are naughty."

Bo ran a hand through her hair, scooping it up into a ponytail and fixing it with the band she had around her wrist. "Mum, I wish I was naughty. Do you know how long it's been?"

Daphne made a sad face and Bo laughed. "You're no help."

Daphne got up and started to tidy the boy's toys. "Bo, I'll tell you what I told your aunt. She kept on at me after your dad left to find someone else. I told her, I've me own money; I've me own 'ouse; and I have full access to the Ann Summers website. Who needs a man?"

Bo screeched with laughter, rolling on the floor. "You never said that to Auntie Rose."

"I did too. And I'm saying it to you—you've made your success, my girl, and you've got that little angel upstairs."

Bo waved her hands. "I know, Mum. Just sometimes, you know?"

"I know. That's why I've got a dog."

"Eww, Mum!"

"To cuddle, you idiot," her mom grinned wickedly. "Look, if you're okay, I'd like to get home."

Bo checked her watch. "Oh, right ... what is it tonight?"

"Supernatural," her mum said excitedly, "Carry on my wayward son ... especially if it's Dean Winchester."

"Dirty. Old. Woman." Bo said but laughed. "I hope that vibrator runs on batteries. I don't want the National Grid going out on me."

"Cheeky cow." Daphne kissed her daughter. "Bye Tiggy-Tiger," she called as Tiger came back in the room, dragging a massive bag of candy with him.

After her mother had left, Bo sat with Tiger, trying to persuade him not to eat the whole bag of candy at once—she checked the sugar count and wondered why someone at school would think it was a good idea to give sugar as a gift. Maybe it was a rogue teacher hell-bent on revenge on the parents who sent the kids to school all hopped up on sugary cereal.

Later, when Tiger was asleep, she lay in her bed and allowed herself to think about Kit Mallory. Yeah, the guy was a dickhead but ... Jesus ... when he kissed her, she'd felt it right between her legs. Never shy, she'd decided on impulse to check out his goods ... and he wasn't lacking. At all. Good thing the director had come up to them—

if Mallory had fucked her right then, right there, she wouldn't have been complaining.

She flicked her phone round and round in her hand. She knew where he was staying in London ... she could call him ... no. Don't do it. You left him wanting more. Don't offer it on a plate.

"Just don't be too fucking long, Kit Mallory," she groaned into her pillow. Sighing, she sat up and flicked the TV on. Then on a whim, switched to Netflix ... search Kit Mallory films ...

There was one, about twenty years old, right at the start of his career. Bo put it on and settled back to watch it. After half an hour of watching his blond-haired perfection, she nodded to herself.

"Yeah, Kit Mallory ... don't you take too long ... '

IN SEATTLE, Randall was having dinner with his eldest and youngest sons. Jakob and Grady—Gray, to his family—had always gotten along best of all his sons and he delighted in their company.

"I haven't met Quilla yet," Grady said to Jakob. "I've heard she rivals Helen of Troy." Grady's amused grin made Jakob grin.

"You heard correct. She's with her friend Marley. Marley's been away on a research trip, so they want to catch up."

"She fully okay now? Quilla?"

Jakob nodded, but Ran exchanged a glance with Grady. "We still have nothing on Gregor Fisk. He keeps sending threats, vicious, evil things he says to both of them."

"I never knew," Jakob said, the desolation in his voice making it scratchy. "I never even imagined he would be this twisted, this full of hate."

Grady put a hand on his brother's shoulder. "Bro, we got this. If he thinks he can hide anywhere in the world, if he thinks he'll hurt any of us again ..."

Jakob winced, obviously recalling the terrible night his beautiful girl was stabbed by his ex-partner. Ran changed the subject. "So, Gray, where's the next adventure to?"

"Local ... well, somewhat. New Orleans. A huge estate sale is coming up with some pretty serious pieces. A couple of minor Rothkos, some Georgia O'Keefe sketches."

Ran's eyes lit up. Even now, art was his first love—the same as his youngest son. Grady had spent his life as a nomad, going to all corners of the globe to first learn his craft, then to help his father build up their portfolio. Rarely did they keep what he found—except for the Hoppers that hung both in Jakob's and Ran's home and some Kahlos in Grady's. Their business was to buy and sell, and they had both made billions doing it. "Rothko," Ran said now, "Always a favorite."

Grady grinned. His dad was like a kid in a candy shop when it came to art. "Say, Dad, have they lifted your restraining order?"

Ran looked confused. "Who?"

"Every major art gallery in the known universe," Grady intoned, and Jakob laughed loudly.

"'Excuse me, sir, but you seem to have picked something up by mistake.'"

"No, no, officer, my jacket has always been this boxy," Grady replied in an uncanny impression of his dad's voice.

"Sir, that's the Mona Lisa," replied Jakob, and they both howled with laughter as Ran chuckled.

"Remind me to write both of you out of my will," he mock-scowled. Then he smiled, sighing. "God, it's good to have you back, Gray. You'll stay for a while?"

"Couple of days, then I gotta get to NOLA," Grady said. "But I promise, afterward, I'll be back for a good long time."

QUILLA CHEN PUSHED the pizza box away. "No more, there's no space left in my belly." Marley Griffin, her oldest and best friend, grinned at her. They sat in Marley's apartment, the scene of many of their fun times together over the years. Now, though, it had been months since they'd gotten together. Marley had left town as soon as she knew Quilla was going to be okay, for a three-month long research trip to the

Brazilian jungle, and now she was regaling Quilla of tales of the Amazon jungle, her research fellows, and the many, many bugs she saw.

"Size of my fist," she told a cringing Quilla, "and its legs were another five or six inches as well."

"Gah, stop, I do not want to know about the tarantulas." Quilla clamped her hands over her ears. "I won't be able to sleep."

Marley grinned wickedly. "Don't forget the jumping spiders ..."

Quilla threw a pillow at her. "The words 'jumping' and 'spider' should never be in the same sentence, ever."

Marley sat back, satisfied she'd scared her friend enough. Apart from the face, she was pulling now, Quilla looked good, if a little tired. Marley fiddled with a slice of leftover pizza.

"How's the love life?"

Quilla beamed. "Truly, truly fantastic. Jakob is ... God, I wish I could tell you how he makes me feel."

"Stabbed?" Marley couldn't help the sarcastic comment that fell out of her mouth. Quilla blanched, and she immediately regretted her words.

"It wasn't Jakob's fault," Quilla murmured. "Please, Marls, don't hate him."

"I don't hate him; I just think he was careless, and you paid the price."

"How was he careless? Should he have not fired Gregor? Wouldn't you have done the same thing?"

Marley was annoyed now. "He knew that asshole for years, and he didn't see that side of him until that day?"

Quilla squirmed in her seat, not wanting to get caught between her best friend and her lover. "Marls ..."

"And he's still out there."

"The police, the Mallorys, they're throwing everything they can at the search."

Marley got up and went to her window. Outside, she could see the black sedan in which sat the two huge, silent bodyguards that had delivered Quilla to her door. Marley shook her head.

"How can you live like this? I know you; you hate being watched or supervised or ... '

Quilla sighed. "Make up your mind, Marls—do you want me protected or dead?"

It was Marley's turn to flinch. "God, Quilla ..."

"He calls me, Fisk; he calls me and says the most disgusting things, most vile, barbaric things. He describes exactly how he intends to kill me and I listen to it because I can't stop listening, because in between the threats he might give something away. And if he thinks I'm not the only one on the call, then he'll hang up and we'll lose the only chance to catch him. He's a psychopath, Marls. If someone else were Jakob's girlfriend, she'd be the one with the scars and the threats."

Marley went to her friend, seeing she was getting upset, and hugged her. "I just worry."

Quilla struggled not to cry for a moment. "Please, Marl, now that you're back, come meet the rest of the family; get to know them. I promise you'll change your mind."

Marley sighed but smiled at her friend. "For you, anything. For you, I'll make friends with the billionaires."

Quilla laughed. "Thank you. I promise, you'll love them as much as I do."

IT HAD BEEN TWO DAYS, and Bo Kennedy still hadn't called. Kit, stalking around his hotel room—he had found himself deliberately extending his stay—couldn't believe that he, Kit Mallory was waiting for a woman to call. Him!

Fuck it, he was sick of waiting around like a lovesick teenager. He grabbed his cellphone.

It rang eight times before she answered. 'Ello."

"Bo?"

Silence. "Christopher Mallory, I presume," she drawled and laughed. It was a thick, throaty, sensual sound. Kit closed his eyes and imagined how the vibration from that laugh would feel with his cock inside her. God, he had to fuck this woman and soon, or his balls would explode.

"That's me," he said lightly. "Listen … I figured I should maybe call, thank you for inviting to be in the video, maybe take you to lunch."

Lunch followed by an afternoon of fucking. That's what he was offering, and he was pretty sure she knew it, too. There was a silence on the other of the phone.

"What hotel are you in?" she said shortly, and he grinned and told her, knowing she already knew.

"Good. Order room service. I like steak. An hour." The line went dead.

Kit grinned. "Victory is mine; victory is mine." He did a little dance and then pulled himself up. Don't be an idiot—this, after all, is what you do best. The Art of Seduction.

It was his turn to win.

Bo Kennedy sat in the cab to the hotel, still not sure she was doing the right thing. Maybe just screw him and then leave; you both get what you want. Finito. Over. Itch scratched.

She hoped.

KIT OPENED the door to his suite and smiled. Not a smug smile. A friendly, conciliatory smile. Okay … Bo went in, confused, and saw he had indeed arranged room service. Two covered plates sat on a table in front of the massive wide screen TV.

Kit nodded towards it. "I thought we might eat in front of the TV, watch some trashy program."

What was this, a move? Bo narrowed her eyes at him, but his gaze was steady. "Hey, you wanted steak, we have steak and fr—I mean, chips."

She grinned at his attempt to Anglicize French fries. "You had me at steak."

Kit's mouth hitched up in a grin. "Promising."

.   .   .

THE MEAL WAS HEAVENLY, Bo had to admit a half hour later, and Kit was surprisingly easy to talk to. True to his word, they watched some trashy tv—some of which Bo had to translate for him, as the regional British accents stumped him.

'What is a 'gobshite'?"

Bo couldn't help but giggle. "It's English for a jerk."

"Got it."

Finally, he turned to her, leaning back on the couch, his arm along the back of it. His fingers were almost touching her hair.

"So, like I said on the phone ... thanks for inviting me to be part of your video. The song's great, by the way."

He was touching her hair now, twisting the ends in his fingers. Bo was slightly discombobulated; this was clearly a move, practiced, maybe, but give her a good meal and a handsome man ... that was her kryptonite. No. No way. She wasn't falling for this.

She gave him a half smile. "This has been fun, but I should go."

Kit just grinned. "Okay."

Okay? Okay? "Fine." She got up and in a flash, he had taken her in his arms.

"Bo, let's stop this game playing. We both know what we want."

Asshole. But he was right, she had to admit. "I don't do commitment," she said. "I don't do flowers and hearts and love. I don't need a white knight."

"I understand."

"Then what do you want, Kit Mallory?" As if she didn't know.

Kit bent his head to kiss her and it was so soft, so sweet, it sent her senses reeling. "You. Now."

His fingers were at the nape of her neck, on the fastening of her halter-neck dress, and when she didn't pull away, he released the tie. The dress slithered down her curves and fell to the floor.

"Wow, oh wow," he said and dropped to his knees, burying his face in her belly. Bo shivered as his lips trailed across her skin, his fingers kneading the soft flesh of her hips.

"You should be naked all of the time, Bo Kennedy, or on the bow of a ship." She giggled. He stood and kissed her mouth again.

Unfreezing, Bo started to unbutton his shirt, flattening her hand against his hard pecs, her fingertips seeking out the puckered nipples, tweaking them before she placed her mouth on them.

Her mind was a whirlwind ... she had expected a full-on fuck fest: hard, fast, dirty and done in twenty minutes. Not this slow seduction. She kept in the back of her mind that this was Kit Mallory, well-known swordsman and player, but ... this was unexpectedly tender. He released the clasp on her bra and let her full, heavy breasts fall into his hands, kissing them, plumping them, taking her nipples into his mouth in turn. She felt the heat between her legs, the rush of arousal, and by the time they reached the bedroom, she was so wet for him that when at last he drove his huge, diamond-hard cock into her, she was more than ready.

"God, you feel so good," he murmured, kissing her eyelids, her cheeks, her mouth. "Not just your delicious cunt but your skin, your breasts, your soft belly. God, Bo Kennedy ..."

His words were turning her on as much as the strong rhythm of his thrusts, and she tilted her hips to take him in deeper. Their bodies fit together so well, she forgot any reservations and just went with it, enjoying every sensation and electric pulse of pleasure, her body was experiencing.

"Not so bad, yourself, Kit Mallory ..." She grinned and he chuckled and then she saw who he was truly, a good man under all that bluster and arrogance. A kind, loving man.

God, she hoped she was right as he drove her inexorably to a shattering orgasm, his own following quickly, crying her name out over and over again.

She was prepared for the quick kiss-off, the 'I'll call you sometime', the 'I'm going to the bathroom and when I get back you won't be here' thing. Instead, with his cock still semi-hard, still inside her, he stroked her face, his eyes soft, holding none of the arrogance she had come to expected, and said one simple word.

"Stay."

. . .

SKANDAR, Hayley, Ran, Grady, and Jakob listened to the recording of Gregor Fisk's latest threatening phone call to Quilla. Quilla wasn't present—she didn't need to go through this twice, but Jakob had told them he needed them to listen, to see if they could glean anything, anything, from it.

"No theory is too small or too big," he said, wearily, "we just need a lead."

The threats were sickening in their violence and now Gregor had added a sexual element that made Hayley clamp her hand over her mouth and rush out to throw up. Skandar went to find her. He found her sobbing in one of the guest bathrooms. She fell into his arms.

"I'm sorry. It's just, until that recording, I never knew for real what this guy's deal was. He's obsessed."

Skandar grimaced "I know. We got off easy, but I'm still not taking any chances. When does your semester close out?"

She told him and he nodded. "At the risk of sounding like I'm controlling you, I think we should go away, far away, for a couple of weeks. We have a private island we can use. What do you say?"

She smiled through her tears. "It sounds perfect, but I still feel for Quilla and Jakob. They can't escape this, wherever they go."

Skandar sighed. "No. Look, come back down. Maybe we can come up with some ideas for Jakob."

BO OPENED HER EYES. Light seeped through under the curtains in Kit Mallory's hotel bedroom, so she could tell it was morning. Kit was still asleep, the sheet pushed down to hips, his broad chest turned towards her, his hand resting on her waist. God, he was beautiful. She stroked a finger under his eyes, along the path of the dark shadow there, and he opened his eyes, the blue eyes twinkling at her.

"Good morning, beautiful."

She smiled. "Mr. Mallory, I presume." He chuckled and kissed her.

"Forgive my morning breath."

"Right back at ya. Good thing about hotel rooms; they always have spare toothbrushes."

"That's right," he said, sitting up and pulling her up, "and it just so happens this one has an enormous shower, too, so I can get you all soaped up and have my wicked way with you."

She giggled. "That sounds just about perfect."

"Get in that bathroom, woman."

HE'D ORDERED breakfast by the time she was finished dressing, and she swooned over the fresh fruit compote and Greek yogurt. She saw him grinning at her obvious enjoyment.

"I love my food," she said unapologetically. "When I was first signed to the label, they did everything to try and get me to lose weight. Real passive aggressive stuff—and when I told them to do one —sorry, that means to fuck off, in English," she grinned at him, "they just got aggressive. And then my debut album sold twenty-seven million copies. Haven't mentioned my weight since."

"Nor should they," he said, shaking his head. "The number of eating disorders in the showbiz industry is horrendous. As long as you're healthy, who cares? Don't change a thing; you're a goddess." He meant it as a throwaway comment, but she suddenly beamed at him through tear-filled eyes.

"That might be the nicest thing anyone's ever said to me, thank you."

He took her hand and kissed it. "Are you free today?"

She shook her head. "I wish, but I have a kid at home who wants to see his mummy."

"You have a kid?" To her surprise, he didn't look wary but excited, interested. Had she misjudged this man that much? Yes.

"I do. Tiger, he's four. Me and his dad, well, it was more of a one-off, but we get on really well, and he loves Tiger."

"That's cool ... my twin brother had Skandar when he was really young, but the mother didn't stick around."

"Usually the other way around. So, yeah, I'd love to spend the day with you but ... unless you want to come along? We're going to the Natural History Museum."

Kit looked surprised. "Really? I'd love to ... are you sure it isn't too soon for him to be exposed to me?"

Bo couldn't help smiling. 'Too soon' implied he wanted to see her again, and the idea thrilled her more than she liked to admit. "Nah, mate, he's cool."

KIT WAS SURPRISED WITH HIMSELF. Normally, spending an afternoon with a brat wasn't on his wish list at all, but he was curious about this woman. This woman who could command audience numbers in the tens of thousands for her live shows; could sell millions of copies of records; and yet still found time to manage herself and look after a kid.

She made him laugh, too, and later, when he was with Bo and her entirely adorable nerd of a son, he found himself both relaxed and happy; yet suddenly depressed. Was this what he had been missing? He had everything—everything—and yet he was having more fun listening to a four-year-old kid tell him about each different dinosaur he'd had than at a million Hollywood events. Tiger had taken to him straightaway—like his mother, he wasn't shy, and when Bo introduced them, he'd looked Kit up and down with clear green eyes and shrugged. "Okay, cool."

Now Tiger was listening, enraptured, to the tour guide. Kit grinned down at Bo. "Such a great kid."

She beamed. She wore a simple navy wrap dress cinched in at the waist to emphasize her curvy hips and bust; her hair tucked up into a loose chignon, her lovely, radiant face bare of makeup.

You are everything the world says I shouldn't go for, he thought, looking down at her, and everything I want.

They were recognized, of course, and frequently stopped for photos and autographs. Kit admired the easy way Bo interacted with her fans, hugging them and posing for selfies with a mad grin on her face. He abandoned his usual ploy of posing like a movie star and followed her lead.

"You're so sweet," he was told, their voices amazed and again, and he felt both happy and sad at their surprise. Was his reputation as a douchebag set for life? Damn. No wonder his family was so distant. He'd been a pig to Skandar, the poor kid—he vowed now to make it up to him, to all of them, when he got back.

"You look deep in thought." Bo, finally free of fans, tucked her hand under his arm. He kissed her temple.

"Bo … do you think it's possible for someone's life to change completely in the space of a few days."

Bo grinned. "Mate, my life changed in a millisecond," she nodded at Tiger, "but yeah, of course. Why?" She studied him. "You're not going to tell me you're in love with me yet, are you?" She was joking, but then she saw his face and her smile faded. "Kit, don't. Please don't. If you say it now, so soon, I won't believe you."

Kit was stung. "I can't help how I feel."

She took his face in her hands. "Look, whatever you're feeling, happiness, desire, lust, heck, even the beginnings of love … that's what I'm feeling, I promise you that. So don't look so down … this is the exciting part. We're getting to know each other."

He stroked the back of his hand down her cheek. "You've changed me already."

She smiled. "Bloody good job, too." Her eyes softened. "Look, I'm not saying don't say it, just make sure you're sure before you do, and I'll do the same. We're not teenagers."

Kit smiled. "Then how come I feel like I am?"

She laughed. "Kit Mallory … are you telling me you're finally tamed by this London girl?"

"I don't know," he said, and kissed her, "but I'm getting there."

SKANDAR GRINNED at Hayley as he drew up to her house in his convertible. "Hayley Applebee, one day soon I hope I have to say 'I'm taking you home' and mean our house instead of this house."

Her eyebrows shot up and she laughed. "Baby, people will talk if I move in with you so soon."

"Bah, humbug."

She kissed him, savoring the taste of his lips. "I'd invite you in, but I think your dad's in there with my sister and you know what happened last time I burst in on them."

He groaned. 'The image is seared into my brain."

She laughed and started to get out of his car but he stopped her. She frowned at the expression in his eyes.

"Seriously, Hays. I hate leaving you here. Please ... go grab some stuff and move in with me. Now. Tonight. Let's just jump in and figure it out on the way."

Hayley stared at the man she loved beyond reason and knew what she was going to say.

"Skandar ..."

Her face was blank, and she could see the sadness in his eyes ... so she grinned widely. "Come help me pack, then."

Skandar blinked, then beamed. "Really?"

She laughed. "Really, truly, yes, yes, yes ..."

INSIDE, Joel and Nan, who were watching them from the window, laughed as Skandar picked his girlfriend up and carried her, shrieking with laughter, into the house.

Quilla Chen bent double over the toilet and threw up again. Ng ... she hadn't felt this bad since she was stabbed—the searing pain in her stomach made her want to scream. Outside the bathroom, Jed, one of her ever-present bodyguards, knocked cautiously. "Miss Chen, do you want me to call a doctor?"

She didn't answer for a second, rinsing her mouth with water. She wiped her mouth, then went to the door. "Not just yet." She smiled at Jed weakly. "It's probably just the stomach flu. I'll call if I change my mind. Thanks, Jed; you're sweet to worry."

Jed nodded. "If you're sure, I'll be in my room." Their guest room was now the bodyguard's room, six of them on a rotating schedule of eight hours a day, three days on, three days off. She was never alone —but she was certainly safe.

Jakob was at work late again, so she got into bed and switched on the TV. She was just falling asleep when she heard her name.

"Chen, a twenty-four-year-old art graduate, is best known for dating billionaire Jakob Mallory. Now that her past is better known, it remains to be seen if that relationship can overcome the revelation that Chen comes from a family of high-end prostitutes and drug addicts ... '

She couldn't breathe, the shock slamming into her; she was reeling, reeling ...

Not knowing where she was going, she stumbled out of the bedroom, trying to get help and reaching for the phone. An all-consuming agonizing pain in her stomach ripped through her, and as she passed out, she heard Jakob's voice calling for her, far away, so far away ...

5

PART FIVE: TROUBLE ME

G rady Mallory stepped off the plane into one-hundred-degree heat and grinned. New Orleans was experiencing a late summer heat wave, and it was just as Grady loved it—hot, sweaty, and sexy.

He caught a cab to his hotel in the French Quarter, showered, and stepped back out onto the street. Whenever he came here, he had a tradition of walking around the Quarter for an hour or two, getting his bearings, soaking in the atmosphere.

He was glad to be away from Seattle—so much drama and upset. After the revelations about Quilla's family had hit the headlines, and her subsequent illness—thankfully just stomach flu and nothing worse—Jakob had been snappy and irritable—back to the wreck he had been before he met her. Grady hoped against hope that his beloved older brother wasn't using again. His father, Ran, was worrying himself into an early grave, because of this thing with Gregor Fisk. That asshole, Grady thought now, if I got my hands on him ...

The streets were crowded with tourists and entertainers. He found a restaurant off the main thoroughfare and went in to grab some food. The diner was filled with, by the looks of it, mostly local people, so he regarded this as a good sign.

He loved this city, so when he heard about the artwork being auctioned here—a very exclusive invite-only auction, at that—he had jumped at the chance. He'd tried to persuade his dad to come, but Ran was too locked into the Fisk situation and taking care of the family. Grady understood. But now, sitting, here he would have loved his dad to be sitting opposite, excited about the new pieces. Grady had no doubt he would get them for the Mallory collection—he was that good at this now. That wasn't conceit, just the confidence of a man who had spent the last twenty years honing his craft.

He was so lost in his thoughts, he didn't see her at first—although to be fair, it looked like she didn't want to draw any attention to herself. She was sitting two tables away, at a tiny table stuffed into an alcove, her laptop out and on, her eyes intent on the screen. Something blue must have flashed on the screen because that's what drew his attention. The girl looked exasperated, and knocked the computer as if annoyed with it.

Grady studied her with interest. Dark brown hair, pulled back into a ponytail, massive black-rimmed spectacles on a small, delicate face, huge blue eyes rimmed with kohl. Geek, Grady thought with a smile, and a very attractive one. He heard her curse—Italian then English—then sigh, shutting the laptop and shoving it into her bag. She got up, throwing some money onto the table, and he watched her slim, athletic frame stumble through the nest of tables, apologizing to the diners who got hit on the head with her overstuffed messenger bag. Cute, Grady decided. Seriously cute. Time was he would have followed her out, got her number. A long time ago. Before Molly, before the cancer that took her less than a year after their wedding. Before Asia. Before Asia and Kit.

Stop it. If Grady was going to break one damn habit this year, it was wondering "what if?". It had been holding him back from living, from loving again.

No more, he said to himself, it's time to start over.

He hoped he could stick to his new plan.

Asia rolled her eyes after Quilla had apologized for the hundredth time. "Sorry you got landed with babysitting duties again," Quilla said ruefully.

"Girl, stop. It's a pleasure spending time with you; we don't do it enough." They were driving along the highway, out towards the Olympic Mountains. Asia had suggested the trip after Jakob had insisted that Quilla not be alone. At all. She was starting to feel trapped both by Jakob's fear and Gregor's malevolence, she told Asia now.

Asia, driving, turned to glance at her. "How are you feeling about the ... you know?"

"A lot better after Ran told me it made no difference to him what my family was alleged to have been, or what they did."

Asia frowned. "Did Jakob not say that to you first?"

Quilla hesitated. "He did. Over and over. But I always felt like he was saying it because he had to. God, what a mess, and what a fucking bastard Gregor Fisk it—what did I do to him? Wasn't stabbing me and threatening me enough for him?"

"Ran seems to think that his obsession with you has become his ... how can I put this, his main focus. Yes, he wants revenge on Jakob and Ran, but it's almost as if he just can't get you out of his head. It's like he stabbed you—then realized ..."

"... He enjoyed it. God." Quilla looked like she was going to throw up. "Can we change the subject? I hate feeling like a damn target."

Asia squeezed her hand. "Sure, honey."

Quilla shot her a look. "How's Sebastian?"

Sebastian Winter was one of the world's most eligible bachelors, from old New Hampshire money. In essence, he was a money man in the city, but really, he was a party boy and a socialite.

Asia sighed. "Sebastian is very, very pretty. Also, very, very gay, but don't tell anyone that. He asked me to accompany him to a couple of things to help throw his father off his scent—he thinks his dad knows about Sebastian's boyfriend and doesn't know how he will react. His father is, well, old school."

"Bigoted, you mean?"

"Pretty much."

"Asshole. So what's Sebastian like?"

"Like a little boy lost. Underneath all the glamor, he's a sweet kid who reacts to his lack of paternal love by acting the big man."

"Gosh," said Quilla hiding a grin, "never let it be said you have a type, Asia Flynn."

Asia conceded with a grin. "Kit can't claim lack of paternal love, just a rampant immaturity. I think Joel stole it from him in the womb, because he never has trouble stepping up to the plate."

"I know. How sweet are he and Nan? I swear to God, one moves and the other moves with them." Quilla sounded almost jealous, but Asia decided not to push it.

"Yeah, so, romance wise ... I'm just doing a favor for a friend. Nothing else happening."

"Shame." Quilla shot her a sideways look. "You know, Ran and I were having a chat, and he tells me Grady is in New Orleans for a week or so."

Asia chuckled. "You are two are like scheming old matchmakers, sitting around hatching your plans."

Quilla laughed. "Can you blame us? We love both of you and now that Kit's, er, 'moved on' ..."

Asia snorted. "Don't remind me of that damn interview. You know, people were coming up to me, this look on their faces like ... oh poor, poor thing, you must be devastated. Ugh."

"If you want, I can bust some moves on him, kick his ass?" Quilla looked like she was serious but Asia smiled, shaking her head.

"Nah, leave it alone. I suspect Kit's being handled properly now."

Quilla giggled. "I love Bo Kennedy. You're right; she won't take any crap from him, will she? Did you see that video of her taking down that pap who tried to take photos of her kid?"

Asia nodded. "Warrior Woman."

"Kit's going to have his ass handed to him if he tries to do what ..." Quilla broke off, looked over at Asia apologetically. "Sorry. I'm about as sensitive as ..."

"Don't worry about it."

They drove in silence for a couple of minutes. "You know," Asia said thoughtfully, "maybe it isn't the worst idea to reconnect with Grady. As friends, I mean, before you get excited. I miss our talks; we were always such good friends."

Quilla tried not to grin. "Just so happens I know where he's staying."

OKAY, this is not happening. No way, nuh-uh. Grady Mallory did not lose out when he went to auction. Ever. Something about having a vast pot of money to dip into, but ... it was happening. He'd had to stop when the two pieces already auctioned went way past their reserve ... way, way past even what they were worth for two rare O'Keefe sketches, and that was saying something.

And what was bugging him, even more, was that he didn't know who was bidding. He'd scoured the room every single time, but no one apart from him was even signaling. Every time Grady nodded at the auctioneer, the man would check the ledger in front of him and hike the price another twenty thousand. In the end, Grady had to forfeit.

Not this time, though. The Rothko was being brought out. Jesus, it was magnificent, a monument to color, depth, abstraction. Grady got that feeling he always did when he saw a piece that spoke directly to his soul. His heartbeat would quicken, his breath would catch in his throat. Only two human beings in the world had ever had that effect on him: Molly and Asia. He struggled to think of one piece of the artist's which didn't incite that reaction in him.

The auctioneer introduced the piece, then looked around the gathering. "So I'll start us off at thirty-two million dollars."

Even though the starting price had been expected, there was still a hum of awe around the room. Grady nodded, and the auctioneer signaled to him. "Thirty-two, I'm bid, thank you, sir, thirty-three." He glanced down at his book.

Not this time, buddy. Grady gritted his teeth. "Thirty-four."

"Thirty-five ..."

The bidding went on, Grady refusing to back down even when the price went past one hundred million. Finally, just as Grady thought he had it at one-hundred-and-seven, the auctioneer was tapped on the shoulder by a clerk who handed him a piece of paper. The auctioneer's eyebrows shot up.

"We have a bid ... goodness gracious ... a bid of five hundred million."

Afterward, Grady would swear you could hear the collective jaws dropping. He felt sick. There was no way he could justify spending that much on a painting, no matter what it was. His dad would kill him. Shit, shit, shit. Grady shook his head as the auctioneer looked questioningly at him. It slightly cheered him that the auctioneer knew he could afford it if he wanted, but Grady hadn't made his fortune by being reckless.

He sat through the rest of the bidding, occasionally making a half-hearted attempt to bid, but whenever he did, he was quickly outbid. It was hard not to think someone was messing with him.

At the end, he got up, and as he stopped to let people pass, he saw her. The girl from the café. Grady blinked. This auction was an invite only, an incredibly exclusive gathering for which you had to have a clear few billion in the bank to be allowed entry. What the hell? The way the girl had been bashing her ancient computer the other night, he was certain she didn't fit the brief. She moved toward him, her gaze flicking left and right, but never at him.

"Hey," he said as she passed. She nodded briefly, and then disappeared. Grady shook his head. This was so damn weird. The secret buyer with the seemingly bottomless pockets and this girl, who looked like she had fallen asleep in her clothes.

He was still shaking his head as he walked back to his hotel. The sun was hidden behind some pretty black clouds, and a few fat raindrops hit him as he entered the hotel. Still preoccupied, he was about to press the elevator call button when he heard his voice being called.

A familiar voice. One that made his heartbeat quicken. He turned.

Asia Flynn was standing at the reception desk, smiling her beautiful smile at him, and to him, the sun came out again.

Skandar Mallory was watching his girlfriend Hayley trying to figure out how to work his very expensive, very complicated espresso machine. And failing miserably. She stuck her tongue out at him.

"You could help."

Skandar grinned his crooked smile. "I could, but then I'd miss your perfect little tush jiggling when you move."

Hayley tried to look mad. "Sexist pig."

"That's me." He grabbed her and swung her up into his arms. They had been living together for a month, and though neither would admit it, both were waiting for the day when they'd regret moving so fast. So far, neither of them had, even the slightest bit.

He hustled her over to the couch and lay down on top of her. She giggled as he rained kisses down on her. "Dude ... I have a lecture at nine, and if you keep doing that, I'm going to be late."

"Ssh, I'm using my best moves."

"Shouldn't you be at practice? Carlos will never take you back if you don't keep up ... what are you doing?"

Skandar was pushing up her skirt and tugging her panties down. Grinning widely, he kissed her. "Just sending you off to class with something to think about ..."

She gave up and wrapped her legs around his waist. "Hard and fast, then, soldier."

"Damn, you sure got a dirty mouth, Hayley Applebee."

"Get busy, Mallory."

Later, as she walked into her lecture hall, she was still smiling, her body buzzing from the high; she didn't notice the stares of her fellow students. Or rather, she ignored them. They'd been staring at her since the 'sex tape' had hit the headlines. Fuck 'em, Skandar had told her, and she had laughed. Still, you'd think, the novelty would have worn off by now, she thought. She sat in the middle of the class defiantly, staring down each student as they glanced at her. So what if she had no special friend here, she thought; jealousy was an ugly thing. That's what she told herself. She had Skandar. Who cared if these idiots judged her?

The professor—a guest speaker today—was running late. Hayley pulled her iPad out of her bag and flicked to her email. Like a lovesick teen, she had set up email alerts anytime there was a news story about Skandar. She didn't particularly relish the myriad of real and fake exes who daily slammed him. She could tell which was which by what they were complaining about. The real exes were complaining about him being the champion of the one-nighter. (Not with me, she thought smugly); the fake ones were complaining about his ... performance. Those stories just made her snort in derision.

She flicked down the list, then her heart seemed to tremble and freeze. Tennis Ace Corrupted My Daughter. Fuck, no, no, no ... her damn mother was selling her own kids out—again. Hayley shoved the iPad back in her bag and got up, and as she stomped down the stairs, she caught the eye of a particularly creepy jock, who smirked at her.

"Go fuck yourself," she hissed and ran out to her car. Locking herself in, she yanked out her phone and called Nan.

"Our goddamned mother is at it again. I'm coming over."

GRADY LOOKED over the breakfast table at Asia and grinned. "I still can't believe you're here. Did you sleep okay?" The hotel had been very accommodating and found Asia a room at the last minute.

Asia smiled. "I'll say. I've got to give it to you, Gray; you always know the best hotels to pick."

She dug into her fruit salad, and as she ate, she studied him. "I had some vacation time owed and nothing better to do so I thought, why don't I go see my old pal, Grady?"

He tapped her juice glass with his. "Good decision. Hey, this is exciting, I can take you around Orleans, do the tourist thing. I do have some more auctions coming up ... God, I hope they're not like yesterday's." He told her what happened, and Asia frowned.

"That is unusual ... but then again, there might just be a new player on the scene, someone who's just made their fortune, wants to get in on the game."

Grady shook his head in disbelief. "Half a billion, though? For a painting, even if—and this pains me to say—it's a Rothko? Damn, I keep thinking about it, Asia; it was glorious. Whoever, he or she is, they're no fan of etiquette. Went straight in, bang, knocked everyone else out of the running." He sighed, and Asia reached out and touched his cheek.

"It is just a painting, Gray, don't get down. You're so like Ran, sometimes."

He caught her hand and held it against his face, closing his eyes. "It really has been too long, Asia." He was gratified when she didn't move her hand away. He opened her eyes and saw her expression; soft, loving, wondering. He lifted her hand to his lips.

"Asia ..."

She shook her head. "Don't say anything. Let's just see what happens."

A thrill flooded down his body. She wants me, too. God, he had been waiting for this day for years. He laced his fingers between hers, his heart thumping against his chest. Asia's lovely face was flushed, her dark eyes, soft, full of desire.

"Do you want to go for a walk?"

Slowly, she met his gaze and shook her head, the flush on her cheeks deepening. He said nothing more but stood and led her back to the elevator. Inside, he pressed the button to his floor and then took her in his arms. He wanted to ask if she was sure, but instead kissed her, tasting the lips he had dreamed about for years, his fingers sliding into the soft, dark hair that clouded around her. Asia returned his embrace, her gentle tongue caressing his, her hands on his chest, her thumbs brushing over his tightening nipples.

His cock was ramrod hard, and as he pressed her against the wall, his body curved into hers, the feel of it pressing against her soft belly made him moan with desire.

"God, Asia..."

In his room, they undressed each other slowly, taking their time, Grady kissing her shoulders as he removed her bra and let her full breasts fall into his waiting and eager hands.

"You don't know how long I've waited for this," his voice broke as his emotion overcame him.

"Ssh," Asia stroked his face, "It's okay..."

He swept her into his arms and laid her back on the bed, not able to tear his eyes away from her incredible body. Athletic but with gentle curves, she was slim, slight, her skin a lovely olive color. He covered her with his body, his cock erect against his belly and as she stroked it with her hands, his own hands slipped between her legs to find her already wet for him, her sex swelling and pulsing with her desire.

The moment his cock pushed into her, Grady knew he'd found what he had been looking for all these years. As her legs curled around him and they kissed and fucked and sweated and cried out the other's name, he could hardly believe it was happening at last.

Asia, Asia ...

HALF A WORLD AWAY, Asia's ex-husband was sitting backstage at a concert venue in Paris, watching his girlfriend get ready to go out and sing for some of the most important VIPs in France. On Kit's knee, Bo Kennedy's son, Tiger, slept, Kit's arms tight around the sleeping child.

Bo grinned back at Kit in the mirror, and then turned. "You're a natural at that."

Kit smiled. "Who knew? But it helps that your kid is awesome." Bo flushed with pleasure and went to kiss him.

"You surprise me every day, Kit Mallory, and I adore that."

"I adore you, Miss Kennedy. How're you feeling?"

"Shit scared," she said bluntly in her London accent, and he chuckled. "I'm serious; I feel like I could chuck up me lunch. It's bollocks that you can't smoke inside anymore. I could do with a Gauloises right now."

Kit shook his head, grinning. "You don't even smoke. And think of your voice."

To be fair, she did look a bit green. "How do you do it, then?" he asked, curious. "How do you stand up in front of all those people every night and not throw up?"

"Not helping," but she grinned and turned back to the mirror to put on her mascara. "Well, it's like ... you know what it's like when you go out on stage? You must have done theater?"

He shook his head. "Not once."

She turned, obviously shocked. "Never?"

"Not even at school."

She blinked. "How'd you get into acting then?"

Kit looked uncomfortable. "At the risk of sounding like a complete asshole ... this." He pointed at his face. "I got 'spotted' at a charity benefit by my agent, Naomi. She put me up for a part, and that's that. It turns out I'm okay at it. Please don't hate me."

Bo laughed. "I ain't gonna hate you for getting a lucky break. Pretty boy."

Kit grinned. "It's painful being this beautiful." He flicked his long hair back, and she threw her makeup brush at him, giggling.

"But you've never fancied doing a stage play?"

Kit shook his head. "Stage fright. So come on, tell me the secret."

Bo still looked surprised. "Well, it's different than acting because with a music set you can really build up the anticipation of the audience. That's why it takes so long for the singer to come on, building that atmosphere. It's great for the audience, but not only that, it gets my adrenaline going and that is crucial to overcoming stage fright."

Kit was fascinated. "Huh. Always thought it was an ego thing, that 'I'm going to keep you waiting so you can beg for me to come out and stroke my huge ego.'"

Bo nodded. "Oh, there's definitely some of that going on, too; we're artists, after all, as insecure and as monomaniacal as the next."

She got up and grabbed her stage outfit, a long, midnight blue sheath that slithered over her body. Kit watched her dress, admiration all over his face. Man, he'd known her only a few weeks, but he'd changed his plans and cleared his schedule—much to the disgust of his agent—so that he could accompany her on the short sold-out world tour. When she wasn't performing, they'd take Tiger to all of the tourist spots in whatever city they were in. Tomorrow, it was Disneyland, Paris, and Tiger, who had been hyper all day, was finally exhausted from excitement.

There was a gentle knock on the door and Tiger's nanny, Felicity, poked her head around the door, saw Tiger asleep and grinned. "I'll take him back to the hotel," she whispered, "give you two some privacy."

"Cheers, pickle, you're a peach." Bo kissed Tiger's forehead. "Night, sweetie. See you in the morning."

When they were alone, Bo checked her watch. "Half an hour till kick off."

Kit took her in his arms. "You'll knock 'em dead, gorgeous."

She tilted her head up for a kiss. "Christopher Mallory, you know what? I bloody love you."

"Beatrice Fenella Kennedy," he made up her middle name and she giggled, "I am so in love with you, it's pretty gross just how much, actually."

"Who'd have thunk?" She grinned. "I'm still not convinced the real Kit Mallory wasn't kidnapped by aliens and you got sent in his place."

"Was I really that much of an ass?" Kit was slightly stung, and then conceded. "Yeah, I know."

Bo kissed him. "Don't be sad; you were never really like that, you just built up a mask."

Kit shrugged. "Tell Asia that. I did not treat her the way she deserved."

"No, you didn't, but that's in the past." Bo's voice had a little edge, and Kit looked at her curiously.

"You're not jealous of Asia, are you?"

"Not jealous … curious. I mean," Bo sat down next to him, "and this is not a criticism, but I've seen her picture, heard you talk about her ... why on earth would you cheat on her?"

Kit sighed. "The simple, awful answer is because the opportunity presented itself. Because I told myself it didn't count as infidelity. I was an insensitive idiot."

Bo nodded slowly. "And now? If the opportunity presented itself again?"

Suddenly he got why she was asking. He shook his head. "Bo ... you are everything to me. Everything. I'm older; I'm wiser; and I'm committed to making us work, to us being a family; you, me, and Tiger."

He could see she wasn't convinced, and his chest hurt with the pain of it. "Guess I'll have to prove it to you," he said gruffly. Bo leaned her head on his shoulder.

"I want to trust you, Kit, I do. It might take some time, but I'll be right there with you, trying to put other relationships, other hurts, other mistakes behind me, too. But I think, it'll be worth it ... don't you?"

"You bet that sweet ass of yours, it will be," he said fiercely, and took her face between his hands to kiss her, but she pulled away, grinning to soften the slight.

"One last question."

"Go for it."

She searched his eyes. "I have no doubt that you love me, Kit, but ... are you still in love with Asia as well? It's okay if you are."

Kit sighed. "I don't want to be. I don't. But yeah, there's a little part of me which still loves her in that way. I'll get over it. You are the only one I want to be with, Bo; I swear to God."

She nodded. "I believe you."

Kit glanced at the clock. "Almost time. You knock 'em dead, beautiful."

She kissed him, and then moaned. "My bloody lipstick!"

They both laughed and quickly, she re-applied her gloss and was out of the door.

A quarter hour later, Kit listened to the roar of the crowd as she went on stage and felt such rush of pride and love that it over-whelmed him.

She was his queen, and he was a slave to whatever she wanted or needed. He would do anything not to mess this up.

GRADY WASN'T CONCENTRATING on this sale—not one bit. All he could think of were the last four days, the days filled with Asia, laughter, love, sex—a wonderful reconnection. It had been everything he'd hoped for, everything he'd dreamed about. Her soft skin against him, the bliss on her face as she reached orgasm, the way her lips moved against his. Afterward, they had talked like old friends, and it was if both of them felt as if an age-old torment had been extinguished.

Now she was flying back to Seattle for work, and he felt empty. He had thought the auction might distract him, but all he wanted to do was to get on a plane and go to her.

Way to act cool, he grinned to himself. He must have laughed out loud, as the elderly women next to him started and glared at him.

"Sorry," he smiled broadly and winked at her, giving her the full-on Mallory charm. She simpered and waved his smile away. Back in the room, Mallory.

The next artwork was a beauty—a little known Italian painter, for sure, but one whose star was rising. Grady was confident he'd get it for a steal and started the bidding off. Two hundred thousand. He didn't expect anyone to follow that, but once again, the price took off until Grady, exasperated, held his hands up in defeat. This went on all throughout the whole sale. Grady had had enough. Walking slowly around the auction room, he tried to see who was taking his legs out from under him.

He stopped when he saw her. Café Girl. Mysterious Broken Laptop Girl. She was facing away from him, her phone in her hand. As he watched, she tapped out a text every time a price was called. She was texting someone. Grady didn't take his eyes off her, and as the gavel came down on another outrageous price, she gave a little smile and put the phone to her ear, talking so low into it, he had no hope of hearing what she had said.

At least he had a lead now, though, and when the auction was over (and he'd once again failed to secure a single painting), he followed her out into the street. She moved so quickly he didn't have the time to call out, and after he'd scrambled after her for a few blocks, he lost her.

"Fuck it," he breathed and turned down the nearest alleyway. The Café Girl hit him from behind like a wrecking ball, shoving him, face first, into a wall.

"What the hell?" he managed to shout, before she waved a blade in his face.

"Why are you following me, asshole?" For a small woman, she certainly had some strength about her. Grady, despite the threat to his person, had to grin and, clearly annoyed, she shoved his face hard against the brick of the building. He held up his hands.

"I'm not following you, you idiot, I was trying to catch up to you to ask you something. I was at the auction. I'm Grady Mallory."

The knife disappeared, and she let him go. He turned—wait, he was wrong—the knife was still there, just not pointed at him. Well, that was progress. He smiled at her.

"Hi."

She was as cute as he remembered, and clearly could take care of herself. She looked at him with suspicious eyes. "I know your name. What do you want?"

"To talk, that's all."

"About what?"

"About how you or someone you work with or for keeps outbidding me."

She shrugged. "What of it?"

"I'd like to talk, is all. Can I buy you a coffee?"

He'd expected an outright 'no', so when she nodded, it took him aback. "Fine. I know a place."

She led him through the back streets of Orleans, places even he didn't know existed, until they reached a small, out-of-the-way bar. It was dark and atmospheric inside, low jazz playing on the sound system. She sat down in one of the booths and signaled to a waitress.

"Dewar's, rocks," she said, and Grady nodded.

"Make that two, thanks." He looked back at her. She was making the most of the free nuts in baskets on the table. He guessed she must be mid-twenties, her clothes cheap but functional. Dark hair tied back in a ponytail. Army surplus, by the looks of it. She carried a messenger bag; he supposed it was convenient for her piece of crap laptop and assorted deadly weapons.

"Who are you?"

She shrugged. "No one. An art student. I like to see the pieces when they're going up for sale."

The drinks arrived, and he took a sip. "But there's more to it, isn't there? You're bidding for someone—or feeding them information as the auction goes on."

Her chin lifted. "How do you know I'm not buying them?"

He didn't even bother to reply to that, and she sighed. "Look, Mr. Mallory ..."

"Grady."

"Mister Mallory," she said firmly, "I don't mean any offense, but how is what I do any business of yours?"

"It isn't," he shot back honestly, and she looked taken back. "I'm just curious—or nosy, whichever suits you. I gotta say, I'm not used to being outbid."

For the first time, she smiled, and Grady was struck by how lovely her face was when she grinned. "I guess that's just tough luck, Mr. Mallory. A bit of competition never hurt."

"Agreed," he nodded. "So, who is it?"

She shook her head, still smiling. "I am not at liberty to disclose my associate."

Grady gave up. "At least tell me about you. What's your name?"

She hesitated for a second, and then relented. "Floriana Morgan."

"American?"

She nodded. "Half. Half Italian, hence the Floriana. If it helps, just called me Flori."

Grady stuck out his hand. "Well, then, hi, Flori. I'm Grady."

She gave a sheepish grin as she shook his outstretched one. "Hi ... sorry about the ..." she mimicked a stabbing motion and mimicked the Psycho music. "Can't be too careful."

"That's perfectly okay. You're like an artist/ninja, then?"

She laughed. "Just an art student, I'm afraid. My attempts at art itself are somewhat amateur. My focus is on the history of art."

"Grad student?"

She shook her head. "No, still an undergrad, sophomore. Had to defer my college place for a couple of years."

"Are you based here?"

"Portland."

"Maine or ..."

"Oregon."

"Then we're neighbors; my family is in Seattle," Grady signaled for some refills, "Only seems right we should be friends. I don't know if you know anything about what my family does, but—"

"Of course, I know," she said gently. "You and your father have done so much for the art world."

Grady's mouth hitched up on one side. "So why are you helping the opposition, whoever they are?"

He softened the question with a smile, but Flori looked uncomfortable. "Mr. ... Grady, I don't want to ... it was never my intention ..."

He put his hand over hers for a brief second. "Flori, don't worry. You're right, a little competition never hurt. Besides," and he leaned back and sighed dramatically, "it was getting a little too easy, anyhoo."

He laughed as she lobbed a peanut at him. "But seriously, Flori, if you need any help with anything ... like that crappy laptop of yours?" He grinned when she looked askance at him, and a little scared.

"I'm not stalking you, I promise. I was just at the same restaurant as you the other night, when you were beating the crap out of it."

"Ah," she said. "Is that why you said hello to me that time?"

"It is."

"Sorry I ignored you; I was freaked out by the bid on that Rothko."

"Join the club. Half a billion." He shook his head, his mind still blown.

"Is it worth that?" She looked genuinely interested.

"Rothko's work has gone for big sums before, the most for about seventy-five million for Royal Red and Blue in 2012, but no painting by any artist has yet to reach that half billion. Some have come close —if you can call a difference of two hundred million close." He smiled. "I was tempted, very tempted, I tell you. Rothko is my hero."

She was looking at him with curiosity. "You're not what I expected, Grady Mallory. Of course, I realize I know very few billionaires, so it's hard to compare, but when I see the exploits of your brother, the actor, and your nephew ..."

Grady half smiled. "Don't believe the crap you read about Skandar; he's a good kid, and now that he's with Hayley, he's a different man. Settled, happy. Responsible. Kit, well, Kit is Kit."

He had no idea why he was telling this stranger so much, but she was so easy to talk to. "What about you, family still alive?"

Her face lit up. "Yep. Working class girl, paid my own way through college, or rather, paying. My mom and dad are good people. They're so happy I'm following my passion."

Grady was impressed. "That's great." He hesitated, then shrugged. "I have to ask ... how did you get hooked up with your associate? I'm only asking because actually it seems like a great idea of his or hers— you get the experience of seeing first-hand how the art market works; he or she gets to keep his anonymity. Hmm."

Floriana nodded. "He contacted me—yes, it's a he—through my art lecturer, asked if I wanted my education paid for, no questions asked. All I had to do was go to the auctions he wanted me to and help him bid most, to win the sale."

And you've no idea why he chose you, apart from your obvious passion for it?"

"Honestly, I heard 'paid college tuition' and 'unlimited travel expenses' and that sealed the deal for me. It was bugging my dad that he couldn't pay for me, that I had to work twenty-hour days to pay for it. So I said yes."

Grady chewed over this information then smiled at her. "You know, it's been really good to talk about art with you. I don't get to do that enough."

"Ditto. Thanks for not being an asshole about the auctions."

Grady held up his hands. "Hey, look, like you said, healthy competition. Flori, would you like to meet again, just for drinks and a chat? I'm in NOLA for another week or so."

Flori grinned shyly. "Wow. Hanging out with a Mallory. I'll get airs and graces."

Grady laughed. "Money doesn't make me classy, Flori, it's just money. Here's my card; give me a call. Where are you staying?"

She told him and gave him her cellphone number. "Thanks for the drinks."

"You're welcome. Can I walk you back to your hotel?"

"Actually, I want to sketch in the Quarter for a while, but raincheck?

"You're on."

QUILLA WAS DYING to get rid of Jakob so she could get the gossip from Asia about New Orleans. She was due to come over any minute, but Jakob was taking forever to change for a business dinner.

"You sure you don't want to come? The place is supposed to have amazing food."

She smiled and kissed him. "Asia's already on her way, and we have an evening of girl talk and Chinese food planned."

Finally, after kissing her thoroughly and wondering out loud if they had time for sex before he left, she got him out of the door. She had just grabbed some wine from the cooler when her phone rang. She was smiling when she answered it.

"Hello, Quilla."

Gregor. Again, the sweating palms, the way her stomach dropped when she heard his voice. He hadn't called for a couple of weeks, and there was a part of her that wanted to pretend he'd simply gotten tired of terrorizing her. Now, though, she rubbed a hand over eyes and pressed the 'record' button on the surveillance the FBI had installed. Every word that was said was sent to them, processed, and scoured for any clue. He never stayed on long enough for a trace, but the FBI had said to her, "Try and stay on as long as you can; get every bit of information from him. Anything could be the key. As long as you can stand it."

Easy for the FBI man to say. It wasn't his own brutal, horrific, bloody murder he was listening to being described in minute detail. Gregor would describe in sickening detail what he intended to do to her, and while Quilla had steeled herself for the worst, it always got to her. The nightmares were unimaginable, and on more than one occasion, she'd woken up screaming and having to be calmed down by a deeply concerned Jakob.

She was tired of it, tired of Gregor's shit. "Hello, Gregor. Calling to give me an update on when and how you're planning to kill me? How original. I tell you what. Why don't you go fuck yourself?"

She hung up the phone and cursed loudly. She grabbed a pillow from the couch and screamed into it. However much she pretended she was fine, she wasn't. She was close to breaking.

She heard a knock at the door and went to open it, smoothing out her expression. She smiled when she saw Asia, but Asia, having spent a great deal of time with the other woman of late, wasn't fooled for a second.

"He called, didn't he?" She walked in and hugged Quilla fiercely. "That son-of-a-bitch."

Quilla relaxed into Asia's hug. "Doesn't matter," she muttered. "Come, let's have a drink."

Asia dumped her purse onto the couch and studied Quilla. "Enough is enough, Quills. This is abuse. The Feds can't expect you to listen to his filth until you break."

A sob escaped Quilla then, and Asia went to her. "Oh, sweetheart."

"I'm okay, really," Quilla said, brushing away her tears. "I'm just so angry all of the time. Please, Asia, please, please distract me. Tell me about New Orleans."

Asia smiled. "New Orleans was great. Grady sends his love."

Quilla, her tears drying, handed Asia a glass of wine and searched her face. "Asia Flynn ... did you sleep with that man?"

Asia tried not to grin. "No idea what you're talking about."

Quilla gasped. "Oh, my God, you did! Hallelujah, hang on; I have to call Ran ...'

She pretended to go for her phone and Asia, laughing, swatted her away. Quilla nodded at the couch, her low mood lifting. "Food's on its way, Flynn, so get on that couch and tell me everything."

Skandar Mallory put his arm around his girlfriend and kissed her temple, as her older sister, Nan, read through the newspaper article. Joel, Skandar's father, and Nan's boyfriend, sat stone-faced beside her. The third one in three days. The paparazzi were obviously doing some sort of series on them, with all of their family secrets laid bare by Zinnia, their absent and errant mother.

"To be fair," Nan said, her voice cracking with her anger, "All of this is bullshit. Practically every word." She looked at her sister then Joel. "Someone must have given her a lot of money, because this is some classic Zinnia fantasy right here."

"Well, Nan, we did 'abandon her as soon as we found ourselves a couple of billionaires,' after all," Hayley spat out. "God, I hate her."

Nan's shoulders slumped. "What you have to understand," she spoke to Joel and Skandar now, her voice low and upset, "is that this is a woman who does not have the capacity for love. Or empathy. Our dad was such a good guy, but he totally enabled her, to our detriment. She would rant and scream at us for nothing, and he'd always excuse it as just one of her moods. But it was worse. It was prolonged, sustained abuse. She had serious mental health problems that she would not take responsibility for. We think it was Narcissistic Personality Disorder."

"Everything revolved around her, everything. When she wasn't downright aggressive, she played the martyr card; she did so much for us, and we never did anything for her. In fact, all we did was cause

trouble again and again—you know, things like wanting to partici-
pate in after-school activities, and getting straight As. Terrible things
like actual parental support and occasionally getting sick and it being
really inconvenient for her." Hayley was spitting out the words; such
was her anger. "If we didn't have video proof of our births (and how
much pain we caused her, of course, and how grateful we should be),
I'd take a DNA test and prove that bitch had nothing to do with us."
She choked up on the final words and Skandar and Joel shared a look
of concern.

Nan put a hand on her sister's arm. "Calm down, sweets; it's not
like this is actually harming us, just more of her bull crap. And look
what paper it's in." She waved the tabloid in the air. "The thing I want
to know is, who put her up to it. She's a bitch, yes, but unless there
were some serious financial incentives, she wouldn't bother. She likes
to pretend we don't exist."

Joel sighed and sat back. "I don't think we have to look far to see
who is behind this."

"Gregor?" Skandar cursed. "I don't get what he gets out of it. This
is some petty shit."

"Yup."

For a while there was silence, all lost in their own thoughts, then
Joel got up. "Look, I say we ignore anything he does that isn't a direct
threat to personal safety. By reacting to every made-up story, we're
giving him the oxygen of attention, of publicity. The more elegant
thing to do is to say nothing. If you get direct questions from the
press, roll your eyes and walk away." He grinned at Hayley. "However
tempting it might be to cuss them out."

Hayley smiled back and high-fived him. "I'll try. You're right,
though, as long as he doesn't threaten any of us physically or the
business, what harm can these stories actually do?"

"Tell that to Quilla," Nan said softly.

"That," Skandar said, sounding twenty years older than he was,
"is a different situation entirely. That's not revenge; that's obsession."

· · ·

FLORIANA MORGAN THANKED the bellboy and took the huge package, frowning, staggering under its weight a little. She wasn't expecting anything; her mom had sent her a care package two days ago. She sat on the bed and pulled open the envelope that had come with it.

Thought you could use these, compliments of the Ran Mallory Art Foundation. It's always thrilling to me when someone else loves art as much as I do, so think of this as both a thank you and a 'way to go'. Enjoy. Grady Mallory. (PS: absolutely no strings attached)

Flori was touched beyond words, and as she began to pull open the package, she had to stop and catch her breath. Inside was the highest-end Apple laptop money could buy, a graphics tablet, and an iPad Pro. She couldn't quite believe it. With trembling hands, she pulled each item from its packaging, turning them over in her hands. She flicked the laptop on and waited for it to boot up.

Could she accept this? Were there really no strings attached to it? She shook her head, blindsided. Grady Mallory was clearly a very generous man—as well as being drop-dead gorgeous. The screen flicked up, and an image opened. Flori started to laugh. It was a picture of Grady posing like the Fonz. Underneath, he'd added "Coffee at the Spitfire at 4:00 p.m. today? If no, text me." He'd left her his cellphone number.

Flori felt a small thrill pass through her. She wasn't sure exactly why Grady Mallory had taken such an interest in her—at first she thought it was just to get information from her, but talking to him that first time had changed her mind. He genuinely loved art.

She would meet him for coffee later, to thank him, if nothing else. As a friend, she told herself, just as a friend.

GRADY SMILED as he heard Asia's voice on the other end of the phone. "Hey, beautiful."

"Hey, yourself. How goes it in the Big Easy?"

"Pretty cool—missing my buddy," he said with a grin. Asia chuckled.

"Gray, you don't know how much I'd rather be there, but work calls. Have you managed to get any pieces yet?"

He told her about the auctions and Floriana Morgan. "Good kid, loves art."

Asia laughed softly. "You're just like your dad, you know, never can resist a good cause. Listen, I do have something I need to talk to you about."

"What's that?"

"Kit. Now, I know I don't owe him anything at all, but as a courtesy, I need to tell him about whatever this—you and me—is. I don't have a definition yet ... and I'm not asking you for one, it's just with you being siblings, it complicates things."

Grady chewed this over. "I know ... look, for what it's worth, I'd like to see how things go, on a more formal footing when I get back to Seattle. What do you say?"

"I'd like that."

"And maybe I'll just tell Kit I'd like to ask you out, test the water."

Asia sighed. "I guess so, and I need to talk to Sebastian. God, why is this so complicated?"

Grady laughed but didn't reply. Asia was silent. Then, in a low voice,

"I should have never married him, Gray. I hurt everyone, especially you, and I can't stand that. I hate that I caused you more pain."

"That's in the past," he said, but his voice broke, and he cleared his throat to cover it. "Just don't do it again."

"I promise."

AFTER THEY'D SAID GOODBYE, Grady called Kit before he could chicken out. Kit sounded happier than he'd ever heard him. There was a lot of raucous laughter in the background.

What's going on there?" Grady said with a chuckle.

"I'm being ganged up on, that's what's happening ... Tiger, no, arghhhhhh!" There was scuffling, and more laughter, then Kit came back on the phone, breathless. "Sorry about that. I was just defeated by the great knight Tiger of Tiggerdom. He might need to work on that name."

"Who are you and where is my brother?" Grady said dryly, and Kit sniggered.

"All me, bro. Just a better version. What's up?"

Grady took a deep breath. "Look, I'm just going to come out and say this ... I'd like to date Asia."

There was a silence on the other end of the phone.

"Kit?"

Kit cleared his throat, and there was noticeably less warmth in his voice when he spoke. "You two been talking?"

"Well, yeah. We've always been friends; you know that."

"Yeah. Well. Gray," Kit sighed, "it's not my place anymore to give my blessing for you two to date. You're both free and single. And it's not like the most surprising news I've had."

Grady frowned. "But I don't want it to affect our relationship."

"Gray, you do what you have to do. Look, I have to go. Speak soon." And he hung up.

"Damn it, damn it, damn it." He might have known Kit would be reticent, but now that he was with Bo Kennedy and happier than he'd ever been, Grady had counted on his blessing. Was he naive, thinking Kit would be happy for them? That he didn't still love Asia, despite everything?

Damn it.

"I CANNOT EVEN BEGIN to thank you," Floriana said again, but Grady waved her thanks away.

"Just promise me you'll keep on following your passion, even through the rough times, and I'll be happy." He picked up his coffee and sipped it. Flori shifted nervously in his seat. Since meeting her, Grady had been preoccupied, edgy, and aloof. It made her uncomfortable.

"So, are you going to the sale tomorrow?" Just say anything.

Grady smiled. "Is it worth me going?"

She flushed, and he relented. "I'm kidding, Flori. Look, sorry, I'm a bit out of it. Let's start again. Yes, I'll probably go. There's a Kahlo sketch I have my eye on. I'm prepared to go pretty high on it, so ..."

He gave her a wicked grin, which she had to return. "Good, I'm glad you'll be there," she said, flushing, "Makes it more fun knowing I'm going to kick your ass."

Grady laughed loudly. "Challenge accepted."

Flori looked around the coffee house. "This place is nice; I hadn't come across it before."

Grady nodded. "Always has the best coffee," he remarked, nodding towards the baristas. "They're properly trained, for years. Makes a difference. I came here on my honeymoon seventeen years ago—Molly was born here and knew all the best spots to eat and drink. She used to say that unless I loved good food and good coffee, she couldn't be with me. Doofus," he added fondly.

Flori felt a small pang of both of sadness and a little jealousy. "Are you still together?"

Grady gave her a sad smile. "Molly died six months after our honeymoon. Stage IV breast cancer."

Flori was shocked. "Oh God, I'm so sorry. That's awful."

Grady nodded. "It was. No denying that, it was horrific. And I lost my best friend. Molly was an artist, too."

He sighed and looked away, obviously not wanting to get emotional in front of her. Flori studied him. His dark blond hair had a light curl to it, cut short and efficient, no need for styling. There was a faint shadow of stubble on his jaw, the dark green eyes rimmed with dark blond lashes. She liked that he had a few scars, a few lines; it made him less perfect and entirely more desirable.

Shit. Desirable? Really, Floriana? Like Grady Mallory isn't way out of your league? She kicked herself mentally and cast around for something else to talk about. Grady grinned at her, not helping her with her crush. She smiled brightly.

"Have you been to the art gallery on Chartres?"

He thought about it, then shook his head. "I think I must have missed it."

"You wanna come with me? If you have time this afternoon, that is?"

Grady nodded. "Sure thing. Then, if you like, we can grab some dinner?"

Flori grinned, trying not to let her delight show too much. "Love to."

Grady drained his coffee. "Deal. Come on then, before it closes."

Yep. Yup. Definitely. She had a queen-sized crush on Grady Mallory. He was so much fun, so knowledgeable, so ... something. Last night they had laughed until their sides hurt at dinner, messing around. She hadn't felt the age gap between them once, and was surprised, in fact, when she got home and Googled him to see he was in his late thirties. Fifteen years between the two of them and yet, when they were together, she couldn't tell. Not that Grady wasn't mature, just, he had little regard for what anyone thought of him.

He'd walked her back to her hotel and kissed her cheek, very gentlemanly, but God, she had wanted to drag him into her bed and fuck him senseless. The Google search hadn't revealed any girlfriends or lovers, but who knew? She read how he'd lost one girlfriend to his brother Kit; a beautiful, dark-haired woman called Asia. Flori felt inadequate as she looked at the lawyer's photograph. Damn, she thought, absentmindedly scrunching her own messy hair up into a bun and fixing it with a pencil. Brilliant, smart, and beautiful. "The golden trifecta," she thought to herself now, as she walked to the auction place.

Grady had called—he was supposed to meet her before, but had gotten a last-minute commitment he couldn't break.

"I'll make it up to you after the sale," he promised, and she couldn't help fantasizing about what that might entail.

After I beat him out for the Kahlo, he walks me out, his hand on the small of my back, shaking his head ruefully. Another one bites the dust, he says. As we walk back towards the Quarter, he takes my hand, then suddenly pulls me into a side street. I'm sorry, he says; I can't wait another minute, and he kisses me. God, that kiss, his mouth soft and yet so passionate, his hands on my body, sliding under my skirt, into my panties. Please, I gasp, and he takes me there, in the evening streets, his cock so big, so hard inside of me and ...

"Wake it up, lady." A grumpy man pushed past her into the sale room. She stuck her tongue out at him and followed him in. She glanced around. No Grady yet. The room began to fill, so she grabbed a seat quickly. There were so many people now that she couldn't see through the crowd to find him. Cursing under her breath, she turned her attention back to the sale. Her phone vibrated.

You there?

She sighed. Yes.

Mallory there?

Flori closed her eyes for a beat, then typed, No. She waited.

If he doesn't show, don't bid on anything.

Even though she had almost expected that answer, she was still shocked. So it was to do with Grady. Hell, what had she gotten herself in the middle of?

Okay.

Let me know what happens.

She turned her phone off and decided to block everything from her mind.

The Kahlo was the fourth lot to be sold. Flori heard a few bids shouted, but none of them were Grady ... suddenly it was imperative she get it for him.

"Twenty-five!" All heads turned towards her, and her cheeks flamed red. The auctioneer took it in his stride and continued. The bidding got up to thirty-three million dollars.

"Thirty-four."

Grady. She turned and looked for him and finally spotted him looking straight at her, grinning, challenging her to top his bid. Everyone else had dropped out. Flori smiled as the auctioneer raised his eyebrows at her.

"I have thirty-four ... Miss?"

Her smile widening, she turned back to the auctioneer and shook her head. "No." Her voice was true and clear as she glimpsed at Grady, to see him looking shocked. She laughed a little.

"At thirty-three million dollars ... going once ... twice ... sold! Congratulations, Mr. Mallory."

Flori giggled as Grady looked astonished—and grateful. He mouthed to her "Why?" and she merely shrugged and smiled.

He caught up with her finally as the crowd dissipated and hugged her. God, those thick arms around her ... "You little dreamboat," he said. "I'm still in shock. How ... why ...?"

Flori swallowed over the lump in her throat. "Because you deserve it. I wish it had been the Rothko."

He looked down at her, lost for words and their gazes locked. Her heartbeat quickened.

"Grady?"

They both turned at the sound of her voice. Flori's stomach dropped to the floor. Asia Flynn stood behind Grady. He took her hand. "God, I'm sorry, As, I got carried away. Asia Flynn, meet Floriana Morgan."

Flori shook the other woman's hand and tried to return her warm smile, but her heart was cracking open. Asia smiled at her. "Grady has told me a lot about you; won't you join us for dinner?"

Flori was about to decline, but Grady was having none of it. "Hell, yes, she will; I need to buy this girl some seriously expensive food."

Flori grinned then. "Gold-plated caviar with diamond ice on top."

"Foie grass made from the bird who laid the Golden Egg."

She giggled. "Grapes handpicked by Bacchus himself."

"At the very least. Come on, women; man feeds you now." He pretended to be a caveman and Asia shot Flori an amused look, rolling her eyes. Damn it; don't make me like you, Flori thought.

HALF AN HOUR LATER, it was a done deal. Asia Flynn was lovely, Flori had to admit. She'd been afraid she might feel like the third wheel, but they were both so inclusive, so welcoming, that Flori had relaxed.

"I feel I might be able to get used to this far too easily." She gestured around the French restaurant, the beautiful layout and atmosphere a reflection of its surroundings. She'd passed on the escargot that Grady and Asia had tucked into so readily, and was quite happily working her way through the soft and fluffy bread, dipping it in garlic butter and swooning. At Grady's recommendation, she'd ordered the Cote de Boeuf. When the food was brought out, she suddenly understood why Grady and Asia were grinning. It was huge, at least a thirty-two-ounce hunk of prime beef.

"It's bigger than my head," she said weakly, prompting loud laughter from the others. Grady wiped his eyes.

"I'm sorry," he said, "I had to. But, I swear, it's utterly delicious and," he leaned forward to whisper, "they do doggy bags."

She boinked him on the head with her fork. "I'll put you in a doggy bag, Mallory."

He sat back and grinned. "Eat up."

It was out of this world; Flori actually moaned with delight as she took her first bite.

"Good?" Asia grinned at her. Flori was glad to see the other woman hadn't ordered salad or something 'light' but instead had a demi-poulet on her plate that she was enthusiastically tucking into.

"So good," Flori replied, "Please, have some."

Asia tried it and swooned. "God, yes. Next time, we'll share one, yes?"

Flori smiled. "Deal."

Afterward, they walked Flori back to her hotel, and it was only then that she felt the pang of sadness as Grady and Asia walked hand in hand back to their hotel and the room they were obviously sharing. Flori waited until they'd turned a corner, then sat down on the stone steps, breathing in the night air. She felt so conflicted; Asia Flynn was so lovely, so kind and warm, and yet ... the thought of Grady making love to her was making Flori feel ill. Sick, actually, sick with jealousy. She breathed in a few lungfuls of the cool night air. I'll get over it, she said to herself, I will. It's just a crush.

But she'd deliberately defied her employer. If he ever found out ...

"Bye bye college," she said. No, to hell with that, friendship was more important. Grady had wanted that Kahlo, and her boss would have to get over it. If he fired her, so be it. She'd find the money someplace else.

Decided, she got up and went up to her hotel room. She was pulling off her scarf when suddenly she gasped and turned. The man she called her boss was sitting on her bed. He stood, his face creased with rage.

"You damn little traitor. I saw you with them."

Flori backed up. "What?" Her knees started to tremble. God, he knows ...

Gregor Fisk smiled without humor. "I gave you everything you wanted. All you had to do was beat out Mallory for those paintings."

"I did," she said, "every time he was at a sale, I beat him out. The paintings are yours." Even to her own ears, the lie was pathetic. She'd backed up, so the door was behind her, her hand on the handle, ready to yank it open.

She tried but Gregor slammed his body into her, banging the door closed. He reached over and locked it. Flori was terrified and could feel his hot, sour breath on her face. To her horror, he pulled a knife out from his pocket. Oh God, no ... Gregor smiled.

"Oh, no ... I'm not done with you yet, girl ..."

And for the next few minutes, Flori could think of only two words.

Help me ...

6

PART SIX: TARNISH ME

P ain. That's all there was now, not night or day, not seconds, minutes or hours, just pain. Floriana Morgan opened her eyes to see a stranger, a man, a man with a kind face, bending over her. He was talking to her, but it sounded a million miles away, hollow, weird. It's okay, sweetie, we've got you now. Her eyes closed again. Pain.

That's all there was.

ASIA FLYNN PRESSED her lips to Grady Mallory's and smiled. "Good morning, handsome."

Grady chuckled. "Good morning to you, angel. Come here." He pulled her on top of him. "God, is it possible you get more beautiful every day?"

Asia puffed out her cheeks and crossed her eyes. Grady grinned. "I take it back." He looked over at the clock. "God, look at the time."

Asia shrugged. "So? We have all the time in the world."

Grady acquiesced. "Or until you have to go back to Seattle."

"Well, there is that ..." she half frowned, half smiled at him. "You talk as if you weren't coming back to Washington ... I thought you were only in New Orleans for a couple of weeks."

He hauled himself up onto his elbows. "I was ... but I've been thinking this last week about the future. You and me, obviously, but more than that, about making a legacy for myself."

Asia looked interested. "Go on."

"Well, it's a lot to do with Flori ... you know she's working for this guy who pays her to screw me over, right?" He was grinning at this and she laughed.

"Yeah, so? Oh wait ... I see something, give me a minute ..." She pretended to be receiving messages from the beyond.

"I just thought she would be a good ..."

"I see pro ... project ... no, I got it, protégé." Asia laughed and kissed him. "Seriously, you are so your father's son, Gray."

He half-smiled. "Not quite. Dad had his students, yeah, but they were all in a classroom. I'm talking about a hands-on mentorship—so to speak. I teach Flori everything I have learned and pay her to be my student on the understanding that she, after a few years, does the same to another art lover. Pay it forward."

Asia nodded but said nothing. Grady studied her. "Asia? What?"

"So you would travel around the world with Floriana?"

He hid a grin. "As her teacher. Jealous?"

She shook her head, but then had to laugh. "A little. Flori's gorgeous."

"And young enough to be my kid."

"If you grew up in a trailer park."

"Snob."

"Hell, yeah. No, seriously, I do think it would be a great thing to do. I'm just jealous she'll see more of you than I will."

He kissed her. "I'll be a cruel, mean tutor. Make her get my coffee and then change my mind about what I want and yell at her for getting it wrong."

Asia laughed, rolling her eyes. "Yeah, right. Go for it."

"Really?"

"Yes, absolutely. In fact, call her now; ask if she wants to meet for lunch, I'd like to see her before I go back to Seattle."

Grady's eyebrows shot up. "Wow. Are you jealous of me traveling with Flori, or of Flori traveling with me ...?"

"Shut up. I need to pee. Call her," she called back as she went to the bathroom. Grady, still grinning, snagged his phone from the night stand and called Flori's number.

"Hello?"

Grady frowned. Not Flori's voice. "Hey, I'm sorry ..." he checked the number—definitely Flori's. "I'm looking for Floriana Morgan; this is her cellphone. Who are you?"

"Dr. Thomas at the Sacred Heart. Are you a friend of Miss Morgan's?"

Grady's heart began to beat unpleasantly hard. He swung his legs over the side of the bed. "Yes, why ... God, is she okay?"

The doctor hesitated. "I'm afraid Miss Morgan has been brought to the hospital in a serious condition, more than that I cannot tell you. We're trying to get in touch with her family."

"I can help with that, Doctor, please, how bad?"

Another pause. "Bad. If you can get her family here as soon as possible, that would be a help."

Grady thought he might pass out from the shock. When Asia came out from the bathroom, she went to him immediately, and he told her what had happened. She was as shocked as he was. Grady looked up at her, his eyes red and scared.

"I have to get to the hospital. Now. God, Asia, I think Flori's dying."

PARKER THOMAS M.D. swept his hand onto Flori's forehead. "Hey, Floriana, can you open your eyes for me?"

No response. God, this poor girl. In his fourteen years, he'd never seen a case like this. Floriana Morgan had been beaten and stabbed in such a brutal attack; Parker wondered how she was still breathing. Bags of blood and saline hung above the gurney she was on. He nodded to his resident. "Yeah, let's get her down to surgery now, get this bleeding stopped. Then arrange for a head CT. I'll be as fast as I can—if she weren't bleeding so badly, I'd be tempted to do the CT first, see if there's a brain bleed, but I don't want her exsanguinating on me."

In the theater, he managed to stop the bleeding but it was touch and go so many times, he had to make the choice several times to carry on and not let her go. She's just a kid, he thought, I have to try. He cursed the person who had done this to her over and over in his mind.

At forty-one, Parker Thomas had made his fortune early by specializing in plastics, but six years into his own practice, he found himself needing more. Needing to help people in emergency situations, bringing people back from the brink, that's where his heart truly lay. His half-sister, Valentina, called it his God Complex and laughing, he'd agreed, yes, it probably was. Valentina, an actress with a flair for the dramatic, now referred to her brother as Dr. Savior. He would grin, but really, knowing that his talent for going the extra mile for his most urgent patients, filled a hole in his heart.

After Flori's head CT, he sat in the booth looking at her scans, satisfied that there was no brain bleed. Thank God. She had a fighting chance, if her brain was okay. He went to see her in the ICU. Coma was a scary word but sometimes, like now, it was the best thing for her. It saved her some of the pain. "Keep fighting, little one," he said.

Out in the corridor, he saw a couple talking with the nurse. The man looked at him. "Dr. Thomas? Grady Mallory, this is Asia Flynn; we're here for Flori – I'm sorry, I mean, Floriana Morgan."

Parker shook hands with them. "As I said on the phone, I'm not able to tell you much because you're not family."

Grady nodded. "I know, just … please …" He got choked up and Parker took pity. He drew them to one side. "Look, I didn't tell you this, okay? Floriana was brought in with multiple stab wounds to the abdomen. She was also badly beaten."

The woman, Asia, made a distressed noise and her eyes filled with tears. Grady Mallory hugged her to him, his own distress obvious. "Do the police know what happened?"

Parker sighed. "I really shouldn't ... she was attacked in her hotel room. I really don't know anymore. You said you could help find her family."

Grady nodded. "Yes, we're looking into that right now, and we'll fly them out as soon as we can locate them. As for press, I don't think we should release her name."

"Agreed. Look, I wish I could tell you more or give you better news, but we are doing everything to help her. She's very sick."

Grady thanked him. "Doctor, I know this is a stupid question, but can ...?"

Parker shook his head. "I'm afraid you can't see her yet. When her folks arrive, it'll be up to them."

"Of course. I thought I'd ask." Grady gave him a half smile, "She's just a kid," he said, echoing Parker's thoughts.

"Yeah." Suddenly, Parker felt bleak. "This world, sometimes."

Asia Flynn put her hand on his arm. "This world. Thank you for looking after her."

He smiled at her. "Thanks. Look, I have to get back. If you can let the desk know when her parents get here?"

"Sure thing."

He nodded, smiled, and left them standing there. Checking again on his patients, he left Flori until last. She was about the same age as Valentina, and the thought made his chest clench up. He would call his half-sister as soon as he got off work tonight. He checked her vital signs—steady, not great, but stable. Jesus, what people did to each other. Her injuries would heal; the bruises on her pretty face would fade; but only God knew what psychological scars would be left.

"Keep fighting, little one," he said to the comatose woman. Shit, why did it always get to him? He was a freaking professional. He went to update his charts. Helena, the ICU head nurse, nudged his shoulder as she sat down next to him. A Mexican woman in her forties, she had taken him under her wing as soon as he transferred to emergency medicine all those years ago—now she was family.

"You okay, punkin? Rough day?"

"Not as rough as that poor kid in there."

"Amen." She studied him. "You ever go out, let your hair down, Parker? Because you look like a guy who needs a big night, some good friends, and an almighty hangover."

He grinned gratefully at her. "Hels, all I need is you to remind me that the world isn't always a bad place."

She smiled. "I'm serious, dude. You need a woman."

Parker laughed out loud. "Ha, you're joking, right? When do I have time for dating?"

Helene gave a chuckle. "Maybe you don't need a date, but you definitely need to get laid."

Parker sighed. "No argument there." He looked at the clock. "You about finished? Wanna get a drink?"

Helena pretended to be shocked. "I am a married woman, Dr. Thomas."

"Shut up and get your coat."

Asia glanced anxiously at Grady. He had been withdrawn since they left the hospital-- understandably so—but she was worried. From what the doctor had told them, Flori was in a very bad way, and Grady was devastated. Was there such a thing as too devastated for someone who'd known her only a few weeks? She immediately felt bad for even thinking such a thing but...

"Gray? She's in the best place." Asia took his hand. The cab ride back to the hotel was almost over, and she couldn't bear to think of the whole evening passing in silence. It was better to talk about it. Grady gave her a sad smile.

"I keep thinking what if ... no, it's ridiculous." He shook his head and turned away again.

"What?"

He didn't look at her. "Later."

. . .

BACK IN HIS HOTEL ROOM, Asia waited for him to speak. He seemed to struggle with something in his mind then sighed. "What if ... Flori's boss ... she deliberately didn't bid on that Kahlo, so I could get it, and what if her boss found out?"

Asia frowned. "But why would he try to kill her for something like that- wouldn't he just fire her?"

"Well, that's what I figured, but her employer is loaded, so maybe I thought it might be someone from a mob background, who didn't take too kindly to her 'betrayal', as they would see it."

Asia wasn't convinced. "It's more likely to be some psychopath seeing a pretty girl and doing what psychos do. God," she suddenly felt sick. "I'm so sick of women being targets for men who can't keep their baser instincts under control. First Quilla, now this."

The idea occurred to them at the same time and their eyes locked. Grady was the first to shake his head. "No ... it can't be."

Gregor Fisk. "Damn it, damn it ..." Grady reached for his phone. "This has got to stop. Yeah, police, my name's Grady Mallory. I'm calling about the stabbing at the Rose Hotel—I think I might have some information. I know it's late, but can I come and see you right now?"

GRADY HAD to hand it to his family, as soon as his dad and Jakob heard the news, they filled New Orleans and Louisiana with private detectives and security, all searching for any trace of Gregor Fisk. Meanwhile, Flori's parents, Mac and Jean, were flown in by private jet and Grady himself drove them to the hospital.

When they got there and saw Flori—still comatose—and the extent of her injuries, Jean broke down and sobbed in her husband's arms. Grady watched as they spoke to Dr. Thomas, Flori's father stone-faced and pale. Afterward, they came to sit with Flori. Grady looked in through the glass door. She looked so tiny and fragile in that bed, he could hardly stand it.

"Please, please, Flori, don't go ..." He hadn't realized he was talking aloud until Asia took his hand.

"Grady ... let's give them some privacy."

He shook his head, not looking away from Flori's still figure. Asia's hand slipped out of his. "I'm going to grab some coffee in the cafeteria, then." There was a slight edge to her voice, but he brushed it aside.

"Okay, see you later."

Asia thanked the server, took her coffee, and looked around for a chair. The cafeteria was busy, but she spotted an empty seat and aimed for it. The other seat was occupied, and she recognized Flori's doctor. She hesitated, but he looked up and smiled, gesturing to a chair.

"Please, it's no trouble."

She sat and smiled gratefully at him. "Hello again."

He looked blank, and she grinned. "Sorry, I'm a friend of Floriana Morgan's—Asia Flynn." She stuck her hand out, and he took it. His fingers were warm and dry and dwarfed her small hand. A little frisson went through her. He was a dark-haired man, pale-skinned, with the bluest eyes she'd ever seen. His dark brown beard framed a handsome, boyish face and she couldn't tell if he was young or just looked it. He was studying her with interest,

"Parker Thomas. Hey, yes, of course, I'm sorry."

She shrugged. "You probably meet hundreds of people every day."

Parker grinned and leaned forward. "There's so many things I could say right now and they'd all sound so cheesy, so I'll just go with I have no idea how I could forget you."

She laughed at his mischievous smile. "Still cheesy."

He shrugged good-naturedly. "Yup, cheesy's all I got. Hey look, Flori's doing a little better. I'm considering bringing her out of the coma, to see if we can test her brain function."

Asia's nausea returned again. "God ..." She rubbed her head and suddenly felt the tears filling her eyes. "Sorry, it's just; we had this happen a few months ago. Luckily that time my friend's injuries weren't as bad, but to have it happen again."

Parker Thomas looked sympathetic. "I'm sorry, I didn't know. Your friend okay now?"

"Oh, yes. But it's just the violence of it, you know. Flori's only a kid."

Parker nodded. "I know. I was thinking earlier, I have a sister about the same age."

"You have a big family?"

"Just me and Valentina. She's an actress."

Asia studied him. "Valentina Thomas?"

"Valentina Rose."

Asia was impressed. "Wow."

Parker grinned shyly. "Sorry, I have to boast about her; she's my best friend."

Asia smiled. "That's sweet. I'm an only child, but I kinda married into a big family. Even after the divorce, I still see more of the Mallorys than I do my own family." She looked thoughtful for a moment. "Valentina is the daughter of Stylo Thomas, right? The banker? Your father, yes?"

Parker nodded. "For my sins. We don't see him a lot; he's always working." He gave a little laugh. "I must take after him."

Asia still remembered something. "I think my ex-father-in-law Ran did some business with your father in the late seventies—aren't they still friends?"

"Oh, those Mallorys," Parker realized who she was talking about. "Wow. Yeah, I think they did, and they might still be in touch, I don't get to see my dad as much as I'd like. So you were married to ...?"

"Kit Mallory," Asia told him, and he nodded. "Now, though, I'm sort of ..." She tailed off, suddenly not wanting to tell him she was seeing Grady.

"Sort of?"

"Nothing." She smiled. "So you come from old, old, money—why are you an emergency room doc?"

"Business was not my forte or my passion. I wanted to help people—I started in plastics," he said and laughed at her expression, "Hey, look, it's important to some people, and I don't mean the celebrity stuff. People who have been in fires, been mauled, attacked, been in car wrecks—you would be surprised by the scope of the field."

"So you worked mainly on those people?"

Parker's mouth hitched up at one side. "No, I mostly pandered to celebrities," and he grinned as she laughed loudly. "But, listen, it made me a lot of money in a short time, so I was able to go into something more fulfilling."

Asia met his gaze. "I'm glad, Parker. You don't seem like one of the bloated Real Housewife surgeons I see on TV."

"You need to watch better shows."

"That's very true. Look, thanks for the company; it's been really good to talk to you. I have to ask," she added as she stood up, she grinned widely, "Do the nurses call you McDreamy?"

Parker groaned loudly. "No, thank God. That's a firing offense."

She laughed. "Good. Because a—thankfully, you look nothing like Patrick Dempsey; and b—because all the screwing in on-call rooms is very unhygienic." She shuddered dramatically.

He laughed. "If only that ever actually happened in real life. Good to talk to you, Asia, but please, watch better TV."

"I'll try." She waved and left the cafeteria, feeling cheered and happier than in days. Parker Thomas was cute as hell, her brain told her. Her body clearly agreed because her skin felt tingly, her nipples hard, and there was a definite beat pulsing between her legs. For a moment, she let herself enjoy the feeling, then shut the feeling down. She was with Grady, wasn't she? She cared so deeply for him, loved the incredible sex, but since Flori's attack he had been withdrawing from Asia so much that she had no choice but to recognize it and deal with it.

She steeled herself for the scene upstairs in ICU but when she got there all was quiet. Mac and Jean had left for the evening, and Grady was sitting in with Flori. He was holding her hand, and as Asia watched, he brought the unconscious girl's hand to his mouth and pressed his lips against it. Oof, gut punch, Asia thought wincing. But something in her understood, told her this had been inevitable ever since Flori had come into their lives. She'd known from the first time she'd seen Grady and Flori together.

Neither of them has any clue, she thought to herself now. She stood back, just watching Grady sit with the young woman, watching his expression as he watched her sleep. Love. Whether Grady realized it, their relationship— his and Asia's—had just ended with that tiny gesture, that kiss against the soft skin of Flori's hand.

And Asia didn't feel as sad as she should have.

JAKOB PICKED at his food while around him, his family chatted and laughed. Only his adored girlfriend, Quilla, looked as subdued and tired as he did. She was working long hours at the college, hoping to make up for some of the negative publicity she thought she had brought them. Her professor had called Jakob to express his concern at Quilla's state of mind, but Quilla had dismissed his worries, even got a little angry that she was being discussed behind her back. It had caused a rift between Quilla and Jakob and he was at a loss for how to mend it.

Marley Griffin, finally persuaded to join the party, met his gaze, and he saw her frown and nod almost imperceptibly at Quilla. He shook his head. Not here. Marley sighed, and when Quilla excused herself to go to the bathroom, Marley scooted into her vacant chair at Jakob's side.

"That's not my friend," she said bluntly. "My friend is funny and loving and excited about life, even when she feels crap. Have you suggested therapy?"

Jakob gave a humorless laugh. "Many, many times. She just shuts down on me. Look, I know you and I have had our differences, but please, help me. You've known her longer than I have, you can ..."

"... tell it to her straight," Marley finished for him, looking grim-faced. Jakob laughed softly.

"Right."

Marley studied. "I'm working on my anger issues with you," she said, her voice softening. "I know it wasn't your fault she was stabbed.

I just, God, I felt so helpless. We're each other's family, you know? I don't know what a world without her would be like."

"Then we have more in common than you think," Jakob said gently. "I just don't know how to reach her."

Marley gave a frustrated sigh. "Just keep on loving her no matter what. I'll be the bad cop, and we'll see if that has any effect."

QUILLA WASHED HER HANDS, avoiding her reflection in the vast mirrors of the restaurant bathroom. She hated looking at herself now; her eyes always seemed wild, scared, and angry. She had tried to analyze what was making her feel like she was on a tightrope without a net. It was him, Gregor; his obsession had become her obsession. She wanted to deal with him herself but knew, frustrated, that it wasn't likely to happen that way. She had even, not to Jakob's knowledge, given her security detail the slip and gone out in the open, wondering if he was watching her, then, if he would strike, if she could drive the knife she hid in her pocket into his heart and be done with this horror forever.

She scared herself. Never, in her life, would she ever have considered harming another human being, but her shredded nerves and fragile mindset made her sure she could kill Gregor if it came down to it.

She dried her hands then stopped, leaning her forehead against the cool tile. She was losing it, she knew it, but sheer orneriness kept her from asking for help. You are not a victim, she said to herself. Grady's friend had it much, much worse than you did. Stop feeling sorry for yourself. She needed something, to reconnect with Jakob, to spend time with Marley and Asia and Nan—her friends, her sisters.

She drew in a deep breath and went back out to rejoin the party. She smiled at Jakob, and his delighted grin broke her heart. She pressed her lips against his. "I love you, Mr. Mallory."

She felt his big body relax into the embrace. "Me too, Miss Chen, and when we get home, I'll show you just how much."

She grinned, then smiled over at Marley, who was watching them.

Marley's mouth hitched up in a knowing grin. "Strumpet", she mouthed at her friend, and Quilla laughed, giving her the thumbs up.

Maybe, just maybe, everything would be okay.

"OKAY, Floriana, I'm going to ask you to open your eyes now."

Flori stirred and slowly, very slowly, she opened her eyes, the lids gummy, sticky with sleep. The bright light assaulted her vision, and she clamped them shut again and moaned.

"It's okay, Flori, I'm sorry, we'll draw the blinds ... nurse, could you ...? Thanks. Now, how about we try that again, Flori?" He had such a lovely, melodic voice. She opened her eyes and looked into the face of the dark-haired man leaning over her and smiling.

"Hey there," he said with a smile. "I'm Dr. Thomas. How are you feeling?"

"Thirsty." The words came out as a whisper. Someone was moistening her mouth, then holding a cup to her lips. She gulped down the cold water gratefully, not taking her eyes from the handsome doctor. "Where ... am?" she said in broken words; her head felt fuzzy, and she couldn't find the right words. "I am ... no ... where?"

He smiled, but his eyes registered concern. "In hospital, sweetheart. Do you remember what happened?"

Pain. A fist being slammed into her face, him, straddling her. The knife. Pain. A whimper escaped her.

"It's okay, darling. We're here."

"Mom?" Her mother came into her field of vision and Flori's eyes filled with tears. "Mom ..." Her voice cracked, then her vision was blurry because of the tears. Dr. Thomas smiled and stepped aside to let her father come in and hug her. As she embraced her parents, she saw him. Grady, standing at the end of the bed, smiling through his tears.

THE POLICE WERE KIND, but after two hours of questioning, she was exhausted. She'd sent her mom and dad back to the hotel; You don't need to hear this, she'd told them. Relieved when they'd agreed, she was glad to have Grady by her side. He'd wrapped his arm around her shoulders and now, when she was drooping from telling them everything she remembered, over and over—he stepped in. "Okay, gents, Flori needs to rest now."

Alone, he perched on the side of her bed, cradling her in his arms. She leaned into his big body, relaxing her tensed shoulders. Her body ached and felt heavy from the dressings. They told her what he'd done to her, the man, her boss ... whose name she now knew. She'd identified Gregor Fisk from his photographs; in the glossy shots, he looked handsome, respectable, and business-like. She'd seen the devil within, the feral creature who had stabbed her repeatedly and left her dying in a pool of her own hot, sticky blood. Gregor Fisk.

"I'm so sorry, Grady," she whispered now and Grady, frowning, moved so he could look at her.

"Why are you apologizing to me? If anything, I should be begging for your forgiveness."

"Why?" she coughed, her throat still raw from the tubes, and Grady immediately reached for the water glass at her side. She took a sip. "I took the job; you had no way of knowing."

"Neither did you. Look, this fucker has been targeting us since Jakob fired him and ..." He trailed off, staring at her as if seeing her for the first time.

"What?" She raised her eyebrows—painfully—at him.

He shook his head. "I never saw it before ... you look like her."

Flori didn't get it. "Who?"

"Quilla. Dark hair, slight, your eye color is different but not by much, both beautiful, both art students ... God, that sick fuck."

"I still don't understand."

Grady sighed, twisted his fingers in with hers. "Fisk targeted you to send us a message. God, Flori, I'm so sorry I didn't see it."

"How could you have? It's insane." Flori shifted uncomfortably; the last morphine shot was wearing off. Grady stroked his hand down her face, and Flori leaned into his touch.

"Hey there."

They both looked up to see Asia watching them from the doorway. She was smiling, but there was something else in her eyes. A resigned look, sadness. She came in and kissed Flori's cheek. "How are you feeling?"

Flori smiled at her. "Better. I think."

Asia squeezed her hand. "Well, look, I have to go back to Seattle for a couple of days, so take care of yourself, won't you? I'm glad you're feeling better."

GRADY FOLLOWED Asia into the corridor. "You didn't mention going back to Seattle."

Asia smiled sadly. "I did, actually, a couple of times. Look, Grady, maybe this is a good thing, get some space, figure out where we want to go from here. We never made a commitment to each other that was anything more than friends with benefits."

Grady's eyes were hurt, confused. "What? I don't get it ... are you breaking up with me?"

Asia chuckled softly, shaking her head. "You really don't see it, do you? Grady, you are my best friend, and you will always be that to me. But I think your heart lies elsewhere." She deliberately glanced back into Flori's room. Grady suddenly understood.

"No ... Flori's my friend; I thought you understood that ... .it has nothing to do with us."

She suddenly grabbed him, hugging him hard. "It has everything to do with us, my sweet," she whispered. Then, dashing away a tear, she smiled up at him. "You deserve a chance at real love. And so do I. When you think about it, you'll realize."

Grady kept shaking his head. "No, this ... this is real, you and me. I've waited so long for this to happen."

"I know, I know, and I will never regret what has happened between us. Never," she said fiercely. "But I can't be a portion of someone's love, and I am not blaming you or Flori because I know neither of you realizes it yet. Try, Grady, and I swear you'll understand what I'm saying. She is your heart, not me."

He was silent then, his mind whirling. Asia kissed him softly. "Goodbye, Grady. I'll see you in a couple of days."

As she started to walk away, he called her name. As she turned, he looked into her eyes. "If you're so sure, why are you coming back in a couple of days?"

She smiled. "Because Flori's my friend, too, and so are you. I'll be here as long as you both need me."

She could feel him watching her walk away. As she pressed the call button, she willed him to go back to Flori's side, not make this harder—although there was still part of her that wished he'd come for her, beg her to stay. A small part. But not her whole heart.

Because over the last few weeks, Asia had realized that Grady wasn't her future. He would always be in her life, but lately, there had been someone else, someone she'd grown close to, met for coffee every day, sometimes, twice a day. Someone with the bluest, sexiest eyes she'd ever seen.

She headed for the hospital cafeteria now, walked in, and saw him.

Parker Thomas looked up and with obvious delight in his eyes, he stood and smiled at her.

MARLEY WAITED until Quilla was strapped into the car. Her friend grinned at her, but Marley could see the dark purple shadows under her eyes.

"So where are you taking me?"

Marley smiled. "Not telling. You'll just have to wait and see."

Quilla smiled. "Fair enough. How have you been, Marls?"

"I'm fine," she said, concentrating on the road. "Have you been sleeping better?"

"A little." She was lying, Marley could always tell, and she shot her a look. Quilla shrugged. "You know how it is."

Marley pursed her lips. She and Jakob had spent hours on the phone trying to figure out how to help her but at last Markey had said, "Right, screw all this, I'm just going to take her to a therapist myself and use extreme emotional blackmail."

Which is what she was doing now. Twenty minutes later, they pulled into the underground car park of a tall office building, Quilla looking confused. Marley parked the car and turned to her friend.

"What's going on?" Quilla was studying her face, her eyes wary.

Marley's face was set. "Upstairs, on the third floor is an office. In that office is one the world's best—and most expensive—psychiatrists. He specializes in PTSD in victims of violence. You are booked in for a course of sessions with him. You will attend every single one of them. Either Jakob or I will bring you, to make sure you attend them."

Quilla was staring at her in horror. "You cannot be serious—who do you think you are? Both you and Jakob need to realize I'm not a child. Switch the engine on and let's leave."

"I haven't finished." Marley's voice was hard now. "If you miss even a minute of a session, that's it. I'm done. You will never see me again. Ever."

Quilla's eyes were filled with tears. "Please don't make me do this," she whispered, "I can't. I can't relive that night."

"You're reliving it every minute! Do you think we can't see that? And it's destroying you, and Jakob, and me and everyone that cares for you."

Quilla was getting more agitated by the second. "For God's sake, of course I'm upset. He's still out there! And he wants to kill me. A man I barely know wants to kill me. Wouldn't you be ...?" Her voice cracked then, and she turned her head so Marley couldn't see her tears. "Why are you doing this?"

"Because I love you," Marley said, softening her tone. "Because you need this. This will help you get stronger, mentally, so you can deal with this other crap."

"This other crap meaning death threats," Quilla snapped. She dropped her head into her hands. "I don't believe what you're doing to me. I can't believe it. Please, Marley, I ..."

"No more talking. Get out of the car, get into that elevator, and get the help you desperately need."

Quilla stared at her. "I'll never forgive you for this." But she got out of the car, slamming it shut, and went to the elevator. A few moments later, Marley's phone beeped. A text message from the psychiatrist's assistant.

She's in.

Marley let out a huge sigh of relief ... then burst into tears.

"You're cheating."

"I am not."

"You are. You're rocking the table so that ..."

The Jenga tower collapsed and Flori groaned, swatting at a grinning Grady. "I told you."

"Sore loser," he chuckled as he swept the pieces back into the box. Flori was looking so much better; the six weeks since the attack had flown by. Grady had spent every hour he could with her, apart from when her mom was with her, not wanting to intrude.

Her father had returned to Portland, work calling him back after a couple of weeks, but by then, they knew Flori would be fine. A long recovery time, yes, but essentially, she would return to full health within a few months. Grady had assured her parents and Flori that all the medical expenses would be taken care of—as well as Flori's college fund. Flori had protested, but Grady would not hear of anything else.

"There is nothing I wouldn't do for you," he'd said earnestly and now, as he looked at her lovely face, so delicately featured, so expressive and warm, he knew that to be true. What Asia had said to him all those weeks ago had made his whole outlook on the world change. She was right—he had fallen in love with Flori. Completely and utterly.

But he was afraid. Afraid of the age difference between them, afraid she would not feel the same way, afraid that if she knew his true feelings, she would feel beholden to him. And God, the thought of that made him feel sick. He wanted her, yes, but only if she wanted him back without condition or hesitation. So he kept his feelings to himself—for the most part. He had a feeling Jean, Flori's mother, could read him like a book. She reminded him so much of his own mother, so kind, and nurturing.

Flori was harder to read. She certainly welcomed him, treated him as her best friend—and that made him a little gun-shy after what Asia had said—but he couldn't tell if she felt anything more for him. They were always holding hands, or touching the other's face, or hugging, but then, Flori was a very tactile person.

Asia had kept her promise and had been back to see them, not showing any resentment or giving Flori any clue to why she and Grady were no longer together. Flori had asked Grady what their deal was when she was on a lot of morphine, and he'd told her they were just friends.

"Sexy friends," Flori had mumbled, just before she fell asleep and Grady had smiled sadly. The more time he spent away from Asia, he realized she had right. Maybe their brief love affair had been just the blissful, short way to resolve unfinished business.

"Earth to Grady," Flori said now with a grin. She stroked his face. "Beardy."

Grady grinned, leaning into her touch. "Want me to shave?"

She shook her head. "Nah, you look good with a beard. So good, you're making me jealous. I sometimes wish it was socially acceptable for women to have beards. I'd rock a little goatee."

Grady laughed. "That medication you're on is really something, huh?"

She smiled. "Actually, at the moment, no pain meds. I'm riding it out. Better for recovery, so I don't strain any core muscles when the morphine fools me into thinking they don't hurt." She winced then and laughed. "Like that."

Grady frowned. "But if you're in pain, surely ...?"

She shook her head. "Only when I move awkwardly. I've got so used to being in pain that now that it's just general soreness, I think I feel great. Maybe they'll let me out soon."

She looked hopeful, and Grady grinned. "Keep dreaming. But I wanted to ask, what are your plans for when you do get out? Will you go back to Portland?"

She shook her head. "I don't think so. I think I'm going to transfer my college credits to somewhere else, start over."

"You know wherever you want to go; I'm going to cover everything, tuition, housing."

"Grady ..."

"No arguments. This is non-negotiable."

She gave him a small smile. "You are the greatest." She hesitated and leaned towards him, and her lips brushed his, quickly, gently. Grady's mouth tingled from the sensation of it and he smiled. He moved nearer to her, taking her face in his hands, and once again covering her mouth with his. He felt her little fingers tangled in his hair as he kissed her, as the kiss became more urgent, he heard her moan softly, the sound of it making his cock harden, his pulse race.

Eventually, he broke away, and they smiled at each other. He ran the back of his fingers down her cheek. "You're so beautiful," he murmured. She nuzzled her nose against his.

"Come lay down with me," she said and shifted across the bed— wincing. He kicked off his shoes and stretched out beside her, her head on his chest, his lips against her forehead. She fit so naturally in his arms that his heart felt like it would burst. He was in love with this gorgeous, fragile, vulnerable girl. And right then, right at that moment, he knew he was lost.

ASIA WALKED STRAIGHT to the cafeteria the minute she got back to the hospital. You should be visiting your friends, she told herself, but she couldn't help pick up her stride. God, she wanted to see Parker. Their talks over coffee had been so flirty, so much fun, that she could barely wait to get back to New Orleans to see him. So far it had all been very casual—coffee, text messages arranging ... dates? Could she call them that?

All she knew was, Parker Thomas was the first thing she thought of when she woke. She grinned to herself now as she walked into the cafeteria and stopped, her heart failing. Parker was at their usual table, but there was someone else there, a woman, a blonde, and Parker was laughing with her. He caught Asia's eye and waved, his smile still in place and slowly, she walked towards them.

The blonde woman turned and smiled at her warmly, and the relief she felt was all-consuming. Valentina; Oscar-winning actress and Parker's sister. Oh, thank God. She nearly said it out loud, but kept her face friendly and open. Valentina kissed both of her cheeks.

"It's so lovely to meet you at last," she said as they sat down, "Parker hasn't shut up about you."

"Dude, way to play it cool," Parker muttered, suddenly seeming less like the medical wunderkind he was and more like a goofy teenager. He grinned at Asia. "Hey, beautiful, good flight?"

Valentina, it turned out, was only with them for an hour, then had to catch a connecting flight to Europe. She was funny, bright, and told them outrageous stories of life on set. Asia grinned.

"God, I remember it well," she said, and Valentina leaned in conspiratorially.

"Between you and me, you were always too good for Kit. He's a nice guy, but an idiot when it comes to woman."

Something made Asia wonder if Kit and Valentina had ever hooked up; then dismissed the idea—who cared now? Kit was blissfully happy with Bo Kennedy. She wondered if Valentina had someone special in her life—maybe you should spend some time on gossip sites, she told herself with a grin.

When they were alone, Parker took her hand, his cheeks flushing pink. "So I was wondering if we could go out of the hospital, on a real date. I'd like to cook you something. If you are free, of course."

She smiled, her own face blushing. "Love too ... tonight?"

Parker grinned, relieved. "If it suits you ... right now?"

God, yes, yes. "Sure thing. You cook?"

The red cheeks were back. "I love food, especially French cuisine, but here, I don't get a chance to cook for anyone."

Asia smiled. "That sounds good."

. . .

HIS APARTMENT WAS NOT as she expected but thinking about it, it made sense. He came from a vastly rich family and his apartment reflected that. A vast open-plan space, exposed brickwork, a kitchen to die for. At the far end, a large bed, swathed in gray, navy, and white sheets. Asia's heart began to beat faster as Parker gave the quick tour. His hand brushed hers and took it, and he gently pulled her to him.

"Are you hungry?" he murmured and as she looked up at him, she shook her head. He smiled.

"Me either," and he bent his head and covered her mouth with his, his tongue gently probing her mouth, massaging her tongue. Asia moaned as the kiss deepened and she felt him lift her into his arms and carry her to that vast bed.

God, she wanted this man so badly, in a way she'd never felt before, so that if she didn't have him inside her now, she would die. She tugged his shirt open, running her hands over the fine smattering of hair on his firm chest. Parker grinned down at her, his fingers on the belt of her wrap dress, untying it and pushing the fabric away from her body.

"Wow, oh, wow," he said with wonder in his voice as he took in the smooth curves of her belly, the full breasts, and her rich olive skin. They spent a long time undressing each other, kissing every exposed piece of skin. Parker was tall and well-built, his body firm, if not defined. Asia felt utterly feminine with him; he made her feel so beautiful that she could have cried.

When they were naked, they lay beside each other for a long time, stroking their hand over the other's skin, drinking each other in. Finally, when neither could wait any longer, Parker gathered her to him and his cock, trembling and bobbing under its own weight, slid into her, filling her, stretching her out in the most blissful way. They moved together, and as they did, they laughed and smiled and had fun and her orgasm, when it came, was mellow and carried on, even after they collapsed back onto the bed. Asia felt warmth flood through her as she looked at his charming, boyish, gorgeous face and knew she'd found something remarkable.

Parker propped himself up on his elbow and gazed down at her, his fingers tracing delicate patterns over her belly. "Asia Flynn, you have no idea what you being here means to me."

She nodded. "Right back at cha. My God, Parker ... if this isn't a weird thing to say, I feel ... free. As if suddenly I get 'it', whatever 'it' is."

Parker grinned and kissed her. "I have no idea what you're talking about, but as long as you're happy."

She chuckled. "I'll explain some other time." She studied him. "How the hell are you single?"

Parker lay back, and she settled her head on his chest. "I just ... it wasn't something I particular cared about, a relationship."

"You slept around?" Her voice held no judgment—he was a good-looking guy.

He shrugged. "Some. I guess I was tied up with my work. Then I saw you and ..." He made a swooning; gesture, and she laughed. "You have the cutest face," he said. "Hey, I'm curious ... what's your deal with Grady Mallory? When I met you, I figured you were a couple."

She sighed. "You know, we were, God, how can I put this? Laying old ghosts." She grinned wickedly. "Literally for a while, but then Flori happened."

"Regrets?"

"None. It hurt, of course, but when you see two people that are so right for each other ..."

Parker stroked her face. "I know what you mean."

She rested her cheek on his hard chest. "Can we just stay here and not deal with the outside world for a while?"

Parker grinned. "You got it, sweet cheeks."

Asia closed her eyes, breathing in his clean scent, and suddenly realized why she was so relaxed with this lovely man. It was because he wasn't a Mallory. She had been too tied up in their world for too long.

Now it was her turn to find the happiness she deserved, outside that world.

GRADY WENT to grab some coffee with Jean as Flori slept. The doctor who had checked her this morning told them with a smile that she could go home at the end of the week. Flori had been so happy but now, exhausted again, she'd fallen back asleep.

Grady carried the tray over to the table, and he and Jean relaxed. "She's doing so well," Jean said happily. Jean, a tiny woman in her sixties, was the spitting image of her daughter, except the dark hair was flecked with white, and the cornflower blue eyes were lined and covered with spectacles. But Flori was there in the easy, warm smile and the plump cheeks which made Jean look decades younger. She was smiling at Grady now.

"That girl's crazy about you, young man."

Grady grinned and tapped her cup with his. "As I am about her."

"Well, I'm delighted, although you may find her father a tougher nut to crack."

Grady sighed, nodding. Mac Morgan blamed him for Flori's attack. "Yeah, but I have to admit, I can't say I blame him. It may have been Gregor Fisk, that damned coward, who tried to kill her, but it's because of my family."

Jean shook her head. "I cannot even imagine what your family has been through these last few months."

Grady was silent for a moment. "Jean ... Flori tells me she doesn't want to go back to Portland. I would like to invite her to come stay with me in Seattle for a while. We, my family, have our base there, security, a home where Flori would be safe. But I wanted to ask you what you thought about that."

Before Jean could answer, Parker Thomas interrupted—with Asia in tow. Grady shook hands with the doctor and kissed Asia, who said hello to Jean. Grady looked between the two newcomers—there was obviously something going on and for that, he was glad. Relieved, which was a weird feeling but ...

Asia pulled him to one side. "Hey, you," she said, her eyes warm. "How's Flori?"

He couldn't help but smile. "She's being released at the end of this week."

"Oh, Gray, that's wonderful, I'm so glad."

Grady hugged her then nodded at Parker. "You and the doc, huh?"

She chuckled. "Pretty much. You okay with that?"

He looked into her eyes and realized that whatever happened, they would always share something special. "More than. You know I love you, right? But in the right way, now."

"I feel the same. I don't regret anything, though, Gray, not one thing."

He smiled. "Me either. Truly."

She snickered and pretended to count on her fingers. "Let me see; that's two Mallory brothers down ..."

Grady laughed and hugged her again. A beeper sounded. Parker, talking to Jean, checked his message and, to Grady's horror, his face dropped. He glanced up at them.

"It's Flori. She's coding ..."

EVERY TIME she went to see the psychiatrist, she got stronger. Yes, it was painful, and Quilla knew as she sobbed all her fear and anger out that something fundamental inside her was changing. She began to feel herself again, to want to be with Jakob, to be more intimate with him as time passed. But it was difficult. No longer did she need the hard, clinical fucking they had participated in over the last few months. Some days she couldn't bear to think of sex at all.

Quilla would never forget Jakob's gentleness, his patience. Not once did he flinch when she would pull away suddenly, fists balled up, panic rising in her, terror choking her. He would simply wait, a hand on her shoulder, her back, or smoothing her hair until she calmed down. She longed for the early days of their relationship where they would fall into bed easily, all of the time, desperate for that connection. Now she felt some of that feeling coming back.

But her relationship with Marley was fractured. Although she had gone to each session as Marley asked her to, the rift was still there, and Quilla felt enormous sadness and guilt. Marley had gone to Antarctica on another research trip—or rather, she had volunteered to go, and Quilla felt as if she was responsible for her friend's absence.

She had reached out to Nan Applebee, Joel's girlfriend, and the two of them had been growing closer but still, Quilla felt Marley's distance keenly.

After a few weeks of psychiatry, Jakob had suggested a vacation, and now they were on the Mallorys' private island, close to the Hawaiian Islands. From the huge villa, they could see the constant stream of lava from the island's volcano from a distance, and at night it was a strangely serene sight.

The island was stunning, a respite, and a haven. They swam and snorkeled and rediscovered some of that joy they'd found so long ago in Venice and Quilla truly started to believe that everything would be okay again.

THEY GOT to Flori's room as the nurses were frantically giving the young woman resuscitation. To Grady's horror, they had already shocked her twice, but still the flat line screamed out. Dead. Dead. Parker went into emergency mood, cool, calm, utterly professional, and took over from the nursing staff.

Grady, Jean, and Asia stood well back, the younger people hugging Jean to keep her from collapsing in terror as they watched them trying to save her daughter's life.

Parker got a rhythm, to their relief, then immediately listened to her chest. "Okay," he said, "I think it's an embolism, air or a blood clot. Let's get her down to surgery now."

In a whirl, they were all gone, and the three of them stood there, not knowing if they'd ever see Flori alive again.

. . .

ON THE FOURTH NIGHT, they were lying on the sun loungers watching the sun set over the ocean. Jakob looked over at Quilla, stretched out on the lounger, white bikini against her tanned skin, full breasts and soft belly, and long, slender legs. She looked so much happier and healthier than for months now. She sensed his scrutiny and turned her head to smile at him. "What are you thinking about, Mr. Man?"

Jakob grinned. "That impossibly delicious body of yours and what I'd like to do to it right now."

She stretched leisurely. "Do what you will with it, Jakob Mallory; it's all yours."

"Anything?"

"Anything."

He thought about it for a moment. Then, sliding his legs off his chair, he moved to her lounger and straddled it, lifting her legs over his hips. His hands went to the halter strap on her bikini top and released it, her ripe, golden brown breasts freed. He grinned and made a 'wow' shape with his mouth, and she laughed. He drew her hands together and, with her top, bound them above her head.

Quilla wriggled, obviously turned on, as his fingers slid under the side ties of her panties. "Side fastenings, very convenient," he murmured.

"I thought they would be," she whispered and sighed happily as he removed them. Jakob spent his time devouring her luscious body with his eyes, watching her belly rise and fall with her breathing, trailing the tips of his fingers in gentle circles around her navel. He did this for a few minutes, knowing she loved the feeling of him touching her belly, before moving down into her groin, his fingers exploring her dampening sex.

"I want to see you," she murmured, but he shook his head.

"Oh, no, tonight you're all mine; do you understand?"

As he slipped a finger into her velvet warmth, she gasped and nodded.

"Good. I want you to spread your legs a little wider, beautiful, that's it." He moved down so he could taste her, taking the hardening clit into his mouth and sucking on it, teasing it with his tongue, feeling it pulse against his lips. His fingers kneaded the soft flesh of her inner thighs and when he could stand it no longer, he bit down on the soft flesh, hard. He heard her squeak, a little cry of surprise, and glanced up to check that she was okay. She met his gaze, breathless, and she nodded, encouraging him. He grinned and crawled up her body.

"Quilla, do you trust me?"

She nodded, her eyes alive with excitement.

"Good. Because I have an idea ... I'll be right back."

He left her tied to the lounger and went to the closet, where he'd stashed some purchases he'd been making. He hadn't known if she would be up for what he wanted to do, but now ... he grinned to himself and took the box out to the terrace. She wriggled with pleasure when she saw him. The light was fading, so he lit some candles and placed them around the terrace. Then he took the oil from the box, followed by a selection of dildos, blindfolds, lube, and other toys. There was a beautifully supple leather harness that he had chosen especially for Quilla. She grinned as he placed each one carefully on the table. When he was done, he looked at her.

"Is there anything on this table that you wouldn't want me to use?"

She shook her head. "I told you ... anything."

He smiled and kissed her. Then, taking the harness, strapped it slowly around her body, the buttery soft leather crisscrossing around her breasts, more straps around her thighs, under her buttocks.

He sat back and admired her. "Jesus, you're the most beautiful thing on this planet, you know that?"

She smiled, blissed out on love and arousal, but said nothing. He grabbed the bottle of monoi oil and, tipping it gently, poured a little between her breasts, so it ran down her belly and into her cunt. He tipped some of the oil into his hands and rubbed them together, then, as she quivered under his touch, began to massage her soft skin, her breasts, and the soft planes of her belly, then finally down into her shaved sex, the oil slick again her skin. His fingers moving against her swelling, aching sex and she moaned, wanting to be fucked by him.

Jakob smiled. She was completely at his mercy, and the thought was giving him the biggest hard-on of his life. He grabbed one of the dildos, sliding it into her wet and ready sex. Quilla gasped as he moved the toy in and out of her, thrusting harder as she cried out, begging him to put his cock inside her.

"Be patient, my love," he smiled as she groaned in protest. With his free hand, he flicked on a tiny vibrator and held it against her clit, making her scream out as the buzz hit the sensitive cluster of nerves at its tip. He couldn't stop looking at her, helpless under his ministrations and when she came, her body arching up, golden in the light of the candles, he could feel the desperate urge of his body. He ripped the dildo out of her and in one swift movement, tore his underwear off, his cock rearing up, and so ramrod hard, he could hardly stand to touch it, pulling her legs around his hips; he plunged into her, his fingers biting into the soft flesh at her hips.

He fucked her hard, brutally, and she screamed his name over and over again as wave after wave of orgasm ripped through her. His gaze never left her as he shot thick, hot spurts of cum deep inside her, his body jerking and convulsing with the strength of his climax.

God, Quilla, Quilla, Quilla ...

As they both started to recover, he brushed the damp hair away from her forehead, gazing into those lovely green eyes and said the thing he'd been wanting to say since the night he met her.

"Marry me ..."

IT WAS a little after four a.m. when Parker came to find them. He looked exhausted, but smiled at them. "We got her back. She's lost a lot of blood, but we've stabilized her. I'm afraid it looks like she'll be here another couple of weeks, at least, but, fingers crossed, she should be fine."

Grady's knees went, to his embarrassment, and he collapsed onto a chair, breathing hard. Jean thanked Parker, throwing her arms around the young doctor. Asia rubbed Grady's back, blowing out her cheeks with the breath she'd been holding in. Grady looked up at her through tear-filled eyes.

"She's okay?"

Asia smiled. "She is, baby. She is."

It was a more few weeks until Flori was released and when she was, they flew back to Seattle. Jean had given Grady her blessing and in turn, Grady had promised to fly their daughter back to see them whenever they wanted and vice versa.

"Just call," he told Jean and Mac, "We can have you together in less than an hour."

Mac had snorted. "Different world," he'd said, looking around the sumptuous apartment Grady had bought for Flori and himself. Grady grinned; there had been a definite thawing in Mac's attitude to him over the past few weeks. Grady suspected Jean had something to do with it.

"Keep her safe, that's all I ask," Flori's father had said gruffly, and Grady had given him his word.

Now, alone, they grinned at each other. Grady had insisted she have her own room. "I don't want to crowd you. I know how I feel, and that's not going to change, but when you're feeling better, you might rethink ..."

He was cut off by her kiss. "Shut up; there's no way I'm going to change my mind, Grady Mallory. None."

Later, much later, she had gone to sleep in her room, but just as Grady was getting into his own bed, Flori, without a word, padded into his room and got in beside him. She still had heavy bandaging around her abdomen, so she wore pajamas, but in bed she snuggled into his arms. Grady kissed her temple, then chuckled softly.

"This is a whole new way of beginning a relationship for me.," He drew a finger down her cheek. "God, Flori, to think I almost lost you before my dumb ass realized how much you meant to me."

Flori smiled sleepily. "I fell for you that first night," she said, and he wondered in amusement if her pain meds were making her say these words, but she went on. "That's the real reason I let that Kahlo go. I couldn't bear to think of it in anyone else's hands."

Grady grinned as her eyes closed and her breathing became regular. He kissed her gently. "I know exactly what you mean," he whispered and cradling his love, he too fell asleep.

"EVERYONE HERE? Good, good. Welcome, everyone, and hello again to Floriana." Ran Mallory smiled down the long table at them all, and Flori, a little awed by being invited to the family meeting, smiled tentatively back at the patriarch. She had met all of the family gradually, individually.

From the other side of the table, Jakob's new wife, Quilla winked at her. She felt a kinship with the other woman, both of them having survived Gregor Fisk's knife, and Quilla had been so kind to her. It was weird, but Flori had loved each and every one of them. She found Skandar and Hayley hilarious. Nan and Joel felt like protective older siblings; Jakob was serious and crazy about Quilla; and Ran—she had adored him at their first meeting. They were nothing like she imagined a wealthy family to be. Only Kit Mallory was absent, still following his beloved Bo Kennedy around on tour.

Ran cleared his throat. "So, what's on the table is this: we step up the search for Gregor, no expense spared, every possible lead followed. We scour the earth for him, even if it means breaking a few laws here and there. We deliberately antagonize him into trying something, so he makes a mistake. I'm still not sold on that, by the way. I don't want any of you in harm's way."

"Too late, Pops," Grady said, taking Flori's hand. "The harm's been done. Let's nail this fucker."

There was a murmur of assent. Ran rubbed his chin. "Then we have to decide what will antagonize him the most."

Jakob leaned forward. "Gregor's weakness is his own ego; that's pretty obvious. So we target that. We've had news corporations reaching out to both Quilla and Floriana to do interviews on their ordeals. They can tell their story and we can plant things about his lack of success with women, in business, his drug taking."

"My experience was nothing compared to yours, Flori, but if you're up for it, we could do that together." Quilla smiled at her, and Flori nodded.

"Anything to help, really ... put me in a room with that asshole and a baseball bat; I swear to God he'd regret it."

Skandar laughed. "Ninja."

Grady grinned back at him. "You have no idea."

Ran smiled, but his eyes were serious. "Let me be clear. None of you is to deliberately put yourself in danger, do you understand?"

He might be a gentle giant, Flori thought, but Ran Mallory's words carry weight.

Later, at home, she and Grady lay together in bed, kissing, Grady careful not to hurt her. They had yet to make love, due to her injuries, but every night they spent together, skin next to skin, she fell in love with him more.

Grady drew his hand down her body. "Sweet thing, are you okay? You were quiet in the car on the way back."

Flori smiled. "I am, I truly am. More than you could know."

She wasn't lying. She truly was better than she had been for months.

He didn't need to know about the nightmares.

IN SYDNEY, Australia, Bo Kennedy's final sold-out night at the Opera House had just concluded to rapturous applause and she and Kit, having just made wild love in her dressing room, escaped their public and made their way to the restaurant, which was staying open late for them.

The meal was raucous, Bo, still high from performing, was making Kit laugh so much, he had barely touched his food.

Eventually, he caught his breath. "God, baby, have you any idea what it feels like to watch you up there? It's better than any pharma-ceutical high. You soar."

Bo kissed him. "Well, babe, home tomorrow, then ..."

Kit grinned. "Seattle. At last. I can't wait to introduce you to my family. Jakob tells me Quilla and Hayley are already fangirling you, so you know they'll give you a warm welcome."

Bo looked nervous, and Kit kissed her. "I swear, they'll love you as much as I do."

She leaned her forehead against his. "I 'ope so, darlin'."

As they were leaving, just after midnight, some paparazzi found them, and they had to run the gauntlet of flashing lights to get to their car.

Kit yanked open the door and tugged Bo towards him ...

Which was the moment the shots rang out ...

7

PART SEVEN: THREATEN ME

S eattle. 6 a.m.

Nan groaned loudly as the alarm clock went off. "Shut that thing off." She burrowed back under the cover.

Joel, already up and showered, chuckled and bent over the bed, tugged the covers from her face and kissed her. "I hate to tell you this, but you have class in an hour, and I have to go close on the new sports club. So, up and at 'em, beautiful."

She stared at him sulkily. "How about if I go sign some paperwork, and you go deal with some feral eighth graders?"

Joel reached under the comforter and grabbed her ankle. "Ha. No deal," he said, dragging her from the bed and hustling her into the shower. She stood obediently while he stripped her, then wound her arms around his neck. "You know what would wake me up?" she purred as she nipped at his bottom lip with her teeth. Joel feigned innocence for a second. Then, growling, he scooped a giggling Nan into his arms and under the shower.

. . .

SYDNEY, 11:00 p.m.

"OH, of course, the paps are here," Bo Kennedy grumbled as Kit helped her into her coat. She kissed him. "Thanks, babe, and thanks for dinner."

"Anything for my girl." Kit leaned his forehead against hers. "I love you, smushface."

"And I love you, you big American gobshite." She grinned widely. "Now, take me back to the hotel and screw me into next week."

"As you wish, your majesty," Kit grinned, holding open the door. "Here, take my hand."

He pulled her through the throng of flashing lights to the car. He turned back to grin at her.

One gunshot, then two more. Quick. Decisive.

Final.

SEATTLE, 6:30 a.m.

SKANDAR MALLORY GRINNED up at his gorgeous girlfriend as she moved on top of him, her vaginal muscles tightening around his swollen cock, gripping and pulling, sending almost unbearable pleasure ripping through his body. He gripped her hips as she breathlessly thrust harder onto him. He came before she did, his body arching up, and as Hayley moaned out her own climax, he gathered her to him and kissed her deeply. They lay facing each other, catching their breath.

"Why can't we just do that all day?" he said, puffing, "Instead of all of this adult responsibility and work and that crap."

"Making billions hitting a ball around some grass," she intoned back at him, then grinning.

"Hey," he said, smiling, "There are clay and hard courts too."

She rolled onto her back. "It's probably best we don't fuck all day; there might be some chafing issues."

Skandar laughed out loud. "Well, that ruined the moment. You are the best part of my day, Hayley Applebee, even if you're killing my hard-on."

Hayley laughed and rolled back on top of him. "That thing would survive nuclear war," she grinned. "At the end of time, it'll be cockroaches, Twinkies, and your boner."

Skandar groaned. "Stop. It'll retract into nothing if you carry on like that."

She giggled and reached down to stroke him. "Hmmm ... wonder what we could do about that?"

Skandar rolled her onto her back and hitched her legs around his hips. "I wonder..."

SYDNEY, 10:30 p.m.

BLOOD. Blooming red on white. Screaming. Panic. Paparazzi scurrying away from the scene, security desperately looking for the gun.

And in the midst of the melee, brokenhearted pleading of "No, please, please ..."

SEATTLE, 8:00 a.m.

HER SMALL HAND on his chest was one of Jakob Mallory's favorite ways to wake up. He looked down at Quilla's divine, serene face as she slept beside him. *My wife.* After he'd proposed to her on the island, they'd flown to the big island and found a justice of the peace to marry them the very next day. Jakob had told her it was entirely up to her whether she wanted to keep her own name and she told him that she would.

"Just so I don't disappear into being a Mallory wife," she grinned, but her eyes were wary.

"That would never happen, Ms. Chen," he grinned.

"How about I'm Mrs. Mallory when it's just you and me and the family?"

"I like that."

Now, he took her hand in his, rubbing his finger over the small platinum band. His wife. He never thought he would be married, especially not after he'd started on the drugs, spiraling down so fast it was almost unbelievable. Then Venice, then Quilla, hauling his ass out of the drink and making him fall so in love with her, then Gregor and his knife. They'd been through so much together in the space of a few months.

Quilla stirred and opened her eyes, smiling up at him. "You're still here," she said sleepily. "No work today?"

"Nah." He kissed her. "Thought I'd take the day off, hang with my woman."

"When's she coming over?"

He laughed and covered her body with his. His cock was already stiffening as she hooked a leg around his waist, arching her body up into his. He buried his face in her neck, trailing his lips down across her collarbone as Quilla slid her hot sex along his thigh. He looked into her eyes and she smiled.

"Take me now," she whispered, and grinning, he launched into her— God, that gasp when his cock found her center—and began to thrust, his cock thickening and swelling inside her. He kissed her throat as she threw her head back, lost in the sweet sensation of their fucking. He knew he would never get tired of making love to her, talking to her, laughing with her. He'd told her once he didn't want kids—he didn't even remember that person now—he wanted a hundred little Quillas running about the place.

Afterward, they showered and screwed again under the hard pelt of water, Quilla shrieking as he turned the cold water onto her hard nipples—Christ, the sight of the water bouncing off them made him so hard, he had to have her again, against the wall of the shower.

She was making breakfast when he finished dressing—Spanish omelets and fresh fruit. He sat across the breakfast bar and studied her as they ate. She finally was looking like that girl he had met in Venice again, happy, relaxed, even though the threat to her life was in no way diminished. Gregor was still out there, still obsessed with her, with killing her. Jakob risked it and asked her.

Quilla shrugged. "Talking about it helped, and now that the FBI have given up on him saying anything when he calls—and I don't have to listen to it— I'm feeling optimistic. Stronger. I don't underestimate the threat; rather, I'm living in the moment."

Jakob was silent for a moment. "Quilla ... my love, I said once to you that I didn't know if I wanted kids. That was monumentally selfish of me and ... no, let me finish," he smiled as she started to protest. "What I should have said is this. I didn't want kids then. With anyone else. But I do want them with you. I want a bunch of 'em. If you want them with me."

She was staring at him, bemused. "What brought this on?"

Jakob grinned. "Just me, growing up at last. I might be catching you up in emotional maturity. What do you say?"

Quilla laughed. "Today on Mallory—life-changing decisions over breakfast. Can I think about it?"

He clinked his juice glass with hers. "Of course. And I don't mean right now, of course, just something to think about for later."

Quilla sipped her juice to hide her grin. "Charlie Chaplin had kids in his seventies."

"I'm not that old, Quilla Chen," but he laughed. He reached over and stroked her cheek, and she leaned into his touch.

"We made it, Mrs. Mallory. We really did."

SYDNEY, Australia, 11:00 p.m.

. . .

RED AND BLUE LIGHTS. Paramedics and police. SWAT scouring the streets. The press, the paps, starting to drift back towards the scene, arguing with the police blocking them from taking pictures, shouting that they were there, they got shot at, too, they could tell them what happened—all to no avail.

The paramedics listening to lungs filling with blood, horrific gargling sounds, shouting instructions to each other, compressions and air. The lifting of a prone body into the ambulance. The comforting voices, the fake optimism.

The sound of someone dying.

SEATTLE, Washington, 9:15 a.m.

FLORIANA MORGAN SAT on the couch gazing out of the window at the panoramic view of Seattle. Grady Mallory had bought this apartment for her; she couldn't quite believe it. Of course, now it was their home; they shared a bed, a life together. It was all so new and unreal somehow.

She shifted uncomfortably in her seat; her injuries from the brutal attack Gregor Fisk had unleashed on her. The healing muscles and organs and flesh were the reason she and Grady had not yet made love ... and it was frustrating as all hell.

She sighed unconsciously. Flori looked around her, everything she could want—except to climb all over Grady's incredible body, feel him inside of her ... God ...

"Hey, cutie." Grady, dressed in a vintage tee and blue jeans, was coming through from the reception hall—obviously having been chatting to their security team. Yup, she thought, we have a security team.

"Hey, gorgeous." She held her hand out to him, and he took it, flopping down next to her, then looking aghast as she winced. Damn you, torn abs— she gritted her teeth against the pain. Grady stroked her hair.

"Still in pain?"

It was useless denying it, but she tried to lighten the mood. "Damn belly doesn't want me to get laid," she grumbled and he half smiled, but she could see the concern in his eyes.

"Hey ... I'm okay. It's just taking more time, probably because of the embolism. But I'm still here." She touched his face and then brushed her lips against his. "Still here."

"Forever. Promise?"

Her heart missed a beat and she smiled, tears in her eyes. God, this man ... "I promise. For as long as you want me."

"Forever."

"Forever, then. I love you, Grady Mallory."

His kiss became more urgent, and she moaned and pulled away. "I can't, not yet. God, I wish ..."

"Ssh, it's okay. I want you so bad, but I'm not prepared to risk your health."

He sat back and ran a hand through his messy mop of dark blond hair and sighed. Flori held his hand. "What did Riggs and Murtaugh want?" she asked, nodding towards the reception.

Grady smiled. "Nothing to report. Look, Jakob gave me an idea, and I want to run it by you. I know you want to see colleges and decide where you want to finish your Ph.D., but what do you say to a vacation first?"

Flori looked excited. "You mean that island? The one I've been dreaming about since Quilla told me about it? That island?"

Grady laughed at her childlike glee. "The very one. Weirdly, I'm the only one of us who has never been, so it'll be new to me, too."

"We can discover it together."

"We can ... the island and each other. For example, I've never asked ... do you like hiking? Swimming? Exploring? Or are you a sun lounger and paperback kind of girl?"

"Definitely the first, but I don't mind what we do, as long as I'm with you."

"Right back at cha. So, I'll set it up?"

Flori hesitated. "Can we wait a couple of weeks? The thing is, from what Quilla has told me, the island has a very sexy, very sensual vibe and I want to be ... ready."

Grady's grin was definitely a shit-eating one. "Oh, yeah," he said, making her laugh. He kissed her. "It's a deal, gorgeous."

Flori was thrilled, and she hugged him, wincing slightly as her stomach muscles protested. "It'll be like the official start of our relationship."

Grady buried his face in her hair. "The beginning of our life together."

"The beginning of our lives ..."

Sydney, Australia, 12:15 a.m.

"GUNSHOT TO THE CHEST, no exit, vitals low and falling. Saline and O-neg were given, but patient is losing it as fast as we can get it in."

Straight to the operating theater, the surgeon ready for their V.I.P. patient. Anesthesia—even though there was still no response.

Ten-blade. Rib-spreaders. Manual heart massage for nearly an hour. The surgeon looked at the clock. "The other one?"

"Gunshot wound to shoulder, not serious."

The surgeon, getting exhausted now. Another half hour. Checking the vitals, shaking his head.

"Not coming back. I'm calling it. Time of death, one fifty-three a.m."

SEATTLE, Washington, 11:00

"MARLEY?"

Marley Griffin turned around in the line to see who had called her name. Randall Mallory, casually dressed, sweater and jeans, waved his paper at her. "Lovely to see you."

Marley looked at the customer behind her in the line. "You go ahead. Hi, Randall, how are you?"

"Good, thank you. We haven't seen you at the big house of late."

Marley grimaced. "I don't think Quilla wants to see me."

Ran shook his head. "Give her a chance. She's a lot better now, more relaxed. "

Marley gave him a half smile. "Ran, I appreciate you trying to mediate, but maybe it's for the best. We move in such different circles now."

The barista called to her. Ran stepped up. "Let me buy you a coffee—do you have time to talk?"

Marley hesitated. She really didn't want to talk about the rift between her best friend and herself—but Ran was such a friendly, warm man, she felt relaxed in his company—and she could do with a stress reliever. "Okay."

They sat in a small booth away from the main café and away from the large flat screen TV which flashed rolling news in silence.

Marley stirred her flat white and smiled at Ran shyly. "Thanks for the coffee, Ran. Look, I wish things had worked out with Quilla, but sometimes friends drift apart."

Ran nodded, but she could see he wasn't convinced. "Look, pardon me for interfering; I have a tendency to want to make peace. Marley ... did you know Quilla and Jakob are married now?"

Marley felt a lump in her throat, but she nodded. "I read it in the paper," she said shortly, and looked away from him so he couldn't see the tears in her eyes. He saw them anyway and she felt his hand cover hers.

"I'm sorry, Marley. I didn't mean to upset you."

"'S okay," she said thickly, then cleared her throat. "Let's talk about something else; I haven't seen you in here before."

Ran smiled. "I'll admit, it's my first time. The coffeehouse I'd been going to for years closed down and I'm loath to frequent the big chains. I found this one by accident; there's a great secondhand bookstore at the end of the block."

Marley's eyes lit up. "You go to The Armchair? I love that store ... although I wouldn't have thought that a billionaire would need to shop secondhand."

Randall laughed and she noticed just how handsome he was, his dark blond hair streaked through with gray, and his hazel eyes kind and intelligent. "Marley Griffin, surely you of all people must know and appreciate the heady scent of old books?"

She inclined her head, conceding his point. "I guess I have a fixed idea in my head of how billionaires are supposed to act. Forgive my prejudice."

Ran studied her. "You still don't like Jakob, though, do you? He can be bloody-minded, surly, domineering," he said of his eldest son, "But he adores Quilla and would do anything for her. He never saw this thing with Gregor coming."

Marley leaned forward. "But that's my point. How could he not have?"

"How many times do you hear the news of neighbors of people who have committed atrocities s saying 'But he seemed like such a good guy? But she loved those kids?' People are blinkered." He sighed, suddenly seeming tired. "We warned Jakob about Gregor. When my wife was alive, she took an instant dislike to the man, but I told her not to say anything to Jakob. Let him make his own mistakes."

He was silent for a long moment, then smiled sadly at her. "So, if you're to blame anyone, blame me."

Marley shook her head, suddenly feeling emotional. "I could never ... you're impossible to dislike, Randall Mallory, gosh damn it." She laughed, and he smiled.

"Good. Listen, this was fun. Say I'm in here tomorrow morning. If you're around, I'd like to buy you a coffee and talk some more. I'd like to know about your work."

Marley flushed pink but nodded. "I'd like that."

"Good." Ran stood and held out his hand. She shook it, smiling, enjoying the feel of her small hand in his big one. "Tomorrow then, Marley Griffin."

"Tomorrow." She watched him walk out, get to the door, and glance back at her before leaving. Lovely, lovely man, she thought. Her eyes drifted around the coffeehouse and settled on the flat screen. A reporter was talking to the camera; a Breaking News banner ribbon across the bottom of the screen. Wherever the reporter was, it was nighttime, she pondered idly.

Then her heart constricted as a photograph of Kit Mallory and Bo Kennedy flashed up on the screen. In horror, she read the words ... shooting ... injuries ... police ... Marley stood and ran. Yanking open the door to the coffeehouse, she darted out into the street, looking around wildly for Randall Mallory. She saw a figure just entering the bookstore along the block, and she started towards it. Pushing open the door of the store, she searched the shop for him.

She heard a cellphone ring and his voice answering it. She followed the sound of his voice and stopped when she saw him.

The look of utter desolation on his face told her everything she needed to know.

JOEL MALLORY WAS ABOUT to sign the paperwork to begin work on his first sports center when he heard the door open. He looked up and was surprised to see Nan, her face pale, her expression one of numb disbelief. He went to her immediately, his arms wrapping around her.

"What? What, baby, what is it?"

She stared up at him, shaking her head. "Joel ... it's Kit ..." She couldn't say any more. Joel pushed her away, staring at her in angry confusion.

"What? Damn it, Nan, what about Kit?"

She gasped in a breath which turned to a sob. "There's been a shooting, in Sydney ... Kit and Bo ... it's all over the news."

Joel kept shaking his head. "No ... no ... what ... I need to call my dad."

He started to walk toward the door when she called him back. She walked up to him.

"Your dad called me, Joel, to come bring you to the big house. He's on his way to Sydney ... Joel, God, I'm so sorry."

He was trembling now, ice in his veins. "Just say it, Nan. Say it out loud or I won't believe it. Say it."

Tears were pouring down Nan's face now. "I'm so sorry, Joel ..."

"Stop fucking saying you're sorry and tell me!"

His roar filled the room, and Nan quailed under it, but took his hand. "Joel..." Her voice was cracking. "Kit was shot in the chest. They took him to the hospital and tried to save him, but they couldn't. Joel, Kit died."

Every single cell in his body was both numb and yet screaming. "Kit's dead?"

Nan nodded and now he couldn't breathe, couldn't think. His brother. His twin. Gone forever. His world collapsed.

Kit was dead.

A MONTH LATER ...

RAN MALLORY STARED out of the window of his mansion. Winter was on its way; the fall leaves had dropped, and the bleak look of the trees outside mirrored how Ran felt deep in his soul. He was at a loss to know how he should cope with the loss of his son.

Kit simply hadn't stood a chance when the shooting started. He had shoved a bleeding and injured Bo into the waiting car and in the second it took for him to steady himself, the bullet slammed into his chest. The doctors at Sydney hospital had worked on him for longer than they usually would, knowing the international spotlight would be on them, but he'd been dead by the time he got to the hospital.

Ran swallowed the scream that always seemed to be threatening to escape him now. For the last month, the family had gone through the motions— public statements with vows to find Kit's murderer, the funeral, the avoidance of the media since then. The press was relentless in their search for new angles, for clues. They'd rehashed every story from the last year, and the coverage was blanket. None of the family dared turn on the radio or the TV.

At the funeral, he'd help to support Bo Kennedy. The young woman, her arm in a sling from being shot in the shoulder, was pale and shell-shocked, her usual merry and gregarious nature smashed by her grief. Ran had liked her very much and asked her to stay with them for a while. She had politely refused. "It's too painful, Ran. At the moment, I just want to be with Tiger and my mum. When I see you all—and especially Joel ... I can't. I'd like to in the future, just not now."

He'd understood, as had the rest of the family. Asia, Kit's ex-wife, had come to the house as soon as the news broke. She was shattered, devastated. Her partner, Parker Thomas, had accompanied her, and Ran had been impressed by the young doctor's grace and compassion.

"Hey."

Ran turned to see Marley smiling at him. He kissed her cheek. "Thank you for coming."

"Of course."

Over the last month, since that day in the coffeehouse, since she'd chased him down to support him, Marley had been Randall's rock. The young scientist canceled plans and put her own life on hold to support him through the worst time in his life. She made herself available twenty-four-seven in case he needed to talk, or to sob. She became his best friend. Ran was also glad that something good had come from the tragedy; Marley and Quilla had grown close again. Not for the first time, Ran realized that the women in his family were the stronger ones.

"How is it today, one to ten?" Marley said as they sat down outside on the deck. The day was cool but sunny, and Ran's dogs ran around, playing, barking, making them smile.

"Maybe an eight," Ran began, then saw Marley's skeptical face and sighed. "A ten. I can't imagine a time when it won't be a ten. How could it be?"

Marley put her hand on his. "I can't answer that, Ran. But I'm here, so talk to me. Or don't, entirely up to you. Have you heard anything from the Australian police?"

Ran nodded. "From the weapon used, they think it was a professional hit ... God..." He choked on the words. Marley interlinked her fingers with his in a gesture that had become natural between them. Ran drew in a breath. "So, they have a few suspects in mind, but I don't have any doubt who is behind it."

Marley grimaced. "Fisk."

"He won't get away with this, any of it, Quilla, Flori, Kit. We're throwing everything at the search; I don't care if it takes every last penny I have. Gregor Fisk is going to pay for what he's done." He looked over at her unhappily. "I am worried that by being here, you'll be on his radar. Selfishly, though, I could not have gotten through this last month without you, Marley."

She smiled at him. "Don't worry about me, Ran; I can look after myself."

He squeezed her fingers but said nothing. Marley tried to say something to comfort him but found herself lost for words. She desperately wanted to take away some of her friend's pain, but had no idea how. The rest of the family was equally fractured. Joel, Kit's twin, had barely spoken to anyone since Kit's death, especially not his girlfriend, Nan.

"He's pushing me away," Nan told her and Quilla, tears rolling down her sweet face. "I can't reach him."

Quilla was having the opposite problem; Jakob, already paranoid about her safety as Gregor's obsession with her grew, was now suffocating her. The independent Quilla was having trouble not becoming annoyed at his constant vigilance. "He tells me if I can go out or not well, he tries to. Then when I disagree, it turns into an argument." Quilla looked tired. Marley regretted the weeks they had spent distant— it seemed so ridiculous now.

Grady Mallory, the youngest of the brothers, had been the most collected of all of them, quietly supporting his father, his brothers, his nephew. His young girlfriend, Floriana, knew Gregor's violence firsthand, having only just survived him herself. She told them that Grady would only drop the façade of calmness at home, with her.

"I think it does him good to just let go at night and be as vulnerable as the rest." Flori had said, and Quilla had hugged her.

"You do him good," she said. The two women, both survivors of Fisk, shared a bond that Marley felt was healthy for them both.

"I don't want to think of the fact that he's out there, planning another murder." Ran's voice brought her out of her reverie.

"Ran, you'll drive yourself crazy like that," Marley said firmly, and he chuckled softly.

"You're right. Stay and have supper with me, Marley?"

She smiled at him. "You'll get tired of me."

"Never."

GRADY MALLORY CAME HOME to find Flori had prepared a romantic dinner for them both, and he smiled gratefully at her. Despite her youth, she had known exactly how to comfort him this last, horrific month. Tonight, she was dressed in a simple pale blue dress that fell to a good three inches above her knees, bare feet, makeup free face, and her dark hair tumbling down her back.

"God, you look beautiful," he said, wrapping his arms around her. She grinned up at him.

"Thank you, baby. I hope you're hungry."

Grady kissed her, savoring the taste of her lips. "Damn right, I am," he said, his words loaded with meaning. Flori pressed her body against his.

"Funny you should say that..." She hooked a leg around his waist, and he picked her up, her slight body light. "I saw my doctor today. Guess what?"

Grady growled, knowing exactly what she was going to say. "This supper you've made ... can it be reheated?"

Flori giggled, her face flushing scarlet, her breath hitching in her throat. "You bet it can." She shrieked with laughter as Grady whisked her into the bedroom and laid her on the bed. She kissed him, her eyes alive with desire, with excitement. "I've waited so long for this moment," she whispered, and Grady chuckled.

"Me, too, so no pressure, then ..." He kissed her throat and trailed his lips across her collarbone, making her shiver with pleasure. His fingers found the buttons of her dress and slowly, he undressed her, kissing every piece of skin as he exposed it until she was gasping. When his mouth found her sex, Flori moaned as his tongue lashed around her clit, his teeth grazing the soft peachy folds of her labia.

"God ... Gray ..."

He grinned up at her. "You're beautiful, baby..."

He crawled up her body to kiss her mouth as she reached to cup his cock through his jeans.

"I want to taste you," she whispered and grinning, took her turn to move down the bed. Her small, gentle hands freed his cock from his pants and then her warm, wet mouth was on him, sweeping over the wide crest as it grew and hardened, the tip quivering under her teasing tongue.

As he grew unbearably hard, he lifted her on top of him, his fingers spreading the labia, exposing her wet and ready vagina for him. As he pushed into her for the first time, they both gave long sighs of release, the waiting for this moment making it even sweeter, smiling and gasping as they make love.

Grady ran his hands down over her slender body; the full breasts plump in his hands; the small brown nipples hardening at his touch. The vivid scars from her wounds, from the surgeries, were still bright pink, but he stroked his finger pads gently over them, sliding his thumb into the deep hollow of her navel. Flori was breathless, her thighs tight against him, her skin dewy with sweat.

As their arousal grew, Grady deftly flipped over, sliding her beneath him so he could drive himself ever deeper inside her, her legs clamped around his hips. His hands pinned hers to the bed, and their eyes met and locked. Nothing existed apart from the two of them at this moment, bodies tangled, moving in rhythm.

Grady watched as Flori came, her lovely face flushing pink, her lips parting as the orgasm hit her. God, you are so, so lovely, he thought, and felt his body tense and explode in a hot rush, pumping deep inside her, pleasure making his head whirl.

As they caught their breaths, they stared at each other, kissing, not wanting the connection to fade.

"I am so in love with you, Floriana Morgan," Grady murmured against her lips, feeling them curl up in a smile.

"You are the love of my life," she said simply, and Grady grinned.

"Damn straight." He cupped her face in his palm. "You make everything better, Flori. Everything. Thank you for this last month."

"I didn't do anything you wouldn't have—that you did do, in New Orleans. That's why my heart is so sure about you. I'm so glad I met you, Grady Mallory; I would rather take Gregor's knife over and over than to have never met you."

Grady winced. "Don't say that, God, please, Flori."

"Sorry." She looked contrite. "That was a poor comparison. What I mean is, it terrifies me to think that we may never have met."

Grady kissed her. "I don't think that was possible—I would have found you somehow."

Flori laughed. "You think?"

"Absolutely. No doubt."

She kissed him. "Are you hungry?"

He considered. "Not really. You?"

"Me neither."

Her hand drifted down his body to his cock and he grinned. "Ready to go again?" He rolled on top of her, and she wound her arms around his neck.

"Always with you ... always..."

QUILLA BARELY HAD time to say hello to Jakob before he was stripping her. He'd been at work all day and had come home angry. She knew he was angry by the way he barked a hello then launched himself at her, kissing her fiercely, his mouth so rough she could taste blood. He'd been like this for weeks, angry, brutal, wanting sex, wanting that release, needing it, and Quilla, a little frightened by his machismo, went along with it. After all, she had felt the same thing after Gregor's attack on her.

Jakob had taken Kit's death harder than anyone, with the exception of Joel. His guilt, his anger, and grief were palpable in the way he talked and moved. He had the same look in his eyes that he'd had all those months ago, standing on that bridge in Venice, ready to end his life. Quilla was terrified he'd start using again, so when he came home, already revved up, she went along with it, letting him fuck her in any way that he wanted to, to get that anger out. Afterward, he would be calmer, so she figured, if it helped ...

He led her over to the wall-to-ceiling windows that looked over the city, the Seattle evening, cloudy. He had dimmed the lights and as he pushed her against the window, the glass cold on her breasts, her belly, he took her from behind, thrusting his diamond-hard cock into her, clamping her hands to the glass with his own. He fucked hard and fast, slamming his cock into her as deep as he could, groaning her name over and over as he buried his face in her hair.

He took her again almost immediately, sweeping her onto the carpet and thrusting in again. His eyes were almost crazed, and Quilla closed her own so she would not feel afraid of him. Later, after they'd showered and eaten a light supper, she curled up against him on the couch. He kissed her forehead.

"Are you okay, baby?" Quilla stroked her husband's face with her fingertips and smiled when he turned to kiss them.

"I honestly don't know, sweetheart. I think I'm pulling it together, then, by the end of the day, I've been thinking about Kit and Gregor and what he's done to us all, and then I'm so angry. You are the only thing that helps, Quilla. Darling ... I'm sorry if I seem to be ... I just need you."

"You have me," she whispered. "Forever. Whatever you need, I'm here for." She pulled his head onto her chest, wanting to soothe him, pressing her lips against his hair. "I love you, husband mine."

He gave a low chuckle. "Is it weird that I can't believe it's only a few months that we've been married?"

"I know. This time last year, we didn't know each other, and now we're an old married couple."

"Pipe and slippers."

She laughed. "Let's just go to bed, baby; I'll make you forget everything."

. . .

LATER, when Quilla was asleep, Jakob lay awake, fighting his fatigue. He didn't want to sleep, didn't want the nightmares that had plagued him for months. They were always the same; Gregor Fisk—or lately, several Gregor Fisks—hurting his family, torturing them, killing them. The worst ones were always about Quilla and when sleep finally overcame him, tonight's was no different.

They were back on the island, lying on the deck, surrounded by candles, making love, Quilla naked and glorious in the leather harness he loved her in. She was on top of him, smiling down at him as she rode him, looking so, so beautiful that he had tell her over and over how much he loved her. She opened her mouth to answer him ...

There was a weird swooshing sound. Quilla gasped and jerked. Jakob, confused, watched in horror as blood started to pour from her navel. Another whoosh. A red wound appeared an inch above the first. Quilla looked confused, scared, her blood, too much blood, gushing from her. Another whoosh—another red dot on her honeyed skin and then he knew. Bullet wounds. Another bullet drilled into her stomach. No no no no ...

And then Gregor was there, laughing as he shot her again and again as she jerked and cried out. Jakob couldn't move, couldn't help her, and couldn't shout as he watched Quilla being murdered in front of him. Please, no, stop, he wanted to scream at Gregor. Now he understood the whooshing sound—a silencer screwed onto the muzzle of an impossibly big gun.

Something in his brain told him this isn't real; this isn't real, but when Gregor pressed the muzzle against Quilla's flesh before bending to kiss her, Jakob finally screamed. Gregor emptied the chamber into Quilla's body then let her flop, at the brink of death, to the ground. Her lovely eyes were staring sightlessly at him, and he screamed her name over and over as Gregor delivered his final blow, a bullet to her heart ... .

"Jakob! Jakob!" How was she calling him? She was dead, he knew that and ...

"Jakob, wake up; you're hurting me, Jakob!"

He opened his eyes and, with a start, realized Quilla, very much alive, was struggling underneath him. He had pinned her, wrapping his thickly muscled arms around her body, and was squeezing her so tightly she was struggling to breathe. He let her go immediately, devastated, begging her forgiveness.

Eventually, she calmed him down, holding him gently, stroking his head. She managed to coax the truth about his nightmares out from him, and although she paled at the description of her murder, she told him calmly over and over that it wasn't real. She made him get in the shower to cool down his overheated body, then made him a drink, scotch, the way he liked it. Wrapped in her robe, she sat with him until he had truly calmed down.

Jakob stroked her face. "I'm sorry I hurt you, baby; you know I would never do that consciously."

"I do know that, I swear. But I think you should see someone, a therapist. Despite my reservations, it really did help me."

Jakob smiled. "I know it did, but I'm not sure I'd be so receptive."

"Why not?"

"Too cynical. Too jaded."

"Bullshit," she said with a smile. "If the next thing that comes out of your mouth is 'too old,' I will beat your ancient ass."

He laughed, grateful for her trying to lighten the mood. "I will think about it, I swear."

Quilla nodded. "Good."

His phone, abandoned on the counter when he'd come in, began to buzz. He accepted the call, checking the time. Three-o-five a.m. He frowned.

"Hey, Dad, what's up?"

He listened as his dad spoke, his jaw setting grimly. "Yeah. Okay, I'll meet you there."

Quilla raised her eyebrows at him as he ended the call and he nodded at her. "Sweetheart, let's get packing. We're going to Australia. They've got the shooter."

. . .

NAN WATCHED JOEL PACKING, throwing clothes haphazardly into a bag. He didn't look at her as he relayed to her what his father had told him. "It might be best for you and Hayley to go to the big house while we're away. There's more security. Hank will drive you to work and back."

Nan nodded, her chest tight. "I could come with you – "

"No. I don't want you dealing with all that. Better you and Hayley are safe. Skandar will be back on Saturday from the tournament."

Nan was silent for a time, not trusting herself to speak. Joel had been distant and withdrawn since Kit's murder, the grief written all over his face. Nan felt him slipping away from her daily; they hadn't made love since before the shooting, and he spent long hours at the construction site for his first sports center. They would eat in silence, Nan having given up asking him about his day.

It was only when they were sitting down together, reading of watching the T.V. that she felt any closeness. He would hold her hand for a time, or leave his arm across the back of the couch, so his fingers stroked her hair but after a time, again, when they went to sleep, Nan felt cold and lonely.

Now, he didn't want her with him in Australia. She got up and went into the kitchen to hide the tears that were threatening. A few escaped as she grabbed a glass and filled it from the tap.

"What's wrong?"

She turned to find Joel watching her from the doorway. She put down her glass and tried to smile. "Nothing. Can I help you pack?"

"It's done. Nan ..." he came to take her in his arms. "Please, I don't mean to be like this. I'm trying to hold it together for my dad, my family, and if I get emotional ... I think I might break. I love you, Nan, please just ... bear with me."

She gazed up at him and smoothed the frown lines between his eyes. "I can help you relax," she whispered and pressed her lips to his. She felt him respond briefly, then pull away.

"I can't. I'm sorry. Look, I'll call you when we get to Sydney. Take care of yourself—don't go anywhere without Hank or Gus."

And he was gone. She heard the front door close, lock, and she let out a sob. Big mistake. She couldn't hold back then, and it was five minutes before she could manage to get to her phone and call her sister.

Hayley knew what was wrong immediately. "Hang on in there, sis; I'm on my way."

RANDALL MALLORY SHOOK hands with the Chief Inspector of Police in the Sydney station. They'd arrived less than an hour ago and were swiftly taken by town car to the place where the shooter was being held.

"His name is Daniel Harland, thirty-two, unemployed."

"He's talking?"

"Singing like a damn canary."

The inspector motioned to a room, and Randall, Jakob, and Joel went in to see two-way glass and a prisoner in the next room. He looked blandly normal. Ran and Jakob exchanged a glance as Joel fixed his eye on the man who had killed his twin brother. Daniel Harland looked relaxed, even amused as two detectives questioned him.

"Obviously, I can't let you into the room to hear what he has to say but, because it's you, Mr. Mallory, I'm going to let you listen in. I'm putting my neck out for you here, so ..."

Randall nodded. "Of course. I appreciate it."

The inspector nodded at Jakob and Joel and flicked a switch. A moment later, they heard the detectives talking.

"So, to go over this again, you're admitting to shooting and killing Christopher—known as Kit—Mallory on the night of the seventh."

"Yeah."

Jakob's eyebrows shot up. "He's American." The inspector nodded.

The questioning continued. "Can you tell us why you murdered Mr. Mallory?"

"I was paid to shoot him and his girlfriend. I got off a shot at the girlfriend, but he managed to get her to safety before I could kill her. I didn't miss him, as you know."

"Who hired you to carry out the killings?"

"Gregor Allan Fisk."

Even Ran couldn't hold back a gasp at the open way he'd just admitted Gregor was responsible. Even the interviewing detectives looked bemused, and Harland grinned.

"You look surprised, detectives. Mr. Fisk asked me to give you a message –give the Mallory's a message."

"And what would that be?"

Harland glanced up at the two-way glass, as if he knew the Mallorys were watching him. "None of them are safe. He's going to kill every last one of them—their women first. He's hired contractors to deal with all of them. All of them except one."

Jakob looked like he knew what Harland was about to say. Ran put a calming hand on his son's shoulder.

"Which one? And why not?"

Harland smiled nastily. "The eldest son's woman. The Asian one. Fisk says she's all his. He's looking forward to doing her properly this time, he says. I wouldn't want to be her at the end."

Jakob looked like he could throw up; Joel banged on the glass angrily, and the detectives looked up.

"Okay, let's go." The inspector gave Joel a withering look, which he ignored. Ran's lips pursed together.

"I think we've seen enough," he said, and Jakob gave him a sharp nod. Ran knew his son would want to get back to Quilla, safe in the hotel with an armed guard, after hearing what Harland would have to say.

The inspector walked them out. Ran thanked him. "But he didn't really tell us anything we didn't already know. Inspector, have your people been looking for Fisk?"

"You can bet we have," the man nodded. "We've had our armed response scouring the city, all airports, train stations and bus stations have been put on watch. If Fisk is here, we'll find him."

· · ·

"THAT MAN DOESN'T HAVE a clue who he is dealing with," said Joel when they were back in the town car. "Does he honestly think that they can get Fisk when we haven't been able to find him? With our resources?"

"Give him a break," Jakob muttered. "What's he supposed to say to us? Sorry, mate, we know we can't catch him, so we're not going to bother at all?"

Joel's grim face suddenly broke out into a smile. "What the hell was that accent? Welsh?"

Even Jakob cracked a smile. "Yeah, yeah."

Ran chuckled. God, it felt good to laugh for once. Ran had felt like he'd been robbed of joy since Kit had died, that he'd never feel that lightness in his soul again. He rubbed his face.

"Well, looks like we'll need to ramp up security and extend the search."

"Where to, Mars?" Jakob asked, incredulously. "Dad, we're looking in every corner of the globe. I think we need to think about changing tack. Draw Gregor out."

Ran shot his eldest son a look. "And how would we do that, Jakob? The only thing we know for sure is that Gregor wants to kill your wife himself. Are you suggesting we use Quilla as bait?"

"Hell, no. God, Dad, I don't know, I'm just thinking out loud." Jakob slumped back into his seat and they drove in silence for a while.

"Quilla wouldn't hesitate," Jakob said eventually. "To save the rest of us, she would sacrifice herself, and that's why this is not even going to be a consideration. Not that I would ever put her in harm's way. Jesus, I don't even know why he's fixated on her."

Ran smiled softly. "Don't you?" and Jakob had to look away.

"There's a difference between desiring someone and wanting to kill them, Dad." His voice broke, and Ran relented.

"Psychopaths don't work to the same logic as the rest of us, son. Anyway, this subject is null and void. No bait. No risking anyone's lives. We do this the right way."

Joel made a noise then, and when his father and brother looked at him, he shrugged. "I hope by 'right' you mean we get the bastard. Because I don't care if it's legal or not, I'm going to kill that man. I'm going to rip him limb from limb and enjoy every fucking minute.

HAYLEY AND NAN, now moved to Ran's mansion, greeted Skandar as he returned from his tournament. He'd been beaten in the second round but, he told them, he couldn't have cared less. All he wanted was to be at home with his family.

"I offered to fly out to Oz, but Dad said he'd rather I was here with you."

Hayley hugged him tightly. "So glad you're here."

Skandar buried his face in her neck. "God, me, too, baby." He kissed her, then grinned at Nan. "Hey, sis/step-mom, how are you?"

Nan tried to smile, but Skandar's merry face just looked too much like Joel's. Skandar frowned and put his arm around her. "Hey, hey, hey, you okay?"

She couldn't help the tears then, and Hayley and Skandar held her while she sobbed out her fears about Joel. When she'd calmed down, she looked apologetically at them both.

"Sorry. It's just been a strain since Kit. I feel so useless, Skandar; your dad, is so remote. I want to help him but ..." Her voice broke again.

Skandar hugged her. "Look, Kit was his twin; he's bound to feel it even more keenly than the rest of us. Just be there, and forgive him if he gets difficult. I promise he'll hate himself for treating you like this; he just doesn't know how to deal with this. He is so in love with you, Nan, I swear to God, he is."

Nan smiled gratefully at him. "Thank you, Skan. If he doesn't buck up," she suddenly grinned, "I might swap father for son."

"Hey, now," Hayley piped up in mock outrage, "do I get a say? Besides," she said in an aside to her sister, "his dong is tiny. You wouldn't want him ..."

"You are so dumped," Skandar was laughing now. "And just so you know, Nan, it's massive."

Nan was giggling now, enjoying the silliness of her sister and Skandar as they busted each other's chops, teasing, and play-fighting. God, she wanted that fun back in her life. She immediately felt guilty for thinking that when Kit was dead. She excused herself from the others and went outside to get some air. Her phone buzzed in her pocket. Joel.

"Hey, beautiful."

She almost sighed with relief at the warmth in his voice. "Hi, gorgeous ... how did it go?"

"It's Fisk, but we knew that anyway. Look, Dad, Jakob, and Quilla are flying back, but I'm going to London for a couple of days. Will you be okay?"

"Sure, I'm at the big house with the others ... what's in London?"

"Just someone I have to talk to. My flight's being called. I'll talk to you when I get to London. Nan?"

"Yes, baby?"

"I love you, honey."

She smiled down the phone. "I love you too, big fella. Hurry home to me."

"I will."

Bo Kennedy shoved her honey-blonde hair into a bun and lifted Tiger from his bath. "Come on, you big oaf. God, you are a heavy little bugger now, you know?"

"Little bugger," intoned Tiger, grinning at his mother, knowing it was a 'bad' word.

Bo made a face at him. "Don't say that in front of your Grandma or I'll tickle you silly."

"No, Mummy!" He yelled a banshee cry, and she chased him back to his bedroom, making him giggle. She wrapped the towel around him.

"Trust you to run around naked, you little exhibitionist." She dried him quickly and pulled his pajamas over his head. After she'd tucked him into bed, she blew a raspberry on his forehead then kissed him. "You want a story, punkin?"

He shook his head. "Mummy?"

"Yes, precious?"

"Is Kit in heaven now?"

God, the pain didn't get any less agonizing. "Yes, sweetheart, he is. Do you know why?"

"A bad man had a gun."

"He did, and do you know what Kit did?"

"He saved my mummy."

Bo's eyes filled with tears as she nodded and she couldn't speak. Tiger reached up and touched her cheek. "Don't cry, Mummy. Kit still loves us, even if he isn't here on Earth anymore."

The tears spilled over then, but she smiled through them. "Yes, he does, and we love him, don't we?"

Downstairs, she turned off the main lights, just leaving the light of the open fire crackling in the grate. She curled up on the couch, listening to the silence of the evening. The property had land for miles around which, usually, she was thankful for. Now, though, she wished there were people closer.

You have four bodyguards sleeping in the guest lodge, all armed, all highly trained; how much more company do you want? But it wasn't her safety she was most concerned with. It was being overcome with the crushing grief. She had canceled the rest of her tour—something she was loath to do—but in this case, vital. But now she wished she could feel that adrenaline. Night after night she would sit here, a bottle of wine, and her iPad, watching the videos she and Kit made during their all-too-brief time together. It was torture, yet every night she would put herself through it. Her shoulder still ached from the bullet wound; she'd hardly felt it when it ripped into her. It had all happened so fast.

Kit's shout of "get down!"; him shoving her into the car; turning, seeing the bullet smash into his chest. His look of surprise, then of regret as he looked at her, the blood blooming across his chest. Her primal, feral scream as he fell, then scrambling out of the car, not caring if she was shot again, falling onto her lover's prone body. Holding his head between her hands, begging him to live. There was blood on his mouth. He smiled at her. "I love you, Bo Kennedy. Know that, always ..."

His eyes closing. The finality of it.

Bo grabbed a cushion and screamed into it, howling her sadness, her pain. She was so distraught, she didn't notice a very awkward bodyguard hovering near the door. She lowered the cushion and started as he cleared his throat.

"God ... Simon, sorry." She flushed, embarrassed. "Just stress relief."

He nodded, gave her a smile. "I do that all the time."

She smiled gratefully at his attempt to make her feel better. Sweet guy. "What's up?"

"There's a gentleman here to see you; he apologizes for the lateness of the hour."

"Simon, I'm really not up for—"

"It's Joel Mallory, Miss Kennedy."

So many emotions flooded through her—joy, panic, and fear— but she kept her expression neutral. "Okay, then."

She walked out with Simon to the foyer, bracing herself for the impact of seeing her dead lover's twin. As she caught sight of him, something inside her broke.

Joel looked up and smiled. "Hey, Bo ... remember me? I'm Joel..."

"I remember who you are," she smiled, her voice cracking, tears dropping down her cheeks. "Of course, I know who you are..."

She threw her arms around him, sobbing, and he gathered her up, hugging her tightly. "It's so good to see you again," Joel said, his voice broken and emotional.

Simon excused himself discreetly and Bo, finally releasing her grip on Joel, motioned him into the living room. "I have two bottles of unopened scotch. We're finishing them tonight."

Joel chuckled quietly. "That sounds good to me."

She poured him a drink, not able to tear her eyes from him. "God, I thought I wouldn't cope with seeing you, of all the family. But in a weird way, it's helping. Do you smoke, Joel?"

He shook his head. "Not for a while now."

"Me neither." She reached into the drinks cabinet and pulled out a sealed packet of Gauloises, waving them joyously. "Terrible for the voice, but the scotch will take care of that. Come out on the patio, mate."

They sat under the stars and smoked and drank and shared stories of Kit. Bo felt her heart lift, as if Kit were still here, sitting in the empty, rolling his eyes at his brother for making him look 'uncool.' She said as much to Joel, who laughed. "He would be incensed, the stories I could tell you."

Just after midnight and Bo sighed. "Thank you for coming, Joel. I needed this."

"What's next for you, Bo?"

Bo flexed her injured shoulder unconsciously. "Get back on tour, then into the studio. Work is the key, I think. Make sure Tiger gets through all of this. He really loved Kit."

Joel looked away from her gaze, and she took his hand. "I cannot even imagine how this must be for you, Joel. I only knew him a few weeks, and I feel torn apart."

He squeezed her hand. "It's been ..." his shoulders slumped. "I have, to be honest; it's broken me. I can't get through a few minutes without remembering he's gone forever. We didn't always have the best relationship, but lately it was getting better."

Bo steeled herself. "So, they have the shooter?"

Joel nodded and told her exactly what the man had said. She paled at his words. "Wow. So Kit really did save my life. It's weird; I've had stalkers before, but never someone who wanted to kill me."

"If it helps, it wasn't personal. Fisk wants to destroy our family and anyone we love."

Bo bristled. "Fucker. If someone wants to kill me, it should at least be personal. Jesus."

"I hear ya."

A light breeze had started up, and Bo shivered. "Let's go in. Listen, I have a guest room. Stay the night."

Joel smiled. "That's sweet but I can't—this time, at least. Listen, none of us back in Seattle want to lose touch with you. It's almost Christmas— bring Tiger, come out and stay with us. Your mom, too. Let us spoil you."

Bo grinned. "I'll talk to Mum about it."

She walked him to the door and hugged him fiercely, not wanting to let go. "I miss him, you know?"

Joel nodded, his eyes sad. "I know."

When she was alone, she went straight to her bedroom, changing into her T-shirt and shorts and got into bed. All those emotions swirling around her mind hadn't stopped chattering. She lay on her right side and imagined Kit's gorgeous golden head on the pillow next to hers. Bad move. So much pain.

"Why did you have to go?" she whispered, and listened for the answer.

It never came.

QUILLA AND JAKOB got back home just after midnight local time. Jakob had fallen into an uneasy sleep on the plane, but Quilla could never sleep when she traveled. Her eyes felt scratchy and sore; her mouth was dry; and she felt unreasonably annoyed--not at anyone in particular, just in general.

Hormones, she thought, and then it struck her. God, not now. She figured out the days since her last period and sighed with relief. It was due in a couple of days. Still, she would snag a couple of pregnancy tests from the drugstore and make sure. After Jakob's volte-face about kids, she suddenly had doubts herself. She wanted a career first, wanted to make a name for herself in the art world. She wasn't so naive that she didn't know the Mallory name would help her, but she actually wanted to do the hard labor herself, instead of just being a figurehead. And children right now would prevent her from giving all of her attention to it.

She had had the idea on the plane ride home; she would talk to Ran and Grady about a new foundation for arts, independent of Ran's own foundation, and get Flori and Hayley, with their respective art and architecture degrees, involved.

She was so absorbed with the idea; she barely noticed when they got back to the apartment and Jakob put his hands on her waist, pulling her to him. Quilla braced herself for another fucking session ... and was surprised when all Jakob did was stroke her face, gazing down at her, his eyes soft. She smiled up at him.

"You okay, baby?"

He nodded but stayed silent, pressing his lips to hers tenderly, his hands cupping her face. His kiss was sweet, passionate, and heady— after a long moment, she had to pull away for air, bemused by the change in him.

He leaned his forehead against hers. "I'm sorry I've been so angry, that I've been so forceful with you. With us."

"Ssh," she said, rubbing her nose against his. "I love you. It's okay."

Jakob smiled. "I don't know where my head has been; something in me said Gregor would never go this far. Now he has ... I have night-mares about losing you, Quilla. He got to you so easily last time."

"Last time, we didn't have any idea that this was his psychosis, his endgame. Now we do, and we have an army, looking out for us. An army." She grinned, nodding back to the closed door to the foyer. Their security detail waited outside, ready for any intrusion. Quilla held Jakob's hand and led him to their bedroom. "Best way to get over jetlag," she promised him.

They made love slowly, tenderly, this time, taking their time, taking care of the other's body, and then fell asleep and slept until the middle of the next afternoon. After they'd showered, Jakob went to the office and Quilla, eager to discuss her ideas with Ran and Grady, asked one of her bodyguards to take her to the big house.

Grady was the only one there and he listened with interest to her ideas. He nodded as she explained how she wanted to set up a foun-dation which would benefit artists without a college degree or access to art classes. "Kind of like Joel's community sports centers, but for art."

"I like it. And you want to get Hayley and Flori involved? I think that's the right way to go. After all, all three of you did get your college degrees, but only after adversity. Would you teach?"

Quilla was surprised. "Do you think I'm qualified?"

"Hell, yes. And if you're worried, we'll poach some people from your alma mater."

His grin was so infectious, she couldn't help but giggle. "Thanks, Grady; now I'm even more enthused. Is Flori with you? Can I talk to her?"

Grady shook his head. "Afraid not. She's visiting a college in Vancouver."

Quilla was surprised. "Moving to Canada?"

"Maybe. At least while her course lasts. It's just one option we're thinking about, but look, come over tomorrow night for some food and we'll talk some more. I know Flori would love to do something with you."

Quilla flushed with pleasure. "She's a sweetheart and damn, she can draw."

Grady nodded. "The two of you put Pa and me to shame."

"Ha."

"It's true. We're more dabblers; you two are hardcore."

SHE WAS STILL THINKING about his words later; if she was honest, they made her feel so good. That her work was worth something was a real tribute, coming from a man like Grady Mallory. Yes, he was related, but she knew without a doubt that he wasn't just blowing smoke up her ass, that he meant what he said. She tried to remember when she'd last picked up a pencil or a paintbrush. Too long. Even at work, she'd been mired in paperwork and essays, her PhD studies having taken a backseat. Not any more, she thought, gazing out a sunny Seattle as they drove towards the city.

She leaned forward in the seat and spoke to her guard, Rick. "Hey, could we go to Skandar's place?"

"Sure thing, Miss Quilla."

Quilla grinned to herself. Rick was an old-fashioned guy, straight out of Texas. Miss Quilla. He makes me sound like Jessica Fletcher. She pulled out her phone and called Hayley, asking her if she wanted to grab some food and chat.

The reply came back. "God, yes, please, Skandar's still at training, and I'm starving."

Hayley was wearing a long plaid shirt and skinny jeans, and her wool hat pulled down over her long blonde hair as she dove into the car next to Quilla and kissed her cheek. "How was Oz? I'm desperate for Skandar to take me to the Open next year, but he says I'll be a distraction."

Quilla grinned. Hayley's natural enthusiasm was catching. "Don't take no for an answer. It's beautiful. Where do you want to eat?"

Hayley considered. "I am supposed to be on a detox, so ..."

"Red Mill?"

Hayley groaned. "You are the Devil. Yes, yes, yes."

Quilla chuckled and asked Rick to take them to the burger joint. "I need fries in my life," she admitted to Hayley. "PMS-ing hard."

"Poor you. "

Rick pulled the car out into traffic and headed towards Ballard. The two women chatted happily, catching up with each other. Quilla told Hayley she had something to discuss with her but, teasing her companion, she kept her mouth shut.

Neither of them nor Rick saw the SUV until the last minute. It came at them from the side, speeding to over a hundred kilometers an hour and smashed the front of the Mercedes, flipping it over and over.

Quilla, barely conscious, opened her eyes to see a man with a gun bending down to look into the car. She heard Hayley moan.

"They're alive."

"Good. Boss wants the Asian one alive."

"What about the blonde?"

"Bring her, too. If he doesn't want her, we'll kill her and dump her body. Kill the driver."

In horror, Quilla watched as the man calmly shot Rick through the head. Hayley screamed. Then doors were being opened; there was a flash of a knife as Quilla was cut free from her belt. Then, as she was dragged out of the car, a cloth was forced over her nose and mouth. Breathing in whatever chemical was soaking the cloth; Quilla heard Hayley cry out.

Leave her alone; she tried to scream. Take me, leave her alone ... oh God, ... help us ...

Help us ...

8

PART EIGHT: TAKE ME

ow ...

QUILLA OPENED her eyes to darkness. A blindfold; she could feel the rough fabric against her skin. Her hands were bound behind her back; she was slumped on a chair, her ankles tied. Her head pounded with pain; her limbs ached from the shock of the accident. She felt strangely calm—she was in no doubt who was behind their abduction: Gregor Fisk. There was a sense of inevitability about it all. Quilla swallowed, her throat dry. "Hayley?"

"I'm here."

"Are you tied up?"

"Yes, handcuffed to the radiator. You're on a chair. Are you okay?"

"I think so. Aren't you blindfolded?"

"No. He ... Quilla, he's tied you up like he wanted to ... God ..."

Quilla didn't need to hear it. She could easily imagine what humiliation Gregor Fisk was going to visit upon her before he killed her. Because he was going to kill her, she knew that, but she was damned if she'd let him hurt Hayley. She lifted her shoulder, bending her head to push the blindfold away from her eyes. She blinked, trying to get used to the light. Hayley, her face tearstained and bloody, sat on the floor across the room.

Quilla looked around ... an old house, somewhat derelict. She could see out of the window that they were in an isolated place, but the tree line looked familiar—pines, mountainous. "We're still in Washington, or at least the Northwest." Had Gregor been close all this time?

Hayley nodded. "I was conscious in the van, though I pretended to be out. We didn't travel for more than two hours, and we climbed, I could tell that. Your ear is bleeding."

Hayley looked terrified, and Quilla tried to smile and reassure her. "It doesn't hurt." She looked over herself. Her white dress had been ripped open to expose her underwear, and the ties that bound her crisscrossed over her body were leather straps biting into her flesh. Quilla strained against them, but they were too tight, too strong. She hadn't noticed at first, but someone had drawn a circle in marker pen on her belly, her navel at the center of it. "What the hell?"

"He said it was for target practice, the sick fuck." Hayley suddenly retched and vomited. Quilla felt sick herself. Hayley sobbed for a few seconds, then wiped her mouth on the arm of her T-shirt.

"He's going to kill us, isn't he?"

"No," Quilla shook her head. "He is not, Hayley. I will get you out of here, I promise. Jakob and Skandar, they'll be scouring the world for us. I won't let you die."

Hayley was staring at her. "Quilla ... I won't let him hurt you either."

Quilla swallowed the lump in her throat. "Sweetheart, we're going to get out of here, I promise."

The door to the room opened then, and they both started, hearts pounding. Gregor Fisk had the widest smile on his face. Hayley whimpered.

"Well, good morning, beautiful ladies. Thank you for joining me here. Quilla, my love, you're up, and looking so ravishing too."

Gregor grabbed Quilla's hair and pulled her head back, grinding his mouth down on hers. Quilla struggled until she felt cold metal against her belly and she froze.

Hayley screamed, and Gregor laughed. He pressed the muzzle of the gun against Quilla's skin and winked at Hayley. "Hope you've said your goodbyes, girls."

And he pulled the trigger.

Now ...

THERE WERE no words to describe how Jakob felt at this moment. Devastated wasn't strong enough; neither was scared, terrified or angry. There were no words.

Sickened, he turned away from the body of his employee. Rick, the young Texan security guard, could not have prevented his own death, a bullet to the brain, nor could he have protected Quilla from the fate that had befallen her. Gregor had taken her, and Jakob knew in his bones that he would never see her alive again.

The FBI chief drove him back to their field office and numbly, he followed the man into the interview room. He answered his questions in a monotone and for an hour and a half, he went through everything that had happened since he had met Quilla, Gregor's campaign of violence, his stabbing attacks on Quilla and Flori ... Kit's murder.

The FBI chief, Carter James, finally looked at him sympathetically. "I know it seems like you're repeating everything ad infinitum, but we never know when the smallest piece of information will be useful. Look, Mr. Mallory, maybe we should go further back, to when you first met Gregor Fisk."

Jakob raised his eyebrows. "You think that will help?"

Carter James nodded. "Maybe. Like I said, any minor detail."

There was a knock at the door and a young African-American woman looked around the door. She smiled kindly at Jakob. "Mr. Mallory, your father and brother are here."

Jakob felt some of the heavy dread lift. "Thank God. Thank you."

Carter smiled at his partner. "Show them in, would you, Ali? Mr. Mallory, this is my partner, Ali Bell."

He shook the young agent's hand and then she left, reappearing a moment later with Ran and Grady. Both his father and his brother looked shocked. Ran hugged Jakob tightly. "This is not your fault, son."

Jakob almost smiled; his dad knew him so well. "I'll try not to think that, Pa." He introduced them to Carter, then filled them in on what had happened. Ran nodded when Jakob told him what Carter suggested.

"Good idea."

Carter picked up on his tone. "You've always had doubts about Fisk?"

Ran hesitated, shooting a look at his son, and then nodded. "Yes." Carter looked at Grady.

"You?"

Grady shrugged. "I never really knew him, but the few times I met him, he seemed like an arrogant jerk. The trouble with this guy," he nodded smiling at his brother, "is that he's fiercely loyal. He never gives up on anyone."

Carter nodded. "Maybe you both should sit in on this and give any info you can while Jakob goes through their history."

He looked at Jakob, who nodded. "Good. Look, get comfortable, I'll get some coffee and sandwiches sent it. The quicker we do this, the more likely we are to be able to find Quilla safe."

Now ...

SKANDAR MALLORY THANKED his practice partner and went to shower. He always felt buzzed after a good session and this one, nearly four hours, had been exhilarating. Good, he needed those endorphins coursing through his blood. Since Kit had died, he had managed to be a support to his dad and his uncles but inside, he was dying. He and Kit had clashed yes, but God ... The press intrusion was getting ridiculous and at the moment, the only thing keeping him going was the gorgeous blonde waiting for him at home. Damn, he loved Hayley Applebee, and lately, he'd been churning an idea over and over in his mind.

He wanted to marry her. He wanted to take her away, like Jakob and Quilla, and get married on a tropical island and call her his wife, hear her say 'my husband' and belong to each other forever. It was crazy—she wasn't even twenty years old yet, but Skandar knew they would be together forever. Done deal, no doubts. He'd even gone online and sought out some unusual engagement rings for her—he knew she wouldn't want a huge diamond, more something that spoke to who she was in herself, something unique.

He drove home a little too fast, eager to see Hayley, but when he got there, the house was empty. Swallowing his disappointment, he read her note. Gone out to eat with Quilla. Oil up that fine body and have it ready for me when I get home, slave. Master Hayley. (PS: I love you).

Skandar chuckled. "Doofus." He threw his sweaty practice clothes in the washer then grabbed a beer from the refrigerator. He flopped onto the couch, flipping through the television channels to find something to watch. After a couple of hours, he got tired and switched it off, not seeing the Breaking News ribbon and the photo of Quilla that flashed briefly before the screen turned black.

Grinning, he wrote Hayley a note. Wake me up when you get in, beautiful. He stuck it to the bedroom door so she wouldn't miss it and went to bed.

Now ...

Hayley screamed, and Quilla let her breath flood out. The gun was empty. Gregor laughed. "Well, that was fun. Just a little warning of what will happen if you try my patience. Dick, Paul? Untie them. Ladies, there is a bathroom through that door. All the windows are nailed shut, are made of hardened glass, and are alarmed. There will be a bullet for each time you try to escape, do you understand? Behave and you," he gestured dismissively at Hayley – "might get to live. You, my darling Quilla, well, you already know what's going to happen to you, but the rules still apply. You try anything, the blonde kid dies."

"Let her go," Quilla begged him. "You have me; you don't need her."

Gregor moaned and kissed her again. "I know I have you, beautiful, and I'm really going to enjoy our time together, but I do need her, mostly to stop you doing anything silly to yourself. You try and kill yourself, try to take that pleasure away from me, then she dies."

He stood, his eyes not leaving her face. "You'll be fed well, and looked after, if you comply. I'll get them to bring a mattress in for you to sleep on. They're under orders to shoot Blondie the moment you step out of line. Until later."

The other two men silently untied them, then locked the door after them. Quilla and Hayley clung to each other. Quilla could feel Hayley's entire body trembling. "It's okay, honey. The fact that we're not already dead means there's hope."

Hayley scrubbed at her face, wiping blood and tears across her hands. "You're just saying that to make me feel better, but thank you."

Quilla sighed, leaning against her friend. She suddenly felt a chill and re-buttoned her dress, spitting on her fingers to try and wipe Gregor's 'target' off her skin before she pulled the material around her. She closed her eyes and drew in a couple of deep breaths, trying to quell the terror. Try to think logically; she told herself calmly. Make a plan—get Hayley out of here. Quilla knew she would do anything—anything—to make that happen.

Even if it meant giving herself to Gregor Fisk in every way.

THEN ... Twenty-Five Years Previously

. . .

"Jakob Mallory?"

Jakob looked up from his blueprints and smiled at the young man in front of him. "Yes?"

The man, dark hair, dark eyes, handsome, polished, held out his hand. "Gregor Fisk. You said to come straight to the site?"

Jakob blinked, then remembered. The dude from his MBA class. "Hey again. Sorry, brain on autopilot. You want a beer?"

Gregor grinned. "Hell, yes. My kind of interview."

Jakob laughed and snagged a couple of cold ones from his mini-fridge. "Mine, too, although this isn't an interview, as such. I don't pretend to be anything than a grad student with an idea. But thanks for responding to the ad; I thought it would be cool to chat; see what your ambitions as far as property are."

"Build stuff, make a ton of money, love my work," said Gregor, his easy smile appearing again. He took a long swig of beer. "My family is all about medicine, but I just don't have that gene. I want to create something physical, build with my bare hands, design something people have never seen before."

Jakob nodded. "Sounds about right. I'm looking to build boutique buildings at affordable prices—now," he grinned at the doubtful expression on Gregor's face, "just listen. There's a whole bunch of graduates like me and you, and even young professionals, who are crying out for affordable housing but also want something polished. I don't believe we can't give them that while keeping costs low."

Gregor considered. "Okay, so where do I come in?"

"Well, you want to build stuff—that's a good start," Jakob laughed, and Gregor joined in. "My family's going to stump up the starting capital. As a partner, you would be loaned your share—if you want—and then pay my dad back if and when we make a profit."

Gregor nodded but still looked unsure.

"Look, I haven't got it all figured out yet. Why don't we go out for drinks tonight and talk some more?" Jakob looked at his watch. "Say nine o'clock at the Oasis?"

Now ...

"So you decided to work together that night?" Carter James asked Jakob now, as they sat in the interview room.

"More or less, maybe a couple of days later. Believe it or not, back then, he was a good guy, always a bit arrogant, but then, so was I at that age. We were young and ambitious, incredibly driven—which is why the company did so well so quickly."

There was a knock and Ali Bell came in bearing a tray full of coffee and sandwiches and a very grim face. "Press has the story," she said. "They're all outside. Also, your brother Joel is here."

Joel came in, his face drawn, Nan behind him. Joel hugged Jakob tightly. "God, I'm sorry, man. Anything we can do?"

"I'd feel better if Skandar and Hayley were here, safe," Ran said quietly, and Nan nodded.

Carter got up. "We'll send a car over for them—has Skandar got security at his house, a physical presence?"

Joel shook his head. "He hates being crowded, but it is like Fort Knox. No one's getting in there."

"Still, I agree with Mr. Mallory Sr. Let's get everyone here."

Joel nodded and Ali Bell went to arrange the escort. Carter looked at Jakob. "You ready to continue?"

Jakob nodded. "Let's get this done."

Now ...

Skandar awoke at the sound of someone leaning on his intercom. He stumbled out of bed, glanced at the clock, and stopped, turning to look at the empty bed beside him. Where the hell was Hayley?

Dread started to spiral through his chest, and when he opened the door and saw the police officers waiting, his heart dropped.

"What, what is it?"

"Mr. Skandar Mallory? We're sorry to disturb you, sir, but we need you to come down to the FBI field office with us."

Skandar stared at them dumbly. "Why?"

"I'm sorry, Mr. Mallory; we can't tell you that."

"Am I under arrest for anything?"

"No, sir, not at all."

Skandar drew in a breath. "Look, my girlfriend is due home soon; I'd rather wait for her. Then I'd be happy to come. I don't want to leave her here alone at night."

The officers looked at each other. "Hayley Applebee?"

"Yeah, she's gone out with a friend, my aunt-in-law, if there is such a thing."

Another loaded glance. "The aunt's name?"

"Quilla Chen, or Quilla Mallory, that is ... look, what's going on?"

The expressions on the officers' faces had gone from professional to concern. "Okay, Mr. Mallory, I'm going to ask you to come with us now. We'll leave someone here to bring your girlfriend in later. It is important that you come with us now."

THEN ... Twenty Years Previously

"DUDE, to our tenth project together and for making Mallory Fisk the biggest property conglomerate in the world. To us, man," Gregor tapped his champagne flute to Jakob's and grinned. They were standing in the as-yet unoccupied penthouse of their latest residential building, and even Jakob had to admit, Gregor had outdone himself on this one.

Yeah, it might be a little ways off the vision for cheap, stylish housing that he, Jakob, had, but Jakob wasn't Randall Mallory's son for nothing. He had his father's eye when it came to beautiful aesthetics and this place ... damn; Jakob was tempted to buy it for himself. He could afford it now, without even tapping into his trust fund.

"I'm seriously thinking about taking this place." Gregor's word mirrored his thoughts and Jakob half smiled but said nothing. "Look at that view."

Mt. Rainier rose out of the gloomy twilight, and the city was a riot of lights, nightlife, and traffic. Jakob could see over to the islands, the ferries moving slowly across the Bay. He loved this city more than anywhere else in the world, and that was saying something.

"Listen, you want to grab some dinner? Padma said she'd love to see you."

Padme Khan, Gregor's stunning girlfriend, was a human rights lawyer. Gregor had been dating her for a year and a half, was crazy about her, and talked about marriage. Padme herself, smart, brilliant and funny, seemed fond of Gregor, her natural reserve making her hard to read. Yes, she was gorgeous and kind ... and for the last two months, she had also been Jakob's lover.

It had been an instant attraction that they fought for over a year until one night; Jakob had been working late at the office when Padme had arrived, looking for Gregor.

"He's with a client," Jakob had told her. He offered her a drink, and she accepted. He joined her on the couch in his office, their knees touching as they sipped their scotch. Then she had put her hand on his knee and that had been that. A glorious, delirious, adrenaline-filled fuck later and Jakob was lost. They'd met every couple of days since then—Gregor's assistant Mandy more than happy to cover for them—Gregor had never treated her, or any of the Mallory Fisk staff, with any respect right from the beginning; the fact that they had any staff was down to Jakob and their loyalty to him. So, Mandy, with more than a little glee, would tell them when it was safe to meet.

Padme, with her large dark eyes, soft pink lips, and killer athlete's body, was an energetic and uninhibited lover.

Both of them felt guilty, but both of them were addicted to the other. They didn't talk about the future, or make plans, or say I love you. In fact, Padme was adamant. "I don't love you; I just want you," she told him, and Jakob was fine with that.

He agreed to the dinner that evening but didn't expect Padme to announce she'd had a job offer in London. Gregor, by the look on his face, hadn't expected it either. Jakob felt sorry for his partner.

"So, you're taking it?"

Padme nodded. "It's too good an opportunity to miss. I'm sorry, sweetheart; I had to make the decision quickly."

"Without me?"

Padme's smile was distinctly chilly. "Of course. It's my career."

Gregor hadn't argued, but he had been silent for most of the evening. The next day at work, Jakob went to see him in his office. "You okay?"

Gregor smiled, his eyes are distant. "Sure. No big deal. I was thinking of breaking up with her anyway."

Yeah, right, but Jakob nodded sympathetically. "Good for you. Moving on."

"Pretty sure she was cheating on me, anyway."

Uh-oh. "Really."

Gregor looked at Jakob for a long moment. Then the corner of his mouth hitched up in a smile. "What do I know? Hey, I could use a drink tonight."

"Sure thing."

That was the first evening Jakob saw Gregor use cocaine.

Now ...

"So even back then, he was using."

"Recreationally. Not my concern, unless it started to affect the business and actually, he seemed to throw himself even more enthusiastically into the projects we were working on. I struggled to keep up."

"So you were sleeping with his girlfriend. His motive for revenge? Seems a little pedestrian for how he's behaving now. Coke psychosis would go some way ... but I'm still not convinced there isn't something else."

Jakob rubbed his head. "Look, can I take a quick break?"

Carter sat back, tired himself. "Of course. Take ten minutes." As

Jakob got up, another officer came in and handed a note to Carter. "Jakob, wait. Forensics is telling us there was another person in the car with Quilla."

Jakob looked shocked. "Who?"

"We don't know; they're bringing up something they've found. Can you wait?"

"Sure."

Jakob looked at his family, seated around the table with him. "Thank you all for being here. It helps; it really does."

Nan got up and hugged him. "They'll find her, Jakob."

Jakob tightened his arms around the blonde woman. "From your lips, Nan ..."

There was a commotion outside and then Skandar was there, his eyes confused. "What the hell is going on? Why are we all here?"

Joel got up. "You don't know?"

"Quilla's been taken, Skandar. Her car was ambushed. Her driver was killed, shot."

With all the blood draining from his face, Skandar's legs gave way. "No ... God ... no ..." Joel caught him before he fell, shooting a shocked and confused look at the others. Trembling, Nan stepped closer, put her arm around him.

"Skandar, where's Hayley?" Her voice broke when Skandar looked her directly in the eye, his pain obvious.

Behind her, a man in a lab coat came in and handed something in a plastic evidence bag to Carter. He held it up. "Anyone recognize this?"

Nan screamed; an agonized howl that tore at everyone's heart, drawing gasps from the others. Skandar looked up, his eyes heavy and tormented. "It's Hayley's hat," he said in a voice so broken and despairing, it barely seemed human, "She was with Quilla. They took Hayley, too."

Now ...

. . .

HAYLEY HAD FALLEN into an awkward slumber, Quilla's arms around her. Gregor's men had brought mattresses into the room for them, but they huddled together on one. Late fall had brought cold weather, and the thin blankets they had were inadequate. Quill couldn't sleep. She guessed it was about two or three in the morning, by the quiet in the room.

She had already checked out anything she might use as a weapon, but Gregor wasn't a stupid man. The food they were given was all finger food, sandwiches, fruit, stuff that didn't require even plastic knives and forks. In the bathroom, the toilet had no lid, either on the seat or the cistern. The shower rod was cemented into the wall. Even the soap was just a plain bar, no bottle that could be filled and used to club someone.

How did I get here? A year ago, I was sketching bridges in Venice and now ... She couldn't believe how calm she was in this situation. She could be murdered any minute and ...

Stop it. Close your eyes, think of something else.

THEIR WEDDING NIGHT. They'd flown to the big Island the day after Jakob had proposed, the day after that incredible, erotic night they'd spent on the terrace. Simple vows and that was that. Married. Two hours later, they'd gone back to their island hideaway and celebrated.

She slid the white cotton dress from her shoulders the moment they stepped inside the villa, and let it fall from her body to the tiled floor. She looked back over her shoulder at him and saw him smiling, obviously enjoying the striptease. He stepped forward to kiss her shoulder, while his fingers expertly popped the clasp of her bra. She let that fall, too, and turned to press her breasts against him, her lips seeking his.

"Take me," she murmured against his mouth and with a growl, he swept her into his arms and carried her out to the terrace. It was evening, and the sunset made her honey skin golden in its light.

Jakob laid her down on the sun lounger and began to kiss her, his lips trailing down her body until his face was buried in her belly. She stroked his hair, turned on by the fact she was naked and he was still fully dressed. She was his, his wife, his love. When he looked up, she was surprised to see tears in his eyes, and he smiled. "God, I love you, Quilla Chen Mallory."

She grinned. "That's my name." Jakob, his eyes full of love, gently pulled her legs apart and then his mouth was on her, kissing and sucking, tasting and teasing, her sex swelling and reddening under his touch. His tongue made her clit harden, and the sensitive nerve endings scream with pleasure, then he plunged it deep into her cunt, licking and tasting and loving. Quilla moaned, her entire body liquefying under his touch, every cell needing more of him.

"Let me suck you," she pleaded, and grinning, he stood and quickly stripped. She gazed up at his perfect, hard body, the wide shoulders, the firm abs, and his cock, so big, so hard. She stroked it upwards from the root and took the smooth tip between her lips, one hand massaging his sac gently, while her forefinger found that sensitive spot behind his balls. Her mouth, wet and warm, enveloped his cock, drawing on him. His hands were in her hair, stroking her tenderly, letting the fine strands fall through his fingers. Jakob groaned as he neared completion, Quilla looking up at him.

"Come on my skin," she said, and he nodded. His cock quivered and lengthened, and he shot stream after stream of hot, white semen onto her skin, her breasts, her belly. Quilla arched back, spreading her legs, running her fingers through the substance and massaging it in and down into her sex. "God, Quilla, yes, touch yourself like that ..." Jakob fisted the root of his still hard cock as he watched her masturbate, her long dark hair tumbling down her back, her golden skin oiled with his cum, her cunt glistening with desire. When he couldn't take anymore, he dropped onto her body and thrust balls deep into her, pressing her legs as far apart as they would go.

Jakob rammed his hips against her, murmuring to her, telling how much he loved her, loved fucking her over and over. Quilla came, one roaring shattering orgasm after another, crying out her love for him. He didn't let her rest, flipping her onto her stomach and pushing into her ass, wanting to possess her in every way. They fucked long into the night, falling asleep with their bodies tangled just as the sun rose over the island.

QUILLA FELT SLEEP COME THEN, just as a tear escaped. Then she was in that semi-conscious state between awake and sleep when the images came to her: Jakob's face turning from happiness to horror; the pain; her own body jerking and spasming as Gregor stabbed her to death ...

She awoke screaming, and it took all of Hayley's will to calm her down.

SKANDAR WANTED TO SCREAM, wanted to howl. If Gregor Fisk walked into this room this very moment. Skandar wouldn't need a weapon. He'd rip him to pieces with his bare hands.

Hayley. His sweet, young Hayley. He tried to take some comfort that Fisk had taken her, that he hadn't killed her in the car wreck like he had the driver. He hadn't needed the FBI agent to tell him why; Gregor would use her as collateral. To bend Quilla to his will. This was hopeful; she was useful, the FBI agent said. But what about when Fisk carried out his promise to kill Quilla? Hayley would have served her purpose, and be of no more use to him. He couldn't help but picture both the women dead, murdered.

Jesus ... He would vomit, but after they'd shown them Hayley's wool cap, he'd lurched to the bathrooms and thrown up and up, his father not knowing who to console first, his son or his girlfriend Nan, Hayley's sister. She was a wreck. She'd hugged Skandar, no sign of reproach in her eyes.

"We'll get her back; we will," she whispered to him urgently.

Skandar knew the fact Hayley would be used against Quilla wasn't lost on Jakob. In his uncle's eyes, there was a deep sorrow, a resignation. He thinks they'll be killed. The thought made Skandar want to howl. He went to his uncle and took him by the shoulders.

"Don't give up hope," he said to him in a low voice, "don't. If you do, I do, and I can't live with that."

Jakob had nodded stiffly.

The field office was filling up now; it was almost eight a.m. Jakob was back in that room with an exhausted-looking Agent James. Agent Bell had taken the rest of them to the cafeteria for coffee and breakfast, but no one felt like eating. Skandar stared out of the window, oblivious to the press pack on the street below them, aiming their cameras at the heartbroken man. He stared up at the dark gray sky that was threatening snow.

Where are you? Skandar thought, sadness overwhelming him. Where are you, my precious, darling Hayley? Wherever you are, fight to stay alive. Please ...

Fight.

HE CAME for Quilla about lunchtime. With Paul leveling a gun at Hayley, Quilla did not put up a fight when Gregor handcuffed her hands behind her back and marched her out of the room. She turned and looked back at Hayley. "I love you," she said.

Hayley nodded. "I love you." As the door closed behind her, Hayley shouted, "Please don't hurt her."

Quilla choked back a sob, not wanting to give Gregor any satisfaction. It was a relief when she saw both of Gregor's goons exit and leave Hayley alone. She had seen the one named Paul looking lasciviously at the young woman, and she would die before she let Hayley be assaulted. Gregor led her to a private room, a dining room by the look of it, and pushed her into a chair, releasing her hands. He grabbed her head, forcing her to look at him.

"Christ, you get more beautiful," he said roughly and kissed her. Quilla gagged and whipped her head away from him, and he laughed.

"Still so feisty. And overdressed." He yanked her already torn dress open, running a leisurely hand over her breasts, her belly.

Quilla squeezed her legs together, but he merely chuckled, gripping her thighs and prising them apart.

Then he walked away, and she sighed in relief. "Quilla, Quilla, Quilla …" he said, and she gritted her teeth. He pulled a chair up to hers and sat down, studying her. She met his gaze defiantly.

He nodded. "Yeah, I can see why Mallory married you, keeps you in that gilded cage. You're exquisite."

Quilla's eyes narrowed. "And that's all I am to you, isn't it? So-called 'beauty' and nothing else. Nothing that can't be cut down with your knife. Maybe that's your problem, Gregor, not seeing people for who they really are. What gives you the right to take what you want? I'm a human being, not your property, not Jakob's property, or anyone else's."

"That's where you're wrong; I do see you. I want to know you, Quilla."

She laughed mirthlessly. "Before you kill me? Did you want to know me when you stuck a knife in my gut?"

Gregor smiled. "That wasn't meant to kill you, Quilla, just to send a message."

"You sent plenty of messages, remember? I have to give you credit for your imagination, Gregor; you certainly thought up some pretty horrific ways to kill me."

He chuckled. "Would you believe me if I said I was rethinking that idea?"

Quilla was shocked. "Then why are we here? Why did you take me? Hayley?"

"Your pretty little friend was just in the wrong place at the wrong time."

"Then, please," she softened her tone. "Let her go. Just drop her off and make an anonymous call. Just please, let her go."

Gregor leaned back in his chair, his eyes roaming all over her body, obviously enjoying her torment. "Well, let me think about it. I'll tell you what, lovely Quilla, I'll make you a deal."

God, she wasn't going to like this, was she? Quilla swallowed. "What deal?"

He edged closer, cupping her breasts, stroking his thumbs across her bra-covered nipples. "A week. A week in which, Quilla, you will be everything to me that you are to Jakob Mallory. In every way. At the end of the week, if I'm satisfied, I'll let the blonde go." He cupped her face in his hands, forcing her to look at him. "If I'm not satisfied, I'll let Paul have her before I kill her. And you, sweet Quilla, will wish you'd never been born."

His eyes were cold, dark, and almost black with malevolence. Quilla couldn't help the gasp of fear that escaped her. He smiled at that.

"Beautiful sound. I wonder, will you gasp like that when I'm inside you?"

Kill me now, she thought, please, just end this. But she couldn't say the words, couldn't let Hayley suffer because she was afraid. So, she tried to smile. "We'll see, won't we?"

God, no, no Jakob, I'm so sorry—but if fucking Gregor Fisk helped keep Hayley—and maybe even herself—then she would be a goddamned porn star for him.

Gregor allowed her to go back to the room now, and Hayley hugged her, crying. "I thought he was going to kill you," she sobbed. "I had my ear to the door, in case you screamed. I was going to try to kick it down, oh God, oh God ..."

Quilla tightened her arms around her young friend. "It's okay, baby. I'm all good, I promise. Look, sit down with me for a minute; my legs are shaking."

Calming down, Hayley did as she asked, but pulled her sweatshirt off and tugged it around Quilla. "I hate seeing you like that—not that you haven't got a great body—but knowing he wants you on show ... it makes me sick."

God, if you only knew ... Quilla thanked her. "At this point, though, I'm past caring. Listen, we may have a way out of here ... I just have to keep that psycho happy for a week. I don't want to give you false hope, but I think he means what he says, so ..."

Hayley narrowed her eyes at Quilla. "What do you mean 'keep him happy?'"

Quilla had to look away from her gaze. "Don't worry about it."

Hayley's eyes filled with tears. "Oh, no," she said in a whisper. "Oh, no, Quilla, don't. Please."

"I don't have any choice, if I want to keep you alive." Quilla's voice broke. "Please, don't make it harder than it already is."

Hayley's tears poured down her cheeks. "Why do I want to blame Jakob for this? If he hadn't fired Gregor, none of this would be happening."

Quilla touched her cheek, smiling. "But then Nan wouldn't have met Joel, and you couldn't have met Skandar ... Grady and Flori, Kit and Bo."

Hayley choked out, "And Kit wouldn't be dead."

Quilla shuddered. "We can't change what's happened, Hayley; we have to focus on the future."

Hayley wrapped her arms around her friend. "I don't want you to ... screw ... him."

"It's just sex. I have to make it convincing; it might be the only way to get you out of here."

Hayley stopped. "You mean us."

"What?"

"You said 'get you out of here'. You meant both of us, right?"

Quilla nodded. "Of course."

But they both knew she was lying.

CARTER JAMES, running on two hours sleep in the recreation lounge, scarfed down a power bar and chugged two cups of lukewarm overly strong coffee. "Jesus." He winced at the bitter taste.

"You could always make some more, you know. It's not out of your skill set." Ali Bell clapped him on the back. She looked as wrecked as he did. He smiled at her. The day Ali became his partner, he'd found both a loyal, smart, kickass partner and a best friend. Seven years later, and their record in investigating high-profile kidnappings and murders was exemplary. Personally, they had a flirty relationship— Ali had a mouth like a sailor and a wicked sense of humor—but they'd also silently agreed—no peeing in the company pool. It had served them well, through two divorces in three years for Carter and a broken arm from when Ali had taken down a perp three times her size.

"Anything?" Ali sat down opposite him, flicking a packet of sweetener. Carter shook his head. "The Mallorys and their team have done a pretty thorough job; nice to have unlimited resources. The trouble is, all those resources are at Fisk's fingertips, too."

"Be honest. You think we'll find those two girls alive?"

Carter looked at her. "I'd like to think so. The younger girl, Hayley, at least. But Mallory's wife? Fisk is obsessed with her." He sat thinking for a while. "Mallory says she's a smart girl, a grad student. I wonder if she's thinking of her options."

"What do you mean?"

"She knows Fisk is obsessed with her—maybe she can play him."

Ali winced. "God." She had immediately guessed what he meant. "That poor girl."

"Yeah."

Ali sighed. "Look, we're trying to find out everything we can on Fisk. Since he went off grid when Mallory fired him, he's left no trail. It's almost as if he'd been planning to go native. A couple of years ago, there were seven hundred million dollars in his current account. That's just his current account. Factor in investments, on and offshore; Jesus, that's more money than we can imagine. Then, just over a year ago, his US investments were cashed out. His account was cleared out. Carter, this guy's got his money stuffed in a mattress somewhere. Maybe we should check out Walmarts around the country for anyone who's been buying shit like the Rapture's coming." She grinned but Carter sat up.

"That's not a bad idea ..."

"Oh, come on, I was kidding."

"No, think about it. If you're right, that would be some lead to follow. So far, we got nada. Any theory at this point is worth investigating."

Ali still looked skeptical but nodded. "Well, okay, I'll go set up a search of big wholesalers ... still seems a bit easy to me."

Carter grinned, a big cheesy smile at her. "You never heard of Occam's Razor?"

Ali gave him a death stare. "Graduated Suma from Harvard, top of my class, and you think I don't? The simplest answer is usually the right one."

Charlie chuckled. "Which reminds me, I need to talk to his professors at Harvard—you got a contact?"

JAKOB COULDN'T BEAR to go home. Not without Quilla, not knowing if she was dead or alive or in horrible torment. *I love you so much, baby; please hang on for me ... I'll find you, I swear.* He booked into a hotel a few blocks from the FBI field office and called Miles to have some of his clothes brought to his room.

His assistant, Miles, answered on the first ring. "Hey, cutie."

"Hey, Miles, can you—did you just call me 'cutie'?" Jakob was bemused.

Miles laughed. "I did. Do you know why?"

Jakob gave a quick laugh. "No idea ..."

"Quilla. She bet me I wouldn't call you cutie when you least expected it. So now, she owes me money. That's how I know she'll be okay; she owes me money. Plus, that's the girl who everyone loves, who everyone pulls for, fights for. That girl doesn't get dead. I know it in my bones."

Jakob didn't know whether to laugh or cry but he was tremendously moved. "Miles, remind after this is all over to give you a huge raise in pay. Damn, man; that's the first time I've felt better in hours. Thank you."

"My pleasure. Now, what can I do for you?"

.   .   .

AT FIVE-THIRTY, Paul came to their room. He threw a plastic bag at Quilla. "Boss says have a shower, put that on. Dinner's in a half hour. You," he leered at Hayley. "You can take off whatever you want."

"Fuck you," Hayley shot back, and Paul laughed.

"I wish. Maybe once the boss has had his share, I'll be allowed to show you a good time."

Quilla stepped in front of Hayley. "Get out. Tell Gregor, I'll be ready."

Paul sneered at her but left the room. "Cocksucker," hissed Hayley, then looked at the bag in Quilla's hands. "Let's see."

Quilla took a deep breath in, stuck her hand in the bag and drew out a handful of white cotton. A dress. Both Quilla and Hayley let out a sigh of relief.

"I so thought that was going to be some sort of S&M gear," Hayley said, taking the dress from Quilla and shaking it out.

"Me too, and thank God, it isn't." Quilla smiled suddenly, "It would have ruined it for life for Jakob and me."

"You don't?"

"Of course, we do. Don't you and Skandar indulge?"

Hayley looked both shocked and amused. "No."

"Not yet," teased Quilla. "Ask me for tips."

Hayley shook her head. "How can you laugh at a time like this?"

Quilla suddenly looked tearful. "Because it's the only thing I can do, Hays. Please, distract me from what I have to do tonight."

Hayley threw her arms around her. "You are the bravest person I've ever known," she whispered, her voice cracking.

But Quilla didn't feel brave; she felt desperate a half-hour later, as Paul led her at gunpoint to Gregor's dining room. The host himself was waiting, resplendent in a tux, with his collar open, his tie undone. Quilla supposed he thought he looked irresistible—he was anything but that. Her flesh crawling, she waited until Paul left the room before sitting down at the chair Gregor pulled out for her. His fingertips drifted across her bare shoulders, and she shivered.

"This doesn't have to be unpleasant, Quilla," he said, bending to kiss her cheek. If she didn't know that this man in front of her was a killer—was planning to kill her—she would swear that he was genuine. His eyes were soft, his touch gentle. He sat down next to her, took her hand. "You look incredible, darling, and so lovely."

She forced herself to smile. "The dress is beautiful, thank you."

He touched her cheek. "You're welcome."

They had dinner, but Quilla's throat was closing up, and she barely touched her food. She dug her nails into her palms, trying not to cry. *I can't do this; I can't do this ...*

"Quilla." Gregor took her hand and pulled her to her feet. "Aren't you hungry?"

She shook her head, and he smiled. "Good. Me neither. Come with me."

He took her hand and led her into another room ... his bedroom. Quilla froze. Gregor had copied Jakob's bedroom from the apartment. *Her* bedroom. Gregor was watching her carefully.

"I thought it might relax you," he said, but his eyes belied his soothing tone. *Bastard.*

Quilla felt his hand slide down her back, and the zipper on the dress being drawn down. *God, this is it. Turn off your feelings; that's the key.*

Gregor's lips were at her ear. "Convince me, Quilla; remember, this is the difference between a bullet in the head for your blonde friend or not ... make it real."

He drew the dress from her shoulders and let it fall to the floor, walking around her. He touched the scar on her belly from his knife. "I'm sorry about that. I didn't know what a work of art you were; I would never have sullied you."

She wanted to scream. This was unbearable. She decided to get it over and done with. She grabbed his lapels and tugged his jacket off. Gregor laughed, casting his tie aside—*in case you try to throttle me with it*—and she unbuttoned his shirt. His body, while impressive, left her cold, but when he swept her up onto the bed, she began to tremble. His kiss was gentle.

"This will be much more pleasurable if you relax, Quilla."

He was already hard; she could feel his cock through his pants, ramrod hard against her thigh. He got up and stripped the rest of his clothes off, then slid her panties down. A tear rolled down her cheek, and he kissed it away. She didn't want to look at him, but her eyes slid to his cock as he slipped a condom on.

This is really happening, she thought and started to panic. She tried to sit up, covering her breasts, her sex, with her hands but Gregor, much stronger pulled her hands away and pinned them to the bed. His eyes burned into hers as he lay on top of her.

"Put your legs around my waist, Quilla."

She complied, her thighs weak and trembling, and when he entered her, she was so dry she cried out. Gregor smiled, beginning to thrust.

"Christ, Quilla, no wonder Jakob Mallory's like a dog on heat ... so sweet ..." He rammed himself deeper into her, and she gave a sob. "Make it real, Quilla," he warned. "Or I'll kill you both tonight. Slowly."

Afterward, he dressed quickly, throwing her dress at her. "Get dressed. Tomorrow night, you had better learn to act real quick, Quilla. Your body is incredible but next time, I want you engaged. I don't want to fuck a corpse."

"You made me a corpse," she whispered, but he didn't hear her. She had never felt as low as she did at this moment. Right now, she wanted him to take his knife to her, to use her as target practice, to make sure she was dead, dead, dead, so she didn't have to feel this pain. She had betrayed Jakob. Even if by the smallest chance they made it out of here alive, nothing would be the same again.

Gregor called Paul and, not looking at her again, told him to take her back to her room.

Hayley was curled up on the mattress, but as soon as she saw the look on Quilla's face, she scrambled to her feet and caught Quilla as she finally collapsed into her arms and began to sob.

. . .

G**REGOR WAS GAZING** at the laptop when Paul came back. He glanced at what his boss was watching and snickered. "You sending that to Mallory?"

Gregor frowned. "No. Not this one. She back in the room?"

"Yeah."

Gregor considered. "Give them some more blankets, some of that bottled water, some chocolate. Maybe a couple of those paperbacks we found."

Paul's eyebrows shot up. "Going soft?"

Gregor gave a snort. "Paul, one day you'll learn, you get more bees with honey. There's no harm in them thinking we're treating them well. They'll be more receptive."

"You mean she will be more receptive."

Gregor went back to the video he was watching, the video of him fucking Jakob Mallory's wife. "Quite. Maybe if she warms up, we'll get the video we need to send to Mallory. The one where she looks like she's enjoying it."

He grinned up at Paul. "Won't that just break his little heart?"

C**ARTER HANDED** Jakob a cup of coffee. "Skandar's on his way? Good." Jakob filled Carter in on the lack of progress his family's detectives had made.

Carter reciprocated by telling him his—what Ali had taken to calling—Survivalist Guide to Kidnapping theory. Jakob was surprisingly receptive. "At this point, I'll take anything," he said when Carter expressed his surprise. "I've learned in business that it's best to keep an open mind. Anything come of it?"

"Maybe. A couple of Walmarts in the greater Seattle area report large stocks of goods being bought by the same men for the last month or so. Could be nothing; we're getting the security tapes. Would you take a look, see if you recognize anyone?"

"Definitely." Jakob suddenly felt his spirits lift. Something palpable he could do, at last.

"How's Skandar?"

Jakob shook his head. "Beyond terrified. It doesn't help that the press are all over him, all the time. He's going to lose it if they corner him."

"You got someone with him?"

"Joel and Nan, and we've hired in some more people, security, and press liaisons. Shit, Carter. I'd say this was an unbelievable situation, but the more I think about it, I should have seen this coming, should have protected her better."

"You had a team of bodyguards."

"It wasn't enough."

Carter shook his head. "Sometimes it really is out of our hands."

Jakob was silent for a long time. "Quilla's a fighter, you know. I keep expecting her to turn up, barefoot and bedraggled on some highway somewhere, with Hayley, having kicked and punched and fought her way out."

Carter watched him. "That's a romantic notion, but that could get her killed. I hope she's not taking risks."

Jakob was silent. God, come back to me, baby, please ...

Carter's phone rang. "Yeah. Cool, on our way." He stood and gestured to the door. "The tapes are here; let's take a look."

THE SECOND NIGHT, Quilla gave the performance of her life. She and Hayley had talked all day about how to deal with the impending ... "Rape," Hayley said firmly.

"God, don't call it that," Quilla groaned, nausea rising in her throat. "Please."

"But it is, Quils," Hayley said, suddenly seeming eons older than her twenty years. "He's using the threat of death to make you have sex with him. Rape."

Quilla knew she was right, but it didn't make her feel any better knowing that technically, her consent was being extorted from her. She had cried pretty much the rest of the night, trying to hide it from Hayley, but her friend had known and had held her tightly. If we ever get out of here, Quilla thought, I'm telling the world how much I love this girl.

"Look, can you make out it's Jakob you're having sex with? Close your eyes and think of Mallory?"

Quilla blew out her cheeks. "I don't want to do that. Because if I ever get to be with Jakob again, I don't want the association."

Hayley made a face. "Of course not. Okay, how about someone from your Hall Pass list."

Quilla looked askance. "My what?"

Hayley rolled her eyes. "The list of celebrities you're allowed to do it with, and your boyfriend can't complain."

Quilla laughed. "Is that right? Have you got a list?"

"Hell, yes. So has Skandar. We locked that shit down the first week we were together."

Quilla shook her head, still laughing. "So the rules are you can pick so many celebrities that if you were to meet and get the chance to have sex with, you're allowed?"

"That's it. So, I'm saying, tonight, use one of yours."

"I don't have a list."

"Everyone has a list. Come on, think of someone."

Quilla chewed her lip. "Matt Damon?"

"You got the hots for him?"

"Kinda."

"Not good enough. I know, pick someone you would have hot, dirty sex with but that would be it. You don't even want to chat with him, just do it against a wall then leave. That's who you want to picture."

"Got it. Hang on then, let me think ..."

"Channing Tatum?"

"Eww, no."

"What, not even as a DF?"

"DF?"

"Dirty Fuck. That's what they're called."

"Man, you've really thought this through." She chuckled. "But you are making me feel a whole lot better."

"What else have we got to do but talk? One of the Avengers?"

Quilla raised her eyebrows. "I can't see past Black Widow when I watch that."

"Oo, little lady loving, nice. Beyoncé's on my list. No, we need a man. Hey, how about Sebastian Winter?"

"Asia's ex? Nope, look, I'll just come up with a composite man in my head. Again with the association thing, I don't want to be watching ... Daniel Craig, and then feeling sick."

"Good plan. But we are going to discuss this further; I can't believe you haven't got a Hall Pass list."

Hayley's attempt to lighten the mood had worked and it wasn't until Paul came to fetch Quilla that the horror set in again.

AGAIN, she was unable to eat but followed Gregor as he led her to the bedroom. It came to her as Gregor was undressing her. She needed to pretend that she was someone else, not pretend this monster in front of her was anything than what he was. As her dress hit the floor, she switched Quilla off.

Gregor kissed her, and she responded, kissing him back. She noted his surprise with satisfaction. I hate you, you scumbag, but you will believe quite the opposite when I'm done.

And she did it; she went through with it, faking every sigh, every moan—not too much, so it was clearly fake—but enough so that Gregor was convinced she was starting to enjoy herself. So absorbed was she in her performance that it was over quickly, and Gregor looked pleased.

"That was much better, my darling," he kissed her tenderly.

When she got back to the room, she nodded at Hayley, almost imperceptibly. Hayley's eyes flickered to Gregor and back.

"After a lovely evening, I'm feeling generous. Hayley, dear, is there anything you need?"

Hayley sighed. "Our freedom?"

Gregor smiled. "Funny girl."

"New underwear," Quilla said suddenly." And tampons."

"Of course. Let Paul know your sizes for the underwear and we'll arrange it."

"Pizza. Hot pizza," Hayley added hopefully.

When Gregor and Paul had gone, Quilla hugged Hayley. "Not so bad tonight."

"Good. Undies and tampons?"

Quilla grinned. "If you saw an oaf like Paul buying underwear, especially in specific sizes, and tampons, wouldn't you suspect something weird? He has hick written all over him. I'm hoping some salesgirl will have some smarts about them and maybe say something to someone. It's a long shot, but you never know."

Hayley squeezed her arm. "You are a genius. Do you want a bath?"

"God, yes, please."

"Good, because there's something I want to show you."

She led Quilla into the bathroom, twisting the faucets on. When the water was filling the tub, Hayley beckoned Quilla over to the wall near the toilet. She glanced over at the door to make sure no one was coming in, then indicated a tile near the floor. She flicked it with her nail and it popped out.

"I found this earlier," she said in a low voice. "I'm thinking, we snap it in two, then use the rough edge to ..." She made a cutting motion against her neck. "We wait behind the door, then when one of them comes in, jumped on his back and kill him."

Quilla smiled at Hayley's excitement. "It's a good plan, Hays ... if we've run out of every other option. This is our back up, right?"

Hayley looked a little deflated. "I guess. I just ... I hate that you have to do this for us. I want to help."

"You are helping, so much, you don't know."

Hayley looked a little tearful. "I feel so useless." Quilla hugged her.

"You know what? Sit on this toilet and talk to me while I soak and get that asshole's stench off of me."

· · ·

ON THE OTHER side of the house, Gregor watched the video of him making love to the most beautiful woman he had ever seen, watched her face as she came, her delicious body undulating under him as he fucked her, saw her kiss him passionately. He smiled.

"This is for Padme, you bastard."

He opened his email and began to type.

"CARTER, DUDE, WE MAY HAVE SOMETHING." Carter sighed as Ali Bell, looking excited, flew into the room.

"Really? Or is this another false trail."

"Debbie Downer," Ali snapped at him, then grinned. "Nope. You know the ex-girlfriend; the one Jakob Mallory was shtupping on the side?"

"Yeah?"

"Padme Khan. Got a job in prestigious London law firm and left Seattle—and her two lovers behind."

"I know this already."

"Patience. Khan was murdered less than two years later, an apparent street mugging gone wrong. But, here's the thing, even the London dicks think there was more to it. Overkill, they called it. The perp wanted it to look like a mugging, but the woman was repeatedly stabbed, more than thirty-seven times in the stomach. No street mugger does that."

Carter was interested now. "Was Fisk ever questioned?"

"Had an alibi. A shady one, but enough for them to drop that line of questioning."

"So he knew about the affair then?"

"I'd bet my ass on it."

"Wow, that's a big bet." Carter grinned as Ali flipped him the middle finger. "So, do we have a motive?"

"Putting my psychologist's cap on—hey, I got some psych credits before I switched—I'd say killing his first love sent him over the edge, and he blamed Jakob. To him, Jakob put that knife in his hand. Jakob took away his love. Now he's going to do the same to him."

Carter looked bleak. "We're not getting those girls back alive, are we?"

Ali didn't answer. Steve, a younger agent, stuck his head around the door. "Sir? We've got a hit on an email Mallory was just sent. We think it's from Fisk."

Ali looked shocked. "You're monitoring his emails?"

Carter shot her a look. "Of course, we are. You really think it's from Fisk?"

Steve nodded. "I don't think there's any doubt. You gotta see this."

JAKOB WAS FLIPPING through the photos he and Quilla had taken of each other since that first meeting in Venice. It was sweet, sweet torture. His email pinged, and he switched over to it, expecting spam or worse, more press intrusion. When the name showed up as unknown, his heart started beating harder. He clicked on it, and his heart dropped.

Love from Quilla ... was all it said. A video attachment. Oh, God, no ... was this Gregor sending him the video of him killing her? Was he about to witness Quilla's murder?

Please, God, no ...

He hesitated for a long moment, closing his eyes, not wanting, but needing, to know what was on that video ... he opened his eyes and clicked play.

"SHIT," Carter hissed and was out of the door before Ali could stop him. He ran the few blocks to Jakob's hotel and took the elevator to the top floor.

Jakob answered the door, and Carter knew he'd seen the video because he was looking at the face of a heartbroken man ...

9

PART NINE: TAUNT ME

F loriana Morgan smiled at Jakob as he came into the kitchen the next morning. "Hey you, can I get you some coffee?"
He looked awful; dark circles under his reddened eyes, his whole body slumped and dragging. He tried to smile at her. "Yes, thanks."

As she poured his drink, she could feel him watching her, and she blushed a little. Jakob gave her an apologetic smile.

"I'm sorry I'm staring. I don't mean to make you uncomfortable," he said gently. "It's just you remind me of Quilla so much."

Flori swallowed her own sadness. In the few months she had known Quilla, they had grown very close, and yes, she could see the resemblance. Both them were dark, petite, curvy; both of them obsessed were with art; both of them were madly in love with a Mallory brother. She put a hand on Jakob's. "We'll get her back, Jakob." But she knew that's not all that was bothering him.

The FBI agent in charge of their case, Carter James, had called Grady the previous evening and told him what had happened. Grady had gone to collect a wrecked Jakob, and when Jakob had retired to the guest room, Grady told Flori what had happened. Flori couldn't imagine that Quilla had slept with Gregor Fisk voluntarily, the man who had tried to kill both her and Flori, never mind enjoyed it. No, she reasoned, he must be coercing her, under pain of death for her and Hayley. That was the only explanation but now, looking at Jakob, she could guess the turmoil in his mind.

Grady, fresh from the shower, appeared and smiled at them both. "Hey, kiddo." He kissed her cheek and then clapped his brother on the back. "Hey, dude. Get any sleep?"

The answer was obvious. Grady shot a look at Flori, then sat down next to his brother. "Dude, there's no way that tape wasn't … manufactured. Quilla would never cheat on you; that's the one certain thing in all of this. If she looked like she was enjoying it, she was probably forced to. We all know the disgusting things Gregor threatened to do to her."

Jakob, hollow-eyed, looked at him. "I should know this; I should be certain. And that's what I can't face, that I don't trust Quilla enough to believe that. And she's done nothing wrong, nothing. It is my fault that she's even in this situation."

Grady sighed. "Padme?"

Jakob nodded. "It all comes down to that. Gregor was always a player, always, I never imagined that he had been so much in love with her that her cheating with me would kick off some deep psychosis in him." He hesitated. "I never told you this but … Padme was murdered. Stabbed to death in London."

Flori couldn't help the gasp of distress and Jakob looked at her in sympathy. "I apologize, Flori. You are as much as victim in this as Quilla or Kit or any of us."

"Not a victim," she said quietly, "a survivor."

Jakob's smile was kind. "Of course. I'll drink to that." He raised his coffee cup. "Look, both of you, thanks for last night but I'll get out of your hair. I need to regroup, talk to Carter, and see where we go from here."

· · ·

WHEN THEY WERE ALONE, Grady sighed and took Flori in his arms. "Have I told you both how proud I am of you and how much I love you?"

She leaned against him. "I know you are. God, Grady, is it wrong that while everyone is so wrecked, all I can think about is how lucky I am to have you?"

"Not at all. Right back at you."

She tilted her head up for a kiss. "Take me to bed, Grady Mallory. I need you."

Grady smiled, his eyes soft. "Your wish is my command, beautiful."

He still smelled of his shower gel, and she breathed him in as they slowly stripped off and tumbled onto the bed, their arms and legs curving around the other, lips against lips.

Flori gazed up at him, and he smiled. "Hey, pretty girl."

She grinned, then moaned as he bent his head and took her nipple into his mouth, his tongue teasing the nub until it grew hard and ultra-sensitive. Flori reached down to cup his cock, feeling it thicken and grow in her hand, brushing her thumb lightly over the sensitive tip, making his hips jerk, his low groan making her wet.

"I want you inside me," she whispered, but Grady, grinning, shook his head. "Not yet ..."

She groaned, impatient, as he sucked her other nipple, the nerve endings in her breasts screaming for him. His tongue drifted down to her belly, circling her navel. He kissed each one of the scars there tenderly, before making his way down and burying his face in her sex. As his teeth grazed her clit, Flori gasped, her fingers knotting in his hair. He brought her to a screaming orgasm with his tongue, then before she could catch her breath, his cock, heavy and thick, plunged into her, and Grady, grinning, thrust hard, knowing he had complete domination over her body.

Afterward, she pleaded with him to stay in bed with her instead of going to an auction. "I wouldn't ask if there were any significant pieces at it," she said, "but I can't bear the thought of not spending the day with you."

"You could always come with me," he said, but she could tell his heart wasn't it in. He smiled and kissed her. "So, vegging out day?"

"Yup. Sexy times and vegging out. Is it wrong that I want to do this while Quilla and Hayley are missing?"

"Not at all. What are we supposed to do that we aren't already doing? We have to keep things as normal as possible—not that sex with you could ever be described as normal."

They were silent for a while. "Be honest," Flori said finally, turning onto her side to look at him. "Do you think they're dead already?"

Grady sighed. "Or they wish they were. God."

Flori felt tears threatening and instead leaned over and kissed him. "I refuse to believe they're dead. Positive vibes and all of that."

He cupped her face with his big hand. "Good idea."

And they began again where they'd left off.

QUILLA WASN'T SLEEPING. Hayley knew, even though her friend closed her eyes and lay curled next to her, that she lay awake all night, every night. Every time Gregor brought her back to their prison room, Hayley could see the pain in Quilla's eyes, and it worried her. Something in her friend was dying. Hope. Faith. Self-respect. She would try to hold her, help her grieve for the part of her that was lost, but Quilla would just give her a half smile and turn away. It broke Hayley's heart.

In the evenings, Gregor would keep Quilla longer and longer, force her to do God knows what—the way he looked at her friend terrified her. Obsession. Psychopathic. Dangerous. Lethal. Gregor Fisk was a man on a knife edge—when he was with Quilla, Hayley would sit alone wondering if this would be the night that he would snap and kill her friend.

Seven days. Seven days without seeing Skandar, touching him, loving him. Seven days where she didn't know if the next moment would be her last. Hayley was a resilient girl, but this was pure torture, and her nerves were shredded. Last night, Quilla had returned with blood on her dress. She had gone into the shower, and Hayley followed her. There were scratches and cuts on her body. She saw Hayley's scared face and tried to smile. "Don't worry; it's all superficial."

"Did he have a knife?" Hayley's voice quivered as Quilla nodded, not meeting her eye. Hayley hated to acknowledge the thought that kept buzzing around her brain; Quilla will not survive this. All it took was for Gregor to lose his temper. Jesus ...

Now, in the pale light of the morning, Hayley lay on her back, staring at the cracking paint on the walls, the blankness of the ceiling. They had to figure something out, even if it cost their lives. They had to take control. She rolled onto her side. Quilla was lying next to her, her eyes closed.

"Quills ... you awake?"

Quilla opened her eyes and smiled at her. "Hey, buddy." Just that simple, affectionate greeting made Hayley feel better.

"We need to come up with a plan."

"I agree. But I've been thinking for days, and I can't think of anything that Gregor won't kill us for even trying. Hayley, I think we need to accept; both of us won't make it out of here."

Hayley gave a sob. "Don't talk like that."

"We have to be realistic."

"You've given up."

Quilla didn't answer, and Hayley wrapped her arm around her waist. "Don't do that; I can't bear it. I know exactly what you mean, and I won't permit it. You are not sacrificing yourself for me. No way, nuh-uh."

She leaned her forehead against Quilla's. "I love you, Quilla; you are my sister as much as Nan is my sister. We may not share DNA, but you are my blood, my family."

Quilla's already exhausted eyes filled with tears. "I won't let him kill you."

"Do you honestly think you're not already doing more than humanly possible to prevent that? I'd have a bullet in my head if it weren't for you." Hayley's whisper was urgent, but she felt sick. Too many images of Quilla, dead, were crowding her mind. No. No.

Quilla kissed her cheek. "I love you too, rug rat."

Hayley smiled. "That's better." But she didn't know how much worse it could get.

But, of course, it did.

ALI BELL WAS CONCENTRATING SO hard on her computer screen that Carter James grinned. "You watching Magic Mike again?"

He expected her to give him the finger, but instead, her face deadly serious, she beckoned him over. "Take a look at this."

He came around to sit beside her. "The tapes from the retail stores? We've seen these."

"No, look, these are from a couple of days ago. This dude," she tapped the screen. "We've tracked him using the same retail outlet for a couple of months, buying stuff in bulk, from one of the wholesale stores near Puyallup."

"So?"

"So, he's been buying pretty standard stuff for two months but then two days ago, he buys women's underwear in two different sizes and tampons. The first time he's bought anything like that. Now, forget that this dude doesn't look like the most enlightened guy in the world; he's been doing the grocery run for two months and has never bought any feminine products before. Underwear, two different sizes, and guess what, they match Quilla Mallory and Hayley Applebee's sizes."

Carter was interested now. "Anything else? How does he pay?"

Ali looked slightly gleeful. "Cash."

"Shoot, no way to trace a card."

She was still smiling. "Cash, Carter. Fifties. Every single time."

"Fuck."

"Yep."

"Christ, Ali, that's the best lead yet. Right, let's get people out there now."

"Already done. We're sweeping the area."

Carter let out a long breath. "Alianja Bell, I think I love you."

Ali grinned. "Tell me something I don't know. Look, I think we should tell Jakob Mallory to come, see if he can recognize this guy now these are clearer photos."

Carter wasn't convinced. "Ali ... I don't want to give Jakob Mallory false hope. If it doesn't pan and out and this dude is on the level, I think it'll break Mallory. He's on the edge."

Ali looked sympathetic. "Poor guy." She was quiet for a while. "You know what's weird? I hope Quilla Mallory was sleeping with Gregor Mallory and enjoying it. Because the alternative is so fucked up, I can't deal with it."

"Quite. But we're not married to her."

Ali stood. "Look, let's get out there and see what we can find."

JAKOB WENT BACK to his hotel after thanking Grady and Flori, but he couldn't stay there for long. He packed his stuff and checked out and drove to his dad's place. Ran Mallory was on the phone when Jakob walked into his study, and Ran waved at him to sit down. Whoever Ran was talking to must be a friend, if Ran's warm tone and smile told him anything. Jakob waited until his father finished the call. His father greeted him.

"That was Marley; I was just updating her on what the police told us yesterday."

Jakob's eyebrows went up. "You're calling each other?"

"For a couple of months now." Was he imagining it, or did his dad flush? Wow. Jakob grinned for the first time in days.

"Go for it, Dad. How's she doing?"

Ran shook his head. "Utterly devastated. She's considering taking a sabbatical from work, but she says all she'll do all day is sit by the phone and watch the endless news coverage and drive herself crazy. If any of that actually had any positive effect, I wouldn't mind, but ..." he sighed. "I said I'd go over this afternoon, talk things out."

Jakob chuckled. "Is that what the kids call it now?"

"Jakob Mallory, I am your father." But Ran was grinning bashfully.

"Darth Vader did that much better. Anyway, I came over to tell you; I'm going to London. I want to talk to Padme's parents, see if they can give me any insight to Gregor's behavior with her before she left him, whether she was scared of him."

"Haven't the British police already done that?"

"I need to hear it for myself; they might be more inclined to talk to one of her ... friends."

Ran got up and hugged his son. "If it helps you. Why don't you see Bo while you're there?"

"Good idea. Are you still hoping she'll come for Christmas?"

Ran nodded then laughed softly. "Here we are talking about Christmas..."

Jakob nodded. "Yeah. I have to keep believing we'll get them back soon."

Ran's eyes were kind. "I understand. Be careful in London; those parents have already been through enough."

THE DOOR OPENED, and Paul, carrying a lunch tray, came in. Quilla and Hayley, sitting against the far wall as instructed, ignored him. But when he closed the door and locked it—from inside—they shared an alarmed glance. Paul set the tray down and waited for them to look at him. Finally, Hayley made a disgusted noise.

"What do you want? Thanks for the shit food, Paulyboy. Now run along to Daddy and kiss his ass."

Quilla shot Hayley a look; don't antagonize him. Paul grinned nastily.

"Better watch how you talk to me, Blondie. One word from me and your whore friend gets a knife in her gut."

Quilla was a second too late grabbing Hayley's hand. The young woman scrambled to her feet and got in Paul's face. "You fucking whiny cocksucker," she spat at him. "Do you think all this makes you a man? Is this what you want from life? Keeping women prisoner and jerking off thinking about them because Daddy won't let you touch them?"

He cuffed her viciously, sending her flying to the ground. Quilla was up then, throwing herself at the huge man, all her rage, her hurt, coming out. Paul just laughed and threw her against the wall. Quilla's head crashed against the window, and she was knocked senseless, slumping to the ground. Hayley screamed.

"You've killed her, you motherfucker!"

Paul grabbed her, pulling a blade from his pocket. "It's about time you learned some manners, you little slut." He pushed her against the wall and yanked her jeans down, using the knife to cut her underwear away. Hayley was struggling, screaming. Quilla, coming around, was immediately on her feet, unsteady and dazed, but she again ran at Paul, using everything she had to get him away from Hayley.

"Get off me you bitch!" She was on his back, digging her fingers into his eyes, trying to gouge them out. Paul roared and backed up, slamming Quilla against the wall but she clung on until finally, he managed to shake her off, dropping her to the floor and crouching over her. Knife drawn.

"No!" Hayley went to help her friend but Paul elbowed her viciously in the stomach, and she crumpled. Paul, one hand pinning Quilla down, pushed up her T-shirt and raised the knife. "Let's add some more to that nice little stab wound, shall we?"

Quilla closed her eyes and Hayley, sobbing, begged Paul not to kill her friend. Then the door was kicked in and in a daze, Quilla opened her eyes to see Gregor, his face one of rage, a gun in his hand. Paul ignored him and raised the knife ... and, roaring, Gregor shot him through the head. Paul dropped instantly, and Quilla kicked his body off of hers and skittered away from it.

"What the fuck is going on here?" Gregor looked wildly around, then pointed the gun at Hayley, who froze. "You. You fucking taunted him, didn't you? Couldn't keep your mouth shut? They should have killed you in that car." He clicked off the safety and Hayley squeezed her eyes shut. Scrambling to her feet, Quilla darted in front of her friend.

"Please," Quilla said, "Please don't hurt her. It was my fault, not hers. Please ... baby."

Gregor squinted, his eyes locked on hers. "Give me a good reason, Quilla."

Hayley whimpered, but Quilla kept her gaze steady. "I'll make you a deal. Her for me. Let her go and I'll go with you. Anywhere. I'll be yours entirely. I'll divorce Jakob and marry you, if that's what you want. And if I make you unhappy, well, you can obviously kill me whenever you want; I won't fight it. Please, Gregor. Let her go."

Gregor stared at her, and Hayley could see the turmoil in him. *God, he's really thinking about this.* But she couldn't do it, let Quilla throw her life away on this monster. *Not for me.*

"Quilla, no," she whispered, but Quilla held her hand up. Quiet. Gregor's mouth hitched up in a smirk and aimed the gun at her belly.

"And what if I don't agree? What if I decide you're not worth it? What I decide I want to put a bullet into you instead?"

Quilla edged forward so that the muzzle of the gun pressed into her. "Then shoot me right now, Gregor. Do it. Because while Hayley is here, while she's not safe, I'll never let you touch me again. Choose, right now."

Hayley felt a chill pass through her. Seconds passed, and it felt like a lifetime. Gregor, his eyes never leaving Quilla's face, clicked the safety off the gun, and Hayley stopped breathing. Her gaze was riveted to his finger on the trigger.

Then he lowered the gun. "Deal." Both Hayley and Quilla breathed out and, trembling, Quilla reached around her to take Hayley's hand.

"How do I know you'll keep your word?"

Gregor considered for a long moment, his eyes flicking between the two girls. "Hayley's phone. She'll video the whole drop, right up until she's picked up by police. We'll watch a live feed. How does that sound?"

Quilla nodded. "Good. Thank you." She squeezed Hayley's hand.

"Thank you," Hayley stammered. Gregor gave her a stiff nod, then gazed at Quilla.

"You're mine now."

Quilla nodded. "I'm yours." She glanced at Hayley. "Gregor, would you give Hayley and me a little time alone to say goodbye? Please?"

Gregor looked down at Paul's body. "Sure. Five minutes. Then Dick will take Hayley to the nearest town, and we'll leave here, Quilla. We'll go away and begin our life together."

After he had left, closing the door behind him, Quilla dragged Hayley into the bathroom and locked the door. She went to the toilet and bent down, grabbing the loose tile. She smashed it and picked up the two biggest, most lethal looking shards. She handed one piece to Hayley, tugging her into an embrace, her lips close to Hayley's ear. "Use it only if you need to, if anything goes wrong. Tell Jakob I love him, and I'm sorry, but this is the only way."

Hayley's eyes were huge, brimming with tears. "What are you going to do?"

"Try to kill Gregor. But it might take me a little while to get him comfortable enough to relax around me. Wherever he takes me, it'll be remote, but he can't take me out of the country; Jakob will have the airports and borders on alert. He'll need sex soon so that it won't be too far from here, probably still in the state. Just tell Jakob and the police everything and anything. I'll try to get away, but Hayley, whatever happens, I love you so much, all of you. I would not have swapped anything for this last year with the Mallorys, with you and Nan, and Flori and Asia. Anything."

Haley started to sob then, and Quilla held her, tears pouring down her face.

"I don't want to leave you with him," Hayley gulped, "Please, Quilla ..."

Quilla stepped away from her. "You have to go, Hayley, please, or all of this will have been for nothing. Hide that in your jeans." She nodded at the tile shard and tucked her own piece into the messy bun at the nape of her neck. She smiled at Hayley's confused look. "It's the only part of me where I can hide things from him."

Hayley looked sick but nodded. "I love you, Quilla."

"And you, Bubba."

Gregor banged on the door. "Let's get going."

Quilla opened the door, and Gregor held out his hand to her. She took it, glancing back at Hayley as she hesitantly walked out. Dick, the other goon, who they'd barely seen, stood implacable as ever. Quilla saw Hayley look at him nervously.

"Look after her, won't you, please?" Quilla looked at Dick, trying to read him. He didn't have that sleazy look that Paul had, and now he nodded to her, meeting her gaze steadily.

"You have my word; she'll be safe with me."

Quilla had no choice but to believe him. Hayley grabbed her one last time, and they hugged, simply holding each other.

Quilla watched as Dick led her out, her heart pounding. It was out of her control now. Gregor took her hand. "I promise you could see her delivered to safety," he said, his voice tender, loving. "I'll keep that promise. Then we'll leave here. God, Quilla, you have made me the happiest man in the world." He cupped her face with his hands, and she saw in his eyes, the complete belief that she was his now. She smiled back at him.

"Our new life together," she said, and he kissed her. She kissed him back, and a certain sense of satisfaction flooded through her. Whether Gregor Fisk knew it or not, whether he ended up killing her or she killed him, she had won. He believed her. His psychosis, his monumental ego played straight into her hands. He actually believed she cared for him, and that put him at such a disadvantage, she could hardly believe it herself.

Live or die; she had won.

HAYLEY STARED BACK at the farmhouse until she could no longer see it, then turned to Dick. The big man was driving, his eyes riveted on the road ahead.

"If you're going to kill me, can I ask you a couple of favors?" Hayley said, not letting him speak. "Make it quick and let my family have my body. If you can avoid the face so they can have an open casket, I'd be grateful, too. A bullet in the heart should do it."

She was surprised when Dick burst out laughing. He grinned over at her. "Thanks for the tips but I'm not going to kill you, sweetheart. You're going home to your tennis player."

Hayley studied him. "You're not yanking my chain?"

"No, kiddo. I realize you've been through hell, and for my part, I'm sorry about that."

Hayley was astonished. "Then why? Why did you go along with it?"

Dick looked uncomfortable. "Sometimes you have to do things that you don't want to do."

Suddenly she understood. "That son-of-a-bitch. What's he got on you?"

Dick sighed. "My brother got into drugs, started dealing. He was Gregor's dealer for years. Gregor, of course, plays the long game. Every interaction documented—he blackmailed my brother until he couldn't stand it anymore. He tried to kill Gregor – which of course, Gregor had seen coming. So now my brother's in debt to him and what does Gregor want? Me."

Hayley was confused. "With respect, why?"

Dick smiled. "Because I was Black Ops. A trained killer. Gregor only likes to kill women. For anything else, he used me. Assassination, abduction."

Hayley suddenly felt nervous. "Why are you telling me this? Is this a trick? Are you going to decide you've told me too much and off me?"

Dick suddenly pulled the car over and took out his gun. Hayley cringed back. "Oh, my God ..."

"Give me your hand." Dick opened the chamber and dumped the bullets into her palm. Then he cranked open the window, wiped the gun free of fingerprints, and threw it out onto the dirt road. Starting the car, he grinned at her, reaching over into the back seat. "Gregor would have set up the feed now. Turn your phone on and call the number I've programmed. And the conversation we had never happened."

She shook her head in disbelief. "Why?"

"Because I've had enough. I don't kill women; I don't kill any innocent person. Fuck Gregor and fuck my brother. When we get to the police station, I'm turning myself and my brother in, telling them everything about Gregor. I just hope we can get to them before he takes Quilla somewhere they'll never find them."

Hayley looked at the bullets in her hand. "Should I dump these?"

"A little further along the road. I don't want some kid finding them and the gun together. Now, I'm going to start driving so ..." He nodded at the phone, but she put her hand on his arm.

"Thank you."

He smiled. "Turn the phone on, Hayley," and he pulled the car back onto the road.

RAN MALLORY WAVED at Marley Griffin as he pulled into the parking lot of her college. Jumping out of the car, he embraced her.

"So good to see you, Marley."

She chuckled. "It's been all of twenty-four hours since I saw you."

He shrugged good-naturedly. "I should have said it's always good to see you. Ready for lunch?"

At his favorite restaurant, he told her about Jakob going to London. "He's just desperate to do anything. Failing trying to comb the country for her on his own, he feels useless. He's hoping Padme's parents will be able to tell him something."

Marley chewed on her lip, and he noticed a wary look in her eye. Ran sighed. Jakob was Marley's breaking point; she blamed him for everything and now Ran wished he hadn't told her about Padme and Jakob's affair. Thank God, he and Jakob had decided not tell her about the tapes.

"Marley? Every day, the police are getting closer. Carter James just called me; they have a lead out near Puyallup."

Her eyes lit up, and she suddenly looked hopeful. "Really? That's great."

Ran nodded. "They're scouring the area for any abandoned buildings; anywhere people could be held."

"How did they come up with that theory?"

Ran shrugged. "He didn't go into details, but he sounded excited, which, if you'd met him, is unusual. I'm taking that as a good sign."

Marley touched the back of his hand. "Ran ... I can't imagine what all of this has been like for you, and I want to thank you for being so ... supportive. What with Kit and everything, you must be in hell."

"You make me feel better, so I suppose I'm selfish. Marley, do you realize what a friend, a confidante you've become?"

Marley smiled, blushing. "And the same to you, Ran. Really. I know I rub against Jakob's involvement with my best friend, but not yours. I'm glad Quilla has you as a father figure; she's never had that before. If she'd never met Jakob ... maybe Gregor would have found her anyway and taken her, but then maybe we wouldn't have your army or the FBI combing the world for her. And I know Jakob loves her. I know that."

Ran took her hand. "For something different, let's talk about you. What's happening with your project?"

Marley told him about her work and Ran listened intently, noting the way her expression got animated when describing things he couldn't understand in a clear, concise way, the way she got excited when he finally got a concept. He smiled at her.

"You would make an incredible professor," he said. "What's your end game?"

"End game?"

"Your goal. Lecturing? Writing a book?"

Marley looked blank. "Um, I hadn't really thought about either ... I just want to carry on the way I am. Science is infinite; there are always new theories to test, new places to go. It's limitless."

Ran nodded, and two pink spots appeared high on his cheeks. "And ... personally?"

Marley colored, too, but he was gratified that she didn't look uncomfortable. "Personally ... I would say for now," she emphasized the 'for now,' blushing furiously, "I need to concentrate on my work. We have a huge cycle coming up soon, late nights, early mornings, very little sleep, living on day-old pizza. But ... after, who knows? I

mean," and her voice wavered, "I'm certainly not interested in anyone
... else."

She was trembling now, and an equally nervous Ran smiled. "Me,
either ..."

Marley looked up at him with large eyes. "Ran ..."

He kissed her. Gentle, soft, and quick but so, so sweet, she closed
her eyes for a second. Ran leaned his forehead against hers. "The
years between us ..."

"Don't bother me in the slightest," she whispered and pressed her
lips back to his. Ran felt breathless, giddy like a teenager. Everything
about this woman drew him in; her intelligence, her refusal to bend
to pressure from her peers, her kindness. And, God, she was beautiful
...

"Ran ..."

"Sweetheart?"

"I don't have to be back at work today ... our research cycle doesn't
start until next week ..."

"Then ..."

She looked up at him, her dark eyes full of desire. "I don't want to
be distracted when I work, thinking of you and me together ..."

He smiled—then his phone rang. He groaned, but Marley
laughed. "That's what Alanis Morissette would call 'ironic', but the
rest of us would call a pain in the ass."

Ran grinned and picked up his phone. "Indeed. Excuse me ...
hello?"

Marley watched as Ran's expression changed—more than
changed – became something she couldn't describe ... excitement,
hope, and joy. "Yes, yes, thank you, we'll be there right away."

He ended the call, staring at her in disbelief. "Hayley's been
released. She's safe—the police are bringing her back to Seattle now."

"And Quilla?"

"He wouldn't tell me anything else; just said to get to the field
office. Will you come?"

"Of course."

Together, they drove through the city and got to the field office twenty minutes later. Just as they were about to get out of the car, Marley suddenly stopped him. "Ran ... what if Quilla ... what if she's dead?"

Ran stopped and saw her eyes were full of fear, of tears. He kissed her. "We'll face whatever comes together, and we'll get through it."

She nodded, and they got out of the car. Holding hands, they raced into the field office to find out what was going on.

SKANDAR MALLORY PACED UP and down inside the interview room, Nan Applebee equally as tense. Seated next to Joel, her legs jiggled up and down, and she couldn't keep her hands still. She'd collapsed when Joel had gotten the phone call from Skandar—she could hear the young man sobbing down the phone, such was his relief. All they knew was Hayley had been freed and was safe and well. No news of Quilla yet.

Now, they waited. Nan looked up and smiled as Ran and Marley joined them, then a few minutes later, Flori and Grady arrived, Flori hugging Nan and sitting beside her.

Skandar kept checking his watch. They had a new agent, Steve Kendrick, sitting with them: Carter and Ali were down, following the trail in Puyallup—made easier now that Hayley was freed near there. Skandar was impressed; their lead had proved to be fruitful. Of course, Hayley had been released before they had found where the women were held, but now she could tell them where to go. He knew no one in this room could stop thinking: where's Quilla? If she was dead, wouldn't they have told them? Or would they? God. Joel had told him not to call Jakob yet.

"He's in London. He might find out something useful and if the worst has happened, well, I want him to be with us when he finds out."

Skandar didn't agree but went along with his father's wishes. All he could think of now was having Hayley back in his arms and when, thirty-seven minutes later, he heard her voice out in the office, every sense left him, and he ran.

Hayley saw him at the same time, and as they slammed into each other, they collapsed to the ground, holding each other, sobbing, kissing, as Nan, hysterical, joined them, the three of them making a human pile in the middle of the FBI field office.

After they'd gathered themselves, Agent Kendrick shook Hayley's hand. "Good to have you back. We're going to have the doctor look you over ... I know, you said you were fine," he stopped her interruption, "but it's a formality for the case. Then you can have a few hours with your family, go shower, eat, and maybe get some sleep. But we are going to need you to help us by answering some questions; I warn you, we go over everything with a fine-tooth comb so be prepared for answering the same questions over and over."

Hayley nodded. "I don't care how long it takes, anything to help Quilla."

When she'd told them what Quilla had done for her, Marley had burst into tears, Nan and Flori looked close to it, and even Joel's normally implacable face colored.

Skandar shook his head. "I owe her everything," he kept saying. "Everything."

THEY MANAGED to book a suite in a hotel, not wanting to run the gauntlet of the press just yet. After they'd eaten dinner together, the others left them alone, Nan hugging her sister tightly, looking at her as if she still couldn't believe they'd gotten her back.

When they were alone, Hayley stripped her clothes off and went to the shower. She turned and smiled at a wondering Skandar; his eyes drinking her in. "Get in this shower, Skandar Mallory, and soap me up."

He didn't need to be told twice. The moment he put his hands on his beautiful girlfriend, Skandar felt a shift inside him, a release, and he kissed her more passionately than he ever had before, feeling her soft skin under his like it was the first time. Hayley sank into his arms and it wasn't long until, still soaking from the water, he lifted her up into his arms and took her to bed.

"Are you sure you want to do this?"

Hayley groaned. "God, yes, this is all I've been thinking about for over a week, please, Skandar." She reached down and stroked his cock, which jerked and trembled under her touch. "God, Skandar, I want you so bad, don't wait, please ..."

With a growl, he kissed her, hitching her legs around his waist, the tip of his cock nudging at her sex before sliding in all the way. Hayley quivered and moaned, tilting her hips up so she could take him in as far as he could, moving with him as he thrust. Their eyes stayed locked on the other—a reconnection, a new beginning, a love solidified—and they moved, Hayley felt all the tension in her body be replaced with pleasure. She kept her mind focused on him and only him, his gentle eyes, his beautiful smile, his dark blond hair which felt so soft as she ran her fingers through it. The feel of his hard chest against her breasts, his belly against her own, the feel of his hips rocking against her inner thighs – God, blissful, heavenly release.

Her orgasm was less of an explosion, more of a gradual build, until she felt Skandar come, groaning and moaning her name over and over until she felt that utterly pure love come from him then it hit her. The climax was so bittersweet, she lost all sense of control, and she started to sob uncontrollably, hysterically, great wrenching sobs of terror and heartbreak and the utter helplessness she had felt during her abduction.

Skandar understood immediately and gathered her into his arms, swaddling her tightly as she cried out and let go. He said nothing; just let her get it all out, his lips against her temple. Eventually, she calmed herself, her sobs turning to hiccups. Skandar rocked her gently, and she burrowed hard against his chest, lifting her chin, finding his lips with hers.

"Okay, baby?"

She nodded. "I love you so much. I didn't stop thinking about you the whole time. God, Skandar, it was ... indescribable, thinking I'd never see you again. And what he did to Quilla ... Jesus ..."

She told him, haltingly, everything that had gone on and Skandar was sickened. "Do you think she's given up?"

Hayley shook her head. "I don't know. I hope not; she plans to try and kill Gregor, but I think ... if she died trying, she'd be okay with that. I'm scared she'll be reckless, and he'll guess what she's planning and ..." She couldn't finish, and Skandar tightened his grip on her.

"Listen, precious one. We know Fisk's weakness is Quilla. As long as she plays along with him, he'll keep her alive. So keep the faith that she knows what she's doing. I'll be forever in her debt for getting you home safely. We're all going to do everything to repay that debt and get her back alive. I promise you."

She nodded. "I know. I'll talk to the FBI in the morning—it might be hours and hours, but I'm willing to do it. Will you be there?"

"I'm not letting you out of my sight, Miss Applebee, and when this is all over, if you'll say yes, I'm going to marry the heck out of you."

She giggled. "That sounds like a fine idea, Mr. Mallory. Nan will be outraged I beat her to it. But ask me again, properly, when Quilla is safe. I promise I'll say yes."

Skandar's eyes were full of love, surprise, joy. "You will?"

"Hell, yes! This is it, you and me, for all time."

LATER, when she'd finally fallen asleep, Skandar lay next to her, drinking her face in, gently stroking his hand down the length of her body. She was home. She was safe. She was his.

Now he could only wish the same for his uncle.

JAKOB TOOK THE NEWS CALMLY. "Well, at least Hayley's okay. That's great news. Quilla's a smart girl; she'll find a way to let us know where she is."

Ran was a little discombobulated by his son's rather cold response. "Jakob ... I don't think you heard me right. Gregor has Quilla; he's taken her away somewhere we don't know."

"I heard you, Pa. What do you want me to say? I have no panic left; all there is left is hopelessness."

. . .

AFTER THE CALL HAD ENDED, Jakob sat in his hotel room. He'd called Padme's parents, and they'd agreed to see him later. He'd also called Bo Kennedy, and she was delighted to hear from him.

"I 'eard the news, love; that fucker doesn't give up, does he? Come over later."

PADME KHAN'S parents were polite, but he could tell they were not pleased to see him.

"Padme told you about us, then?" He couldn't help ask the question and her father, a serious-looking man with rimless spectacles and a full beard, nodded.

"She did. For what it's worth, she told us that she regretted the affair but not that it was with you. She cared for you deeply, Mr. Mallory."

"As I did for her. I'm not proud that we had a fling behind Gregor's back but I can't change that. I'm so very sorry that she died. Dr. Khan, be straight with me. What were her true feelings for Gregor?"

Padme's mother muttered something under her breath, then looked at her husband. He nodded.

"Gregor's intensity concerned her; part of the reason why she moved back to London was that she was beginning to feel afraid of him. He called, of course, after she'd come home, begging her to come back. Then after a while, the calls just stopped. Then, one night, she was coming home on the Tube. It was only a couple of streets from where she lived. She was stabbed to death a few seconds from where she lived. Fisk was questioned, of course, but he had an alibi and after a few months, the investigation was quietly dropped."

"I'm sorry," Jakob said softly. "Her murder not being solved, it must be awful."

"You make the mistake of thinking that if the law has said so, it must be unsolved. We know different," Padme's mother held his gaze. "We know who killed our daughter, Mr. Mallory."

.　.　.

JAKOB WAS at Bo Kennedy's door by eight-thirty. Despite only meeting her once before, he immediately felt at ease in her company.

"You look like shite," she said and Jakob, relieved to be with someone without an agenda, laughed.

"I feel like it."

Bo had made dinner, a divine beef casserole that warmed him to his soul. Two good bottles of red and he was as near to relaxed as he could be with his wife missing. He told Bo everything, and through her gentle questioning, he was finally able to admit his doubts.

"Why would she go through with it?"

"Easy. To stay alive, to keep Hayley alive."

"Everyone keeps saying that but ... she looked like she was enjoying it."

Bo studied him. "You know what a psycho Gregor is. Come on, Jakob; this is a no-brainer. She was forced to act the part. So what is this? Please tell me it's not your wounded male ego because I'll scream." She was grinning at him, and he laughed softly.

He sighed. "I don't know. God, this is killing me, Bo, knowing he has her, that he's doing God knows what to her. And it's my fault—if I'd acted more responsibly when I was younger ..."

"We could all say that, Jakob. All of us."

Jakob nodded then looked around the vast living room. "This is a nice place, Bo. Kit loved it here, you know."

She smiled, a little flush coming onto her cheeks. "I still can't believe he's gone, he was just so ... present, you know? Even when he was a numpty."

"Numpty?"

Bo snickered. "An idiot. That's why I loved him; he was everything, good and bad, his kindness, his massive ego, his ability to piss me off one minute, then make me fall even more in love with him the next. People are flawed, Jakob. Kit, me, you, Quilla. She's not perfect; she's a survivor. Do you know how many women are put through this kind of thing every day? It happens to us all in some manner. When Quilla is freed—and I have no doubt she will be—don't ever let her know you've felt like this. She's been through enough."

. . .

THEY WERE high in the Cascades, a small cabin—one room, but luxurious—the snow ten-feet deep outside. The nearest cabin was just across a snow field, but Gregor had already warned her. "Try to contact them and I'll kill them without a second thought." Quilla would not risk anyone else's life.

But every day she thought about killing Gregor. All day, every day. It consumed her and fueled her 'performance'. For the first few days, he'd held a gun to her while he fucked her, obviously not trusting her after the threat of killing Hayley was removed. But now, she had been so responsive, apparently, that he'd laid the gun aside and caressed her body. She felt dirty, sullied, but she switched her feelings off and smiled prettily at him, even murmuring encouragement.

Gregor had fallen for it all. She drove him crazy with her body, yet still, she had to listen to him fantasizing about killing her. She expected to die every day, whenever Gregor picked up the gun or used a knife. It had shredded the last of her nerves, and now she was close to the edge, struggling to keep it in.

So, killing Gregor was all she thought about.

CARTER JAMES and Ali Bell exited the interview room where they had been interviewing Richard Danks, the man who had delivered Hayley Applebee to freedom. Danks had been open and had given them a lot of information ... but not the location where Gregor had taken Quilla Mallory. "I would tell you if I knew," Danks had said, and the agents believed him.

Hayley Applebee had been a star, patient and responsive, and she'd even told them, with feeling, that Danks had been kind to her on the drive to freedom.

"He didn't have to do that; he could have killed me; he could have done anything. They had all the cards. And he was never abusive like the other guy."

They'd found Paul Mines' body in the farmhouse Hayley had

identified. With Skandar, she'd agreed to show them where the house was, and had shown no fear entering it with them. To Carter James' frustration, there was no evidence of Gregor's plans there either.

They all agreed he could not have taken Quilla far. Their pictures were all over the press; the airports, ports, and all other transport services had been alerted. Danks had told them Gregor was paranoid about being caught; that he'd kill both Quilla and himself before going to prison.

Carter ran a tired hand over his eyes. Ali, wan and pale, shook her head. "This case ... man, I don't think I've ever been this ..." She couldn't finish, but Carter nodded.

"I know."

Ali looked up at the board containing every scrap of information they'd gleaned and threw her hands up. "What next? We have nothing more, no clue to where they are. We're not getting Quilla Mallory back alive."

Carter wanted to argue but he couldn't form the words because he knew she was right. They'd exhausted every last resource. He didn't look forward to telling Jakob Mallory that.

Ran put down the phone and sat back, his hands covering his face. The FBI had no leads. Ran had told them he would talk to Jakob, see what they wanted to do next. But he felt drained. He didn't want to have to tell his oldest son that Quilla was more than likely dead. He couldn't bear to think the lovely young woman, who had saved Jakob's life, might be dead. Quilla had become a daughter to him and now ...

"Ran?"

Marley entered the study looking for him. She took one look at his face and went to him. She wrapped her arms around him. Since the day they'd declared their feelings, they'd barely been able to spend any time together; tonight they were supposed to have dinner, but Ran had asked Marley to come to the house, rather than go out. Since Hayley's release, the press had been all over all of them, all the time.

Ran sighed, his face in her hair, his arms around her. "Thank you for coming, darling."

He looked up, and she stroked his face. "You look exhausted."

Ran tried to smile. "But better now that you're here. Look, I have something to tell you." In halting words, he told her that the FBI were out of ideas. Marley took it calmly at first, then her face crumpled, and she started to cry. They held each other for the longest time before Marley, her face streaked with tears, finally shook her head.

"I knew it was a longshot getting her back, but ... goddammit," she whispered. Ran pressed his lips to her forehead.

"I'm so sorry, Marley."

She leaned into him. "Ran?"

"Yes, honey?"

"Can we forget dinner? I just want to be held." She gazed up into his eyes. "Please, Ran, let's just be together and forget everything else."

Ran nodded, and they walked to his bedroom Ran was suddenly nervous as he closed the door but Marley, sensing this, pulled her T-shirt over her head and unhooked her bra. Ran watched her as she stripped, her toned athletic body, her firm breasts and flat belly. He wanted to tell her she was beautiful, but something told him that no words were necessary here.

Marley walked to him and kissed him, her little fingers at the buttons on his shirt. Everything seemed to be going in slow motion. He hadn't felt like this in years—since his wife had died, he'd dated off and on, slept with a few women, but had never felt like he did right now. Marley stripped him of his clothes and smiled up at him, stroking his thickening cock against her soft belly, feeling it growing and thickening.

He ran his hands down her body then cupped her breasts, dipping his head to his each one, flick his tongue around her nipple, her little gasp making his cock tighten and swell. They lay gently on the bed and Ran moved his body over hers, and they took their time, exploring the other. Ran knew he had kept himself in good shape, that he had the taut, hard body of someone half his age, but still, he was nervous about what she would think. He shouldn't have been. Marley caressed and kissed his body before taking the sensitive of his penis into her mouth, the sensation of her tongue driving him crazy, and by the time he pushed into her warm, wet, velvety sex, he was lost in this woman, this brilliant, charming woman.

Afterward, they lay, smiling at each other. Ran stroked her damp cheek, looking into her shining eyes. "I love you, Marley Griffin. I think I've loved you since we met. Even with the age gap, I feel I've met my soulmate. Will you have me, Marley? Forever, I mean? I know it's fast, but I don't want to wait. Marry me."

Marley smiled at him. "I will, Ran Mallory. I will marry you. You are the best thing to happen to me, and I'm so in love with you. Despite everything that has happened, that is still happening, you are the one bright star, and I cannot wait to be your wife."

Ran kissed her, overjoyed. "I want us to be married as soon as possible but at the same time, with what's going on ..."

"Then we should keep it a secret until everything is ... settled." Marley said firmly. "I don't want to wait. We've done enough waiting. If Quilla were here, she'd be dragging us to City Hall right now."

Ran chuckled. "Yes, she would." For a moment he hesitated, then he said, "Marley ... I know that it seems bleak at the moment and to even hope is so painful, knowing that, in all probability, Quilla is gone. But we shouldn't forget ... Quilla negotiated Hayley's freedom. She could do the same for herself."

Marley nodded. "I know. That's the only thing stopping me from screaming. Quilla's always been resourceful, but Gregor is pure psychopath."

"Keep the faith, my love."

They married two days later at City Hall, Ran making sure that their privacy was respected. Two clerks served as their witnesses, and afterward, Ran and Marley moved what few possessions she had—no more than a carful—to the big house. They had decided to tell the others that she was moving in with him; his sons weren't surprised—only Jakob seemed a little ... what? Marley could not make out the expression in his eyes. It wasn't until later that it came to her.

"God ... it's because if Quilla dies, I'll be here as a permanent reminder of her."

Nothing Ran could say would ease her heart, and the relationship between his wife and his son did not improve.

QUILLA SLEPT FITFULLY; her wrist handcuffed to the bed stand, and it was almost dawn when she felt Gregor lay down beside her and curl his arm around her waist. She hated every time he touched her, no matter how affectionate his caress. He must have sensed her being awake because he gave a low chuckle.

"One day you won't cringe when I touch you, my love."

I wouldn't bet on it. She opened her eyes and looked at him.

"Who is Padme?"

Gregor looked surprised. "How do you know that name?"

"You said it in your sleep last night."

"What else did I say?"

"All you said was 'Padme, please'"

Gregor sighed. "Padme was my first love. She was everything to me, the way you are now. But she betrayed me; she fucked around on me. You can guess who with."

"Jakob." A lump sat heavily on her chest.

"Bingo." Gregor pushed her onto her back and stroked her stomach. "I loved Padme with everything I had and in the end, I took that love back, vowing I would never fall so hard again. And I waited. Waited for Jakob to find 'the one'." I knew as soon as I saw you."

She studied him. "So that's why you've done all of this. Revenge for Padme cheating on you?"

Gregor smiled coldly. "Not just that. Jakob, by betraying me, by driving Padme away from me, made me do something I never thought I was capable of. Jakob took her love, but I took her life. I sobbed as I stabbed her to death; my heart broke."

Quilla shivered, and Gregor smiled. She shook her head, frowning. "Why didn't you just kill me that night in the bar? You had me right there; you stuck that knife in my gut then walked away. You could have finished it then, left Flori, left Kit out of it."

"You don't get it, do you?" He was angry now, and he got up off the bed and stalked around the room. "I had to have you ... entirely, completely before I killed you. I had to make him suffer like I suffered. He made me kill her. He took her and threw her away. Now I get to take you away from him."

Quilla drew in a deep breath. "So, you are going to kill me then?"

He stopped and stared at her for a long moment. "I don't know yet, Quilla. Don't make me do it."

She almost laughed. That's all he was, a spoiled little boy who took no responsibility and whined about it. A damn crybaby toddler. It was at that moment that she stopped being afraid of Gregor Fisk and knew what she had to do now. She held her hand to him.

"Come back to bed and show me how much you love me, Gregor."

For a moment, she thought he'd laugh in her face, but then he took her hand, climbing back on top of her and kissing her. Quilla made sure every part of her performed as she forced a genuine smile onto her face. "I won't make you do anything you don't want, Gregor. How could I? I'm yours ... just yours ..."

Gregor grinned. "That's right, beautiful, all mine ..."

And he began to make love to her again. Quilla closed her eyes, mimicking ecstasy, but the whole time, thinking, thinking, thinking ...

She knew now she was his weakness, and how she would make him pay. For Hayley. For Flori. For Kit.

And for herself.

"HOLY SHIT." Carter read through the report again, looking up at Agent Kendrick. "This is all confirmed?"

Kendrick nodded. "Every word. Gregor Fisk has form. His first girlfriend back in college, Sue-Lin Chang, was murdered, stabbed to death, gutted, practically. Fisk wasn't even questioned, so powerful was his family."

"Was?"

"They died in a car wreck, mother, father, and eldest son. Convenient, huh?"

"Wow. Just wow. Anything else."

"Oh, yes." Ali came in, looking excited. "Steve asked me to run a check on the first victim. Wealthy Chinese family in Seattle and guess what ... they have a private snow cabin in the North Central Cascades up near Mazama."

Carter was on his feet. "Let's get everyone together ..."

"Already on it. Let's go."

LIKE EVERYTHING IN LIFE, the moment came unexpectedly. Quilla was almost dropping from exhaustion; the physical strain the constant demands for sex placed on her was shattering. Gregor had made her go on top, riding him, and as she moved, he gazed up at her.

"How come you wear your hair up so often now?"

Quilla smiled. Because I'm hiding something, moron. "Just gets it out of the way."

"Let it down. I love the way it falls across your tits."

Quilla winced; she hated the coarseness of the word. "Really, you want it down?" Oh God ... here it comes ...

Gregor nodded. "Take it down."

Your choice, asshole. For a moment, she went through her plan. Get him to the point of orgasm, take the sharp edge of the tile ... she closed her eyes, increasing her thrust, hearing him moan. She went through her checklist. Clothes near to hand, tire iron to break the door down, grab his gun, put a bullet in his head ... run ...

It was time. She drove herself on and on, hearing his groan, knowing he was near. "Gregor, grab my hips, help me take you in ..."

Grinning, he did so, his fingers biting into her fleshy hips. She smiled and reached behind her to undo her hair, her fingers closing around the tile shard, feeling for the sharp edge, locking her grasp. Gregor grinned as her hair tumbled down over her breasts.

"Christ, Quilla, you're so fucking beau ..."

Lightning quick, she slashed across his throat with the tile, using all of her strength. Blood, hot, sticky blood, spurted out and covered them both. Gregor clutched at the wound, his eyes wide, terrified, and furious.

"Fucking bitch!" The curse was gargled out, full of venom.

Quilla tipped herself off him and dove towards her clothes as Gregor rolled off the bed, his hand clamped at his throat. He came for her, grabbing her leg as she went for his gun. The pistol skittered out of reach as Gregor pulled her back to him, his fury all consuming, the adrenaline making him superhuman despite his injury. The tile had obviously not severed a major artery and Quilla cursed herself. Gregor forced her onto her back, his face set in a grim smile.

"I told you not to make me do this, Quilla ..."

He grabbed his knife and she felt the cold steel against her belly.

"Goodbye, beautiful Quilla ..."

Quilla kicked and fought but then ... pain. Unimaginable pain.

Gregor drove his knife into her belly mercilessly, over and over, quick, deep stabs and Quilla groaned in agony. No ... no ... this is not the way this ends. She plunged her thumbs into his eyes, deep, and Gregor screamed, dropping the knife. She kicked him away and scrambled, bleeding heavily, towards the gun. She flicked the safety off just as Gregor, roaring, came at her again.

Quilla didn't hesitate; she rammed the muzzle against his head and fired. The back of his head exploded, and he collapsed, dead, but she kept firing, emptying the gun into Gregor's head until, sobbing, she dropped the empty gun. It's over.

Bent double, desperate to keep the blood inside her, she managed to drag her clothes on, packing a clean shirt against her wounds. The pain was so intense, it was almost unbelievable. The evening had fallen and across the snowfield, she could see lights on in the cabin.

Every movement was agony, but she searched Gregor's pockets for his keys. The jeep stood outside, but she'd bleed to death before she made it down the mountain. The other people in the cabin across the snowfield were her only hope. Dragging on her T-shirt, her jeans, grabbing a flashlight, she staggered out into the snow. It was deep, the snow, the fresh powder having fallen earlier that day, and each step brought a moan of sheer agony. The shirt covering her wounds was soaked through; her blood started to spatter the pure white snow, and she could feel her body shutting down. She used the flashlight, blinking it urgently at the opposite cabin, praying, hoping against hope, that they would see it.

Help me ...

She staggered another few steps, then collapsed into the snow, all her strength leaving her.

I'm sorry, Jakob, my love, my heart, I tried ...

She lay there, her finger still on the flashlight's on/off switch, flicking it with the last of her strength.

I'm dying ...

There was more light, voices, male voices ... was it Gregor? Come to finish her off? No, it couldn't be; he was dead; she'd killed him ...

"Sweetheart, can you hear me? God, she's covered in blood. Let's get her inside ..."

Hands lifting her, cradling her. "Can you hear me, lovely?"

"She looks familiar."

Warmth, the cold air had gone, she was inside. Her clothes were being pulled away. "She's been stabbed. Oh, God, poor kid."

"I'm calling 911."

Quilla. My name is Quilla. I don't want to die. But she couldn't speak, black spots encroaching on her vision. Lightheaded now.

"I can't stop this bleeding ... Jesus, I think I've lost her ..."

No, no, I'm still here ...

I'm still here ...

I ...

10

PART TEN: TREASURE ME

enice ...

QUILLA OPENED her bedroom door a crack and peeked out. Jakob Mallory heard the door open and sat up, looking at her, watching for her reaction. Quilla padded quietly over to the couch, her face splitting with the widest smile he'd ever seen, and from that second, Jakob knew he'd found the one. He wanted to pull her onto the couch with him and kiss her. Instead, he gazed up at her, drinking in every feature, the soft face, still holding onto the last vestiges of puppy fat, the color of her honey skin, the dark green eyes, the long dark hair, messy. That smile.

"You stayed," she said, and her voice broke a little and Jakob realized how much it meant to her that he had made the decision not to run out into Venetian night and find another fix.

"I did. You were right. I want to be better, Quilla. I want to get straight, be the man who deserves a woman like you risking her life for him."

She perched on the side of the couch. She smelled of cinnamon and sleep, and he breathed the scent in, his entire body responding to her.

Her big eyes searched his. "Would you like me to help? Like I say, I've been through this—well, not me personally, but my mom used to try and come off heroin periodically, so I know the drill. I know you're not on heroin but ..."

"Cocaine. And yes, please. You're the only one I trust to get me through this."

She flushed with pleasure. "Then you'd better grab a shower, because we need to get you some new clothes and some supplies."

He smiled, wanting desperately to brush that lock of hair that had fallen across her cheek back behind her ear. "I should call the airport; see if my bags were taken off the plane. Otherwise, yes."

His bags were still at Venice airport so after a good breakfast, they took a cab and retrieved them, Quilla helping to lug them up to her apartment—"Their apartment," she'd called it absent-mindedly, which made him feel strangely warm inside.

He took her to lunch at Quadri, where they ate langoustine with lemon aioli and drank an entire bottle of wine. Quilla grinned at him. "Enjoy that, because it's water and juice from now on."

He loved that she could make light of something so serious—for the love of God, they were talking about addiction— but her attitude was so matter of fact, it gave him hope that he could do this, could drag himself back from the edge. He would do it for himself, but also for her. Her mom ... he would get the entire story from her, he decided. She was an unusual woman, this Quilla Chen.

She might have made light of it, but there was no doubt that she knew what she was doing. His body bucked against the with-drawal; he became edgy and tired, desperate for a fix one moment, then raging at himself the next. Quilla did not back down even when he was begging her to unlock the door; at night, she dragged her mattress from the bed and slept in front of the door so he couldn't pick the lock or bust his way through. There was enough reason still left in him, even at the worst of it, that he knew every minute meant his life got better. Even when, on the fourth night, he awoke screaming from the most gruesome, terrifying nightmares and lashed out, his arms flying everywhere, she launched herself onto him, wrapped her arms around him and held him down, soothing him, calming him until exhausted, he fell asleep in her arms.

When he woke up the day that he'd declared to himself, that they'd made love for the first time, he'd known something was going to happen; his gut instinct told him that this, she and him, them, was inevitable ...

Now ...

Now, as Jakob sat on the place, crossing the Atlantic on the ten-hour journey back to Seattle, he closed his eyes and tried to capture that feeling. Those feelings ... .all of the firsts—the moment his lips touched hers, the first time he'd kissed those gorgeous breasts, felt the hard nipple against his tongue, the taste of her, the moment his cock slid inside her.

Anything, anything to try and forget that once again, she was lying on an operating table, her life hanging in the balance as surgeons tried their hardest to repair the violence that Gregor Fisk had visited upon her—again.

The phone call at the hotel had been the best and worst of his life. His father. They've found Quilla ... Gregor's dead ... but she's been stabbed and, son, I'm so sorry, it's bad. Please come as soon as you can ...

He'd been in a cab to the airport moments later; he hadn't even bothered to pack the few clothes he'd brought with him to London. As the cab weaved its way through heavy London traffic, Jakob called the airline and begged them to put him on the first plane. He'd have to change in San Francisco, but he could be home in fourteen hours.

Now, as the plane flew over the coast of Greenland, Jakob stared out at the view below him, not seeing anything, but imagining he was hearing the doctor's voice telling she didn't make it.

No...no ... she will; she's a fighter. He wondered if Grady had called that doctor in New Orleans, the one who had saved Flori. God, so much pain, so much violence ... knowing that Gregor was finally dead didn't help matters. The damage he had wrought would not be easy to repair.

Stop it. Try and think positively. Think about the time in Venice with Quilla, think about ...

Venice ...

It was evening, and they were walking hand in hand through St Marks, disturbing the pigeons on the palazzo. He couldn't take his eyes off her; the sultry heat, the low sun, made her honey-skin glow, her lovely dark hair pulled up into a messy bun at the nape of her neck. Her back was bare, her pale pink dress tied as a halter, and he trailed a fingertip down her spine. Quilla shivered, then chuckled. "That feels good."

He stopped walking and took her in his arms. "You feel good."

"Cheesy."

"You bet your sweet ass."

He kissed her, her soft lips warm against his own. Her little face fit so perfectly in his big hands, she made him feel like a giant of a man, a hero instead of the screw up he really was. She pressed her insane body to his, and he felt his cock jump instantly, swelling and thickening with longing for her. He pressed his lips to her throat. "God, I want to fuck you so bad, right now, Quilla Chen."

She gave a throaty chuckle. "Well, Mr. Mallory, I do believe you promised me a night on the balcony, and I'm going to take you up on that."

He grinned. "Then let's get a water taxi and go home right now ..."

.   .   .

ON THE BALCONY of her apartment, there was a streetlight immediately adjacent, so Jakob threw a towel over it, much to Quilla's amusement. Then slowly, he stripped her, his lips against the skin he revealed. He made her sit on one of the chairs while he went down on her, Quilla gasping quietly as his tongue lashed around her clit. He grinned up at her as he trailed his tongue up her belly and took her nipple into his mouth. She knotted her fingers in his hair and let her head fall back, her eyes close. When his lips found her throat, she murmured, "I want to suck you," but he just chuckled.

"Not tonight, Miss Chen; tonight is all about you …"

He stood and peeled his clothes off quickly, his cock heavy, bobbing under the weight of the blood engorging it, ramrod straight against his belly. He fisted the root of it, smiling as he watched her admire him. "You like what you see, beautiful?"

"God, yes."

"Show me."

Smiling lazily, she slowly spread her legs, and trailing her hand between her breasts, down her belly, she stroked into her sex, parting the peachy folds to show him how wet she was, how red and swollen she was, for him, only him.

"That is the most fucking beautiful sight on this Earth," he hissed and suddenly he was pulling her to the floor and plunging his cock deep into her, her legs curling around his waist, her eyes locked with his as they fucked, clawing at the other, both tender and animal, Quilla urging him deeper …

JAKOB OPENED HIS EYES. There were so many emotions roiling around inside him. He would give anything, every penny he had, every material thing he owned, to turn back time and go back to that day on the balcony. Or the day after, when Quilla had suggested finding an empty gondola after night had fallen and they'd fucked in that, trying not to laugh or moan too loudly, having to hide hurriedly as two Carabinieri passed by, their flashlights sweeping over the line of silent boats.

But so much had happened between then and now. Gregor. If his end game had been to shatter Jakob's psyche, he'd succeeded. And then there was the fact that Quilla had slept with him. Had been intimate with her would-be killer. Jakob hated himself for thinking it, but he couldn't deny the torrent of jealousy, of betrayal he felt. He knew, he knew, it wasn't fair, that she'd done it to save Hayley, to save herself ... but he couldn't get that image of her face on that video tape.

And now she was dying, and he might not get the chance to tell her he loved her, or to hear her tell him that she had hated every minute being with Gregor, that she loved only him, Jakob, that she was sorry ...

Sorry? What the hell is wrong with you, man? He swore under his breath. Quilla had nothing to apologize for; she had made a huge sacrifice for the people she loved and what was he? A fucking idiot. He didn't deserve her.

Many hours later, when he landed in Seattle, he got into a cab, but when the driver ask him where to, he choked on the word 'Hhospital' Instead, after taking a deep breath in, he gave him an address across the city. One he hadn't been to in over a year.

Flori, Nan, Hayley, and Asia looked up as Marley came back, balancing hot coffee on a tray. The Mallory men were with the police, going through everything. Asia's partner, Dr. Parker Thomas, was indeed the surgeon trying to save Quilla's life—he'd flown into Seattle at the moment Grady had called Asia.

"You know what's weird?" Nan said quietly, "We're back to the beginning. First time I met Joel, we were right here, in this room."

Marley nodded. "I remember. Quilla had been stabbed by Gregor then, too. What the hell is wrong with this world?"

Hayley, whose quiet devastation was written all over her face, sighed. "I can never tell you how much Quilla did for me in that prison. Even if I described every single minute, I couldn't tell you."

Nan started to cry at her sister's words and gathered her into a hug. Flori wiped her face. "I just hope, somehow, she can fight this last fight."

"She will," Marley said gruffly, her voice breaking. Asia put her arm around the woman.

"Look, I'm a great believer in positivity. We need to tell happy stories about Quilla, or about our lives or whatever. Send good energy out into the ether."

"Good idea," said Hayley suddenly, then she looked at her sister. "I'm marrying Skandar. Soon."

Nan grinned. "Really? That's amazing. Congratulations."

Hayley looked comically disappointed. "What no 'you're too young' No 'Are you knocked up?' Darn it; I was hoping for some drama."

The others laughed, and Nan shook her head. "No way— although I had better be your Maid of Honor."

Hayley shook her head, and Nan's face dropped. Hayley kissed her cheek. "I want you to give me away, Nan. I know it's a traditionally male role, but fuck the patriarchy. Will you do me the honor of giving me away?"

Nan colored and burst into tears, smiling through them. "Of course ... oh God ..." She sniffed, trying to stop crying as Hayley rolled her eyes. Nan wiped her nose. "Just to check, though—you're not knocked up, are you?"

"No, don't worry." Hayley smiled but Asia, whose face was scarlet, put her hand up.

"Um ... I am."

They all gaped at her, and she laughed, her face returning to its normal color. "Afraid so. It wasn't planned. Parker and I both want kids, but we also don't want to get married yet."

Flori gave a dramatic gasp. "I am clutching my pearls! This new-fangled way of living ... oh, hell, I can't even be bothered to make fun of you. Congratulations, I'm so happy for you both." She hugged Asia, who chuckled.

"Thank you, boo."

Marley went to the window and gazed out into the gloomy light of the evening. She desperately wanted to join in with the women, but she felt distanced from them, even though, technically, she was the only one of them married to a Mallory. It was her best friend on that operating table—again, and she wanted to scream and curse and punch something.

What she couldn't believe most was that finally, Gregor Fisk was dead. Although they didn't know exactly what happened, it looked like Quilla had killed him, and that's what worried Marley as much as the hideous injuries Quilla had received while escaping. Knowing she killed another human being would change Quilla—possibly irretrievably. Marley knew her too well—sweet, sweet Quilla would grieve for the man who abducted, raped, and stabbed her. That she was the wife of Jacob Mallory would only exacerbate and fire up the press stories—Marley could see the headlines now: Killer Quilla.

Christ ...

"Marley?" Nan's voice was soft, and she felt her hand on her back. "This must be even worse for you, I know, but we're all here for you, sweetheart."

Marley smiled and turned back to the group, flushing when she realized they were all looking at her. She drew in a deep breath. What the hell? "I married Ran. A few days ago. We also didn't want to wait," she smiled shyly at Asia, who beamed.

"I'm so glad, Marley. You make such a wonderful couple."

The rest of them murmured their assent, and Marley felt a tension leave her. "I love him so very much, and it's weird, it's not the mad, crashing love you think you'll find. It's just ... right and solid and adoring."

Flori smiled at her. "You're such an old soul, Marley, or what I mean is, you are mature beyond your years. You're right; it makes so much sense for you to be with Ran."

"Thank you, Flori ... and what about you? What's your news?"

Flori smiled. "Nothing new to tell ... except I think I love Grady Mallory even more each day. Since we've been able to ..." She trailed off, flushing, shooting a look at Grady's former lover, Asia, but the other woman nodded encouragingly. "Well, since then, it's just gotten better every day. I have to be honest, I'd been living under fear that Gregor would find me again or do what he did to Bo Kennedy and take Grady away from me. I'm so glad he's dead."

"You bet your butt he is." They all looked up as Grady came back into the room with the others. Skandar immediately pulled Hayley into his arms; Ran slid an arm around his wife's waist; Joel, planted a kiss on Nan's forehead.

Grady smoothed Flori's hair. "And the police just confirmed: Quilla killed him." He looked at Hayley. "They think she used the tile fragment to slash his throat, but it wasn't enough to kill him. He went after her, stabbed her, but she managed to grab the gun and shot him. She emptied the gun into his head and then tried to reach help. She collapsed in the snow, but luckily the people from the cabin across the way found her and called it in."

"Has Parker given you an update?" Asia asked him, her eyes wide.

Grady shook his head. "Not yet."

Ran cleared his throat. "The police say her injuries were life-threatening. The cold may have slowed her heart down so that she didn't lose as much blood, but still. It's touch and go."

Marley gave a little sob, no longer able to hold it in. Ran wrapped his arms around her and let her cry. Asia glanced at them sympathetically but not knowing what to say.

"Where the hell is Jakob?" Skandar, who had been in shock for days now, and had not let Hayley out of sight for long, glanced at his watch. "His plane got in a couple of hours ago."

"I'll call him." Joel got up and went out into the corridor to use his phone. Nan went with him."

All them sat in silence for a few minutes. Hayley, exhausted, burrowed into Skandar's arms, and he pressed his lips to her temple, his own eyes full of sadness and fatigue.

Asia got up as her boyfriend, Parker, came in, still in his scrubs.

He looked grim-faced, and Marley felt Ran's arms tightened around her.

"We've managed to stop the bleeding," Parker said, "but she's very, very sick. I wish I could give you better news, but it is a waiting game now. The knife nicked her abdominal artery, and it was leaking, but we've managed to stabilize it, for now. She just needs time now for her body to do its job and heal."

"Can we see her?"

"She's in recovery, and I wouldn't advise too many of you go in. She might get overwhelmed if she wakes up. For now, I think Jakob ... and Marley?"

"Jakob's not here yet," Marley said, a hint of annoyance creeping into her voice.

"I'll go in with you," said Hayley quietly. "I need to see her."

Just before Marley pushed open the door to Quilla's room, she balked. Hayley looked at her with surprise, then, understanding. She linked her fingers with Marley's. "Together." Marley nodded, and they went in.

Quilla was, as expected, surrounded by machinery, wires, and tubes all over her body, the hiss and click of the breathing equipment the only sound in the room. Quilla was paler than pale, her usually honey-colored skin wan and tinged with yellow. There were dark purple bruises on her skin, cuts and welts; her abdomen was heavily bandaged, blood seeping through in some places.

"God." Marley felt her legs give way, and Hayley hurriedly steered her into a chair. She went to Quilla's head and stroked the matted hair away from her face.

"I love you," she whispered and kissed her friend's forehead. Marley watched the young blonde woman, a growing fondness inside her. Whatever Quilla and Hayley had been through had forged a bond as unbreakable as her own with Quilla.

Quilla, deeply unconscious, was so still, Marley and Hayley could only watch the rise and fall of her chest as the machine breathed for her. They each took a seat either side of her and took one of her small, cold hands in their own.

Marley didn't know how long they sat there, but she glanced over at Hayley and was appalled to see tears pouring down the younger woman's face. "Hayley ..."

"I keep watching her chest go up and down and thinking that the next time, it won't move. That she'll just go, and we won't get to say goodbye."

"Oh, sweetheart ..."

Marley could not think of anything else to say to comfort her friend. She glanced at her watch and wondered again: Where the hell is Jakob?

JOEL HAD NOT BEEN able to get hold of his brother on the phone, but he'd called the airline. "He definitely got to SeaTac, and he definitely got off the plane."

None of them knew what to do next. Ran rubbed his hands over his face. "Look, why don't you all go home? I'll wait for Jakob and the girls, but there's obviously not much you can do here."

Grady nodded. "Asia, why don't you come back with us?" Flori nodded and took Asia's hand.

"Yes, do come, you need looking after."

The men looked confused. "I'll explain another time." Asia waved away their questions. "I will, thank you both."

Joel and Nan followed the others out, but Skandar shook his head. "I'm not leaving Hayley."

Ran smiled at his grandson. "Well, then, I'm grateful for the company."

It was another hour before Hayley came to find them. She looked red-eyed and upset. "They're checking her at the moment, asked us to step out. Marley's gone to find more coffee." She smiled at Ran. "You might have to go home without the missus tonight."

Both Ran and Skandar looked up. Ran, a slight flush on his face, grinned. "She told you?"

"She did, and we're all very happy for you," Hayley grinned at Skandar's surprise, "those of us who know. You have a new step-Nana, Skan."

Skandar actually smiled for the first time in weeks and congratulated his grandfather, who nodded gratefully. "Well, look, you two should go home and get some rest. I ..."

He stopped as someone knocked and FBI Agent Carter James stepped into the room. "Hey, folks. How's Quilla?"

Hayley made a face. "Not out of the woods, yet."

"Sorry to hear that. Ran, could we speak privately for a second?"

Randall followed the agent out into the hallway. He looked grim-faced and awkward. "Ran, there's no easy way to tell you this ... Jakob's been arrested."

Ran felt like a sledgehammer had slammed into his chest. "What the hell for?"

Carter blew out his cheeks. "He was trying to buy cocaine. The trouble was, we were in the middle of a sting and Jakob was at the wrong place at the wrong time. Look, the arresting officer knows of your family and the case but says his hands are tied. Jakob's at the county lockup. He'll be arraigned in the morning; I'm pretty confident bail will be set."

"Charges?"

"Probably possession. Look, I'm sorry. I haven't seen him, but I guess he's pretty messed up about Quilla, which is why he spiraled down. I'll let you know where he's been taken."

Ran went back into the relative's room and told Skandar and Hayley what had happened. Skandar cursed and shook his head, furious, but Hayley put her arm around his waist. "Skan ... if I was Quilla, what would you feel like right now?"

Skandar's jaw clenched, a nerve flickering in his cheek. "Yeah, okay," he muttered eventually. Hayley kissed him. Ran sighed.

"Go home, the both of you, get some sleep. When Agent James comes back, I'll go see Jakob."

.   .   .

QUILLA SLID BACK into consciousness but didn't open her eyes for a moment. She could tell the hand holding hers wasn't Jakob's—it was too small, but it was familiar. Marley.

She opened her eyes to see a darkened room and her oldest friend, her head laid on the bed, turned towards her, her eyes closed. Quilla tried to smile but the tube in her throat was so bulky, she couldn't. Her throat was scratchy and a terrible thirst raging inside her.

And the pain ... God ... the lightheadedness she felt she knew was from morphine, but it wasn't touching the burning ache in her belly.

She squeezed the hand that held hers, and Marley sat up instantly, blinking her eyes. "Quills?"

Quilla tried to nod her head, and Marley burst into tears, smiling through them. "Oh God, honey ... welcome back."

She tried to hug her but with all the wires and tubes, it was difficult. Quilla couldn't speak but pointed to her throat. Marley understood. "I'll go get a nurse, darling, hold on."

Alone, she listened to the silence being broken by the machines keeping her alive. She tried to move any part of her body, but everything screamed in pain. At least she could move her arms, write things down, like ...

Where the hell is Jakob?

HER HUSBAND, locked in a cell, had his head in his hands. This is the lowest you've ever been, Mallory, he told himself. In a strange way, he was glad he hadn't had the chance to take the coke—that would have been infinitely worse than this. Still ... he felt incredibly guilty—he should be with Quilla right now. How was he going to explain this to her, to his family, when he didn't have an answer for himself?

"Jakob?"

Carter James looked at him, and Jakob could see the empathy in his eyes. It didn't help. Jakob got up and went to the door. "How are you doing?"

Jakob shrugged. "Okay. It was a dumb, stupid thing to do."

Carter nodded, gave him a half smile. "Yeah, it was. Look, your dad's on his way—no, don't worry, Quilla's doing not great, but okay —but your dad wants to see you. You'll be arraigned in the morning, and I'll be putting in a report to the judge. Bail should be set, and under the circumstances, I think you'll be out pretty soon after that. What possessed you?"

Jakob sighed. "Stupidity. Wanting to escape. Not having to face the fact my wife is dying."

"She's not dying," Carter interrupted him. "Quilla is in a bad way, yes, but she's not dying. Parker Thomas thinks she'll pull through, although it won't be easy. But I think deep down you know that ... Jakob, this is to do with that video tape, isn't it?"

Jakob felt a wave of sorrow, of guilt, of hurt flood through his body. "I can't stop thinking about it; it's consuming me."

The door opened behind Carter and Ran walked in, his expression neutral, his eyes tired. Carter shook his hand, and then turned back to Jakob. "Talk to your dad. I'll see you in the morning."

Alone, Jakob couldn't meet his dad's gaze. "Dad, I'm sorry. I don't know what I was thinking."

Ran hesitated before he spoke. "Jakob, I love you, so this is not going to be easy for me to say. I don't think I've ever been more ... ashamed ... than I am right now. In you, in myself."

His words battered and bruised Jakob's fragile heart, but he nodded. "That's fair. But the fault is mine, Dad; you have nothing to be ashamed of."

"I thought I had brought you up better than to run away from things and be that guy who would rather stick his head in the sand and let other people carry the load. Quilla was stabbed fourteen times, by Gregor, fifteen, if you count the first time. She had to kill him, take another human being's life, and still, she tried to make her way back to you. She had to turn over her body to him to save Hayley's life, and she did it. She deserves more than this, Jakob, and if you cannot provide that for her, then let her go. But know this; Quilla is my daughter, and if you turn away from her, then you are no longer welcome in this family. That's all I have to say. I'll see you in the morning; I have to get back to my family at the hospital."

Jakob wanted to scream, wanted to beg him for forgiveness. Ran, always mild-mannered, had never spoken to him, or anyone, like he just had to his eldest son. He watched his father, his hands trembling, grip the door handle to leave.

"Dad ..."

Ran turned back, and he could see the tears in his eyes. Pain ripped through Jakob at the sight. "I'm sorry, Dad."

"I'm not the one you should be saying that to. When the bail is posted tomorrow, I've booked you into rehab. Just a week. You're not permitted to see or talk to Quilla before that week is completed."

Jakob was up now, panic starting. "Dad, I didn't take it. I'm not addicted, please. I have to see her."

Ran gripped the door handle tighter, closing his eyes, the turmoil inside him obvious. "You should have thought of that when you got off that plane." Then he was gone, Jakob staring after him.

PARKER THOMAS, his cornflower blue eyes crinkling as he smiled, stroked Quilla's head. "Now, I'm going to ask you to give a big cough, then I'll take the tube out ... after three, sweetheart. One ... two ... three ..."

Quilla coughed, then gagged as Parker pulled the tube out. The nurse with him, Julia, passed her a cup of water. "Don't gulp it, sweetie, just sips."

Quilla did as she was told, the water giving blessed relief to her throat. She was still laid back on her pillows, but at least she was halfway to sitting up. It had been a day and a half since she'd woken and according to the smile on Parker's face, she was doing well. Now that the tube was out, she could suck in lungfuls of air herself and start to feel alive. Marley and Asia were at the other end of the room watching and smiling. At last, Quilla gave them a wave. Marley was smiling through her tears, leaning against Asia for support.

Quilla felt a wave of gratitude come over her and she caught Parker's arm. "Thank you," she croaked, her throat still scratchy. He grinned—damn, he was so handsome.

She told Asia that when he and the nurse had gone, and Asia laughed. "You're not falling for your doctor, are you? That old cliché?"

Quilla smiled, and then looked at Marley, who was wiping her eyes on her sleeve. "Dude, stop that, I'm okay."

Marley tried to smile. "I'm sorry, honey. I think the floodgates have opened."

The three women chatted lightly, then Quilla steeled herself. "Okay, you wouldn't tell me anything about why Jakob wasn't here, so I need to know, because it's driving me crazy. Come on."

She noticed the anger in her own voice and saw they hadn't missed it, either. "I'm not mad at you," she said softly. "I don't know who I'm mad at."

Asia and Marley shared a long look, then Asia nodded. "Jakob's in rehab, darling. When he thought you were dying, he flipped out and tried to buy coke. Luckily—if you can call it that—he was arrested before he could actually take the stuff. He's been bailed, but Ran sent him to rehab for the week. Banned him from coming here."

Quilla frowned. "I don't get why ... surely the fact that I was back was a good thing, even in the state I was in ... I don't understand. What aren't you telling me?"

Another loaded glance between her friends. "Quilla ... when Hayley was released, she told us everything that you had done, what you had sacrificed for her."

Panic was starting to build inside Quilla's chest. "But, surely, Jakob knew I had to do it; I had to sleep with Gregor, or he'd kill both Hayley and me?"

"It's not just that," Marley said gently. "Gregor videotaped you having sex."

Quilla's stomach dropped. "What?" Barely a whisper.

"Hayley explained that Gregor had made you ... act the part. It was one of those times that he taped—and sent to Jakob."

"Oh no, no, no ..." Quilla's head was in her hands, and Marley shot Asia a concerned look. Asia nodded and slipped from the room to find Parker. Marley got her arms around Quilla.

Her body was trembling violently. "I had to do it. He was going to kill her," Quilla sobbed. "So I pretended I was somebody else, that it wasn't me he was raping. And he was raping me, Marley, how can Jakob think I would have slept with that ... monster ... voluntarily? He was going to shoot Hayley in the head unless I did it. He only let her go because I did such a convincing job. I only escaped him because he'd started to trust me enough to fuck him without being tied down. So, what, Jakob thinks I'm unclean now? How could he?"

Her voice was getting louder, more hysterical, her entire body in motion, and Marley had to fight to keep her from tearing her stitches, hurting herself. Quilla's eyes were wild—fear, anger, hurt and Marley cursed Jakob Mallory and Gregor Fisk over and over.

Parker came in and took one look at Quilla and muttered an instruction to his assistant. Marley got out of the way as Parker tried to calm Quilla down from her panic attack, his tone steady and soothing. When the assistant came back, Parker took the hypodermic needle from her and slipped it into Quilla's IV. Her breathing slowly returned to normal and in a few minutes, her eyes closed. After checking her vitals, he beckoned Asia and Marley from the room.

"She can't get overexcited like that. Her core muscles have been ravaged. Any hysteria risks tearing, which means infection might get in."

Asia put her hand on her boyfriend's arm. "Sorry, Parker, but she asked about Jakob."

"I should have waited to tell her," Marley fretted, "or fudged the truth."

Parker sighed. "I think she'll be okay, but yeah, soften the blows, would you?" He smiled kindly at Marley. "Kiddo, if we keep her calm, she has a chance of a quicker recovery. Whatever bullshit Jakob is dealing with, Quilla's health is the main concern."

Marley smiled gratefully, comforted that Parker wasn't impressed with Jakob either. She felt like she had an ally in the surgeon. "Thanks, Parker. For everything. For keeping her here with us."

"My pleasure. Look, why don't you go home, get some rest? I gave her a pretty strong sedative so she'll be out for a few hours. And you," he kissed Asia's cheek, "you go back to Grady's and look after yourself and Bean."

"We're not calling him or her Bean."

"Yeah, we are." Parker grinned and waved as he left them. Marley said goodbye to Asia and drove home, acknowledging to herself that she was shattered. She wanted to sit and howl, then sleep for hours and hours.

RAN, not looking much better himself, met her at the door. Marley sank into his arms. "God, take me to bed, please. I need to feel good again."

He chuckled. "How about a long soak first, candles, a back massage, the whole nine yards?"

Marley smiled up at him. "You really are perfect; you know that?"

IN THE TUB, his hands moved over her body, gripping the tight muscles in her shoulders, his thumbs pressing firmly into the sore flesh. Marley groaned. "That's so good."

Ran kissed her neck. "Better?"

She leaned back against his chest. "So much." She sighed. "Did you speak to Jakob today?"

"I did. He's doing well, working hard."

Marley didn't say anything and Ran pressed his lips to her temple. "Give him a chance, Marley."

She sighed, turning around to face him. "Ran, I love you, but I think I've given that man plenty of chances. Because of him, Quilla has been raped, stabbed, and abducted ... been subject to the worst a human can do to another. And now, added to that, she had to kill another human being. Where was Jakob? And when he needed to step up, his pathetic male ego made him run away. Again."

Ran flinched at her words. "Marley, he's made mistakes."

She relented. "I know he's your son, Ran, and you love him. But even you must see; he's terrible for Quilla."

"I think we need to see how Quilla feels."

Marley looked away from her husband's gaze. "Yes."

Ran stroked her face. "Don't let this come between us, sweetheart. We should be in our blissful honeymoon phase. Speaking of which, when Quilla is recovered, I'm taking you away for an actual honeymoon."

Marley tried to smile. "Sounds good."

Ran sighed, and then held out his arms. "Come here, beautiful." She went into them, and he kissed her. Marley closed her eyes, letting the sensation of his lips against hers consume her. For Ran, she would try to accept Jakob; for Ran and Quilla, she would try.

SEVEN DAYS. Seven days he had turned up for any and every counseling sessions, group meeting, had helped out in the kitchens ... everything, and now, as Jakob waited for his dad to come pick him up, he felt optimistic for the first time in days, hell, months. Ran had called him every evening with updates on Quilla's condition; still a long way to go, but every day she got stronger. Of course she is, he thought now, his heart full of love. She's a fighter. She always has been.

He couldn't wait to see her, take her in his arms, and beg for her forgiveness. He would spend the rest of his life trying to make it up to her, not that it was possible. God, what had I been thinking? He shook his head now, then looked up as his father came into the room.

Ran nodded, but Jakob could see in his eyes, the pride, the thankfulness that Jakob had done so well here. He hugged his father. "I'm so sorry, Dad."

Ran embraced his eldest son. "I'm proud of you, son. Let's go and see Quilla."

·   ·   ·

JAKOB'S HEART was thumping as they rode the elevator to Quilla's floor. Ran had told him that she was recovering, but he still was nervous about seeing her so hurt, so brutalized. Ran warned him not to get too physical; Quilla's wounds were still healing, and she was still in a lot of pain.

They walked along the corridor to her room, and as they reached it, Marley came out, shutting the door behind her and blocking it. She glanced at Ran with apologetic eyes, then looked at Jakob, her eyes cold. Jakob's heartbeat quickened.

"Hi, Marley."

"Jakob. She doesn't want to see you. I'm sorry." She didn't sound sorry at all. Ran shot her a sharp look.

"Marley? What's going on?"

Marley's expression was soft as she looked at her husband. "I'm sorry, Ran, but Quilla doesn't want to see Jakob."

"Why?"

"I think you need to ask Jakob that."

Jakob stared at her in horror. "No ... no, please, I need to see her. I need to explain."

Marley fixed her gaze on him. "Jakob, Quilla does not want to see you. She does not want to talk to you. She doesn't need you to explain your behavior. It's pretty clear, and her decision is final."

Ran sighed. "Come on now, Marley."

"I'm sorry, baby," she said to him, "but it's Quilla's choice."

"Bullshit," Jakob exploded. "It's not Quilla, it's you. This is what you've always wanted, isn't it? Me out of the picture?"

"This is the result of your actions, Jakob."

"Quilla! Quilla, please, I need to talk to you!" Jakob was yelling now. He stepped forward and Marley moved, immediately bracing herself against the door jam. For a moment, it looked like Jakob would simply shove her out of the way and everyone froze, Marley and Jakob staring each other down. Then Ran, his face pale, stepped between them.

"Jakob, back off. Marley ... is this really Quilla's final decision?"

She nodded. "It is."

Ran put his hand on his son's shoulder. "Come on, Jakob. Let's go."

Jakob, seething, stared at Marley a beat longer then stalked off. Ran looked at Marley. "Will I see you at home?"

"Of course." Her face softened. "I'm sorry about this, Ran."

He kissed her forehead. "It's okay ... do you want me to come pick you up?"

She shook her head. "I'll get a cab; it's okay."

JAKOB WAS PACING around the parking lot when Ran found him. Jakob opened his mouth to speak, but Ran held up a hand. "Before you say something you regret," he said firmly, "just remember ... Marley is my wife, and I love her very much."

Jakob shook his head. "Dad, she's never liked me, and if this is her dripping poison into Quilla's ear ..."

"Stop it," his father's voice was sharp. "Quilla had every right not see you, after what you did. Do you not understand that? You made a decision, Jakob, and these are the consequences. That girl has been through enough, and I can't say I blame her for this. In any way. Marley didn't say forever, just not yet. Respect that."

Jakob had no answer for that. His shoulders slumped, and he rubbed a frustrated hand over his head. "I want to go home."

AT THE EMPTY APARTMENT, Jakob showered, then poured himself a large drink and sat out on the balcony, even though the night was bitterly cold. He felt he needed the cool air to calm the hot, angry blood that flowed through him. He went through his arguments in his head: Marley had persuaded Quilla to ignore him; Quilla was being unreasonable; Quilla was being petty. But he knew, inside, that none of that was true.

It was him. He needed to step up now and prove to Quilla that he was worthy of her. Jakob stared into the Seattle night, looking over to the Space Needle. The Seattle Center was dressed for Christmas;

thousands upon thousands of twinkle lights. He couldn't imagine Christmas without Quilla in his arms, in their home, in their bed.

He would do anything to get her back … anything. Even if that meant backing off until he could prove to her finally, that he was deserving of her love.

"YOU'RE CHEATING."

"Am not."

"You are. You're picking from the discarded cards."

Quilla grinned at Hayley. "Man, you're a bad loser."

Hayley gave up and scrambled the cards up. "I'm so bored of this game."

"Me, too."

Hayley packed the cards into their box. "So, Parker said you could be discharged soon?"

"He called from New Orleans yesterday and spoke to my doctor. Maybe another couple of weeks, less if I'm lucky. Thank God. My muscles are starting to atrophy. Here, help me up, would you? I need to walk around for a bit."

Hayley helped Quilla onto the floor, steadying her when she swayed. Quilla had been in the hospital for a month now and had made remarkable progress—at least, physically. Hayley knew her friend was fragile mentally; although Quilla tried to hide her red eyes and the dark shadows under her eyes, Hayley worried that she would break soon. It gave her hope though that Quilla was seeing the psychiatrist again, had requested him herself. Christmas had been the hardest but they'd all come in to see her—separately, so Jakob's absence wouldn't be so obvious. Hayley and Skandar had spent most of Christmas Day with their friend, talking wedding plans until Skandar rolled his eyes and pretended to call the whole thing off. "One more mention of fabric and I'm outta here."

They walked out into the corridor, Hayley supporting her friend as they took their usual route to the elevators and outside—almost outside— January had brought with it deep snow, and so they settled for the long corridor near the big glass window at the front of the hospital.

"So, how's the wedding planning going? Skandar forced you to finalize a date yet?"

Hayley laughed. "Ha, you jest. Nope, despite teasing Skandar, the only thing I have locked down is that Nan will walk me down the aisle. My next job is to ask my maid of honor if she'll be so kind to stand up with me. So, will you?"

Quilla gave her a delighted but shocked laugh. "Hell, yes! My God, Hayley, I would never have expected ..." she turned away, but Hayley saw the tears in her eyes and squeezed her. Quilla chuckled, dashing away the tears. "I'm so honored, Hayley, truly but don't you have friends you've known longer than me? I know you do."

Hayley smiled, shrugging. "They'll be my bridesmaids. And listen, I talked to them, and they agree with me. It's the least I could do after what you did ..." She choked up but rallied, forcing a grin onto her face. "There's no one I'd rather have, Quilla. No one."

Quilla chuckled. "That means so much, Hays, it really does. So, a double-double meringue for you, then?"

Hayley nodded. "And all of you in salmon taffeta, 80s style."

They both laughed, Quilla putting her hand on her stomach. "Laughing still hurts, huh?" Hayley said, noticing the gesture.

"Force of habit by now. The pain is definitely manageable."

They walked some more, then Hayley spoke again. "Quills ... have you thought where you'll go when you leave the hospital?"

Quilla nodded. "Grady and Flori have offered me their guest room for as long as I need to find a place."

Hayley sighed. "Good, because I had visions of you renting some tiny apartment on your own."

Quilla smiled gratefully at her young friend. "You are so like your sister, sometimes."

"Thankfully, neither of us is like our mother, though.," Hayley rolled her eyes.

"I hear ya." Quilla sighed. "I'm going to have to find a new job, though, if I want to get an apartment of my own."

Hayley was confused, and then her heart sank. "So, there's really no chance of you and Jakob ...?" Hayley felt tears threatening. She so wanted the couple to find each other again. "He's been doing really well, Quills, and he's respected your wishes about staying away. He's working on the foundation project with Flori and Grady."

Quilla was surprised. The foundation had been her and Grady's brainchild, an arts foundation that would help low-income artists fulfill their dreams of a college degree and mentoring in the art world. She had been talking to Grady about it the day she and Hayley had been abducted.

"Really? It was just a vague idea, last time I was involved."

"Grady told Jakob about it, and Jakob swung into action. I've helped out too, in between classes and coming here."

Quilla smiled at her gratefully. "Skandar must hate me, stealing so much of your time."

"Are you kidding me? Skandar hero-worships you – or 'she-ro' worships you, ha, ha—I think if we both went full lesbian on each other, he'd cheer us on. He keeps talking about what he can do for you."

"Just keep being him, and always look after you, love you, treat you like a goddess and we're good," Quilla grinned. She drew in a long breath. "Lord, I think I need to go back to bed now."

Hayley helped her to the elevator and got her settled back in bed. Quilla smiled wryly. "I get puffed walking, but as soon as I get back in this damn bed again, I want out."

IN AN HOUR, Quilla was asleep, and Hayley kissed her forehead and crept silently from the room. Driving home, she thought about Quilla and Jakob, wishing that she could think of a way to bring them back together.

When she got home, she met Skandar, returning from practice, in their driveway. Now that Gregor Fisk was dead, they had been able to shed a few layers of protection, although Skandar had insisted on Hayley's security guards being in place whenever she went out in public. She wouldn't admit it, but she was grateful for it, and they were so discreet, she hardly noticed they were there.

Skandar, his skin tawny from playing outside in India over New Year's, grinned at her. His skin was covered in a fine layer of dewy sweat, his blonde hair sticking up each and every way.

"Wanna help me shower?" He grinned, and she laughed.

"Why, yes, I do."

In the shower, he kissed her as the cool water ran over their bodies, and she pressed her breasts into his chest. "God, I love you, Skandar Mallory."

He picked her up and stepped out of the shower, lowering her to the tile. Grinning, Hayley wrapped her legs around his hips, reaching between his thighs to stroke his hardening cock and Skandar spread her labia with his long fingers, the crest of his cock nudging at her entrance as he fingered her clit. With one long thrust, he took her and Hayley moaned with pleasure as his huge cock filled her, the friction on the sensitive nerve endings of her vagina utter, utter bliss. She never wanted this feeling to end, and she looked up at the glorious, wonderful man above her and felt such an overwhelming love for him, which tears sprang from her eyes. Skandar grinned, knowing they were tears of joy, kissed them away, and gathered her to him as they fucked.

Afterward, they ordered take-out and sat on the couch in their robes, idly flicking through the TV channels. "I wish I could think of some way to bring Quills and Jakob back together," she told him, but Skandar shook his head.

"Not yet, Hays. If it gets to a critical level, then maybe we need a rethink. But at the moment, don't get in between them. Quilla needs her space, and Jakob is giving it to her. Believe it or not, that's a good thing just now."

Hayley wasn't convinced. "How can it be? They need to be talking this shit out."

"And maybe they will, but us interfering will not help. Just leave it, boo."

· · ·

MARLEY WAS WORKING LATE AGAIN. It had been a long week, but now she was looking forward to going home and enjoying a weekend with Ran. She flicked off the lights in the lab she was working in and walked slowly back to her car, half reading some notes she had just completed. When he spoke, she jumped violently.

"Hey, Marley."

Jakob. "Shit, Jakob, you scared me half to death," Marley put a hand on her chest, breathing deeply.

"Sorry." He grinned sheepishly. He was dressed casually in jeans and a T-shirt and looked healthier than he had for months. "Come to think of it, I shouldn't really be skulking around a parking lot, but I was trying to get up the courage to talk to you. Sorry if I scared you; I didn't mean to."

Marley shot him an annoyed look, then laughed softly. "Don't worry about it. Look, why don't we go grab a quick drink and talk. But, Jakob, I warn you, I won't try and persuade Quilla of anything she's not ready to do."

"That's fair."

They went to a small bar on 7th. Both of them were driving, so it was soda for Jakob, sparkling water for Marley.

"How's my pops?" Jakob asked, obviously nervous. Marley smiled to herself.

"He's great, thank you."

"You make him happy, you know? I like that."

Okay ... "Jakob, why don't you just tell me what you need?" Marley took a long sip of water and waited.

Jakob fidgeted nervously. "Obviously, I wanted to talk about Quilla, but don't worry; I just need your advice."

Marley nodded. "Go on."

Jakob sighed. "I love her, and I miss her every day, but I know I messed up. I know what I have to prove."

"Sometimes, Jakob, people just need some time apart to see things clearly."

"I know, and believe it or not, this separation has been good for me, too. Cleared my head. Shown me what I want."

"Which is?"

"Quilla. I want to make a home with her, have kids, dogs, cats, pet snakes, even. I want to work hard at my job; I want Quilla to achieve the success she deserves in her work. I'll be a stay-at-home dad, if she wants, no problem. Anything."

Marley studied him. "Why do I feel there's a 'but' coming?"

Jakob grinned sheepishly. "But I don't know how to prove all that to Quilla. At the moment, it's just words and I wouldn't blame Quilla for never trusting me again. I didn't protect her—it was my actions, albeit twenty- odd years ago—that kickstarted Gregor's psychosis. I cheated with Padme, then left her to Gregor's mercy."

"I know all this and yet you're here, asking for my help."

"No, not your help, that's the thing. I know this has to be all me. Your advice would be welcome, though."

Marley considered for a few moments. "What you don't want to do is control what Quilla wants to do, or what she does when she leaves the hospital. I know you've been working on the Foundation, but don't take it over. Make sure Quilla knows it's just being set up for her and that she can change anything she wants within the organization or even not go ahead with it at all."

Jakob nodded, his eyes looking more alive. "That's good; that's good stuff."

"The important thing is to do the work but don't take the credit. Just be the investor, which you would have been if Quilla had had the chance to set this up before she was taken. Let Grady or Flori make any public announcements. Be the foundation stone, but be invisible."

"I got it. Man, thank you, Marley ... but there is one thing. I want to make sure people know that it was Quilla's idea without me going on TV and gushing—she'll see right through that. Any ideas?"

Marley gave him a smile, her expression soft. "Actually, I do."

"And you're sure you feel up to it?"

Quilla smiled down the phone. Parker had called three times to make sure she felt okay to leave the hospital. "Honestly, Parker, I feel good. It's not like I'll be running a marathon when I get out of here. Flori has already told me she has box sets and snacks for us both."

Parker chuckled. "Well, okay, then. Look, Asia and I will be up to Seattle soon to see you all."

"Can't wait."

GRADY AND FLORI were accompanied by a very excited Hayley. She hugged Quilla. "Marley says she'll be over to see you later, unless you're feeling too crowded. I said you'd send her a text message."

At Grady and Flori's apartment, Flori showed her the guest room. "All new furniture and a flat-screen," she muttered to Quilla, "I still can't get used to this 'money is no object' thing'"

"Me, too," Quilla whispered back. "It looks lovely in here, thank you. That bed looks like bliss after that hospital one."

Grady left the woman and went to work. Flori tucked Quilla onto their couch, and Quilla grinned, enjoying the fuss. Flori dragged over a crate. "Box sets," she explained, then stuck her head into the crate. "West Wing, Grey's Anatomy, Grimm, Orange is the New Black, Friends ...?"

"Oh, Friends, definitely."

"Are you sure? You might laugh and..." Flori put her hand on her belly and pulled a face. Quilla grinned.

"Good thinking ... but no hospital stuff ... Grimm? A lot of fine looking men in that."

"Perv."

"Yep."

They all laughed and Flori put the disc into the Blu-ray player, the familiar theme tune starting.

SITTING, watching TV and chatting, munching on the snacks Flori had provided, Quilla felt relaxed, her family around her. She still got fatigued quickly, but her body felt better, lighter. She couldn't push herself too hard, but she found she didn't want to. She wanted this. Chilling out with much loved friends, feeling relaxed, as if she didn't have to worry about anything. She had locked Jakob away in a corner of her heart until she was ready to deal with him. After a few episodes of the show, she felt her eyes closing.

A few hours later, she opened her eyes to find Hayley gone and Flori moving silently around the room. Quilla sat up stiffly. "God, I'm sorry. I didn't mean to fall asleep on you."

Flori grinned. "Don't worry; Hayley said she'd come back tomorrow, if you want. You're going to be tired for a while; I was, even after I came home from the hospital."

She came to sit by Quilla and the two women smiled at each other. "We survived," Quilla said to her and Flori grinned.

"Yeah, we did. And now that asshole has gone for good, thanks to you. How do you feel about that?"

"About killing Gregor?"

"Yeah. I know Marley's been worried that it would affect you, maybe even more than what he did to you."

Quilla shook her head. "Honestly, I thought it would, too, but I can't feel bad. His knife was in my gut. I kicked him off; I grabbed the gun, and I shot him. If I had to do it again, I would. I don't spare a moment's thought for Gregor Fisk."

Flori nodded. "Good. Good. That's how I would feel. No one knows unless it's happened to them, so don't let anyone guilt you. Gregor made his own bed."

Quilla hugged her. "Agreed. And now he's gone, and we can get our lives back."

Flori held onto her for a long moment. "Quilla? Have you thought about ...?"

"Jakob? Of course. I'm just ... I haven't got it straight in my head yet."

"Maybe you should talk."

"I'm starting to think that. I just don't know if I'm ready yet."

. . .

BUT BY THE end of the second week, she was ready. Not wanting to reconcile with Jakob over the phone, she asked Grady to set up a dinner for them.

Jakob was waiting for her when she entered the restaurant and for a moment, they just stared at each other.

"Hi," she said in a gruff voice, her hands trembling badly. Jakob saw her shaking and stepped forward, taking her hands in his. His big dry hands felt so comforting, so familiar, she almost lost her composure and threw herself at him; only her pride and her still-healing body stopped her.

"You look beautiful, sweetheart." Jakob's own voice was shaking, and she gave a half smile.

"I feel like we're on our first date."

Jakob led her to their table. "Well, if that's the way this evening's going to end ..." He grinned wickedly and she laughed, relaxing. She knew he was kidding—her body wasn't ready for that kind of reunion, even though, when she saw him, a familiar ache started inside her. Desire.

But there was still too much to be sorted out. They ordered and made small talk before Jakob reached over to take her hand.

"How are you, Quilla, really?"

She didn't pull her hand away. "I'm okay, really. You look ... well."

He smiled. "Am I allowed to say that you look lovelier than ever? That you make me weak?"

Quilla grinned. "Seriously, dude, if you're trying to get me to put out ..."

They both laughed, and then Jakob's smile faded. "Baby, I want to ask for your forgiveness. I was scared and immature, and I messed up. Big time. I couldn't handle what Gregor had done to you, and so I freaked out. It was monumentally selfish and hurtful, and I'm so very, very sorry, baby. I love you so much."

Quilla found her throat closing. "Jakob ... I have to say this out loud so, please let me finish."

He nodded, his eyes wide and scared. She drew in a deep breath. "I did not sleep with Gregor voluntarily. He was going to kill Hayley and me if I didn't make it look … real. I had no idea he was taping it, that you'd ever see it, so I acted the part—overacted, if you ask me—but he was convinced. I'm not going to apologize for that."

Jakob nodded. "Nor should you have to, darling. Call it immaturity, call it male ego … it killed me to see that, and when I thought you were going to die, I couldn't handle being left with that image of you —and him."

Quilla nodded, looking down. She was knotting her napkin, twisting it around in her fingers. "All I could think of was you. The whole time, I kept reasonably sane by thinking of you and me and us, in our little hideaway in Venice, especially. On the island, when we got married. I built this image up of a fairytale and the crash to reality was hard. I needed time. You hurt me, Jakob, more than anyone I loved ever has. Even my mom. You broke my heart."

Jakob's expression was soft, regretful. "I know, sweetheart. What can I do to make it up to you?"

Quilla smiled. "You're doing it. You gave me the time; you didn't harass or pressure me. Ran told me you're going to NA."

"Every week, without fail. I might not have taken that coke but the thought that I might have scares the crap out of me."

"Good for you. God, I'll always remember that first night in Venice. You stayed then, and you're staying now. This is the way to make it up to me. Be the man I fell in love with so deeply. I'm not ready to give up on us."

Jakob was quiet for a second, and when he spoke, his eyes were fierce with passion and his voice shook. "I love you so much, Quilla Chen. So goddamned much. Can we start again?"

She smiled at him. "I would like that. Let's take things slowly, this time. Let's do the whole dating thing."

"Whatever you want, baby." Jakob was beside himself with joy. "I'll court you good. I'll court you like a boss."

She burst out laughing. "Seriously, have you been hanging out with Hayley and Skandar too much? Like a boss? Ow, oww," she clutched her belly as she giggled and Jakob joined in with her laughter.

"There's one more thing I have to talk about with you," he said, and she raised her eyebrows, finally stopping her laughter. She wiped her eyes.

"What's that?"

"Your foundation." He reached into his pocket and pulled out a sheaf of papers. "Everything is set up for you. Grady, Flori, and Hayley are all ready to go, so you just have to say the word. Any changes, anything, we'll change it, but it's yours, darling." He handed her the papers and she took them, smoothing them flat to read them.

THE QUILLA CHEN Foundation for the Arts.

TEARS PRICKED her eyes as she read the title and mission statement. "To open the world of art to everyone," she quoted and looked up at Jakob with shining eyes. "I don't know what to say ... it was just an idea and now ... wow." She shook her head. "Thank you, Jakob, my beloved Jakob, thank you. This is ..." She couldn't go on, the tears dropping down her cheeks. Jakob got up and moved his chair next to her so he could take her in his arms.

"It's just the start, Quilla. It's just the beginning of what we could achieve together."

He kissed her, his mouth gentle at first, then as she responded, they both forget where they were. Finally breaking away, they gazed at each other for a long moment.

"There is just one change I would like to make," she said softly, stroking his cheeks with her fingertips. Jakob smiled at her.

"Name it."

"Could we change the name to The Quilla Chen Mallory Foundation ... that is my name after all."

Jakob grinned delightedly. "Yes, of course, my love, and yes, it is ..."

The End

ABOUT THE AUTHOR

Mrs. Love writes about smart, sexy women and the hot alpha billionaires who love them. She has found her own happily ever after with her dream husband and adorable 6 and 2 year old kids. Currently, Michelle is hard at work on the next book in the series, and trying to stay off the Internet.

"Thank you for supporting an indie author. Anything you can do, whether it be writing a review, or even simply telling a fellow reader that you enjoyed this. Thanks

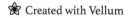 Created with Vellum

Lightning Source UK Ltd.
Milton Keynes UK
UKHW021935180822
407522UK00003B/143